Phoenix

Collisa

Book One of the Outsider series.

by
Aiden Phoenix

Collisa

Copyright © 2023 Aiden Phoenix

No part of this book may be reproduced in any form or by any electronic or mechanical means including information storage and retrieval systems, without permission in writing from the author. Except for the purposes of making reviews or other cases permitted by copyright law.

ISBN: 9798393045234

Cover created by Aiden Phoenix.

This book is a work of fiction. Names, characters, locations, and events are products of the author's imagination. Any resemblance to any persons living or dead, locations, or events are coincidental and unintended by the author.

Phoenix

Welcome to Collisa!

Collisa is a new world brimming with opportunities for adventure and growth. It is also brimming with chances for romance and fun. This is the story of Dare and the life he builds for himself with the women he meets and falls in love with.

As you can guess, it is a harem tale, with all that includes. Be aware that it features varied and explicit erotic scenes between multiple partners. It is intended to be read by adults. All characters involved in adult scenes are over the age of 18.

Table of Contents

Prologue: After Life 5
Chapter One: Wood 26
Chapter Two: Progress? 50
Chapter Three: Opposite of Hostile 67
Chapter Four: Contact 86
Chapter Five: Questing 115
Chapter Six: Helping Hand 137
Chapter Seven: Healer 161
Chapter Eight: Companion 184
Chapter Nine: Unpowered Leveling 201
Chapter Ten: Abur 215
Chapter Eleven: Gone 237
Chapter Twelve: Hero's Reward 260
Chapter Thirteen: Driftwain 273
Chapter Fourteen: Catching Up 295
Chapter Fifteen: The Rhythm of Things 316
Chapter Sixteen: Visitor 332
Chapter Seventeen: Dungeon Mouth 349
Epilogue: A Gift 356

Prologue
After Life

Dare wasn't sure why he screamed the moment he became aware of himself.

It wasn't a scream of surprise or fear, either. It was pure, unadulterated torment, tearing its way free of his throat with enough intensity to damage it. A raw, wrenching sound that came as a shock to his own confused ears.

That, plus the fact that he wasn't actually in pain, made him choke off the sound into silence after a few seconds. He sucked in a dozen ragged breaths, eyes clenched shut around a few burning tears. His throat ached slightly from its recent abuse, and now he was starting to feel confused and frightened.

If he was hoping that opening his eyes would make him feel any better, he was wrong.

He'd been too focused on his scream to pay more than the slightest attention to his surroundings, but the only impression he'd gotten was gray. And now, looking around, he confirmed that he was indeed in a blank gray void, which could've either stretched into infinity or ended just out of arm's reach, and he'd have no way to tell.

That was because he wasn't lying on any surface, or sitting, or standing. He wasn't weightless either, and he didn't feel any gravity. He assumed there was air because he was breathing and he wasn't dying painfully in a vacuum, but he felt no hint of it moving other than his own breath.

He was just there, floating in empty gray. Waving his arms and legs didn't seem to do anything; he didn't begin to rotate endlessly like he would in a weightless environment, so it was like he was in gravity. He just couldn't feel it.

Dare couldn't feel much of anything, aside from the pain in his throat. In fact, not even the weight or friction of clothes; a glance down confirmed he was naked.

"What's going on?" he said, staring around frantically. The fact that there was nothing *there* was making his head spin dizzily, not to mention freaking him out.

"YOU'RE DEAD."

He screamed again, this time in terror, as a female voice loud enough to make his entire body vibrate assaulted his ears, immediately making them ring. The volume of it was so overwhelming that it took him a few seconds to realize it had been a statement of fact, not a threat.

Not that he cared about the words themselves; the voice could've said anything and it would've been agonizing. "Stop shouting!" he said, covering his ears.

The voice spoke again, at a more reasonable volume this time. It had a calm, soothing lilt to it, putting him at ease. Although there was the barest hint of woodenness there, something artificial. Like the latest model text-to-speech apps that sounded almost like the real thing. It also had no source that he could see, nothing and no one that could possibly be speaking to him.

"What do you remember, Darren Portsmouth?"

Dare frowned, rubbing at his head. "I, um, remember everything?" he said hesitantly.

He could look back on his life with no difficulty, and in fact remembered the vague details lost to time better than he had since those memories were actually fresh. Not the most noteworthy of lives, maybe, but it was all there.

Except his claim couldn't be true, because he had no idea how

Phoenix

he'd ended up here.

"What's the last thing you remember?" the unseen woman's voice said, as if she knew what he'd been thinking.

Dare wasn't sure he wanted to know. But he rubbed at his head again. "I think I was, uh, at work?"

"At the chemical plant," the voice prompted.

"Right." The haze cleared a bit. "I was moving barrels on a lower level. Then the alarm rang and we all began evacuating."

"A man in front of you hit his head on a closing door and was knocked out," she said soothingly. "You dragged him up two flights of stairs, then managed to hand him off through a doorway to a security guard."

Dare nodded slowly. "I think, yeah. But then I don't remember anything after that."

"There is nothing after that, Darren Portsmouth. There was an explosion in the hallway behind you. The guard and man you carried both survived, although in critical condition."

The voice fell silent and Dare swallowed, feeling sick as he waited for the inevitable. And waited.

And waited.

Finally he wondered if he needed to prompt the disembodied voice. "What happened to me?" he whispered. It seemed almost cruel she was making him ask.

"You were effectively vaporized. Only a few bone fragments remained."

Holy shit. Dare closed his eyes against a surge of nausea. This creepy place, the voice coming from nowhere, and now this, was too much.

He sat like that for almost five minutes, silently freaking out.

And in all that time the voice said nothing, did nothing.

Finally he got enough of a grip to address the voice again. "So this is the afterlife?" he asked hoarsely.

"It is after your life, so technically," she said, sounding amused. The first sign of emotion he'd heard from her. "I'm not at liberty to give you any clues about what happens to the people of your world after death."

Again the voice paused, the silence dragging on agonizingly until he realized she wouldn't continue on her own. Did she just like to make sure he was engaged in the conversation by forcing him to offer frequent replies?

Dare looked around the gray space again, then down at his nude body. Obviously he knew what was happening right now, that he was dead and here in this odd gray void. So if she couldn't give him any clues about what happened after death then he had to be experiencing something different.

"But it didn't happen to me?" he guessed.

"Correct." The voice seemed pleased by his question. "In my searching I found you and took interest, bringing you here."

"Because I died saving a coworker?" Dare concluded; there were all sorts of stories about people being given a second chance after some heroic death.

"No, I just thought your life was interesting."

Dare looked ahead (which for the sake of his sanity he had decided was the source of the voice) in disbelief. "Interesting?" He couldn't help but laugh. "I spent most of my life playing video games, mostly RPGs and RTSs, when I wasn't at my dead end job moving barrels of dangerous chemicals around on a hand truck or forklift. I barely talked to people online, aside from friends in games. The highlight of my empty, isolated life was when I could get the occasional game night going at a nearby game store, although it was a bitch to get people to attend. What's interesting about that?"

"Yes, games. You experienced hundreds of stories, hundreds of unique and interesting gameplay systems. You spent a great deal of time on theorycrafting and min/maxing, as well as general problem solving. Always excelling in the game through your own ingenuity and effort, rather than seeking the solutions from others. Most of the people of your world live comparatively boring lives, but to me your life is endlessly fascinating."

Well, that was interesting. He never would've expected to be dragged out of line for the usual afterlife because he'd wasted his life playing video games instead of doing the usual things like getting married, having kids, and rising in a lucrative career.

"You're not fucking with me, are you?" he asked cautiously. "Who are you anyway?"

She continued as if he hadn't spoken. "As luck would have it, I happen to know of a world that was structured by its creators in a way similar to the roleplaying games you most enjoy. Would you like to see it?"

"Sure," Dare said cautiously.

"How badly?"

Dare jumped as two doors appeared in front of him. They opened into some sort of mind-bending tunnels he wasn't sure he could even describe if he'd wanted to, which vanished in opposite directions.

The disembodied woman's voice continued solemnly. "The door on the left will take you to the world I spoke of, where I will give you a second chance at life. The door on the right will return you to where you should be in the grand scheme of things."

Wow. How did he even begin to make a choice like that? Especially when he had almost zero information to go on. "Which choice would be better for me?" he asked, hoping for an easy answer from her.

Collisa

"I would not have given you this choice if I did not think the option I offer would appeal to you," she replied. "You could live a life like the games you love, except far more real and expansive. A whole world of possibilities."

That was definitely tempting. Although was it potentially fucking up his afterlife tempting? "What about when I die on your world, hopefully of old age?" he asked. "What happens to me then?"

He wasn't too surprised when she replied, "I'm not at liberty to tell you."

Dare thought carefully, trying to make the best choice with the information he had. If he was being honest Earth, while beautiful and great in many ways, had also left plenty to be desired. Especially considering his former life.

He wondered how interested he was in an afterlife attached to the place.

Not to mention the fact that for all he knew, there might not be an afterlife at all. The disembodied voice could've recreated him out of oblivion when otherwise he would just be gone, and if he took the door on the right that returned him to "where he should be in the grand scheme of things", he'd go back to ceasing to exist.

That possibility, combined with the prospect of having a whole world to explore that was modeled like an RPG game, was enough to tip him over the edge.

He tried to step towards the door on the left, and to his surprise where before he hadn't moved no matter how he flailed his limbs, now he drifted forward as if his mind was willing him in that direction.

The other door disappeared, taking the other tunnel with it. "I'm pleased you chose to accept my offer," the woman's voice said warmly as Dare drifted through the remaining one.

What followed was a mind-wrenching trip through sensations,

dimensions, possibilities, memories, and phenomena too odd to describe. It could've lasted an eternity or a split second.

Then Dare emerged from the door, which winked out of existence behind him, and found himself . . . floating naked in a gray void.

"What the fuck!" he shouted, sure he'd been tricked.

"Calmly, Darren Portsmouth," the disembodied voice said soothingly. "It may seem as if nothing has changed, but everything has. However, there are a few last details to iron out before you start your new life. For your own benefit."

Dare supposed he couldn't argue with knowing more about the world he was going to. If it was similar to a game, the better he understood the mechanics and world the better. "All right, what sort of world are you sending me to?"

A large map appeared, what he supposed was a complete map of this new world. There were eight continents on it that featured extensive mountain ranges, deserts, large stretches of forests, plains, lakes, and streams. Surrounding the continents were several oceans as well as a few large islands, some island chains, and what looked like a seamount in the middle of one of the oceans. The poles were covered with snow, like on Earth, and he assumed that meant the equator was tropical.

The map was surprisingly detailed, including territory lines for countries or kingdoms scattered over every continent and on some of the islands, within which were marks with the names of towns and cities that meant nothing to him.

The map abruptly vanished. "Ah ah ah," the disembodied voice said playfully, "I'm sure you'll want to discover the world on your own, without a map just telling you everything."

Actually, Dare would've liked to inspect the map longer, so he'd have some idea of where he was and where to go when he was sent to the world. Or maybe get a copy of it. "Where will I start?"

"On the continent of Shalin," she said, which going on memory was the largest one. That was all she said, which was hardly helpful.

But from what he remembered of the map, Shalin had had several different kingdoms and some large patches of unclaimed wildlands. In other words, your standard fantasy setup, teeming with opportunities.

"The world works on a simple leveling system, wherein you gain experience through killing enemies close to your level, gaining proficiency in abilities, completing quests, exploring, and earning achievements, with a few opportunities for special bonuses. Each level you will receive an increase in stats, and occasionally free class-based abilities. But most importantly you will be granted points which you may use to purchase abilities, class-based and universal, of a vast variety to help you tailor your life to exactly what you want to do.

"The leveling system is augmented by the ability proficiency system, wherein you rank up your abilities by using them and gaining proficiency. As your proficiency increases you'll be able to use that ability with more effectiveness, and occasionally will also unlock new abilities specific to that ability that you may spend level up points to purchase. As well, you will earn free abilities specific to that ability. You may also occasionally unlock new abilities, based on a combination of your class and the abilities you've elected to focus on, as well as specific ability synergies."

Okay, Dare thought he could wrap his head around that. The level up system was basically the same as what you saw in just about every RPG game. As for the ability system, ranking abilities up based on use was fairly common. Although this one seemed far more complex.

Which made sense, if basically everything you did in life became an ability; that was going to be a huge variety. As for the last bit she'd said about the ability system, he'd have to scratch his head over it for a while. But he thought it meant that if you selected, say, a warrior class and ranked up a universal ability like unarmed combat, you could unlock various unarmed attacks suited to a warrior.

Although he supposed he'd have to see, since this was all guesswork.

"Is everything you do on that world dictated by abilities?" he asked.

"Within reason," she replied. "Obviously you wouldn't have an ability for eliminating waste. However, eating, drinking, sleeping, and other basic necessities do have an ability attached to them, which you can gain more proficiency in to gain better results."

Something like sleeping, Dare thought he could wrap his head around, but . . . "You can get better at eating and drinking? How?"

"The way babies do, I assume," she said wryly. "Eating faster, without making a mess. Drinking faster, without choking."

Ah. That was a bit disappointing.

The disembodied voice continued briskly. "However, anything that isn't a specific ability you can do, as long as you're aware it can be done and can figure out how to do it. Like on your world. And similarly if you want to do something but don't have the ability for it, you can. But abilities are usually faster and easier and put created items in the official item tree, where their quality is known and they can be traded, sold, or given as gifts."

"So if I didn't have a woodcarving ability, but I decided to carve a pointy stick?" he asked.

"You'd have a pointy stick. Basically the same as it would be on your world. If you used it to try to injure something then its sharpness, hardness, and other statistics would be used to determine damage and durability loss."

Interesting, and potentially a headache. But if the ability system had been designed around people living their lives, he assumed there wouldn't be many times where he needed to do something that went outside of it.

Not unless he wanted to go full on living the time traveler fantasy, and try to bring technology to a fantasy world. He could just imagine the chaos it would cause if he introduced guns (assuming the world didn't already have them), or bombs or even electricity.

Of course, he didn't know how to create any of those things. Besides, although he'd use knowledge from his world to his advantage if he could, he kind of didn't want to turn this new place into Earth 2.0.

Also he kind of doubted the beings in charge of this world, including this unseen woman, would even let him.

"All right, what else do I need to know?" he asked.

"A great deal," she replied, sounding amused. "In order to make sure everyone can level up, the world spawns large amounts of monsters of various levels that can be hunted for experience. The world also ensures that animals breed at a faster rate and grow to adulthood faster, so they can be hunted and the more dangerous ones can be fought for experience. Many animals are also given higher levels if they can be found near high level monsters, so you can kill them to augment your experience gains.

"You can also gain experience for fighting members of your own or other intelligent races, most commonly as bandits or pirates or other scum that have turned to preying on others, or those that have turned to outright evil such as necromancers or mad scientists. I leave it to you to decide if you're willing to kill others, although if it helps in most kingdoms there is a bounty on bandits and the like, and brave citizens are encouraged to kill them on sight."

Interesting. In games Dare had had no problems with killing other humans or intelligent creatures, but those were games. In real life he supposed he'd have to see what the situation was, and how he felt about such a drastic decision. He didn't know if he'd even be able to, except at the most dire need.

"Anything else?" he asked, eager to move away from the grim topic.

"Well not so much giving you more knowledge, although if you pay attention you'll learn more about this world. I've yet to give you your gifts."

Dare perked up. "Gifts? Like magic gear or gold so I can buy equipment to level faster?"

"Not quite, I can't offer you anything tangible." The disembodied female voice sounded amused. "However, there are other things I can offer worth far more than any item. And I'm inclined to be generous . . . since I went to all this trouble bringing you here, you'll understand if I have some motivation in protecting my investment."

Again she paused, giving him an opportunity to parse her words and say what she meant. "Keeping me alive?" he said.

Her laugh was like tinkling bells. "Improving your chances, at the least."

Dare frowned. "At the risk of pissi-displeasing you," he said carefully, "you're going to a lot of trouble on my behalf. I'm curious to know what you expect to get out of it. Was there something you wanted from me?"

There was no response. In fact, the silence stretched over a very uncomfortable minute before Dare finally gave up. Looked as if the unseen voice really didn't want to talk about herself. "You may not want to tell me, but this is something I need to know."

After another pause, not quite as long, she answered. "I expect you to entertain me."

His frown deepened. "Um, what?"

Collisa

"I believe that needs little explanation. I want to see how you do on a new world, given your proficiency with games from your world. I want to see you prosper, and the direction your life will take. Your victories and failures, your loves and losses. I want to see what you're capable of."

Well that was more . . . basic than he'd expected. Also a little cynical, if he was being honest; she'd disrupted his afterlife for her amusement? No great quest to save the world, no challenge to right some terrible wrong? Just "have fun living your life and I'll have fun watching you"?

"Is that all?" he demanded.

Yet another pause . . . he could almost *feel* his benefactor's displeasure at this subject. "If I do have other motives, which I make no admittance of, I give you my assurance they will in no way negatively impact your safety, happiness, or autonomy."

Dare wasn't sure he could fully believe that a god, or whatever she or it was, would resurrect him and transport him to the world of his dreams just to watch him live his life there. It was something for nothing, too good to be true, and his unsatisfying life on Earth had left him highly suspicious of that.

But he'd already stepped through the doorway, so he supposed he'd have to take his benefactor at her word. "All right, thank you for answering. What gifts did you have for me?"

Again an image popped up in front of him. A simple disembodied eyeball looking around alertly. "My first gift, the Adventurer's Eye." Her voice turned pensive. "Although perhaps not the most apt term, since only a relative few adventurers have ever unlocked the prerequisites to attain it."

Dare stared somewhat queasily at the image; he thought he'd seen far more creepy things, but something about the way the eyeball moved as if it was still attached to a person just going about their day made it oddly eerie.

Phoenix

"What does it do?" he asked, since he was now certain she liked him to be engaged in the conversation. Even if he was just asking obvious questions or making obvious observations that most people would quickly get impatient of.

"It allows you to assess the basic information and power level of the people and creatures around you. Whether they're stronger or weaker than you. About how much effort it would take to kill them, their "hit points" you might say. The attacks they might use against you."

The disembodied voice gave Dare an opportunity to mull that over. Although it didn't take long to come to the conclusion that such an ability was not only extremely useful, it was lifesaving.

If he was being thrown into a world where he'd grow in power by killing monsters (or the occasional evil intelligent creature), then knowing which monsters he could hunt without committing virtual suicide would mean everything. If nothing else, it would save him time if adventurers had access to creature compendiums that listed their levels.

"That is an . . . incredible gift, my Lady," he said.

"Lady." She sounded amused. "This voice has been carefully selected as one you'd find most soothing, nothing more."

"Then could I ask about your nature?" he asked.

There was no response; he took that as a no.

After an uncomfortable silence, when he was beginning to wonder if he should apologize, the voice spoke as if he hadn't said anything. "In addition, I will give you another gift. A more fun one, for me at least, for it will require you to choose between options."

Dare leaned forward intently, then bit back a curse when she didn't elaborate; he was getting tired of having to goad her along at every step of the conversation. "What are the options?"

Collisa

The eye vanished, replaced by three pictures. They were stylized, liked you'd expect to see for an ability tooltip in a game. The left one had a brain with swift movement lines behind it, the middle one had what looked like a cutout view of an underground cavern half full of water, and the right one had an arched foot with swift movement lines behind it.

To his pleasant surprise, the left image enlarged without him needing to prod the voice. "The first option is Quick Study. You level up 50% faster. That includes increasing your abilities through usage and experience gained through killing monsters, earning achievements, and completing quests." There was a long pause. "You may ask one question about each ability."

Dare stared at the speedy brain, thinking carefully. She'd given him a surprising amount of information just by explaining the ability. Most of it stuff she'd already told him, but there were gems there he'd have to think over.

"Is there a level cap?"

"Yes." She didn't elaborate.

Well, that wasn't helpful. What was the cap? How hard was it to reach it? Was it a soft cap, where his level from experience might be capped but he could continue to increase his power through working on his abilities? If he could level up all the different abilities then potentially there was no limit to the power he could gain, if only through versatility.

But that seemed to be all he was getting. He anticipated her clamming up and asked, "What about the second ability?"

The left image shrank and the middle image of the cavern with the pool grew. "The second option is Bottomless Pool. Your mana reserves are doubled."

Interesting. That confirmed that the world had magic, as he'd hoped. But it was hard to glean much from just that.

Phoenix

No way to tell if magic was prevalent, or easy to learn. Or just how useful a doubled mana pool would be. Dare had played games where you could spam your most powerful spell without your mana bar moving a notch, especially with items.

"Is it possible to cast powerful spells that use significant portions of your mana pool?" he asked.

The disembodied voice sounded almost pleased by his question. "Yes."

Again, not helpful. Although by the way he'd worded the question, he at least knew that powerful spells were possible. Although there was no way of telling whether "powerful" meant capable of scouring the world or just burning up a wagon or something.

He bit back a sigh. "And the third option?"

The middle image shrank, and the foot with swift movement lines grew. "Fleetfoot. You are 34% faster."

Dare snapped to attention. "Is that just movement speed or everything that involves speed?"

Again, the voice sounded pleased. "Everything. Your arm movements for weapon attacks and spellcasting, modifiers for dodge, parry, block, acrobatics, etcetera. Your reflexes will also be enhanced by 34% to compensate for your physical-"

"I choose Fleetfoot," he interrupted without hesitation.

There was a very long pause. "That was . . . swiftly chosen," the voice said carefully. "You don't wish to consider the options, or even hear the rest of the answer to your question?"

Dare grinned. "No need. In my experience speed is the most valuable attribute in just about every game I've played. I might've been tempted to take it even if it just applied to movement, since that can have such a huge impact. But since it basically gives a major speed enhancement to pretty much every ability, and even *reflexes* . . ."

There was another pause. "Yes?" the voice asked politely. She obviously didn't understand trailing off for emphasis.

"It's an incredible ability," he concluded.

"I see." She sounded . . . he wasn't sure. Definitely some strong emotion. "Would you like more information on the options now that you've made your choice?"

He wondered if she was offering that just to punish him for his seemingly cavalier choosing, even though he was 100% confident in his decision. "Please."

It looked that way as she continued. "Quick Study. While there is a level cap, it is virtually impossible to reach based on continually increasing experience requirements per level. At the higher levels it can take decades to reach another level. Even an immortal devoting all their time to the effort would take centuries to reach it."

The voice sounded almost smug. "You would've swiftly surpassed other adventurers and in your lifetime come closer to reaching the cap than just about anyone ever has. A god among mortals."

Dare grimaced. Well, knowing that certainly would've affected his decision.

He was still sourly mulling on the missed opportunity when to his surprise she continued without waiting for his prompting. Probably delighted about being the bearer of bad news. "Bottomless Pool. At high levels mages are capable of casting spells that devastate hundreds of meters around them, or focusing their power into a needle of such intensity it can pierce the scales of an ancient dragon and shred its heart.

"Their most powerful spells take a significant portion of their mana pool, and mana is their greatest constraint. Double mana would turn them from deadly weapons to gods. As well, at higher levels there are spells that can be learned that the mage can technically cast, but require more mana than their entire pool holds, usually requiring them to gain more levels or use cripplingly expensive enhancements to increase their capacity."

That sounded absolutely sick. Which was kind of how he felt at the thought he might've passed up the chance to become the world's most powerful mage. "And Fleetfoot?" he said through gritted teeth.

"Your assessment of it was fairly sound," the disembodied voice said, that hard to decipher emotion back. "If I may ask, what made you pick Fleetfoot over the others?"

Dare thought it over. "Quick Study could be amazing, but I had no way of knowing how easy it was to reach the level cap. It's possible I might've been stuck with a useless ability after a short leveling period."

"I see. And Bottomless Pool?"

He shrugged. "It's a fairly limited, if powerful, ability. I had no way of knowing how prevalent magic was, and even if it was useful there are so many other areas I'd be missing out on. Meanwhile Fleetfoot is universally useful, and always will be."

For a few moments of silence he stared at the Fleetfoot tooltip, which slowly began to spin. "You didn't tell me anything about Fleetfoot, like the others."

She made a unique sound, somehow managing to sound pleased and displeased at the same time. "It was a good decision. By most perspectives the best option, particularly if it fits your style. With the enhanced speed you'll find everything easier, each fight less risky. And at any level you'll be more powerful than your peers."

"So if I was at level 30, I'd basically be as powerful as a level 40."

"Not quite, speed is only one attribute, after all."

Collisa

Dare shoved aside any thoughts about the other to options, which he still considered less desirable and in any case were now out of reach, and let himself be excited again. "My fastest sprinting speed was about 15 miles per hour. So now I'll be able to run at 20? And for just jogging around I can go at 8 miles an hour instead of 6 for the same amount of energy. That's better anyway, since humans are known for stamina more than speed, so with such a huge speed bump I can do more without having to exhaust myself. Heck, even walking I go from 3 miles and hour to 4. That adds up quick."

The voice sounded amused. "Those estimations of your max speed, jogging speed, and walking speed are inaccurate. On our world you'll have more . . . idealized attributes. Consider your attributes more on par with the top athletes and intellectuals from your world."

He stared at the Fleetfoot icon in stunned disbelief. "Another gift?"

"If you wish to view it as such. Considering your body was obliterated, I saw no reason why you should not have the best possible replacement. After consideration I have made your body's age 18, adult and accountable but with the prospect of a full adult life ahead of you. And it will be a full life, because longevity is another of your new body's attributes. Assuming you don't die."

Dare frowned. "So in other words you decided for me that I should have 18 less years of my new life."

She again sounded amused. "I assumed you wouldn't want to relive a childhood, especially an early childhood, with all your memories intact."

Well, 18 was better than 27. He'd get to relive what everyone called the best years of his life. And on a fantasy world with all sorts of exciting opportunities.

"Do I already have the increased intelligence?" he asked. He hadn't noticed any change, and a part of him was a bit uneasy about

Phoenix

his unseen benefactor messing with his mind. Even to improve it.

"No. But I assure you that you were already well above average on your world. The improvements will be distinct, but perhaps not as noticeable as your other enhancements."

Noticeable . . . a thought occurred to him. "What about, um, appearance?"

If the voice was amused before, now she sounded on the verge of outright laughter. "Yes, you'll be on par with the most physically appealing men of your world." She finally did laugh. "You'll have no reason to complain about the size of your reproductive organ, either."

Wow. "It sounds like you're really setting me up to succeed in this world."

The voice paused a moment. "With any luck, which by the way you'll have a high base stat for, you'll be very successful. I'm looking forward to seeing the heights you achieve."

"What do you get out of it?" he couldn't help but ask, even though she'd already answered that. Although her answer sucked. "You're really doing all this just so you can watch my life like a TV show?"

There was a long pause, and Dare thought she was going to ignore it like other questions he'd asked about her. "Yes," she finally said.

It seemed like a lot of effort to go to for some entertainment. Then again, for her maybe all this was as easy as snapping her fingers. If she even was a "her", after what she'd said about choosing this voice to put him at ease.

Either way, he had no reason to complain about her motivations considering the results. "I suppose I don't have to ask, but I should anyway. If I somehow die . . ."

Collisa

"There are no respawn or resurrect mechanics," the voice said somberly. "Death is death. Squander the gift I have given you in bringing you to this new world, and you will find yourself in the afterlife again."

He'd sort of figured that was the case: no gentle game where he could die and just run back to his body, with at worst a debuff or penalty to experience.

"What sort of world is it going to be?" he asked. "I know it'll have magic, and it sounds like a typical fantasy RPG world. Including game mechanics. And you mentioned monsters. And other intelligent races . . . what races specifically?"

She laughed. "All the races you may have heard of from your fantasy stories and games, and perhaps some you haven't."

Dare couldn't help but grin. "So I'll be able to marry an elf if I get the chance?"

"That is certainly an option." The voice became oddly flat. "Bear in mind, however, that this world is more brutal than the world you know. It will be up to you to decide whether you'll live up to the sensibilities you were raised with, or if you'll embrace the opportunity to use your power for your own benefit, as many on this world do."

That was less hopeful. "Brutal how?"

"In all the ways you might expect when the strong do as they wish and the weak have no choice but to submit to it." She sounded almost hesitant as she continued. "In such a world you might find people are surprised, and disproportionately grateful, at even the most offhand display of kindness or civility."

Her voice lightened. "So if you wish to cavort with elves, humans, or females of any other race, a gentle word may go a long way to helping you achieve your goal."

Dare got the feeling she was hoping he'd hold onto the morals he carried from his world. Which he certainly planned to do.

Although if he had the option to have safe sex, with women from *multiple races*, he wasn't going to pass it up. He wasn't a prude.

Chalk it up to a lifetime of few and far between romantic opportunities. He had a lot of experiences to catch up on. "You sound like you don't mind if I have a bunch of sex," he half asked, half stated.

"If anything, I encourage it," the disembodied voice said. Her voice turned teasing. "It'd be a shame to give you an attractive body and a huge manhood if you never use it. And if you're going to go to a new world with many opportunities for exciting adventures, you should be able to experience the most enjoyable adventures of all."

She paused. "And believe me, you'll have plenty of opportunities. Harems are common here, and many women would be happy to share a wealthy, powerful adventurer who can offer them a good life."

Dare liked the sound of that.

"Preparing to send you to your new home," the voice said abruptly, making him jump.

"Wait!" Dare shouted frantically, caught flatfooted. Weren't they just in the middle of a conversation? "You can't send me yet, I still have so many questions."

He could've sworn she had a smile in her voice as she answered. "And you'll find answers in your new life. Good luck, Darren Portsmouth."

Before he could say or do anything, he abruptly felt blackness closing in around his vision. He blinked, struggling to fight off the unconsciousness sweeping over him like a tide, but it was futile.

Within moments he was pulled under.

Chapter One
Wood

Dare gasped awake to find himself standing in a clearing in a light, airy woods.

The air he drew into his lungs with that involuntary breath was shockingly clean and fresh, in a way that would be difficult if not impossible to find on Earth. His first clue that he was on a new world, one where advancing technology hadn't taken its toll.

He stumbled and nearly fell flat on his face, as if he hadn't been supporting his weight before and now had to; it was an extremely disorienting sensation to wake up already on his feet. But in spite of his surprise he recovered with surprising quickness and grace.

Was that Fleetfoot?

Dare put that out of his mind as he stared around in awe. He could've been camping on Earth, except some of the trees and other plants around him had completely unfamiliar leaves. And, of course, the incredibly clean air.

It was slightly cool but not unpleasantly so, probably early spring or late fall, an Earth-like sun near its zenith filtering light through the canopy overhead and a chilly breeze blowing past his skin. That breeze made him look down, realizing he was wearing a simple sleeveless, knee-length tunic of some rough cloth that looked homespun, of far poorer quality than the machine made clothes he'd worn on Earth.

He also wasn't wearing underwear, which made him feel surprisingly vulnerable as the breeze swirled beneath the hem of his tunic and blowed across him freely.

He had shoes, at least, clunky leather things with thick laces.

Phoenix

They weren't anywhere near as comfortable as sneakers or even dress shoes, but at least they weren't painful and they'd protect his feet. No socks, though, which he was going to have to remedy fast; even if socks weren't a thing on this world, he'd have to see if he could hire a tailor to make some. As well as boxer shorts and pants.

Dare put that out of his mind for now and started looking around at this new world again, trying to spot any differences from Earth or signs of its game-like system.

But just a few seconds later a sharp buzzing noise sounded, making him jump and stare frantically around the clearing.

Then text appeared in front of him, read aloud by the same disembodied female voice from that odd gray space he'd just been in. "Alert. You are over the age of 12 and have not selected a class. Please select a class now."

"Hey again," he said. "You're the voice of game alerts?"

There was no response; another question she didn't want to answer? Or was this automated voice part of the system, and had nothing to do with his disembodied benefactor?

After all, she'd said she picked her voice as the one he'd find most soothing. This world's system might've done the same.

"How do I select a class?" he asked the system.

A very odd sensation occurred in his head, almost like he had an options menu in his brain. The text in front of him shifted to a list of terms, with the banner "Select One Now" at the top.

"Wait!" Dare said hastily. "Can I change class later?"

More text appeared in front of him, read aloud by the female voice. "Number of available class change tickets: 3. First class change incurs a 10% penalty to total experience. Second class change incurs a 30% experience penalty. Third class change incurs a 50% experience penalty."

Collisa

Wow, that was steep. Especially from what the voice had told him about the level cap and leveling up. It looked as if people were expected to either pick a class and stick with it, or at most change early on before they'd wasted too much time leveling up.

Still, 10% wasn't ruinous. And it might be better to select a class that would help him starting out, then when he knew more about the world change to the one that suited him best. Although he had to remind himself that it would mean a tenth of all the work he'd done on this world would be wasted.

Ouch. And that was the *first* one. Usually noobies were given a free pass the first time for choices they regretted, with at most a small penalty.

It meant he was going to want to pick a class that would be good for starting out, and that he could conceivably be happy with for life, so he wouldn't have to spend so much XP.

This was actually kind of BS, not fair at all. Dare assumed children on this world grew up learning about the various classes and receiving tons of advice about what one they were best suited for, as well as a lifetime to decide which one they wanted.

But in his case, the disembodied voice in the gray space hadn't even *mentioned* that he'd immediately have to pick a class, with no real knowledge of this world or the classes themselves, and no context to help him make that choice.

"Is there a time limit for class selection?" he asked.

"No. But you cannot move from this spot until you have selected a class."

Dare stared at the text in disbelief. "In other words there is, when I either collapse from exhaustion or die of thirst. Or some monster comes and kills me."

There was a long pause. "Technically," the voice said. Her tone thus far had been completely emotionless and formal, with no sign of the liveliness or humor of his disembodied benefactor.

He bit back a sigh and looked at the list of available classes.

Even if this was complete bullshit, there didn't seem to be any other option than to suck it up and make the best choice he could on short notice: as he'd already settled on, a class that would be good for starting out and that he could see himself being content with for life.

Well, first things first it looked as if he was in the middle of a forest. He wasn't sure if it showed any signs of human cultivation or at least presence, travelers or hunters or loggers. He just didn't know enough to recognize those signs.

Still, there was no sign of civilization anywhere nearby, no roads or buildings on the horizon or anything. And he didn't hear anything but the muted sounds of forest creatures in the presence of a sudden intruder.

He might've been thrust right into the deep end here, and needed a class that would help him not starve to death before he could find other people. As well as probably protect himself from the inevitable monsters that teemed in the wilds.

Besides, what sort of opportunities would he have in a town or city anyway? If he was an adventurer leveling up then he'd get the most benefit out of being out here for long periods of time anyway, or ideally living here.

Then there were his special gifts. He should take those into account, especially Fleetfoot. "Show me archer classes," he said.

The list of classes shrank to a subsection of ranged classes. Which wasn't exactly what he'd asked for, since some involved knife throwing or weapons he had no chance of getting his hands on anytime soon.

Not that he had a chance of getting a bow, either.

Collisa

Or . . . maybe not.

"Can I get more information on the Hunter class?" he asked.

A details page immediately popped up, headed by the picture of a man holding a bow and four arrows in one hand, and drawing an arrow nocked to the bowstring with the other.

The Hunter differed from the Archer or Marksman or other ranged classes in many ways, most of which had to do with exactly what Dare was looking for: woodscraft, crafting, and survival.

First and foremost, selecting the class immediately unlocked numerous abilities. He assumed that was the same for all the classes, but he wondered if any other class's initial unlocked abilities would be so uniquely suited to his exact situation.

For woodscraft, the class's initial ability unlocks included things like Find Prey, Track, Forage, and Forest Perception, which made him more aware of the details in the forest around him and their importance, and which would reduce the speed penalty incurred by moving through underbrush and other obstacles in the woods, and gave him a 2% movement speed increase in woodlands at that level.

Those were pretty exciting, but more pragmatically by picking the Hunter class he'd also unlock the ability to create snares from vines or various braided things found in nature, the ability to create a stone knife, the ability to create a simple bow from wood and sinew, and the ability to skin animals and tan the hides to create leather. It also unlocked the Leatherworking ability tree as the class's mandatory subclass, which would allow him to craft things like shelters, bedrolls, sacks and backpacks, clothes, and eventually leather armor.

Although he'd incur an experience and ability proficiency gains penalty to Leatherworking for it not being his main class, as well as a significant quality reduction modifier.

The Hunter class seemed pretty good, not just for his current situation but moving forward. Ranged damage meant he wouldn't have to run up and try to kill dangerous enemies with a sword, and he wouldn't have to worry about depleting his mana pool either.

And if he wanted to stay out in the wilds long term to farm monsters and level up, having skills that let him survive in the wilds would be hugely beneficial.

Then there was also something to say for the fact that he'd immediately gravitated to it. If he was looking for a class he could he happy with forever, his first pick wasn't the worst idea.

Of course, it might turn out that Hunters were garbage. Although if that was the case then he could always take the XP hit and change to something better.

Dare set it aside as an option and kept looking through the classes, seeing if he could find something better. He was methodical about it, at least as much as he could be considering he was trapped standing there, on a ticking clock until he made a choice.

There were all the standard classes he would've expected to see, like Mages, Warriors, Paladins, Rogues, and Clerics. And all their various subsets like Thief and Assassin for Rogue, or Priest and Healer for Clerics. There were also specialized classes, not only ones available to pick immediately like Brawler, Swashbuckler, etc, but also more "hero" class ones that you could earn once you leveled your class up sufficiently or unlocked certain abilities.

All in all there were probably 100 combat classes. Then there were the profession or talent specialty classes, which seemed endless and included all the crafting ones, as well as things like Artist, Sculptor, and things like that. Not to mention ones like Scholar, Inventor, Bureaucrat, Manager, and various entertainer classes like Musician or Actor.

Not to be confused with the combat classes like Bard.

Dare had zero desire to pick a non-combat class, and after

perusing the combat classes he didn't find any that he thought would be as useful at the moment as Hunter, and that he thought he'd like more.

The magic classes were tempting, of course. Especially since apparently he immediately started with the basic class spells, without needing to worry about training or spellbooks. Although it looked as if some of the requisites for more advanced class spells, especially at the higher level, included training, spellbooks, or even quest chains to go out and find spells.

It was confusing enough to make him hesitate, and since he didn't know much about the magic system he was leery of diving into one if its classes.

Especially because his closer inspection of the magic classes showed that none had any abilities in the way of survival; Mages were obviously meant to be a class that started established in a settlement and worked from there.

Sure, maybe there were abilities in the universal tree that would help them when they went out to hunt monsters and needed to make camp or something. But Dare didn't like the idea of trying to blunder his way into figuring out how to be a Mage, all the while starving to death in the woods.

Besides, what if Mages turned out to be a class that needed a group to really function, and for them solo leveling was close to impossible?

Dare figured hours must've passed while he stood there in this level screen. His old body would've slumped to the ground in exhaustion by now, but with his new body his legs were barely starting to ache.

Still, he felt the weight of passing time and decided he should probably make a choice. He had a good basic idea of all the information for the classes he had even the slightest interest in, and at this point browsing around more wouldn't really make his decision any easier.

He was just procrastinating because it was such a major decision that would affect the rest of his life. Which was perfectly justified, especially on short notice like this, but eventually he was going to have to just bite the bullet and go.

So he did. "I pick Hunter class."

He heard a soft chime, and the disembodied woman's voice accompanied new text. "Congratulations, Hunter. May you level quickly and have many adventures, with lots of loot."

That seemed like an oddly juvenile thing to say, and Dare had to remind himself that aside from special cases like him, it was 12-year-old kids who'd just selected their class who were given that sendoff.

The command screen disappeared, and Dare was left back in the clearing as a brand new Hunter. And almost immediately his class selection took effect, giving him all his new abilities, perks, and stat increases.

He now had access to more detailed information about his Hunter abilities. As well as tantalizing hints about ones he could unlock in the future, as the information screen helpfully informed him. He also knew more about general Hunter stats and how they meshed with his basic stats.

The rush of knowledge and new abilities Dare now had just from selecting a class was almost dizzying. But he pushed aside the impulse to spend hours in the command menu theorycrafting and min/maxing with the available data and focused back on the clearing around him.

He'd been almost immediately interrupted from his first experience of this new world by the system demanding he pick a class, and he wanted to get back to it.

He began wandering around the clearing, more closely

inspecting various plants and the few insects buzzing around. Most were familiar, although he saw a distinctly odd beetle with wicked looking spines all over its carapace, and a bulbous plant with a single pale red flower that seemed to be spinning slowly.

He could "select" an object by focusing on it, and a small information screen popped up. Unfortunately, he didn't know what any of these things were, so those screens were blank without even a name for the object.

Aside from obvious things like rocks, that is. But even plants and insects Dare recognized, like grass and birch trees, showed up blank. As if his knowledge from Earth no longer applied.

How would people on this world learn about these plants and identify them? From being told, most likely, unless they had a specific spell or ability that let them identify them.

He decided to try something. "That's a birch," he said, pointing at a nearby tree. "It grows in cool northern climates."

Dare focused again, and was a bit pleased when the information screen showed the name and details he'd provided. The question was, had that information populated just because he'd said it, or because it was accurate?

Only one way to find out.

He pointed at a maple tree. "That's a gadrogul tree. It bears pleebus fruit in the winter."

He focused on the tree and was satisfied to see that the information didn't show up. Looked as if the system would populate the information screen with any accurate information he learned, and filter out the bullshit.

Which was actually an advantage from the real world. Or more accurately Earth, where he'd come from; this world seemed real enough.

Phoenix

Since it was an easy and obvious thing to do, Dare quickly moved around identifying as many things as he could in the clearing, along with whatever information he could think of them. He managed to get grass, dandelions, a few other varieties of trees, butterflies, flies, worms, centipedes, roly polys, and a few other insects.

Then, while lifting and flinging aside a rock to try to unearth more insects, he ended up launching the moderately heavy stone all the way across the clearing. He also got an indicator at the edge of his vision that his throwing skill had slightly improved.

Dare stared at the rock, then with a grin found one that fit better in the palm of his hand. He took a pitcher's pose, focused, and then threw it as hard as he could towards a patch of sky overhead so it could fly as far as possible.

The small rock disappeared from view, and after a surprisingly long pause he heard a faint crash as it fell back through the trees in the distance.

He was pretty sure he'd never thrown anything half that far in his previous life. Courtesy of the incredibly athletic body his unseen benefactor had provided him?

Grinning, he broke into a sprint for the other side of the clearing. He took off like a rocket, blowing right past his previous best speed and still accelerating. The wind whipped him as he ran at speeds more suitable for a car than a human, he guessed close to 25 miles per hour, and he whooped in excitement.

Fleetfoot. This was *awesome.*

Rather than trying to skid to a stop at the edge of the trees, Dare leapt over a fallen log and tore into the underbrush, ducking around bushes and leaning trees and hanging branches.

He'd run through forests before, of course, but never this fast. It felt like the obstacles rushing towards him came in slow motion, his nimble body easily able to dodge them. Courtesy of Fleetfoot's boost to his reflexes, he assumed.

Laughing, he tried jumping over a bush that was probably five feet tall and at least six feet wide. He cleared it easily; he'd wondered whether Fleetfoot would affect jumping, but he supposed it was reliant on initial speed as he pushed off from the ground, which meant his benefactor's gift would apply.

Just for fun, he stopped in a clear area with space overhead and tried jumping in place. After a few tries he was able to jump up to the height of his own head, *without* needing to tuck his legs close to his body for extra space.

And it hadn't even required his best effort. With a laugh he took off into the trees again.

Dare spent a while jumping over and ducking under things, not to mention sprinting full out and laughing like a lunatic at how fast he could go and how easily he avoided obstacles and kept from tripping. The forest was like an obstacle course, and while he'd never really done any parkour he now went out of his way to try things that looked challenging.

The body his unseen benefactor had given him was incredible. Lean and strong and seemingly tireless, at least compared to his old body, with athleticism he couldn't even have dreamed of in his old life. Combined with Fleetfoot, it made him feel like he had super powers.

Another thought struck him as he caught sight of a pool reflecting the trees waving above it, and he veered over to look down at the water, trying to see his reflection.

Water gave terrible reflections, unfortunately, but he got the impression of a square jaw, high cheekbones, an ideally sized aquiline nose, and piercing blue eyes. His black hair was cropped short and slightly tousled from running around, but even so seemed to fall naturally into aesthetically pleasing positions. His shoulders were wide and muscled, bare arms similarly well defined with lean muscle, and his legs were similarly muscular and well defined.

In other words, Dare was movie star level good looking and built like an elite athlete.

That brought to mind the other thing the disembodied woman had said, and Dare quickly straightened from inspecting his reflection. Then, after sheepishly looking around to make sure he was alone, he lifted the hem of his simple tunic to check underneath.

He had a perfect ten pack and a well muscled chest, but he was only distantly aware of them because his focus was on his dangling penis.

The sight was unexpectedly jarring, although in a good way.

In his old life he'd gained and lost weight and muscle definition at various times, and also tanned and faded over summers and winters. Which meant his body changed frequently enough and significantly enough that his new one, while incredible, wasn't quite as shocking. The fact that he was also about the same height, although a few inches taller at 6'3" or 6'4", also helped.

But the same wasn't true at all for Dare's old dick. He'd come to trust in its familiar appearance every time he took a leak, showered, or of course jerked off. It didn't change.

Only now it hung heavy between his legs, almost as large flaccid as he'd been fully erect before. And he'd been average sized.

It was also uncircumcised, which added a whole new level of unfamiliarity. Although he had to admit that while he wasn't an expert on cocks, his new one seemed to have a better shape and proportions than his old one.

The same applied to his balls: they were decent sized, not overlarge but definitely hanging with a reassuring weight. They also had an ideal, uniform size and shape and hung perfectly symmetrically in the scrotum.

Collisa

He'd always thought his old balls were good sized and looked normal enough, but the sight of these ones would have given him body image issues if they weren't part of his new body.

Just like the rest of his old body compared to this one.

There was just one more thing to check. Dare dug into his spank bank for something that would reliably get him hard, and watched with disbelief as his cock grew to its full size. A lot faster and with less effort than he'd expected, too. The sensation of it expanding was a new one as well, which made sense because his cock was now entirely different, and he had a *lot* more of it to feel sensations from.

Sensations that were more intense because he still had his foreskin.

"Damn," he muttered as he looked at his wood in all its glory, "this'll definitely help my popularity with the ladies."

Looking at his size flaccid he'd assumed he was a shower not a grower, but he had to change that opinion. Without a tape measure it was hard to be sure, but using his old body's dick as a measuring stick he judged he was around nine inches.

And the *girth*. He was going to have to pay more attention to foreplay and taking it slow while his lovers acclimated to this monster, for their sakes.

Out of curiosity Dare gave his new tool an experimental rub, and his knees weakened at the surge of sensation. Sensations which went up, up to where his old cock's tip would be, then up some more, past the end of his old cock, and kept on going until finally he reached the new tip, feeling around the foreskin.

At the risk of sounding crass, he couldn't wait to get this thing inside a girl. He was pretty sure it would blow the limited sex he'd had in his old life out of the water. Especially since there were so many more tantalizing options here.

He couldn't wait to see his first elf girl. In fact, at the thought of it he began absently stroking himself while thinking of the sexiest image of one he could remember. He was temporarily distracted by the fact that he had a lot more to stroke, a pleasant sensation, and for the fun of it tried double fisting his shaft.

Something he'd never been able to do before.

Dare felt the first tinglings of serious pleasure when he handled his new foreskin, and closed his eyes as he imagined the scantily clad elf in his head stripping off what little she'd been wearing, revealing pink nipples and a glistening pink slit. She began to grind on his thigh, skin silky smooth and the copious juices of her arousal dripping down his leg, and moaned wantonly as she took his hand and guided it towards her glistening-

Crack!

His eyes flew open in alarm when he heard the sound of a stick breaking in the woods nearby, completely pulling him out of the moment. Cursing to himself in a panic, he hastily dropped his tunic over his cock (or at least left it to puddle around it) and whirled towards the noise, tensed to run for safety.

It was just a squirrel jumping from tree to tree.

Dare felt his cheeks heat as he watched the small animal frolic in the treetops; he was all alone out here and he still felt embarrassed about his response.

But it was a good reminder that there were probably bigger and more dangerous things than squirrels in these woods. He needed to prepare so he could be ready, and sooner rather than later, or he might be killed while he was literally standing around holding his dick.

He'd picked a combat class for a reason, because he expected to fight monsters and he needed a way to do it well. And the sooner the better, which meant he had no time to waste on wanking around until he got his bearings.

Collisa

Dare focused on breathing for a few seconds, letting his heartbeat settle. His cock also began to shrink as he calmed, and he finally pulled his tunic down over it and put it out of his mind for now. Plenty of time to have fun with it later.

Although he did take a moment to admire the almost absurd tent his dwindling erection made in the front of his tunic.

Then he turned his gaze back to the squirrel. Now that he thought of it, this was a good chance to test out the Adventurer's Eye his benefactor had given him. He could use it to look more closely at the small animal.

Embarrassingly, it took a bit of fumbling to figure out how to use the ability. He'd found that all abilities could be used instantly, as if they were all on a hotkey bar, as long as he was aware of them. But he had to hunt down Adventurer's Eye in his universal abilities before he could do the same with it.

After Dare found the ability he stared at the squirrel, trying to figure out how to inspect it.

It turned out he couldn't because it had no level. It was designated "Squirrel, prey critter, normal stats". Which he assumed meant it had the same health and abilities as any normal squirrel from his world, and would be about as difficult to hunt and kill.

Would that be the case for all animals? Even predators like wolves and cougars? If Adventurer's Eye only applied to monsters and intelligent races then it lessened its value, because he'd have no idea whether he could take on a pack of wolves, say, or even a single surly badger.

And he was in the woods, surrounded by wild animals.

Frowning, he began walking, looking for other things to scan. He spotted some sort of rock chuck scuttling into cover, and it displayed "Potgut, prey critter, normal stats".

Then, to his relief, he spotted a small deer in the woods ahead. It

Phoenix

showed a yellow icon above it to his naked eye, the Adventurer's Eye's automatic threat assessment. Then when he inspected it with the ability he saw: "Spotted Deer, animal. Attacks: Flee." and a full hit point bar with a max HP of 28. The spot for a mana bar was blank.

From the looks of things, the deer was completely normal in that it would try to run away from predators. He assumed yellow must be pretty weak, since the threat assessment had assigned it to a deer with no attacks.

Although considering he had nothing to his name but the knee-length tunic he wore, he wasn't sure if he could even kill a deer. What was he going to do, punch it to death? Try to pin it and break its neck? In fact, in that sort of fight was it possible the deer could actually beat him, with its hooves and teeth?

"Information," he said.

The command screen came up, offering him a list of options to browse, and Dare frowned at hit.

In some ways the command screen was really nice, but in others it was frustratingly unhelpful since it didn't offer much more than the class and universal ability lists, ability point allocation, class information, and the info screen for his personal statistics.

But maybe he could get more specific information if he asked. "I need clarification on the Adventurer's Eye color threat system."

To his pleasant surprise, a list quickly popped up, narrated by the disembodied female voice. "Threat assessment: Silver sickle icon, more than ten levels above you. Avoid at all costs. Capped greatly improved experience gains. Charcoal, ten levels above you. Avoid at all costs. Capped greatly improved experience gains. Red, five to nine levels above you. This will be a fight you likely cannot win. Greatly improved experience gains. Pink, from two to four levels above you. A challenging fight, improved experience gains.

"Blue, within one level of yours above or below. A worthy opponent, normal experience. Purple, between two and four levels below you, good hunting, reduced experience gains. Yellow, five to nine levels below you, very poor experience gains. Light grey, ten levels below you, extremely poor experience gains. Gold critter icon, more than ten levels below you, will not provide experience or progress towards achievements."

Okay, that was more useful information. Although honestly since the Eye told you an enemy's level anyway, the color threat system seemed a bit redundant. Fancy, pretty, and maybe useful for a quick assessment, but unneeded.

Where possible Dare was going to be looking over everything the ability could tell him about an enemy, so he didn't expect to make much use of the color system. "Does the Adventurer's Eye do anything else beside show the power of living things around me and their combat abilities?"

"It will passively display all creatures within an area equal to twice the range of your perception circle, and alert you when a creature of bright green or higher level enters your perception circle. You will then have the option of inspecting the creature. It will also pulse when you are nearing the perception circle of a silver sickle or charcoal creature. Other abilities not unlocked."

Okay, those were definitely useful. And he liked that bit about it getting even better as he used it. "How big is my perception circle?"

"Perception circle is determined by level, class abilities, and universal abilities. Yours is currently twelve meters thanks to a 20% boost to perception in forest environments provided by Forest Perception."

So his Eye would work to within 24 meters? That . . . wasn't very far. "But I can see things for miles away. Can I use my Adventurer's Eye on anything I'm looking at directly?"

"You can only use your Adventurer's Eye within the specified range."

Damn. "Do other creatures of similar level have the same perception circle range as mine?"

"Same base range, affected by the previously listed modifiers. Stronger enemies like party and raid rated monsters will have a larger perception circle, in most cases."

Damn, that was going to make things tricky. He'd have to pay serious attention when his Adventurer's Eye pulsed that dangerous enemies were approaching. Which wouldn't help him against red or even pink enemies, depending on his items and abilities.

Even more annoying, he wouldn't be able to use his Adventurer's Eye on much stronger enemies without aggroing them. Unless he could find some way to improve his perception circle's range or if improving his proficiency with Adventurer's Eye let him see even farther with it.

Maybe ranking up the ability would even increase the range of his perception.

Although as it stood the color threat assessment may not be strictly accurate since he doubted he could take on a similar level blue, or even purple enemy. At least not until he could craft a knife and then a bow. That, or use his trapping abilities with snares and whatever other traps he unlocked to catch animals he could skin, then tan the hides and sell them to buy equipment.

Looked like he had his work cut out for him.

He just hoped he'd been dumped in a noobie zone, and not one populated by a bunch of Silver Sickles that were a hundred levels above his. Or however many . . . the voice had never told him what the actual level cap was. For all he knew it could be just twenty or so, the minimum needed to justify the Adventurer's Eye threat ranking system, and levels were incredibly hard to get.

On the plus side, he hadn't encountered any monsters or other enemies while running around in these woods like an idiot. So as long as he stayed in the area he'd already explored, and no roaming monsters made an appearance, he should be able to get his feet under him and make his weapons without having to worry about getting into a fight.

Either way, he should probably stop dicking around and get to work.

If he wasted too much time he might end up starving to death before he figured out what he was doing. And then there was thirst; he'd have to find a way to purify water, assuming that microbes existed in this world. Which he was sure they did.

Speaking of which . . . Dare hurriedly looked through his abilities, then was left stunned when he realized that creating a campfire wasn't among them.

Of course he knew how to make a fire. He'd done a bit of camping with his family as a kid and with his friends in his teens and early twenties. But he knew that trying to rub sticks together using a string was hugely frustrating and took hours, and that was probably his best option since he had nothing else that could help him.

"Information." The command screens came up, and he looked at his class screen. Then, frowning, he looked at his statistics screen.

Ah, right. The universal abilities everyone had access to, which were shown on the stats screen. And there were a ton of them, too. Including a lot of greyed out ones with no identifiers that he guessed he'd have to unlock by discovering them or unlocking some sort of prerequisites.

In the meantime, though, it looked as if everyone started with "build campfire". Or maybe it was just one of the abilities he was expected to have unlocked by now, and his disembodied benefactor had done him a solid and given it to him.

Either way, the requirement was two rocks and between ten and

Phoenix

thirty seconds of clacking them together. Which was ludicrous, like something out of a cartoon, but he wasn't complaining since it beat hours of rubbing sticks together.

He quickly moved back to the clearing he'd appeared in, where he gathered sticks and kindling and built a circle of rocks. Then, a bit hesitantly, he raised the rocks and tried to use his first ability.

It was . . . unnerving. He was definitely making the motions, but it was like his body was on autopilot. Like he was doing a task he'd done a thousand times so he could let his mind wander. It made him wonder whether abilities more complex than banging two rocks together would also be done automatically like this.

As promised, the rocks struck a spark in no time at all. The spark hit the kindling, which began to smoke before a small flame appeared, and from there the fire acted the way it would on Earth.

To Dare's amazement, when he inspected the campfire he saw that along with providing a few comfort buffs, it also provided a deterrent to hostile enemies: 75% reduced chance of aggroing wandering enemies within 5 yards of the fire.

That was a huge advantage for a basic fire everyone could create. Doubtless whoever created this world's system hadn't wanted people to get murdered by monsters as they slept. He wondered if houses or settlements had an even bigger deterrent.

Well, he'd get his answer when he found one.

Dare turned away from the fire and rubbed his hands together. All right, now that he'd learned a bit and covered a few basics, it was past time to craft a knife so he could actually defend himself.

The recipe, if that was the right word, called for a Sharpened Stone, Twined Vine, and a Wooden Grip. The sharpened stone he could create with another basic ability which had subsets for knife blade, arrowhead, and axe head. The finely twined vine was also a required material for snares and other crafted items, and like sharpened stone had its own ability to create it.

As did the wooden grip. Although there was an alert that the quality would be affected by the hardness of the wood he found and his skill gouging out the notch that would hold the sharpened stone.

Since Dare expected to be making snares soon, he gathered every single vine he came across as he searched for the other materials. Then he searched around until he found two likely stones, one for the knife and another for an axe head, and another larger stone to bash against the stones to sharpen them (which seemed like it would be more difficult and complex than that, but that's what the ability called for). Last last of all he found a sturdy oak branch he could carve to make the handle.

That all took a fair amount of time and effort, but then crafting the Sharpened Stone, Twined Vine, and Wooden Grip were even worse. The crafting was time consuming and laborious, especially sharpening the stones, which tired him out and made his muscles burn. Braiding the vines also felt like it took forever, although he could relax by the fire and think as the ability did the work for him.

And using the sharpened stones to hack off the branch at the right length, smooth it to make the handle, then carve the notch, was just a complicated pain in the ass.

On the plus side, he was right that he could basically do all the ability tasks on autopilot. His body moved on its own, needing almost none of his attention, which allowed him to make plans and think things through as he worked. He also got a few notifications that his ability proficiency rank improved with use.

Hours passed, and the sun which had been overhead when he first woke up in the clearing was steadily sinking towards the horizon, but finally Dare finished making all the components and could combine them to make the knife.

After all the other frustrating effort, the last step was surprisingly quick and easy. He just jammed the stone into its notch, tied it with the vine, and he was done.

Text scrawled across the edge of his vision. "Achievement unlocked: Baby's First Weapon. Hold a weapon for the first time. 100 experience rewarded."

"Seriously?" Dare said. "Screw you." Was he going to be getting a bunch of achievements that people on this world got as young children?

On the plus side, though, he saw his experience bar move. Not much, but it was a start. Especially if he kept getting more ridiculous achievements like this one.

He raised the newly crafted knife and inspected it, and an information screen popped up. "Stone Knife. Quality: Trash. Damage: poor. Durability: poor. Significant reduction in quality for items produced from skinning and crafting with this item."

Well scrud.

He wondered just how accommodating this world's crafting system was. Was it like some survival games, where he could work his way up to harvesting ore and creating metal tools and weapons?

That seemed optimistic. But either way, he was going to need to prioritize getting a good quality knife. From what he knew, a proper knife was right there at the top of the list when it came to survival. And no matter what other weapons he used or what the situation, a good knife would always be a fallback for defense in the last extreme.

Which left him the frustrating double bind of needing a good knife to produce quality skins and craft quality items so he could make money, but not having the money for that knife. He'd probably have to take ten times as long harvesting inferior skins and crafting inferior items with this stone knife to earn that money.

What a pain.

Collisa

Well, if nothing else he'd be getting experience and leveling up his abilities from the efforts. And he probably shouldn't be making assumptions when he hadn't even tried the skinning and crafting systems yet. And he needed to catch game before he could skin it, anyway.

As if on cue, as he thought that he felt his stomach growl with the first pangs of hunger. He was relieved to see that this world didn't have a hunger meter, like a lot of survival games; he hated those things.

On this new world it looked as if it was just good old fashioned needing to eat and drink like back on his old world.

Still, that didn't make the hunger pangs any less painful. They were a good motivation to start looking for vines and other crafting materials the game was willing to designate as "Unrefined Rope Fiber: Trash", and get to work making snares.

Dare had no idea how to do any of that, but thankfully like with everything else the ability did it for him. He soon found himself holding a nice little snare, which it turned out he could place anywhere he wanted.

Considering he had at least the most basic commonsense knowledge of trapping, he went in search of rabbit runs, spots at a stream where animals came to drink, and other likely spots to place a snare. His Forest Perception helped with that, although since it was at the lowest rank not by much.

Still, he finally found a good spot where a lot of animal tracks met at a stream and placed the snare right on top of the tracks.

He spent the rest of the day making snares and placing them in good spots. By sundown he had a dozen made. Unfortunately, that didn't do anything for his growling gut. He ended up curling up by his fire with no blanket, just his simple tunic, thankful the weather wasn't too cold as he tried to sleep.

Phoenix

Dare just hoped that tomorrow would work out better.

Chapter Two
Progress?

The next few days were frustrating and borderline discouraging for Dare.

It turned out the crude snares he was able to make had a prey capture chance of .2% per hour. Doing the math on how long it would actually take for one to capture something, *on average*, was too much of a headache, but he knew it would be a long time.

Worse yet, digging deeper into the snare's information showed that there was another chance percentage, for the prey that would be in the snare when it actually did catch something. Kind of like a random loot generator.

And it turned out that the highest percentage chances were things like mice, rats, voles, and other tiny critters. The good news was the snare could actually catch prey as large as deer, which in real life no snare that flimsy would ever be able to do. The chances were just abysmally low to the point of not even being worth hoping for.

But the possibility *did* exist.

And to top off the suck, the snare had a RNG roll for when prey was caught, with a percentage chance of the snare breaking rather than catching the prey. And for a Trash quality snare with terrible durability, that was a depressingly large chance.

The only solution Dare could think of to the challenge was to just craft an absurd number of snares, to increase his odds that at least one would catch him something. It was a daunting task, one that required running around gathering materials and then spending hours crafting them.

Which, thanks to the ability system, was even more monotonous than crafting real snares would've been.

One pleasant surprise, however, was discovering that with every snare he crafted the quality slightly improved as his proficiency in Traps increased. Each one had slightly better stats than the last, giving him some hope that at *some* point he might be able to craft snares that actually had a chance of catching large prey with reliable regularity.

In the meantime, though, he had several dozen snares scattered in the woods around his campsite, and no faith whatsoever that any of them would be providing him food anytime soon. Assuming they didn't all just break.

His hunger wasn't going to wait for his first bit of good luck, though. It already hurt so much he felt like a weasel was trapped in his belly and trying to gnaw its way out. So he had to put snares in the "possible" category and look for another source of food.

Thankfully his class was suited for that. He also had the ability "Forage", which allowed him to find food in the wild. Of course, the ability was at its most basic at this level, which meant that he just had the *ability* to determine whether the things he found in the woods were edible, but not any list of actual edible items.

There was a also fairly high chance of foraging food that would make him suffer food poisoning, and even chances of suffering actual poisoning or exposure to toxins. Which sucked.

Best of all, the sort of food he was foraging at this level were things like thistle leaves, dandelions, common mushrooms, and bugs. Yes, bugs. None of it was appetizing, and most of it gave him a stomachache even though his stats didn't show any poison or toxin effect.

By the third day, he would've killed for even a bite of venison harvested from a deer. Which, he supposed, was technically how he would get that venison.

Collisa

On the plus side, he at least had the most basic idea of what was likely to be edible or poisonous, based on his knowledge of foods from Earth. It allowed him to only forage foods he was fairly certain were safe, reducing the risk of encountering something toxic.

Wouldn't that suck . . . to be given a chance for a second life, only to eat a poisonous mushroom and die like an idiot after the first few days.

Thankfully, that concern at least was quickly solved. On his second day of foraging his proficiency in the ability leveled up enough to gain a free ability in the foraging tree: Test Edibles, which allowed him to take more time testing an unfamiliar food to make sure it was safe.

The ability gave him an 80% success rate at detecting poisons or toxins, and better yet just about every time he used it the percentage rate increased by about a point. Which meant he had it maxed out at 100% within a day.

Apparently whoever designed this world's system didn't want all the Hunters out there dying of poison while trying to survive using one of their abilities, either.

One nice thing was that, in that strange way of video games, eating an edible food identified it to him and gave him the name the plant, fungus, insect, or whatever else was known by to the people of this world. Or at least he assumed so, because he sure as hell wasn't making up all the names the system automatically assigned to everything. It also made it so he could spot food items he'd already identified more easily in the wild, and recognize them as safe.

But best of all was that it told him the water was safe. As in, completely.

Dare had been feeling like he was dying of thirst, to the point of drinking from a stream in desperation while he tried to figure out a way to get water to his fire and boil it without destroying whatever container it was in. He knew he was risking all sorts of nasty

Phoenix

infections and parasites by doing it, but the thirst was too painful to ignore.

So it was no surprise he used his Test Edibles on the water in the stream near his camp almost as soon as he got it.

What *was* a surprise was that after he'd identified the water as safe, the information screen for the water showed that it was *all* safe. It claimed, and the voice in his command screens confirmed, that any water he drank, from the purest spring to the most stagnant puddle, would be safe. No waterborne diseases or parasites.

The only exception seemed to be water sources that were clearly tainted or poisoned, but the ones he found exploring the woods were all fine. Although realistically animals pooping in them all the time should've counted as being tainted.

Still, Dare wasn't complaining; if the creators of this world's system wanted to make sure that people wouldn't die of thirst or have to suffer awful illnesses like dysentery, he was fully on board with it.

By the third day, Dare was able to forage enough food to quiet the painful growl in his belly. It was ridiculously time consuming and the food was about as low quality as it could get, but it kept him alive.

That still seemed unrealistically easy, considering that even expert survivalists on Earth often went hungry for days trying to survive in the wild.

Not that he was complaining, considering the alternative.

Even better, his dozens of crude snares finally began to produce results. Granted, most of those results were broken snares, but there was the pleasant surprise that he could salvage the broken snares for a portion of the Twined Vines he'd used to make them. Which would save him a lot of time in gathering components.

He finally began to catch woodland critters, too. All about the size of a rat or smaller, and only four by the third day, but better than nothing.

The critters provided no meat, and skinning them produced what was quantified as a hide fragment. When hovering over the fragment he saw he could combine a hundred to them to create a small hide, which made no sense but was the sort of thing you'd expect to see in a game.

Unfortunately, what the critters didn't provide was sinew.

Considering his class and the fact that he was in a wilds teeming with monsters, Dare was desperate to craft his bow. He had a feeling it would be as shitty as the stone knife and snares, but it would at least let him begin hunting enemies and gaining levels.

Unless of course he wanted to get started right away leveling up with his knife, which seemed pretty stupid.

Lacking any better options at the moment, he at least got to work carving the wood part of the bow. Then, when he realized that it gave a tiny bump to his bow crafting proficiency, he began crafting more of them.

The bow staves he carved could be repurposed as spears or spikes for traps. Not with abilities, of course, since ironically for a survival class he couldn't craft either. Or at least not yet. But since they were simple to make and he knew they existed, he made them even so.

Actually, it was a nice change to actually have to do something by hand, rather than sitting back and letting an ability do it.

To his pleasant surprise, spears were classified as a thrown weapon. And as a Hunter he was qualified to use them, although he didn't want them to be his weapon long term.

Still, short term it solved his problem of the snares not doing the job and him not being able to craft a bow. He began practicing throwing the crude spears he'd made, and by the afternoon of the

Phoenix

third day tried his hand at hunting the woodland critters around him.

In most games killing critters was ridiculously easy, although they usually didn't provide much in the way of loot or experience, if any at all. Unfortunately, while a lot of things on this world had turned out to be easier than expected, hunting wasn't.

Dare shattered the tips of half a dozen spears throwing them at squirrels and potguts and even a small deer in the distance. He could just sharpen them again and keep going, although their damage and durability took a serious hit, but it was frustrating.

Especially since he wasn't crafting them with an ability, so he didn't get any proficiency for making or repairing them.

He *did* get proficiency for throwing the spears, at least. And after almost a full day of practice and completely destroying half of the weapons, he finally brought down some sort of medium sized pig-like creature, or maybe mole-like if much larger, that his Eye identified as an abbar.

To Dare's delight, the critter provided not only a small hide but four cuts of meat and, most important of all, a small length of sinew. As he roasted the meat over his campfire he started the sinew and hide curing, the tantalizing scents of roasting meat making it hard to focus on anything else.

From the looks of it he'd need three more lengths of sinew to create his bow, and given how long it had taken to get the first critter that might take another full day as his spear throwing ability leveled up. Still, it gave him hope that he was getting there.

He went to bed with a full belly, content and optimistic.

By the end of the fifth day, he had enough cured leather to create pants. Which were almost as high a priority as his weapons, since he was sick of his ass hanging in the breeze beneath his tunic in early spring. Especially since as he slept biting insects found their way *everywhere* and he woke up covered in irritating welts in the worst places imaginable.

Pulling on his new pair of pants felt like a major victory. They looked like shit, sure, but they were warm and protected him from insects and the elements.

Even better than the pants, Dare finally got all the materials to make his bow. He was relieved when crafting the bow unlocked the ability to create stone-headed arrows, and he hastily made a dozen as the light waned towards nightfall.

The snares had produced a mouse and a skunk today, and 13 had been destroyed. Dare had been starting to lose enthusiasm for them, considering active hunting was doing so much better anyway and required much less effort. Especially now that he had his bow.

But to his pleasant surprise as he was grudgingly recreating the destroyed snares, contenting himself with 10 since he didn't want to bother with gathering more materials, he unlocked the next tier of the Create Traps ability. It gave him the free ability Snares 1, which let him craft an improved snare that required much harder to find materials, but had drastically better chances of catching prey and better percentages for catching larger prey as well.

But much more importantly, it unlocked Traps and gave Dare a simple spike trap and the ability to craft spikes. The trap's stats for catching prey were almost as bad as the basic snare, but Dare didn't give a shit about that because the traps could be used against enemies.

According to the stats, the trap would do roughly the same damage to a target as an arrow from his new bow. Which meant it would be worth putting them down in a line and kiting an enemy across them until it died, or laying them in front of where he stood to finish off a wounded monster closing the distance to him.

Unfortunately unlike with snares, using a spike trap on an enemy destroyed it and the materials made to build it. So he was going to be gathering a *lot* of sticks and sharpening them. Which would increase his ability proficiency and continue to rank up Create Traps, Traps, and Basic Spikes.

Yay.

It was an hour past full dark when Dare finally abandoned his preparations and settled down by the fire to sleep. Although he was so excited that it took what felt like forever to settle down.

The last several days had been fun and challenging in their own way, sure. But it felt like his adventure on this world was finally getting started now that he'd managed to get the basic items needed for his class.

Tomorrow, he'd finally be able to hunt his first monster.

* * * * *

Dare had yet to see a monster or animal predator.

Of course, he'd been pretty much hiding in his explored area of the woods, unwilling to risk aggroing an enemy when all he had was a basic stone knife. And honestly, he still wasn't willing to risk going out just yet.

Instead he used his bow to hunt game all morning, ranking up his Bows skill. The nice thing was that even his basic bow was way better than spears, and he was able to collect a decent haul of meat, hides, sinew, and the few other things critters dropped.

He also took the time to craft leather bracers with the last of his cured hides, because he'd quickly figured out that using a bow without wrist protection, at least on the wrist holding the bow, *hurt*.

On the plus side, the bracers also gave him a small armor bonus. Very small, since just like the rest of his crafted gear the armor pieces were Trash quality, but every little bit helped.

Honestly, the pragmatic part of Dare wanted to keep on focusing on hunting for another few days, rank up his Bows skill and gather more hides. He still had a lot of things to craft just for basic comfort, like a tent and a bedroll. And a coat, and cloak, and leather armor so he'd be better prepared against enemies.

And he also kind of wanted to try his hand at making a collapsible camping chair like he'd used on Earth, although he'd have to design it himself and create it without the help of an ability.

But although working on all that would probably be the better (and certainly safer) way to do things, Dare was impatient to actually start *acting* on the potential this world offered him. He wanted to see his first monster, he wanted to fight it, and he wanted to kill it and see what loot it dropped.

He wanted to get experience and level up and actually get some proper abilities. Feel like an actual adventurer, instead of a transplant from Earth stumbling around trying to pretend he belonged here.

So Dare spent only a few more hours making some final preparations before setting out to begin leveling up.

First he turned a few of the uncured hides and some sinew into a hide pack, which he loaded all his spike traps into. When he realized he still had room he went to the laborious effort of crafting twenty more arrows, in case they were inclined to break like the rest of his shitty gear.

You could never be too prepared.

Finally, bow in hand and knife tucked into the belt he'd crafted with his pants, he hefted his pack and set out.

To scout out monsters and prepare . . . he wasn't going to hunt his first enemy just yet. Not until he was as sure as possible that he could beat it.

Since Dare had no idea where he was it didn't really matter which way he went, so he traveled west in the direction the sun was traveling. That way he could have it at his back when he returned to his camp later this afternoon.

Phoenix

He set out at a jog, which without Fleetfoot and his athletic body he would've considered a sprint. It was quick enough to eat the miles beneath his feet, but slow enough that he could keep a cautious eye on the forest ahead and make sure he wasn't about to blunder into danger.

As it turned out, he didn't need to worry about that since the first danger he saw was just hanging out in the middle of a clearing, in plain sight.

Dare could tell it was a monster even without using his Eye, since it looked like a hideous cross between a pig and a human. It stood upright at about five feet tall, thickset but looking as if it was mostly fat rather than muscle, with a tusked face, tiny aggressive eyes, and a boar snout. It had bristly pink skin, was clothed in a shirt and skirt of crude hides, and even from a distance he could smell a rank stench coming off the creature.

If he had any doubts that the pig-man creature in front of him was a dangerous threat, it was dispelled when he used his Eye on it and it was identified as "Level 3 Boarite. Monster.", with the threat color Pink. The attacks it might use on him were listed as Charge, Gore, Tackle, and Pummel.

All fairly self-explanatory, and not exactly pleasant sounding. Also not hard to guess that it was an unarmed fighter. Which, if he played his cards right, meant he might be able to kill it before it could even get him.

Or, with Dare's enhanced speed from Fleetfoot, he could run circles around it and kite it while he filled it with arrows. Although the Boarite's Charge ability might cause him some problems with that plan, depending on what exactly it was.

Too bad the Adventurer's Eye was so sparse on details about what the attacks actually did. Dare hoped that was something that would improve as he ranked up the ability.

On the plus side, since he was able to see the hit points of larger prey like deer, and having killed some prey earlier with his bow, he knew how much damage it did and how many shots it would take to kill the Boarite: twelve, possibly fewer with critical hits.

That was too rich for Dare's blood, so he cautiously circled around the Boarite in search of a lower level one.

Apparently he'd stumbled across a Boarite camp, or wallow or den or whatever, because he encountered regular sentries a few hundred yards out from it, and separated by a few hundred yards from each other. Beyond them could see hints of crude tents and signs of habitation through the trees.

The Boarite sentries ranged in level from 1 to 3, with the Level 1s being drastically weaker than the others, with a major step up to Level 2, and then a more moderate step up to Level 3.

Dare was pleased to see that he could kill a Level 1 in three to four shots, maybe two with a critical hit. Which meant he should definitely single them out as his targets until he either gained more confidence that he could handle a Level 2, or he actually leveled up himself.

Given all the time he'd taken with his earlier preparations it was already later in the afternoon, maybe around 5 p.m.; it seemed like this world had the same length of day as Earth, which made him hope it had the same seasons as well.

He had time to kill one Boarite with the precautions, and if it went well maybe risk taking out one or two more before he needed to head back to camp.

Dare selected the farthest Level 1 Boarite from the camp, then made careful preparations for his fight with his first enemy on this world.

First he set up a hunting blind within range of the monster, complete with a carefully prepared escape route in the treetops that he hoped his Fleetfoot would give him the agility to traverse. A few days ago he'd tested out tree hopping to be sure, and found that while a bit precarious he *could* leap from branch to branch.

It was actually exhilarating, something he *might* have been able to do back home but never would've been crazy or stupid enough to attempt. But with his enhanced speed and reflexes, not to mention the amazingly athletic body his unseen benefactor had given him, he could easily leap from branch to branch.

Even when one had broken underneath him, threatening to send him plummeting to the forest floor fifteen feet below, he'd almost casually found himself latching onto the tree's trunk and swinging to a sturdier perch.

It was good to know that in a pinch, Dare's speed would give him that extra edge over another Level 1.

Just to be safe he made a second knife, in case the impossible happened and he found himself face to face with the pig-creature, forced to defend himself in the last extreme. He wasn't sure if he could dual wield, but if it would give him extra damage he was damn well going to try.

Finally, with everything done, he climbed up into the blind and selected his best arrows, laying them out in front of him so he could grab them quickly. The picture of his class showed a Hunter holding arrows in the hand holding the bow, so he could shoot three or four in quick succession.

He knew that was possible, and very effective, from watching videos of archers doing it on Earth. But his attempts to copy the tactic resulted in him fumbling arrows everywhere and not being able to hit the broad side of a barn. He could keep practicing until he got it, but it was probably an ability he could learn anyway as he leveled up. Which would make the effort a waste of time he could be spending on gaining experience and ability proficiency.

All his preparations made, Dare nocked an arrow to his bow, raised it, and took a deep breath as he prepared to take aim, draw and loose.

From his observations the Boarite sentries mostly just stood there, and when they did walk around they all seemed to follow a fairly similar routine and stayed in their own general area.

He wondered if that was a characteristic of monsters and other similar threats in this world, or if these ones were simply stupid and predictable. Either way, it made planning for hunting them much easier.

Now he just had to hope that his target didn't have some sort of call that would send every single Boarite in earshot running to help it. That would be a grossly unfair ability for a monster that adventurers were expected to solo hunt, especially a Level 1, but that was one of the reasons he'd prepared so carefully.

And if these Boarites *did* do what any half intelligent creature would and call for help when under attack, better to know sooner rather than later. It meant Dare would have to either change his plans or abandon them as targets.

The Level 1 he'd picked out ambled into the far side of the clearing, well within bowshot, and Dare tensed and prepared to loose his first arrow.

He'd had a crappy plastic bow with a loose string as a kid, which if he was lucky could send an arrow twenty feet and might actually let him hit the target. That was the extent of his archery talent, and it wasn't great.

But he now had a class based around bows, and while his aim left a ton to be desired, as he'd proven by how many shots he'd had to take earlier while hunting before he'd finally hit his first target, he had to hope that his class abilities and stats would help him do better than he realistically would've.

Hope very, very hard.

Please don't let me die to my very first mob, he thought as he took aim, breathed to settle his heartbeat, then in a smooth motion drew and loosed.

His arrow hit the Boarite in the thigh rather than the center of its chest like he'd been aiming for, but he was satisfied that he'd hit it.

Under normal circumstances an enemy, especially a stupid one, would either be confused about where the attack came from and take a few moments to find Dare in his concealed perch, or would never figure it out and die pincushioned with arrows.

But instantly finding the source of an attack seemed to be a characteristic of creatures of this world, at least the monsters, because the Boarite bellowed and without hesitation turned to charge Dare's position, waving the crude club it held.

Dare bit back a curse and nocked another arrow, drawing and loosing. This one hit the monster, which was quickly closing the distance with the help of its Charge ability, in the side just above the hip. It stumbled but kept coming; obviously neither of Dare's attacks had hit anywhere that would provide a crippling effect.

He had time for a third shot, assuming he didn't panic and fumble. And also assuming the Boarite could climb. That reassured him a bit, and he took the time to make sure his final shot would hit.

It did, a critical hit right in the Boarite's head this time, and the monster flopped bonelessly to the ground less than five feet from the blind. It didn't so much as twitch.

Dare stared, wondering if it was really that easy. Then again, the head *should* be a killing shot. Except in most games it would just do an extra amount of damage compared to a hit in a less vital spot, reducing the enemy's hit points while it kept coming undeterred.

How much was this world like a game, and how much was it like real life? For instance, the fact that the monster had immediately seen through his concealment and charged him.

An important question, but first he needed to confirm that the

Boarite was actually dead and it was safe to go down and loot it. Also, Dare realized while looking around nervously, he hadn't checked to make sure the monster hadn't brought any friends as adds.

The area seemed clear, no sign of Boarites trying to sneak up on him. Dare activated his Eye just to be sure, then cursed his own stupidity and turned it on the downed pigman.

Of course his Eye showed an enemy's hit points, and at the moment the Boarite's were at "0". More pertinently, beside the other information about the monster was the word (DEAD) in parenthesis.

Dare sighed in relief, took one last look around to be sure the coast was clear, then climbed down from the blind to check the body.

Had it really been that easy? Just shoot a few arrows to kill a mob of equal level? He wondered if Level 1 enemies were made weaker on purpose since they were the lowest possible level, to give Level 1 adventurers a better chance of beating them and leveling up rather than dying to an equal level enemy.

Since he knew how much damage he did and could check an enemy's hit points before attacking it, he could just calculate the number of arrows, on average, it would take to kill it. Even so, it might be wise to use his Eye to regularly check enemies he was fighting, to see how his hits were landing.

It might give him hints about the monster's own attributes, like if it was weak to piercing damage or had extra armor or damage reduction abilities. That sort of thing would be good to know right near the start of a fight, before an enemy was able to soak up twice the damage he thought it could, so it managed to reach him and rip him to pieces before he could kill it.

The Boarite's stench got more and more unbearable the closer Dare got, and he wondered if he could really bring himself to search it. But he was pleasantly surprised to find that, like with the animals he'd killed, a screen popped up with all available loot.

Which in this case was one copper piece, tattered rags, and Boarite tusks.

He took it all, on the reasoning that vendors were usually willing to purchase anything in most games, even if they didn't pay much for the trash loot. Still, the amount he'd gotten for the enemy wasn't exactly thrilling.

It was probably intended to discourage high level adventurers from just running in and slaughtering camps of low level enemies to farm gold. Which meant that the loot would probably only get marginally better with each level, aside from rare drops or special loot.

Dare stared down at the dead monster, frowning as he considered the fight. Especially the way the Boarite had managed to immediately spot him as soon as he attacked it.

He'd gone to some effort to conceal his position in the hunting blind, but apparently it hadn't mattered. Did he have to use some sort of stealth or concealment ability in order for attacking from hiding to work against monsters? Or did he just lose some sort of detection roll against the Boarite, and otherwise it would've worked?

Was this an example of how real world attempts to do clever things didn't matter because they weren't part of the ability system? That would almost be disappointing if it was.

Well, the only way to answer some of those questions was to keep hunting Boarites, and other monsters, and see what happened. Although he'd need to take another look at his ability tree to see if concealment or attacking from stealth were in the Hunter class.

It certainly seemed like they should be.

Another interesting question . . . if stealth was determined by an ability, would concealment improve it? Or could he just stand out in the open stealthed in front of a monster, and be invisible because he was outside stealth its detection range?

He liked to think that concealment would at least provide a stealth modifier: it required effort that should be rewarded, and it just made sense. But he'd have to see.

In any case, Dare had managed to kill a Level 1 monster pretty easily. He thought it would be safe to go pick off the other Level 1s around the perimeter before he headed back to camp.

Between his Fleetfoot speed and killing everything in around three shots, it took less time than he'd expected. Unfortunately, soon enough there were no more Level 1s, and he didn't want to risk himself against a Level 2 without making some preparations. Like he had with the first Boarite.

So he decided to swing wide on the way back to his camp, explore the area a bit more and maybe find more enemies to fight.

Tomorrow he'd return to the Boarite camp and see if the Level 1s had respawned. If not, he'd try to approach the camp through an opening where one of the Level 1s had been and see how strong the enemies in it were.

But all in all, it had been a successful trip. He hadn't earned much loot, but he'd managed to make some decent experience; he thought that killing another twenty or so Level 1s would get him to Level 2.

As long as nothing went wrong, he should be able to manage that tomorrow. Then he'd just have to see what sort of jump in experience to level he'd be facing for Level 3.

Chapter Three
Opposite of Hostile

Dare had played some games where you could aggro a mob, and the enemy standing right next to it wouldn't so much as bat an eye, continuing to wander around aimlessly.

It turned out that adds were a lot more alert on this world. As he learned when he risked picking off a Boarite in the camp that was twenty yards away from another Boarite.

Now he had two pissed off pigmen after him, one of which was a Level 2.

Discretion was the better part of valor, especially when there was an entire camp of Boarites not far away that still might aggro if he wasn't careful. So he turned and bolted back the way he'd come, using every ounce of speed he could muster with Fleetfoot.

Well, now was as good a time as any to see what sort of effort it took to escape a fight once you'd aggroed an enemy. That was definitely information he'd want to have when confronted with a dangerous situation.

Such as, for instance, right now.

He'd previously seen that even with Charge, Boarites weren't all that fast. As in, they could almost keep up with his fastest speed while Charging, but the ability only lasted ten seconds.

That let him stretch his lead on the two pursuing enemies, and he started to feel more confident in his chances.

If all enemies were this slow then he'd never have to worry about being able to run away. Not to mention that he'd be able to run circles around enemies, shooting an arrow and then running back and shooting another.

He was busy enough relishing in that prospect that it took him longer than it should've to realize that the Boarite sentry he'd killed to get to the camp had respawned and was now in front of him.

Fuck, how did that happen?

None of the other sentries, not even the first he'd hunted this morning after confirming they'd respawned overnight, had shown any sign of coming back anytime soon. Was it possible that attacking the camp had triggered the respawn? That was going to be a pain in the ass.

Dare hadn't aggroed the hideous monster yet, but he needed to stop now or he would. Which meant he'd have to either change directions or turn back and fight his pursuers.

He glanced back over his shoulder, then nearly shouted in alarm when he realized the Level 2 Boarite was only twenty or so feet behind him.

Obviously its Charge was better than a Level 1's. Which was strange, because usually enemies of similar levels had similar rank abilities.

Dare could worry about the mechanics later, though. He spun, lifted his bow, and loosed at the raging pigman. Then he started running again, slinging his bow and drawing his knives as he listened to the Boarite close the distance to him.

At the last second he spun and reversed direction, dodging his enemy's clumsy punch and punching one knife into the pigman's armpit. His enemy squealed and tried to throw another punch, but before it could Dare slipped around to its other side and slashed at its throat. The sharp knife began to cut deep, then to his irritation snapped at the handle, the knife blade flying away.

Even better, the other Boarite finally caught up at that moment, and Dare found himself backing away and dodging desperately to stay ahead of attacks from both.

At least they were only using punches. If they'd actually had weapons he would've been in trouble.

The Level 1 had about half the health of the Level 2, so he switched targets and began slashing his knife at the Level 1 with all the speed Fleetfoot gave him and the weapon was capable of.

He saw the monster's hit points slowly dropping as bloody slashes opened on its arms and back, and felt a moment of hope that he might be able to find a way out of this.

Then the Level 2 landed a punch square in his face that sent him reeling backwards, a small chunk of his hit points vanishing off his bar. The Level 1 used the opportunity to Tackle him, and Dare found himself on the ground with the reeking pigman atop him, viciously swinging its head in an attempt to Gore his face and neck with its tusks.

Shit shit shit!

Dare desperately held the creature off with one forearm while he slammed his knife into the Boarite's neck over and over. He watched the monster's hit points go down in steady chunks from the repeated critical hits, dropping towards zero.

Then the Level 2 began kicking him in the ribs, and he gave a strangled grunt of pain and lost hold on the Boarite. His speed gave him barely enough time to jerk out of the way as the monster's tusks bore down on him, and he cursed through gritted teeth as one sliced across the meat of his shoulder.

With a last surge of panicked adrenaline he managed to stab the Boarite in the neck again, hoping against hope that would do it. Then he cursed aloud as his enemy showed a sliver of health and raised up to Gore him again.

He stabbed one last time, and to his immense relief the monster finally slumped in death, weight dropping to pin him.

Collisa

The Level 2 kicked him again, hard enough to bruise his ribs, and both Dare and its dead friend went flying away from the force of the blow. That freed him from beneath the Level 1's corpse, and he scrambled to his feet.

Just in time to take another punch to the face. Then another and another in rapid succession, blows landing on his face and abdomen as the Boarite Pummeled him.

Dare leapt backwards and then sprinted to one side, managing to stay just out of range of the flailing monster. When the Boarite squealed in fury and pursued, he saw with vast relief that it didn't seem to have Charge back.

He'd lost his bow back when he'd been tackled, and he wasn't in the mood to try to chunk his enemy's health down with dozens of hits of a knife that might break at any minute. So he led the monster a short ways off, then doubled back at his top speed and grabbed his main weapon.

He was panting like a bellows as he nocked an arrow to the string and raised it, barely taking the time to aim before loosing. To his relief it hit the approaching Boarite in the chest, causing it to stumble.

Dare bolted away again, managing to buy himself enough space to shoot another arrow. It hit the monster in the shoulder and barely slowed it, although its hit points dropped to half.

Kiting his enemy, keeping just ahead and loosing arrows when he had a moment, he managed to shoot it two more times. Then his luck ran out and the Boarite's speed drastically increased, closing the distance in moments.

Dare dropped his bow and began desperately dodging as the monster continued to try to Pummel him. Half the blows landed painfully, but he accepted them as he looked for chances to stab his enemy with his knife.

Phoenix

The Boarite only had a sliver of health left, maybe four more hits with the crude stone blade. He got one good slash on the Boarite's forearm, another good stab into its side, a slash across its snarling face, slicing deep into its snout . . .

Then his knife finally broke.

Dare punched the pigman in the face with the hilt, the heavy wooden grip acting like a fist weight and giving him extra force. His enemy stumbled back a pace, missing with its continuing flurry of punches. It was *so* close to death, hit points not even visible on its bar, which meant it had to have just 1 or 2 left.

He fumbled for an arrow, and with a defiant shout stabbed the stone head into the Boarite's eye.

It dropped bonelessly, and he got several text notifications at once.

"Achievement unlocked. Desperate Measures: Kill an enemy with a previously unused ability. 100 experience gained."

"Ability unlocked: Unarmed Combat."

"Ability unlocked: Fist Weapons."

"Ability unlocked: Arrow Stab."

Dare barely noticed the notifications, panting in pain and exhaustion as he stared down at his fallen enemy, then over at the dead Level 1 nearby. His hit points were at 69%, which wasn't nice, and he'd come dangerously close to being pinned and killed while he was helpless.

Fleetfoot had saved his ass there. And it confirmed what his disembodied benefactor had told him about the ability, that it would basically make similar level fights easy mode. Or at least possible mode.

It also confirmed that he'd been way too cautious in avoiding Level 2s. Sure, the stronger Boarite had been a challenge. But if he was fighting one alone, from a distance, he should be able to beat it without too much trouble.

He'd also gotten a small but decent bump to experience for it, which was nice. Although most importantly he was still alive.

The behavior was beneath Dare, and he wouldn't have done it in a player vs player game (most of the time), but to relieve some of the tension of the terrifying encounter he spat on the Level 2's corpse. "Should've minded your own business," he told it.

He looted the two enemies, then killed the Level 1 that had respawned to block his escape and got well away from the Boarite camp. Once he felt a bit safer he stopped to clean his gored shoulder and bandage it, hoping it would be fine without stitches he couldn't manage at the moment.

Then he settled down to rest and assess his options.

The Level 1 sentries he'd hunted yesterday had been back today, so he'd once again circled the perimeter of the camp picking them off. Then he'd ventured closer to the ramshackle structures to see what things looked like.

As it turned out, what it looked like was that there were around 20 Boarites, most within 20 yards of each other. Which he now knew was within range to become an add for an aggroed enemy.

Actually, at some point he should probably test that range to find the minimum. Assuming it wasn't different for different enemies, as he was fairly sure it was for levels. But he wasn't keen to have to either flee or fight multiple enemies, so he'd save that for when he was high enough level that he could test it on enemies far weaker than him.

In the meantime, he couldn't clear this camp unless he was either part of a group or was way higher level. Which was going to slow his leveling a bit since it limited the number of enemies he could hunt. Especially depending on respawn: was it every day? Every 12

Phoenix

hours? Shorter, but he hadn't been around to see it?

He did want to see how long it took for monsters to respawn after he killed them. And at some point, see if they'd respawn at all if he cleared the entire camp. But he was also in the mood to get experience today, try to reach Level 2, and the only reason to stick around was for the remaining sentries.

Dare laboriously crafted two more knives, then a third one just to be safe. It ate up precious hours of his time, and he'd probably end up breaking them if he had to use them in a fight, but he didn't fancy trying to kill an enemy with Unarmed or Fist Weapons or Arrow Stab; all three abilities did even worse damage than his shitty knives.

Once that was done, he circled the perimeter again and picked off the Level 2s, managing to kill them without too much trouble. Most managed to close the distance to him with some hit points left thanks to their improved Charge, but he was able to keep ahead of them long enough to finish them off.

He managed to clear all of them without losing any more hit points, and better yet he saw that his hit points were regenerating at a rate of about 1% per hour.

Hopefully eating and sleeping would help him recover his hit points at an even faster rate. Although he wondered how this world handled serious bleeding, broken bones, or internal injuries that on Earth would *need* to be treated or he would die.

With any luck Dare would never have to find out. He certainly planned to be more cautious from now on.

Soon enough there were only Level 3 sentries and the Boarites in camp left. The ones he'd killed hadn't respawned yet, and Dare didn't really feel like risking going for a Pink so early in his leveling experience, especially when Level 2s were just difficult enough to be touch and go at the end.

So instead he decided to explore around the area and try to find more Level 1 monsters to hunt.

His mysterious benefactor had made it sound like monsters would just be all over the place in this world, so he'd have plenty of enemies to kill. He hoped that was the case, but at the same time he also hoped they wouldn't be *too* numerous or close to each other because that would make things a lot more dangerous. Like in the Boarite camp.

After running around for a few miles, which wasn't too time consuming since he could basically jog a mile every six minutes with his enhanced speed without tiring himself out at all, he discovered two things: first, that monsters *were* fairly common, because he found spawn points for two different kinds within a mile of each other. And second, that monsters tended to be well spread out in their spawn points, and the spawn points had plenty of buffer space between them and the locations of other monster spawn points.

It meant he could hunt enemies without having to worry about adds, and should also be able to get around higher level monsters if he needed to.

The first spawn point Dare found was for Level 4 and 5 Mange Wolves, nothing he wanted to tangle with just yet. It was interesting to see that even though they were animals, his Eye classified them as monsters.

Maybe because of the mange descriptor? Or because they spawned rather than repopulated by breeding? Did monsters breed?

So many questions. He needed to find some people soon so he could get some answers from them.

The second spawn point featured Level 1 to 3 Giant Toads. They were also classified as monsters, with acid spit and long tongue attacks. Those could be dangerous, but as if to make up for it they had fewer hit points than Boarites.

He eagerly began killing the toads, hoping that clearing all the

Phoenix

Level 1s and 2s would be enough to level him. The Level 1s died in 3 or sometimes even 2 shots, and dropped Toad Meat, Frog Legs, and Rubbery Pelt, which could be used in some crafting recipes. Although the drop rate for all 3 was frustratingly low.

It was interesting that hunting animals produced pelts with every kill, but monsters didn't. Maybe it was a way to discourage adventurers from getting all the materials they needed solely from leveling up?

Dare killed all the Level 1s and checked his experience bar, pleased to see that it was close to the top; he'd level with one or two more kills, depending on of the experience bonus for Level 2 Giant Toads was similar to what he'd gotten from Level 2 Boarites.

Only one way to find out. He targeted a Level 2, found a good position to aggro it from, and took aim.

Five seconds later the furious toad, an arrow protruding from its bulbous body, was spitting acid with enough force to send it flying at him. At maximum bowshot range.

Dare cursed, only his enhanced reflexes allowing him to avoid the glob aimed right at his face, and fumbled for another arrow as the toad hunched in on itself and prepared to spit again.

He loosed another arrow at the toad, then tried to dodge a second glob. It hit his hide pack instead of him, and as he drew a third arrow to shoot at the monster he heard the alarming hiss of the acid eating through the uncured hide, and smelled the queasy stench of acid and disintegrating fur and leather.

With a curse he shrugged out of his pack, then took his shot. Thankfully the weak toads had few enough hit points that even a Level 2 died in only five or six shots, so he already had it down below half health. He focused even harder on dodging *before* the toad spat, and managed to stay ahead of its globs of caustic saliva as he loosed his final two shots to finish it off.

Dare should've expected it, because he'd been tracking his experience and had calculated that he'd level up soon.

But even so he literally jumped three foot into the air, aided by his enhanced reflexes, when as soon as the monster dropped dead from his final arrow he found himself bathed in golden light, and a roar like a triumphant army filled his ears.

In front of him large golden letters said, "CONGRATULATIONS, YOU'VE REACHED LEVEL TWO!" bracketed on either side by golden banners showing his Hunter image.

Dare wasted no time looting the toad, then retreated back a safe distance in eager anticipation and wasted no time pulling up the level menu.

He got some overall stat increases, the old stats in yellow with an arrow pointing to the new stats in green. They were small increases, but he wasn't about to complain. He also unlocked some new abilities he could spend points on, and some small improvements to his hunter and universal abilities.

But to his dismay, he only got 1 ability point to spend.

"I only get one point per level?" Dare demanded incredulously. There were already so many abilities he needed to get, including putting points into ranking up abilities he already had to keep them maxed to his level. And he was certain that there'd be even more as he unlocked new ones with levels or ranking up his abilities.

Words formed in the air in front of him, along with the familiar disembodied female voice. "Ability points awarded increase with each level gained."

Ah, that made more sense. Getting his first level had been relatively easy, and not too dangerous either aside from a couple of crises caused by his own mistakes, so it stood to reason the rewards for it would be small. "By how much?"

A chart quickly populated, showing ability point awards up to Level 20. Up to Level 4 he'd get 1 point each level, then 2 points each level from 5 to 9. At 10 he got a 1 point bonus on top of starting to get 3 a level, and then at 15 it went up to 4 a level. Up to Level 20, when he got 5 a level as well as 2 bonus points. He assumed the trend would continue like that moving forward.

Okay, that was a bit better. But he still faced the choice of what to spend his first point on.

In the end it wasn't really a choice. As a Hunter there was one thing he desperately relied on, and that was his bow. No other ability he could see, either in the class or universal lists, came close to being as important.

At the moment he had Bows, which wasn't so much a level of the ability as simply unlocking his ability to use bows, with no modifiers. It also allowed him to gain proficiency in the ability.

"Show me Bows 1."

A description quickly populated. The upgraded ability would make him more competent with all bows and crossbows, reducing his chance of fumbling it, dropping arrows, getting the bow or quiver caught on branches as he moved, and things like that. It would also increase his range, accuracy, damage, and speed drawing, nocking, and shooting.

Dare was interested to note that while range and damage went up a small but decent amount, and accuracy went up an even more decent amount, the speed increase was almost negligible. He supposed it was like with a real bow, where archers trained for years to reach the point where they could shoot an arrow every 3 seconds.

That just made his Fleetfoot improvements to speed that much more major; being able to shoot arrows 34% faster from Level 1, or Level 2 now, was an even more powerful advantage than he'd thought.

Collisa

Although now that he'd checked his stats and selected an ability, it was a bit disappointing that, after all the anticipation, the event of leveling up was over just like that. Dare took a moment to admire his increased hit points, although his overall health remained at 72%.

That dashed his hopes that leveling up would fully heal him and restore his mana, like it did in some games.

With a grimace he looked down at his hide pack, which had a patch of blackened char where the spit had touched it. He wasn't sure if it had eaten all the way through, although he wasn't about to test it until he had thoroughly washed the thing to make sure there was no more acid on it.

Dare gingerly picked the pack up by one strap, carrying it in front of him, and set off in search of water. There were plenty of streams in the woods, and he assumed one would probably be nearby.

Instead he found a river, and along its banks the most glorious sight he'd ever seen.

* * * * *

Dare stared at the creature sliding its way along the bank beside the river, one of many in view in the large meadow the river ran through.

It was a nude woman made out of some clear, viscous blue substance. Her head and torso were clearly defined, even showing flowing hair and large breasts with medium sized nipples. At about waist level, however, the figure collapsed into a pile of its substance, which it moved along the ground in undulating waves.

Not quite able to believe what he was seeing, he checked his Adventurer's Eye.

"Slime (non-toxic), level 1. Monster. Attacks: Envelop, Stimulate, Devour Excretions."

No way. Was he actually looking at a slime girl? As in, one that

Phoenix

he didn't have to kill but that he could actually fuck? Those "attacks" really didn't sound like attacks at all.

Dare instantly felt himself hardening at the prospect, cock straining against his leather pants. He wanted that to be true so desperately that if he'd listened to his raging libido, he would've stripped and gone right for the transparent blue woman.

Which probably would've been stupid. But oh god, if it wasn't . . .

He settled back at the edge of the trees, watching as the dozen or so slimes in view undulated around with the aimless patterns he'd noticed in other monsters. He wanted to think of a way to test if the slime girls were safe, maybe approach and see if he was attacked.

But what if the slimes didn't attack until they had you fully vulnerable? He could just imagine being balls deep in one of those sexy mouths, and then the monster girl ripping off his cock and then proceeding to tear him apart while he rolled on the ground wishing for death.

Absurdly, he was still debating the issue an hour later, completely forgetting his acid-burned pack, and leveling, and everything but the debate of whether or not the slime girls were safe.

Then the question was answered for him when he noticed a Level 3 Boarite eagerly approaching the river. Dare perked up as the pigman tore off its clothes when it came close to the slime girl he'd been watching, then continued its beeline straight for it.

For her part the slime girl moved forward just as eagerly to embrace the hideous monster.

What followed was downright disgusting, and Dare did his best not to watch too closely as he continued observing to see what happened.

Maybe five minutes later the Boarite, sated and with tusked mouth pulled back in a stupid grin, dressed and returned back the way it had come.

Dare stared at the slime girl the brutish monster had just left after very clearly fucking it. It even had ropes of the Boarite's semen suspended in its transparent belly, slowly drifting apart and dissolving.

Was really it possible that this world would include a slime monster that didn't attack you, but would have sex with you instead? It seemed too good to be true, like a self-serving fantasy.

But on the other hand, it made a sort of sense. There the slime girl was, oozing along contentedly as it digested the come it had been fed.

Why go to the effort and risk of fighting when you gained the nourishment you needed from bodily secretions? The slime wouldn't even have to go out of its way for food if it made itself look like a beautiful woman; plenty of men would be happy to come and feed it while asking for nothing in return, thinking they were the lucky ones in the deal.

Even monsters, as he'd just witnessed.

In fact, if slime girls had evolved naturally they would probably be almost perfectly adapted. A lifeform whose source of nutrients came to her, and had incentive to come back regularly, and she didn't have to do a thing in return but change to an enticing appearance and wait patiently to be fed.

And he desperately wanted to feed one of the slime girls in front of him.

It was probably stupid, even crazy, to consider going down there. Not to that slime girl, of course, since she'd just screwed a disgusting Boarite, but to one of the others gliding along the riverbank.

How did he even know one would do the same for him? Maybe they only serviced monsters.

Phoenix

Collisa

But in spite of his reservations, the power of boners was stronger. Besides, they were only Level 1 and he had his Fleetfoot if things went wrong.

Dare found himself cautiously emerging from the trees and making his way to where another slime girl, smaller and more delicate than the first, slid along on a less extensive pool of its substance.

He set aside his gear and quickly undressed, then came within the perception circle of the monster. He was already rock hard, trembling in a mixture of excitement and nervous anticipation.

Here went nothing.

The slime began to glide towards him, a delighted smile spreading across her delicate features. Closer up they weren't quite as sharply defined as he'd hoped, but still an impressive job looking realistic.

Even better, as the transparent blue girl approached her pile of substance molded itself into two long, slender legs, small but curvy hips, and a shapely little ass that just begged to be rubbed. A flat tummy led down to a narrow hairless mound that ended in a small slit framed by plump lips.

Dare moved towards her, cock throbbing with every step. Especially when the slime girl grinned impishly and lay down, every part of her that touched the ground beginning to dissolve into a puddle but the rest of her clearly defined as vaguely girlish. Although the facsimile was a bit rough, as if she was struggling with the finer details.

She spread her legs, and he watched in fascination as the monster seemed to focus *very* hard on the one detail that mattered. The simple shape of her slit and labia began to resolve into a careful recreation of a woman's pussy opening like a flower, inner folds glistening with arousal.

Phoenix

He bit back a groan and continued forward, dropping to his knees over the slime girl as she lifted slender arms to embrace him.

Dare expected her slime to be cold and clammy, but to his pleasant surprise it was invitingly warm and had the slick consistency of, well, female sex fluids. As if some giant woman had had the mother of all squirts, and now her nectar was oozing around in search of partners.

The only exception was the smell, a slightly ripe, too-sweet aroma that made him decide not to actually taste the slime, even if his Eye said it wasn't toxic.

Now that he was in the slime girl's arms he had one last hesitation, wondering if this was a mistake. But before he could change his mind the monster acted for him.

Warm, slick legs wrapped around him, and he felt a wet, clearly defined surface begin to rub the head of his cock. He could even feel the slime girl's pussy lips parting to welcome him in, and groaned as she lifted herself up onto his cock, fully enveloping him in her slick heat.

He looked down at the slime girl's face, then immediately regretted it and looked away. Her features were still as a doll's, and from close up the details were more blurry. Also the slime was constantly flowing along her surfaces, as if it wanted to dissolve into a puddle and she was only holding it in this shape through sheer force of will.

Altogether it made her face distinctly unnerving.

Dare looked down instead, confirming that her body was beginning to melt into shapelessness as she focused on accommodating his cock. He could see his huge shaft moving through her transparent blue torso, piercing deep into the slime. He could also see the slime bunching and concentrating around it, trying to give him the sensation of tightness with a substance that wasn't intended to grip or become firm.

Collisa

The slime girl's body began to flow up and around his hips and torso, face nuzzling his neck and hair sliding up to cover his shoulders and upper back. It was like being in a bath of warm, viscous oil. All except his cock, which he finally began to thrust deep into the slime.

An immediate plus was that he could go as hard and deep as he wanted without causing discomfort to the translucent woman or hitting her cervix. And the slime around his cock continued to bunch and tighten, until it almost felt like he was getting a firm handjob *inside* the pussy he was fucking.

He'd been so aroused coming into this, and the sensation was so novel and pleasurable, that he barely lasted a few minutes before stiffening in the slime girl's warm enveloping embrace and beginning to spurt into her. He looked down to watch jets of his seed fly out and become suspended in her transparent belly, and groaned at the erotic sight.

As Dare fired off his last spurt his strength finally gave out. He collapsed onto his monster lover, which dissolved into slime and flowed to cover his entire body up to his chin, briefly tightening around him as if to give him an affectionate squeeze.

Before he could worry that this was some sort of attack, and she was about to try to smother or strangle him, the slime began sliding off him.

It pooled on the ground nearby, once again molding to form into the shape of a lovely young woman. She rose from her puddle in a graceful step, his cum still suspended in her flat tummy, and with a final playful wave goodbye began to walk away, every sashaying step drawing attention to her small shapely hips and firm ass.

So that was his first experience not only with a slime girl, but with his new cock. And good god, it had felt incredible. Seriously, absolutely out of this world.

Dare rolled onto his back with a groan of satisfaction, feeling his skin. To his surprise there wasn't even the slightest residue of slime, which he supposed made sense; she wouldn't want to leave a bit of her body with every man she fucked.

    Reason finally broke through the haze, though, reminding him he was on a dangerous world and monsters frequently visited these slime girls. He hastily dressed and retrieved his gear, taking a few moments to wash his pack in the river, then retreated back into the woods and started back for his camp.

Collisa

Chapter Four
Contact

Dare would've liked to say that he began regularly visiting the slime girls for better reason than that he was a degenerate. Or at least, not entirely for that reason.

It was true, too.

Since the slime girls drew monsters to them, it was a perfect place to farm. Especially since the monsters would take off all their gear, and in their distracted state were ridiculously easy to ambush.

Dare was careful never to attack a monster that was anywhere close to a slime girl, though. He definitely didn't want to antagonize them, and even more seriously didn't want to hurt one. Monsters or not, just interested in devouring his fluids or not, he was growing very fond of the transparent blue women.

He definitely found at least one to fuck every time he was there at their river, taking pains to approach a different one every time so he could feed them all equally.

Also, for a more enjoyable reason, because each slime girl had a slightly different size and look, including females from other races: he encountered a faun girl, a massive one that looked like some sort of orc, and best of all what he thought was a nymph or a sylph. Which he was delighted to discover, and ended up visiting the beautiful nature maiden twice.

Even better, every slime seemed to use a different position, as well as access to a different "hole". Some gave him blowjobs, his cock piercing deep down their slender throats, others offered him their pussy in a truly impressive variety of positions, and some offered him their tight assholes.

Phoenix

Dare actually really enjoyed that last category. He'd only tried anal once, and had really enjoyed it. But it had to be said that using that hole required a bit of extra cleaning afterwards.

With slime girls, though, there was really no difference between their orifices aside from where they decided to invite his cock into their transparent bodies. It was more for his benefit than theirs.

So with them he got to grab a plump ass and drive between the cheeks to his heart's content, with none of the smell or mess.

Every girl he fucked dissolved into slime and fully enveloped his body after he was done. And after half a dozen times, he finally figured out why.

The large orc hadn't been content with just one load of his seed, probably due to her size, and had patiently kept stimulating him until he became hard and fucked her again. He'd worked up a real sweat with her, but after she covered his body with her slime before leaving contentedly he realized that the sweat was gone.

It appeared that when his Eye said "devour excretions", it meant it.

Visiting the slime girls turned out to be beneficial for a different reason, too. On the tenth or so day of hunting around the slime girl spawn point, having gained two levels in the process, Dare arrived at their section of river and was surprised to find another man, a human in his mid 20s, already there.

The man was fully occupied with the nymph slime girl, a sight Dare didn't need to see, so he retreated into the woods to wait for him to finish.

He was always mindful of his unseen benefactor's warning about how brutal Collisa could be, and in any case he would've been wary of another intelligent creature anyway. Even someone of his own race; he knew what people could be capable of.

So he waited until the man eventually wandered back into the woods, dressed in rustic clothes and looking pleased, and began making his way purposefully east and a little north. Then instead of introducing himself Dare simply followed him.

He was hoping the man lived in a village, one where Dare could trade and find out more about the world. After he determined the villagers were friendly, of course.

It was an unexpectedly short walk, maybe a half hour before the trees opened up on a well tended farm. Probably a mile and a half at most; Dare could run that in ten minutes. Although it was closer to a half hour's run from his camp.

Maybe he should move it.

The man circled around the farm and kept going, and Dare continued shadowing him until he spotted the thatched roofs of houses ahead.

Dare broke off then, not wanting to risk being seen, and hurried back to his camp.

Although he wanted to keep leveling, he wasn't about to pass up this opportunity. He resolved to spend the next day or two hunting, collecting leather, dried meat, and crafted goods to sell in the village. Along with all the loot he'd gathered so far, of course.

Dried meat was an ability in the cooking tree that he'd learned after cooking ten cuts of meat. It allowed him to preserve all his surplus meat, vastly increasing its durability and freshness timer. He'd had to construct a drying rack, of course, but that had been pretty easy.

Dare still had to make a tent and bedroll, but he prioritized making gold for the moment; his goal was to find a good bow in the village and he wanted to be able to afford it. Or if not that, at least a proper knife that wouldn't break halfway through a fight.

Speaking of his gear breaking, it was probably a good thing he took a break from leveling when he did. As he was hunting his bow

Phoenix

abruptly snapped, startling the deer he'd been targeting and sending it bolting away. It also whacked his arm hard enough to leave a bruise.

He was just lucky he hadn't been gouged by one of the jagged ends.

Dare had to pause his hunting to craft a new bow, which had the minor benefit of being slightly better than his original one. Then he got back to work.

Two days later, he had enough trade items to not only load his pack, but also several hide-wrapped bundles that nearly overloaded him. It was all heavy enough that as he set out for the village he got infrequent notices that he was slowly increasing proficiency in his carry ability, and even slowly raising his strength and carry capacity.

Very slowly, but it was satisfying even so.

The trip that had taken a half hour when running took almost 2 hours with his burden. Dare just hoped he'd be able to sell most of these items so he'd at least be able to run back. Although that was his smallest motivation for getting good sales.

Having decent gear might literally be a matter between life and death.

Dare passed the farm he'd seen before and saw a woman with a pitchfork at one of the hay piles near the barn. She was tossing hay into a small cart, and the open barn doors behind her suggested she was at work filling the hayloft.

Dare hesitated at the treeline, building his resolve.

This would be his first interaction with a person, someone he could actually communicate with, since coming to this world. He was worried he might make some mistake, offend her, and right off the bat sour his relationship with this village. Or, even worse, that she'd be unfriendly or hostile and not even give him a chance.

Collisa

Then a new worry struck him: what if the farm girl didn't speak English? Or, more accurately, what if he didn't speak her language? How would he communicate? How long would it take to learn a new language so he could even operate in this world?

Especially when he had to stay out in the wilds farming monsters to level up.

Well, whatever his fears the only way to know was to try. Besides, it was possible she wouldn't even want to talk to him, the way most people would with a stranger approaching their home, and he'd just end up exchanging a few words before continuing on to the village.

Dare hiked his overloaded pack higher on his back, adjusted a strap, then with a deep breath stepped out from under the shadow of the trees and began walking along the fence that surrounded the farmyard. There was no proper path, but the grass and weeds were trampled in a faint trail from frequent passage.

"Hello!" he called in his most friendly voice as he neared the working woman.

She paused and looked up, briefly knuckling her back. Her expression was slightly wary, but also curious. At least until she got a better look at him.

Her eyes widened with something like awe, and she licked her lips and hastily brushed at her dress and fiddled with her hair, pulling out a piece of hay. Her cheeks were flushed, and she practically drooled as she stared at him.

Right, his unseen benefactor had given him movie star good looks along with everything else.

"Hello!" the farm girl called back with a very friendly smile. She glanced at his bundle. "Coming in to trade?"

"That's right." Dare felt a surge of relief that she either spoke his language, or more likely the system that ruled this world was translating for him. Maybe because they were the same race and should be speaking the same language.

Or maybe his unseen benefactor had implanted the language in his brain, similar to how he was able to do things he wouldn't be able to do in real life thanks to the ability system. Or the fact that he could read the information systems.

Out of curiosity, he checked his universal abilities and saw "Haraldaran: Fluent".

He didn't know what Haraldaran was, since Shalin was the continent they were on. Maybe it referred to this kingdom? Or the humans in it? The information suggested that there were different languages on this world, or the language wouldn't have had such a limited name. It also suggested that there was probably no common language.

Or maybe there was, but the people of this kingdom didn't speak it. He quickly checked for other languages in his universal abilities, but he didn't have any other ones unlocked. And if there were other languages available, he couldn't see them because he hadn't discovered them yet.

In any case, at least Dare wouldn't have to spend months or even longer just finding a way to communicate with the people of this kingdom. It was a start.

And hey, maybe the language system would let him learn future languages faster, like with other abilities.

As he continued forward he looked the woman over, curious about this person from another world. She seemed human, like the man he'd followed from the slime girls, not particularly different from anyone he'd seen back on Earth.

A quick use of his Eye confirmed that she was a Level 6 adult human female. No age specified, although if he was any judge she was somewhere in her early to mid 20s. Her class was Tiller, with no combat specializations he was aware of, and the names of the attacks she could use against him were borderline humorous.

She was closer to plain than pretty, although he could admit that in his old life he probably would've been interested in asking her on a date. Dare would say her height was close to average, so several inches shorter than him, and she was plump, with long brown hair in a braid and expressive dark brown eyes that were probably her best feature. Aside from maybe her large chest and round ass. Her skin was brown with a farmer's tan, although he caught paler skin peeking out beneath her clothes.

"I'm Dare," he continued as he reached the closest spot to the farm girl along the fence.

She hesitated, then approached a few steps closer and gave him a sultry look. "Ellui," she said, absently brushing more hay and dust off the front of her plain tunic. It had a low cut that revealed ample tanned cleavage, with a hint of a line of pale skin where the sun hadn't touched that made him want to see more.

"Nice to meet you, Ellui," he said with a smile, which he noticed made her tanned cheeks blush even redder. "I'm new to this area . . . would you be willing to tell me a bit about your village?"

"Of course, Dare." The farm girl quickly wiped at her face and plucked more hay out of her hair. "Not hard to guess you're not from around here, though, considering the direction you came from." She waved vaguely towards the village. "Not many people come this way, and none from the west. No roads that way, at least not anywhere near here."

Dare had seen as much from his own limited explorations. "I ended up coming here through interesting circumstances with nothing but the tunic on my back," he said. "I've been working to establish a camp nearby, level up, and produce trade goods to get what I need."

"Well there's always call for meat, sinew, leather, and worked leather goods," Ellui said. "Even hides, if you don't want to go to the effort of curing them yourself. And depending on the monster loot there are usually people willing to take it off your hands."

That was good to hear. Hopefully he could earn enough for a new bow and a few other things that would make his life easier. "What sort of crafters do you have in the village?"

She shrugged. "A few Leatherworkers. A Woodcarver. Most of the women put enough into weaving and tailoring to clothe their family, and a few level it up a bit farther as a side income."

Interesting. So the people here spoke of the world's leveling system, suggesting it was a significant presence for them just like it was for him, and not some background thing running behind the scenes as they lived their lives.

"How about you?" he asked.

The farm girl laughed. "I'm one of the former. Just enough so I'm not dressed in rags, and I can turn my focus to other things I need more." She grimaced around the farm. "Lots I need to be able to do, and only so many ability points."

Dare gave the farm a closer look as well. It was in good order, the buildings and fence well tended, the fields growing well, and everything neatly in its place. Ellui was obviously hardworking and took pride in her home. "You've done a good job with the place," he told her.

She blushed again, biting her lip around a pleased smile. "That pack looks heavy and you've probably been traveling awhile," she said. "Would you like some bread and milk and a place to sit while we continue our conversation?"

He blinked, then smiled as well. "That's very kind of you, thanks."

The farm girl motioned. "Come on in, then. You can sit on the back of the cart while I fetch the food."

Collisa

Dare shrugged out of his pack and heaved it over the fence, then vaulted it and made his way to settle on the back of the cart. Ellui fussed a bit making sure he was comfortable, then disappeared into the farmhouse.

She returned a few minutes later with a hunk of bread and two glasses brimming with milk. He couldn't help but notice that she also seemed to have taken the time to wash her hands and face and more carefully brush off her clothes.

The farm girl settled on the back of the cart next to him, the space narrow enough that her curvy hip nearly touched his, and handed him a glass before tearing the bread in two and giving him the larger piece.

"Thank you," he said again as he sipped the milk. It was buttermilk, as it turned out, cool and tart, and went well with the heavy, slightly sweet bread.

"So what did you do before winding up in our little backwater?" Ellui asked as she nibbled on her bread, shooting him almost shy glances out of the corner of her eye. She shifted as if making herself more comfortable, bringing them slightly closer together.

Dare would've preferred to ask more questions, since he had a million and thought of more by the second. But she'd been very forthcoming and generous with him, and it wasn't like he was in a hurry.

"I worked in a che-" he cut off, not knowing if this world had industrialization. "As a crafter," he amended. "But there was an accident and I lost my job. After a while I ended up here."

True enough, if a bit of a stretch.

"A crafter, huh?" she said. "How vague."

He couldn't exactly say the plant had produced dangerous chemicals that probably hadn't even been discovered on this world. Or that he hadn't actually known the process for creating them; he'd just hauled stuff around and worked some machinery.

"Anyway I decided on a fresh start," he said, "so I chose to become a Hunter and began my new life in the woods west of here."

Ellui's expressive brown eyes widened. "You took the 10% experience penalty?" she asked in disbelief.

He could understand her assuming that, since if he'd been born on this world he would've had to pick a class at age 12. And if he chose to become a Hunter now that was the only way he could've done it.

And he could understand her surprise, since in her eyes it would've represented losing a tenth of all the progress he'd made since picking his first class. Six years worth of experience.

Which might make the fact that he was only Level 4 more believable.

"I lost a lot coming here," he said truthfully. "But I'm excited to make a new life for myself."

"It looks like you're making a good start of it," the farm girl said, glancing at his heavy burden of trade goods and all his handcrafted leather items. "You must've been busy, unless you've been here a long time and just never bothered to visit Lone Ox."

Dare assumed Lone Ox was the village. "I've been here about three weeks," he said. "And yes, I've been busy."

She grinned and nudged his shoulder with hers. "Well, stretch out your legs and eat up. You can take five minutes at least."

He chuckled and obliged, tearing off another chunk of bread with his teeth.

They ate and chatted for a while. Dare learned that the area they were in was Kovana, a small, mostly wild and unsettled region of the kingdom of Haraldar. Ellui seemed a bit puzzled when he wanted to know the name of the world, glancing at him sidelong as if she

Collisa

thought he might be teasing her, but obligingly told him it was called Collisa.

Collisa. His new home.

The farm girl really pressed the point home that people didn't come to Lone Ox, with even traders visiting only infrequently, and that most of the monsters in the immediate area were low level. Nothing happened, and even the frequent festivals to divert people from their lives of toil were humble and rustic.

It sounded as if she was bored, discontent with her life, and a bit bleak about her future. Even so she was cheerful and friendly, quick to smile and laugh, and Dare found himself liking her.

The feeling was apparently mutual, because over the course of the conversation her shifting around eventually ended up with her sitting with her hip and thigh pressed against his. She also leaned close to him as they talked, occasionally brushing her ample bosom against his arm.

He was starting to get optimistic about how this visit was going to end.

His heart beat a little faster when, after they finally finished their meal, Ellui set aside their glasses and then rested a hand on his leg just above his knee. "Now that you've rested a bit," she said coyly, brown eyes dancing with mischief. "Maybe there's something you can help me with to repay my generosity."

If he had any doubt what she meant by that, it was dispelled when her hand boldly slid up his thigh to cup his crotch.

Dare felt himself begin to harden beneath her touch and sucked in a breath that wasn't quite a gasp as she began to rub him through his pants. The farm girl *did* gasp, looking surprised at his size, and the gleam in her eyes sharpened.

"It only seems fair," he answered in a strained voice. Ellui wasn't sexy and exotic like the slime girls had been, but the fact that he

Phoenix

could talk to her, and she was so eager for him, more than made up for it.

Besides, he thought she'd be fun, and he could admit he looked forward to playing with her curvy little body. And considering her attitude towards the entire encounter was so casual, he had a feeling she was just looking for some fun too.

"Well then," she teased, abruptly pulling her hand back and standing. "Maybe you could help me find something over by the barn."

Dare wasted no time following as the plump farm girl strode over to the barn and leaned forward with her hands against the wall, looking back at him and licking her full lips. "I think it's somewhere around here," she said with a playful smile as she reached back with one hand to flick up her skirt.

Apparently women of this village didn't wear underclothes, or maybe she'd taken them off when she went to fetch the food, because Dare found himself staring at a pale round ass and plump thighs.

Between those sexy thighs was a thick brown bush, framing a pussy with meaty inner labia crumpled tightly together in a slit that was already glistening with arousal. Her pale legs were also covered with a fine fuzz, and he concluded that women in this area either didn't or couldn't remove their body hair.

Well, he wasn't complaining. His eyes were fixed on that pale round ass, and the pouting pink pussy lips that parted slightly to reveal a glistening interior as she spread her sturdy legs.

"Well?" she asked impishly. "Don't know how it's done? What are you waiting for?"

Dare stepped up behind her, fumbled at his breeches and let them fall to his knees to release his rock hard cock, and grabbed Ellui's ample hips, sliding his hands along the smooth, yielding flesh and making her gasp.

Collisa

Phoenix

She pushed back against him, trapping his cock between her thighs in a forest of soft brown pubic hair, and with a moan of delight began to rub her pussy against it from above, squeezing the sides tightly with her thighs at the same time. Before long the friction of her ministrations was eased by the juices slowly leaking from her pussy, until within a minute or two his cock was well soaked and sliding easily between her plump thighs.

He had a better appreciation for just how well endowed his unseen benefactor had made his new body when she finally pulled away and waggled her ass impatiently at him, signaling the foreplay was over. Dare positioned himself at her entrance, his tip slightly parting her meaty labia, and then began to slowly push himself in.

"Oh gods and goddesses," Ellui moaned, fingernails scraping over the weathered wood of the barn. "You're fucking huge."

The farm girl definitely wasn't a virgin, considering how much she seemed to be enjoying his size and how easily he slid inside her. Still, her cunt was tight and intensely pleasurable compared to the looser feel of a slime girl before she managed to compress enough slime around him to finish him off.

Soon he bottomed out in her warm, velvety tunnel, with a few inches of his shaft still outside. He rotated his hips, pressing lightly against her cervix, and as she moaned he began to pull out again. A glance down showed her pussy stretched around his girth, creating a tight ring that pulled outward slightly with his withdrawal as if begging him not to go.

"How you holding up?" he asked, pausing with his tip just inside the entrance to her pussy.

Ellui moaned again and wiggled her hips. "I'm not sure whether to tell you to take it slow until I'm used to you, or beg you to mount me like a stallion and pound me until my legs give out."

Dare's cock twitched at her language, and with a grin he began pushing back inside her. "Let's try for somewhere in between."

Collisa

He only went a bit faster and more firmly, but even so she squealed as he bottomed out in her again. Grinning wider, he reached between her legs as he began to pull out more quickly, questing through her thick bush until he found her clit. He gently rubbed to one side of it as he once again thrust into her, faster than the last time.

"Oh Goddess of Fertility," the farm girl moaned, pounding one fist against the barn wall. "You're making my year." She began bucking her hips, either to press herself harder against his fingers or push back against his thrusting cock. Maybe both.

"Keep going like you're going," she panted. "But feel free to abuse the hell out of my clit. The little lady can take it."

Dare obliged her, pressing directly on her love button and swirling his finger firmly, while pulling out more quickly so he could thrust into her again. Then again.

Ellui's hips bucked and she squealed. Then with a throaty moan that went straight to his most primal self she collapsed with the side of her face pressed against the barn, and her tight walls clamped down on his cock.

He felt a fresh surge of her juices flow out of her, splashing against his crotch and trickling down his thighs as he thrust into her again. "You motherfucker," she gasped through panting breaths. "Oh gods and goddesses, you fucking fucker." She bucked her hips back against him. "I'm ready, take me like a bitch in heat."

Dare didn't need a second invitation.

He grabbed her wide hips tight, squeezing the soft yielding flesh, and with a grunt pulled almost all the way out of her and slammed in. As she squealed he pulled back and slammed in again, then again, faster and faster. As if he really was trying to match the frantic pace of a dog.

He was dimly aware of Ellui collapsing against the barn again with a wail, velvety walls rippling around his invading cock as she again climaxed. He felt a spray of wetness over his thighs, either her juices squelching out of her pussy at the force of his thrusts or her squirting from her orgasm.

"Ooooh goooood Daaaaare!" she moaned, voice shaking from her climax and the force of his thrusts. It was the first time she'd called him by name since putting her hand on his crotch.

The restraint Dare had built up with the help of the slime girls finally collapsed as the pleasurable sensations finally overwhelmed him. "I'm going to come!" he warned.

The farm girl obligingly hitched her skirt up higher, fully exposing her thick ass and muscular lower back. "Paint me," she squealed.

Dare pulled free with a squelch and took aim, spurting jet after jet over her luscious round globes. Then he sagged in sudden weariness, stumbling back a few steps to sit on the back of the cart. Rough wood and poky hay grated against his bare backside, but he barely noticed as he lay back in the hay and worked to catch his breath.

Ellui stayed desperately pressed against the barn wall for a few more seconds, as if it was the only thing keeping her up. Then she took a final panting breath and straightened briskly, flicking her skirt down without apparent care for his seed cooling on her ass.

She turned to him and beamed, flushed face radiant and eyes sparkling. "That was . . . gods, I can't tell you how much I needed that," she said in a breathless voice. "Any time you want to come around for another go, you're more than welcome."

He chuckled weakly and with some fumbling raised his hips and tugged up his pants, tying the laces. "I think I'll take you up on that."

"You'd better." Ellui looked around as if slowly coming to herself, then grimaced. "You should probably go. The kids will be back from their lessons soon, and that worthless husband of mine could return from the forest at any time." She sniffed. "Probably in there fucking slimes or cunids or whatever other vaguely woman-shaped creature with a cunt he can find."

To say her words hit Dare like a splash of cold water was a vast understatement. It was more like a ball of ice straight to his nose at Major League pitcher fastball speeds. "Husband?" he said with a choked voice. "Kids?" The farm girl's easy smile faded slightly as she turned back to look at him. "You're married?"

She snorted. "What, did you think I still lived with my parents? Of course I'm married. I'm 24 and have a farm to run."

Dare stumbled to his feet and backed towards the fence. "I didn't know you were married!" he protested. "I-I never would've done this if I'd . . ."

Ellui rolled her eyes. "So what, my useless lump of a husband gets to go off and stick his dick in anything that moves, but I can't have any fun myself? At least I do him the courtesy of having my lovers come outside, so he can be sure all our kids are his."

She sniffed. "Meanwhile he'll paint the insides of every moist slit he finds. He's probably got half a dozen cunid offspring hopping around in those woods."

He had no idea what a cunid was, but that was the last thing on his mind right now. "I'm sorry, I don't want to be part of any infidelity," he said, grabbing his pack and throwing it over the fence. "Thank you for all your kindness, but this won't happen again."

She scowled at him. "I'm guessing you'll change your mind and be back in less than a week," she called as he vaulted the fence. "And you know what, I'll take back that fat cock of yours if you apologize for being such a smug asshole."

"Goodbye," Dare said as he shrugged into his heavy pack and started towards the village.

Phoenix

"Come back if you want, as long as you lose the attitude!" the farm girl, or farmwife he supposed, shouted after him. "I'll even let you come inside me . . . screw Brennal and his slime-covered cock! Come in the morning or early afternoon and he'll probably be out in the woods finding beast girls or monster girls to fuck, and the kids will be in the village at their lessons."

Dare quickened his step. He suspected Brennal was the man he'd followed back from the slime girls. The man had walked right past this farm before, but maybe he'd been headed into the village to try to pretend that's where he'd been all along.

Best to avoid the couple entirely . . . they seemed like nothing but trouble.

On the far side of the farm he found cart tracks carving a path through the grass and weeds, headed towards the village, and gratefully followed them. It was a relief when the farm fell out of sight behind him, and he resolved to circle it at a good distance on the way back to his camp.

To his deep chagrin, just as the houses of the village of Lone Ox came into view up ahead he spotted two children headed his way, a boy of about six and a girl of maybe five, escorted by a young woman in her late teens who wore quilted cloth armor and had a sword at her hip.

The kids had to be Ellui's and Brennal's, especially considering their brown hair and similar features, and Dare felt another flash of guilt as he passed them, nodding politely to the woman guarding them as she stared at him warily.

He hadn't known the farmwife was married, but he probably could've guessed if he'd thought about it. That didn't change what he'd done. He just felt a bit bad for the kids, considering how dysfunctional their parents' relationship seemed.

Hopefully they'd be okay.

Collisa

Just a few steps further on he got a text notification. "Discovered: Lone Ox. 25 experience earned." Which was a pitiful amount, but he supposed it was better than nothing. He kept going until he could see the place more clearly.

The village was about what he'd expect. It had more the layout of a place you'd expect to see in a fantasy game, rather than a true medieval village, and didn't seem to take into account some practicalities that people living in these circumstances probably would've already addressed.

No doubt there were abilities that rendered those issues moot.

There were a few people out and about, mostly women chatting or doing errands and children playing. Dare spotted an older man seated on his porch carving a chunk of wood with a small sharp knife he couldn't help but envy, and made his way over to him.

"Well met, traveler," the older man said jovially. "We don't get visitors often out here. I'm Nassor."

"Dare," he replied, extending his hand. "I'm looking to sell or trade meat, leather, and hides, as well as some monster loot and crafted items."

"Ah." The man shifted his knife to his other hand and returned his handshake. "Only so much demand for things like that here. You might not sell everything, and if you're looking for better prices you'd probably have more luck in the town of Driftwain, a day or so north of here. Or better yet Kov, a week's walk to the northwest. It's the capitol of the Kovana region, a pretty big place."

Those distances would be less for Dare, with Fleetfoot, but even Driftwain would still be a long way to go to sell goods that at this level probably weren't worth much. "I'll be content if I can get a bow and knife and a few other things," he admitted, then grinned. "And now that I said that, I hope you're not the man here who'd be buying from me."

Phoenix

"Might be a few things I'd be interested in." Nassor laughed. "Although for your particular trade goods, you'll probably want to try the tailors and leatherworkers. And Olern at the tavern for the meat."

"No local merchant or trader I can sell everything to, and he'll resell at a profit?" Dare asked without much hope.

The older man laughed again. "Not in Lone Ox."

Well, looked as if Dare had his work cut out for him. "Okay, can you point me to those people?"

"Sure." Nassor joined him on the street and pointed out several houses, briefly describing who lived there and what they might be willing to buy. He seemed to know everyone well, which Dare supposed wasn't surprising for someone living in such a small village.

"All right, thank you for your help," he said politely as the older man finished speaking and retuned to settle in his seat.

"Now hold on, lad," the Woodcarver said, motioning him back. "Before you run off to sell your loot, maybe we can help each other."

Dare paused, turning back. "How?"

Nassor held up his knife. "Been noticing you admiring this," he said with a chuckle. "Good steel, good quality. Good for skinning, crafting, and of course self defense."

That certainly sounded tempting. "How much?"

"Well now, wouldn't be much point for me to sell my knife," the man said with another chuckle. "I doubt I could sell it for what I paid, and it's something I use. I've got another, but still . . ."

"So what's the idea?" Dare asked. "Some sort of trade? Did you want me to do something for you?"

"Yes and yes." Nassor pointed west into the woods. "I carve tusks as well as wood, but it's hard to get my hands on any. However, there's a boar out there that has the biggest tusks you've ever seen." He scratched at his jaw. "It's not your usual boar, though. Level 5, and nasty for its level."

He waved at Dare. "You're a bit low, still, but the offer's open for as long as you're interested."

Dare blinked. "You can see my level?" He'd thought that was a feature of his Adventurer's Eye.

Nassor looked at him like he was an idiot. "Of course." He glared suspiciously. "Why, you got some weird ### that makes it so people can't?"

Dare frowned; it sounded like the Woodcarver had practically mumbled a word. Or maybe a stray breeze had muffled it? But he didn't want to get even further off topic by asking the man to repeat himself. "No, of course not. But I come from a place where we're not properly taught all this stuff."

"What's to learn?" The older man scratched his jaw, still giving him an odd look. "Everyone can see the level of intelligent creatures."

Dare frowned; he shouldn't be bothered that other people had a skill he'd thought was limited to his Eye. And honestly for social interactions he supposed it was important to know how powerful the other person was.

"Just the levels?" he asked, to be sure.

Nassor snorted. "As opposed to what, having the Adventurer's Eye? We can't all be Level 50 or higher grand heroes." He shook his head wryly. "Anyway, if you're ever able to kill the beast and bring me its tusks, you can have my knife."

Dare let the matter drop. "I've got some Boarite tusks," he offered.

Phoenix

The older man chuckled. "I'll take 'em off your hands for 2 copper apiece, but if you want the knife I need the tusks from that boar."

"I'll keep it in mind," Dare said slowly.

As he spoke the words text appeared in one corner of his vision. "Quest accepted. A Boaring Request: Bring Nassor the Woodcarver the tusks of a great boar."

"Good man!" the Woodcarver said cheerfully. "You can find the boar about 5 miles to the northwest of here, in a big clearing along a river. It doesn't usually stray far."

Of course it didn't.

Dare withdrew his Boarite tusks, and after a bit of haggling managed to wheedle an extra 2 coppers from Nassor. He also prevailed on the man to purchase one or two pieces of the other loot he had, although the prices were all terrible.

At least as far he knew; he needed to get a better handle on the economy and market system of this world. Although he hoped the older man at least was dealing fairly, if for no other reason than that he wanted Dare to bring him those tusks.

He thought Nassor was, since he seemed a decent sort.

Once their business was concluded Dare was 51 coppers richer. Since he didn't know what that could buy he wasn't sure whether to be pleased or not. But it was a start.

He put away his money, and the older man held out his hand in farewell. "Best of luck with your trading, lad."

"Same to you with your carving," Dare said. "I'll see what I can do about that boar."

For a quality knife, and all he had to do was kill a monster, he was definitely going to do it. But no point looking too eager.

Collisa

Dare made his way around to the houses Nassor had pointed out. He had a lot of success with his first visit, to the tavern keeper Olern. Although instead of a proper tavern what the man had was a slightly larger than usual house and a big outdoor patio with a long table, which apparently served the same purpose for the small village. The tavern keeper was more than happy to purchase Dare's fresh and dried meat, as well as a few of his higher quality foraged food items.

Dare saw silver for the first time off the deal, and couldn't help but grin as he shook hands with the man and walked away.

Unfortunately, after that initial success what followed was a frustrating hour or so of having doors slammed in his face, haggling for every bent copper, and the discouraging discovery that the vendor trash loot he'd hoped to sell was as uninteresting to everyone else as it was to him.

The Leatherworkers didn't have the recipes to use his Rubbery Pelts, and with their laughable offers he finally decided to keep them in case he could eventually use them for crafting himself. And their offers for his leather and hides was so low that he finally broke off the haggling in disgust, deciding he'd just use them for crafting his tent and bedroll like he should've done in the first place.

To his pleasant surprise, he finally managed to unload the Boarites' tattered rags on a poor woman who lacked the materials to make clothes for her family. She paid him a measly 5 copper for the lot, and both of them walked away from the deal unsatisfied.

As he walked away from the ramshackle house she lived in, he was hailed by a well dressed portly man trotting down the street towards him. "Good sir!" the man called, puffing as he caught up to him.

"Dare, please," he said, offering his hand.

The man shook it vigorously. "Durrand, Mayor of Lone Ox. I've been told you're selling goods in the village. And that you might be not just hunting in the woods, but actively trying to level up. That you're an actual adventurer, not just gathering meat and hides to sell as a profession."

Interesting. Did that mean that most people preferred not to take the risk of adventuring and hunting monsters, and no one else in Lone Ox was leveling up? "That's right," he said cautiously.

"Gods and goddesses be praised," Durrand said. He clapped Dare on the shoulder and began ushering him down the street. "Come, come. Let me offer you a drink and say my piece."

This was smelling a lot like another quest, and Dare went along willingly. Although honestly, the prospect of alcohol would've been enough to lend the Mayor his ear; he hadn't had a good drink in what felt like forever. In fact, he'd resolved to return to the "tavern" and buy himself a mug of beer after his other business was done, as long as he had the money to pay for it.

The Mayor led him to one of the largest houses in the village, and by far the finest, and invited him inside. The place was well furnished and cozy, and he heard the clatter of someone working in the kitchen farther in, a woman's voice humming cheerfully.

Durrand ushered Dare to a chair near a cluttered area with a desk that he obviously used as his office space, then moved to a table by the wall and retrieved two glasses, filling them a finger's width with dark golden liquid from a plain glass decanter.

Brandy? That was a lot better than the beer he'd been hoping for.

"Thank you," Dare said, accepting the glass and taking a sip. The liquor had a smooth, smoky flavor. Not exactly top shelf, but it warmed his stomach nicely. "What was it you needed help with?"

The Mayor settled in a chair across from him, taking a longer sip of his own drink. His grimace had nothing to do with the bite of the alcohol. "Bandits have begun operating in this area recently, since the snows melted. They've hit a few farms, and attacked some people who ventured into the woods east of here to forage and got too close to their camp."

"Bandits. Okay, that was a change. "How many?"

"A dozen, perhaps, ranging from Level 6 to their Level 10 leader." Durrand gave him a narrow look. "I know you're a bit low to tackle this, but if you can gain some levels, the sooner the better, or find more adventurers or brave villagers to accompany you, you should be able to handle them."

"A bit low" was putting it very generously. After Dare's disaster at the Boarite camp, he was leery of trying to hit any group of enemies that might pull as adds. Not unless he was a high enough level to easily take multiple enemies at once.

Actually, that reminded him that he should probably head back to the Boarite camp after one or two more levels and clear it. He wanted to see if there was any good loot in there, and if nothing else it would be a good source of experience.

Assuming he didn't aggro a dozen at once and have to run away.

The bandits, though, he wasn't sure he'd even want to try to tackle until he was at least Level 11. Especially since they'd be humans or some other intelligent race, and unlike monsters following game mechanics they'd be a lot more likely to all charge him at once.

If he was careful and clever he might be able to pick off one or two without being spotted. But at that point the others would start searching for him and he'd be facing ten pissed off enemies. Including some sort of boss in the bandit leader, probably.

"You might have trouble finding them," the Mayor said, continuing his spiel. He motioned Dare to join him and went over to his desk, grabbing a rolled piece of parchment. He quickly unrolled it, using paperweights to hold it down.

Then the portly man grabbed what was clearly a primitive fountain pen and began marking the parchment. "Here, this should

Phoenix

help."

Dare looked over his shoulder to see a crude map labeled "Kingdom of Haraldar". It showed nothing but topography, although that in surprising detail, as well as marking the locations of a handful of large towns and cities.

"The map seems pretty incomplete," he said.

"Mmm?" Durrand looked up absently from where he'd been marking a location on the map where the bandits could be found. He glanced back down at the map. "Ah, right. The more detailed a map is, the more difficult it is to copy and the more expensive. I purchased several simple maps for various purposes."

He gave Dare a thoughtful look. "Although I've heard adventurers like to buy a simple map and then add their own notes about the areas they visit such as monster spawn points and levels, locations of dungeon entrances, special discovered locations, and smaller towns and villages. The smart ones also borrow or rent a monster compendium and use the back of the map to write down the levels and other known details of the most common monsters in their area. As well as the details for the monsters closest to them in level, so they can be on the lookout to hunt them."

That sounded incredibly useful, even in its incomplete form. Although of course Dare wouldn't need to bother with a monster compendium thanks to his Adventurer's Eye.

He *would* probably record the information of all the monsters he encountered, start creating his own compendium. If the Adventurer's Eye really was rare then that knowledge might sell for a lot, and if he found adventuring companions they'd want to know that stuff.

"Here," the Mayor said, briskly shaking some sand over what he'd written and then rolling the parchment up. He offered it to Dare. "This will help you find the bandits."

"You're just giving me a map?" Dare asked in disbelief.

Collisa

"Giving?" the man chuckled. "I was going to let you borrow it until the job was done." He scratched his chin thoughtfully, inspecting Dare. "Although if you don't already have a map, and want this one, I'd be happy to deduct it from your reward." He held out the fountain pen. "This too."

Dare had planned to accept the quest anyway, even if it turned out when he checked out the bandit camp that he wasn't sure he could beat them. In most games it was a good idea to accept every quest you got, and then abandon the ones you couldn't or didn't want to finish. Like those that you had out-leveled, which no longer offered experience or a reward worth doing it anyway.

But being given a free map just for accepting the quest was icing on the cake; even if he wasn't able to complete the quest, he could just not abandon it to allow him to keep the useful tool.

"All right, I'll do it," he said, offering his hand.

As Durrand gratefully shook it, text appeared at the corner of Dare's vision. "Quest Accepted. Bandit Brutality: Slay the bandits operating east of Lone Ox."

A few hours in the village and he'd already found two quests. Ones with good rewards, too. "How much are you willing to pay on top of the map?" he asked.

The Mayor rubbed his jaw, expression turning shrewd. "I think I could part with 10 silver for such an errand."

Dare laughed; he would've thought haggling would be a pain in the ass, and it certainly was when he was trying to offload low value trade goods. But it was also an invigorating challenge, more interesting than just handing a cashier some money and collecting his bags of groceries.

"An errand that involves cutthroats who are attacking your people and scaring away travelers and traders," he countered. "You want me to go alone against a dozen outlaws, or find others to help

Phoenix

who'll want their fair share of the reward. 10 silver isn't even a joke, it's an insult."

Durrand frowned. "Then what would you think is fair?"

Dare thought it through; in most games, like in real life, if your counter offer was too outrageous the other person just walked away from the table. He would've liked to push for 30, but that was probably way too high. "20."

The Mayor held up his hands helplessly. "That seems excessively high, but more importantly we're a poor village. We couldn't afford such an outrageous payment." He rubbed his chin. "11 silvers, 50 coppers."

That was a poor counter offer, but it hinted the man wasn't going to go too much higher. "I might do it for 18, since you're also giving me the map. It might be worth risking my life for that much."

Durrand shook his head. "You can press all you want, but reality is reality. We can afford 13 silver, perhaps. And you're welcome to keep all the loot you get in the bandit camp, even what they stole from our village."

Dare was close to 100% sure that that would've been the case anyway, a bonus that wasn't actually the Mayor's to offer. "16, but only because I don't want to see the people of this village suffer." That was true enough.

The Mayor closed his eyes in pain as if offering up his firstborn child. "14 and 50 copper, and I'll have to pay some out of my own coffers. If that's not enough then there's not much I can do to change your mind . . . we'll have to send to Driftwain or even Kov for help, and hope they're willing to act before more of our people are hurt."

Damn, that was some unsatisfying haggling. Although he'd bid up the reward by almost half again, which he supposed was pretty good. "Deal," he said grudgingly. "On the condition that starting immediately, Lone Ox agrees to purchase all monster loot I bring you at fair prices."

The portly man's expression soured, but he sighed as he returned the handshake. "We'll have to pass most of it on to traveling merchants at a terrible profit, but at least it's a solution that doesn't immediately strain our coffers. Deal."

Dare grinned and opened his pack, beginning to pull out his remaining unsold loot.

A short while later he trotted out of Lone Ox with an emptier pack and a fuller purse. He'd earned almost 2 silver from all the loot he'd sold, which was satisfying considering his low level and how little priority he'd given up to this point on gathering goods specifically worth trading.

But now he had a better idea of what the villagers found valuable, and next time would be able to bring more of those things. Especially foraged foods like mushrooms and herbs that could be made into spices.

In the end he'd only found one bow for sale, a Level 4 weapon with a price of 7 silver. Out of his reach for now, and at the rate he was leveling it would probably be useless by the time he could afford it.

Since he was already going to get a knife from a quest reward, that pretty much covered what he'd really wanted to buy. He hadn't found anything else to buy that really interested him, so in the end he'd decided to hold onto his money.

Maybe he'd take a trip up to Driftwain sometime soon. He could haul up a load of trade goods he couldn't get a good price for in Lone Ox, and he'd have a better chance there of finding things he could use. Maybe even at better prices.

Still, he was satisfied with what he'd accomplished on his trip into the village. And eager to tackle his first quest.

Chapter Five
Questing

Considering that the bandits were intelligent, Dare didn't even want to risk approaching their camp until he was more confident he could take out any scouts who might spot him before they could raise the alarm.

Although he still had his doubts about whether he'd be able to take the place on anytime within the next month. Or if at that point it would be worth the effort.

He definitely had no intention of trying to get a group together to fight the bandits. He didn't know enough about the world yet, he didn't know any people here other than from business transactions or casual conversations (as well as casual sex he regretted), and most importantly he didn't know enough about combat and group mechanics.

At this point he'd as likely get his entire group killed, and him with them, as succeed in taking out the camp. And even if they did win that fight, unless the bandits had some serious loot in their camp the village's reward just wasn't worth the effort.

Also he really wanted that knife.

So for the moment Dare put aside the bandit quest and turned his attention to A Boaring Request.

The river the boar was located along was actually the same one the slime girls spawned by, about a mile further downstream. Which obviously meant that Dare took a detour to visit them.

He had more reason than to just empty his balls, although he certainly did that. With a petite little woman that looked like some sort of human-sized fairy, complete with surprisingly delicate wings that only dripped a little, and managed to turn her slender throat into a vise as she took his entire length until he released in her with a groan of ecstasy.

But he also wanted to hunt the monsters that came to visit the slime girls. He'd just barely reached Level 4, but he still held out the hope that he might get to Level 5 quick enough to challenge the boar at an equal level. Or if nothing else, at least improve his ability proficiency so he'd be more effective.

In fact, he should probably be trying to find ways to rank up his abilities as efficiently as possible, outside of whatever organic proficiency he gained while leveling. Although only the abilities he really needed.

Dare had come to a few conclusions by now.

First off, abilities. When he'd first learned how this world's system worked, with a seemingly endless number of class and universal abilities he could rank up without apparent limitations, he'd assumed that he could use that to increase his power above and beyond the level system.

But in the grand scheme of things, increasing his proficiency in abilities he didn't actually need and didn't intend to use often was pointless. It would only take time away from exploring, questing, hunting monsters, farming gold and crafting materials, and increasing his proficiency in useful abilities. And the small experience gains he received for increasing proficiency in an ability couldn't compare to even hunting yellows with their minimal experience awards.

Second, killing weaker enemies that died more quickly was obviously faster than trying to kill tougher enemies that took more hits and proved more of a threat. However, what took more time than both was finding a new spawn point for monsters to hunt, so he usually killed everything he was able to before moving on.

That was another thing that was nice about the slime girls;

monsters arrived in a constant trickle for him to hunt, so he didn't have to wait for respawns.

After a few hours of hunting, though, Dare realized it was going to take longer to level than he wanted to wait. He was impatient to check out the boar, see if he could kill it, and go get that knife.

Once he had it he'd immediately be able to craft a higher quality bow, higher quality arrows, and could even take a look at leather armor.

He'd used his saved up leather to finally make a tent and bedroll when he'd arrived back in his camp from the village last night. They'd been surprisingly comfortable, and better yet the night's sleep with them had given him a buff that slightly increased his stats and stamina.

Honestly, those basic amenities should've been a priority from the start. The only reason he hadn't been more motivated was that the weather wasn't bitterly cold and he was able to sleep by a fire.

Dare killed one more straggler that came onto the slime girl riverbank, a hideous Level 2 imp-like creature that he was extra motivated to kill before it started mating a slime girl. Then he headed downstream to find the boar.

It was a trip of fifteen or so minutes at the speed he ran, and the clearing was easy to find. His first view of the boar was a daunting one; it stood up to his shoulder and was thickly built, obviously strong and dangerous, with vicious looking tusks as long as his forearm.

If that wasn't intimidating enough, his Eye showed that the boar's hit points were nearly double any other Level 5 he'd seen, and it had several dangerous sounding abilities. Including, of course, Charge. And Gore.

Dare swore under his breath; this was going to be harder than he'd hoped.

Collisa

He dropped into a crouch to stare at the huge boar, which in spite of its monstrous size and dangerous abilities was classified as an animal. It was rooting around the clearing, finding things to eat but as promised not showing any signs of wanting to leave its spot.

Okay, so he'd massively over prepared for fighting that first Level 1 Boarite. But those same preparations here might actually do the job and let him kill the boar and get his knife.

Then again, fighting the equivalent of two even level monsters in one surly package might be more than he could manage even if he laid down dozens of spike traps. Especially since he'd been neglecting his Create Traps ability and his bow now did significantly more damage than them.

So it looked as if his first priority should be to gain at least another level. And finally get around to creating the improved snares he'd unlocked a while ago and putting them out, both to get hides to make leather armor and to maybe gain proficiency in his Create Traps ability.

That, plus making more Spike Traps, would hopefully unlock a better version of those that would help him more.

Either way, Dare should clear the spawn points around here, including the Boarite sentries, and then make his way back to his camp. That should get him about halfway to level 5.

He was high enough level to hunt the Mange Wolves now, but had found them to be a pain. They didn't have the Charge ability, but in its place they had a passive ability called Lope that increased their speed by 50%. They also had a Howl ability that let them call for help when they were low health, aggroing an add within fifty yards.

As for their melee damage and abilities, well, they made Boarites with their fists and tusk goring look like bumbling idiots.

Dare could get around Howl by simply pulling the wolves back farther than fifty yards. But with their increased speed he had a hard time killing them before they reached him. He'd been solving that by putting half a dozen spike traps down between him and his target, since they approached in a straight line, which did the last bit of damage needed to finish them off.

Although at the cost of all the traps.

Even then, he sometimes had to pull out his knives and stab the thing half a dozen times while hoping not to be savaged by those vicious teeth.

They weren't worth the bother right now, so he contented himself with the Giant Toads and the Boarites. Then he started back for camp, already planning for what he'd try to get done the next day, and maybe the day after that, before finally feeling comfortable going after the boar.

He was so lost in his thoughts, loping along at what for most humans would be a sprint, that he almost stumbled on the roaming monster before he noticed it and skidded to a halt with a muffled curse.

Dare immediately looked away and ducked behind a tree, activating his Eye. This was a good opportunity to see if he could inspect a target without actually looking directly at it; as it turned out he had to at least have it nearly in his vision, slightly out of focus.

He looked away as soon as he got the monster's information and immediately checked its attacks, then breathed a sigh of relief when he didn't find Petrification or Stone Gaze or any similar skills.

The creature ambling along through the woods in front of him was either a basilisk, or something that looked just like one. A lizard-like monster that stood about up to his knee but long and squat, with powerful legs like a crocodile's, spikes along its back, and frills around its head. Its long, whip-like tail ended in a vicious spike that had a telltale glisten at the tip, confirming its poison attack Tail Sting.

Collisa

It was called a Juvenile Basilisk Runt and was Level 5; all things considered, Dare definitely didn't want to run into a full-sized adult.

Dare looked around nervously. He'd never met a roaming monster, and while that was his first assumption, he couldn't dismiss the possibility that a new spawn point had appeared. Dangerously close to his camp, too.

He was ready to retreat if this had become basilisk territory. But he saw nothing but empty forest around him, and his Eye didn't show him any other enemies in range.

Curious, he nocked an arrow and followed the monster.

As he'd first assumed, the basilisk runt was roaming, its path taking it near the Boarite camp. Dare didn't want to follow for too long with the sun setting and his new bedroll beckoning, but since the monster didn't have any ranged attacks or Charge abilities he decided to risk bringing the higher level monster down.

To his disappointment, the young basilisk was almost disappointingly easy. It went down just like any other Level 5, before even getting close enough to menace him with that barbed tail, in fact.

Not exactly what he'd expected for his first basilisk kill. Although to be fair, it wasn't much more than a hatchling.

The Juvenile Basilisk Runt dropped a few of its back spikes, a poison sac Dare didn't want to risk touching because he didn't know what the rules for safe handling on this world were, and three cuts of basilisk meat.

Well, at least he had dinner. And a novelty from the venison he usually had; he'd never eaten lizard meat before.

Dare continued on to his camp, where he lit a campfire and settled down on a log to cook his basilisk steaks. He'd started work on a collapsible camping chair, complete with armrests, but it was proving to be a lot harder than he'd expected because he had no idea

Phoenix

what he was doing without the help of abilities.

Still, he was looking forward to settling into a fur seat in true comfort.

The basilisk meat turned out to be delicious. It tasted a lot like chicken, with a tender, flaky texture, and he wolfed the first steak down eagerly and reached for another.

He had just taken his first bite of his second steak when his stomach gave a loud rumble. Not just a little growl but a prolonged thing that started near the top of his belly and moved its way down.

Then the pain started. Dare hunched, clutching his stomach with a grunt of dismay, and swallowed a sudden surge of saliva in his mouth. From experience that was the last warning sign before he threw up.

He launched himself from his seat and bolted for the nearest tree, clutching its trunk as he hunched over and emptied his guts. It felt like nails were tearing through his stomach, now, and another alarming rumble warned him just in time to drop his pants before he began spewing from both ends.

In the middle of that torment text appeared at the edge of his vision. "Achievement unlocked. Gonna Be A Long Night: ingest a major toxin. 100 experience received."

Seriously? "Motherfucker," Dare groaned, stumbling away from the mess he'd made and curling up by the fire as the knives continued tearing at his insides.

Basilisk meat. He'd assumed that meat that dropped as loot was safe, without taking into account what that meat dropped from.

Like, say, a fucking basilisk, renowned for their poisonous bite and stone gaze and, in some games with some basilisks, fouling the ground beneath them. And on this world a poisonous tail.

And he'd been feasting on a couple of their goddamn steaks.

Collisa

Dare felt his guts surge again and stumbled a safe distance away to spew from both ends again. The achievement's title and explanation had been pretty clear on what was going on; he was in for a world of hurt.

Hopefully the title also meant he'd actually survive, at least. And that if he was patient, eventually this nightmare would be over.

Although from now on, he was going to use his Forage ability to determine if food was safe on everything he hadn't already identified. And he wasn't going to trust that just because something dropped as loot and didn't show any sign of being dangerous in its details, that meant it was safe.

After all, he'd avoided the poison sac for just that reason.

Once his guts settled slightly Dare dragged himself back to the fire, feeling like he was freezing while streaming sweat, and settled in for what was going to be an awful experience.

* * * * *

It was the worst night of Dare's life. Or lives, more accurately, since on Earth he'd never suffered anything like this either.

His vain hope that his stomach would eventually settle down was dashed when he literally flushed out what seemed like everything in his body. But if he thought that would be the end of it, he quickly realized he was wrong as a desperate thirst overwhelmed him, forcing him to take tiny sips of water just to end the torment.

He would've thought that such a small amount of water wouldn't make a difference, but without fail only minutes after drinking he'd erupt like a volcano from both ends. It got to the point where eventually he said to hell with it, and just guzzled down water and let it all flush through him like a tsunami. Accompanied by brutal cramps that made him feel like someone was pulling razor wire through his guts that lasted the whole night.

Phoenix

He made a huge mess all around his camp, all over himself, and even in his tent when he made the misguided decision in one of the better moments to try to get some sleep. But he was so miserable that he didn't care that he was basically covered in his own filth.

Dare genuinely wished for death on more than one occasion. And near the end of the night, when he was delirious from thirst and lost electrolytes, he actually spent several minutes holding a rock, tempted to smash himself in the head so he could spend the rest of the ordeal blissfully unconscious.

Thankfully his survival instinct prevailed, and he chose to endure the torment.

Just after dawn the cramps finally eased, his heaving stomach calmed, and he was able to sprawl on his filthy bedroll and pass out. He woke up around midmorning to guzzle some more water, in which he mixed a few pinches of salt he'd looted from a monster, and then he gratefully passed out again.

Not long before noon he woke up lucid and alert, if still feeling like shit. Which was also the stench that assaulted his nose in the close confines of the tent. Along with the queasy smell of vomit.

He dragged himself outside with a groan, and even though his limbs trembled with exhaustion and weakness got to work cleaning his clothing and gear.

After that Dare decided to move his campsite far from this one, and upwind. He also decided to look for a place near higher level enemies to hunt, since he'd been contemplating doing that for a few days now anyway.

So he shambled around packing his gear, avoiding spots he'd soiled in the night, and after what felt like forever gratefully left the place behind, not even looking back. Mostly because if he tried he'd probably lose his tentative balance and fall flat on his face.

He was so weak he could barely walk, and starving, but the

thought of eating made his stomach heave. His character sheet showed serious stat debuffs due to illness, deprivation, and exhaustion, but the last vestiges of the tainted basilisk meat seemed to be well gone.

Dare managed to make it a mile closer to the river before collapsing, and reasonably decided that that would be his new campsite. He hadn't gotten that much nearer to stronger monsters given the short distance, and had no idea if this was even a good place to camp.

But he lit a campfire anyway and set up his tent. Then he climbed inside it and slept for another few hours.

When he woke up his stomach was rumbling, but with the more familiar and far less painful pangs of hunger. He gratefully dug into his pack for some of his highest quality dried meat and wolfed it down, along with some of his tastier and higher quality foraged foods.

He felt almost human again after the meal, and while his stomach gave a few unsettling pangs, he wasn't sick again.

After his ordeal he had no desire to try hunting anything, so he spent the rest of the day making and setting the new snares and making the better traps. He wasn't able to rank up to anything new in his Create Traps ability tree, but he looked forward to seeing how the snares did.

He ate a bit more food, then crawled back into his tent and slept until the next morning.

The next day was a busy one of hopping from one monster spawn point to the next, then camping the slime girl area to farm approaching monsters. Given his recent ordeal he didn't feel much temptation to go enjoy himself with the transparent women, but in any case he soon abandoned the area because monsters didn't seem to be interested in them either today.

Phoenix

Instead, as a last resort, he headed for the Mange Wolves. He was close to Level 5 now, and he wanted to try his hand at that stupid boar already.

He might've been in a bit of a bad mood after the wasted day.

Dare got lucky on the first wolf, critting twice and killing it even before it reached him at its increased speed. The second wolf was more of a challenge, although he was able to stay ahead of it enough to loose a few arrows and finally finish it up with his daggers.

He got lucky there, too, since the monster managed to catch his arm in its jaws, but it was on his bracer which mitigated some of the damage. Instead of his arm getting ripped open by those razor teeth he got a few nasty punctures and a large bruise on his wrist.

The third wolf, though, was the opposite of lucky.

It was one of the Level 5s, which was fine. What wasn't fine was that Dare missed a shot, something he'd been doing less and less as his proficiency with bows increased and he'd put more points into the skill.

Because of that, the wolf was still about half health when it reached him. He did his usual thing, sprinting to outpace its Lope and loosing an arrow when he'd put enough distance between them. And as usual it worked, although with the monster's higher health it took longer and was more dangerous.

As was proved when just after he loosed an arrow into the wolf's chest and was turning to sprint away again, he stumbled on a root and nearly fell.

By the time he recovered the wolf was almost on him, and it was too late to try to run. Too late to try to drop his bow and draw his knives either, for that matter. Instead, acting almost on instinct, he rolled desperately to the side, nearly dropping his bow in the process. The monster, clumsily skidding to a halt, took a few seconds to turn and charge him again.

Enough time for him to nock an arrow, draw, and loose at his enemy's head.

It was a critical hit in the wolf's eye, vaporizing the remainder of its health. Better yet, as the monster collapsed to the ground he heard the increasingly familiar triumphant army shout and saw the text bracketed by golden Hunter banners.

"CONGRATULATIONS, YOU'VE REACHED LEVEL FIVE!"

Below it was more text, "Free class ability unlocked: Roll and Shoot."

Dare stared, then quickly pulled up his abilities to get more information. The ability was just what it said: swiftly roll up to 10 feet in any direction to escape danger, grabbing another arrow as he did so, and as he came back to his feet draw and loose.

The question was, had he unlocked it by reaching level 5, or because he'd actually done the ability in combat? He already knew he could unlock certain abilities by actually using them, and had realized it was going to require some adjustment to his thinking to find and unlock those.

And potentially some embarrassing attempts to do novel things while in combat.

On one hand, what he'd done hadn't exactly been that ability. And a lot of games gave abilities or better level rewards for reaching levels like 5, 10, etc. On the other hand, it seemed like too much of a coincidence.

Gah, Dare wished he had someone to ask about all this. He supposed he could try the villagers in Lone Ox, but since none of them were adventurers or actively hunted monsters anything they knew would probably just be common knowledge.

Still, that was better than what he had.

He would have to wait until Level 15 to be sure, but it opened the possibility that, just like every ten levels from level 10 he earned bonus ability points, every ten levels from 5 he'd earn a free class ability.

In the meantime, Roll and Shoot was the first ability he could use in combat that was active and had a cooldown, rather than some sort of passive bonus. And better yet, he was getting it just when it would probably be useful against that overpowered boar.

Grinning in excitement, Dare selected a spot 10 feet away and activated the ability. Immediately he threw himself into a roll, in the same automatic way as when he was crafting. A timer appeared at the corner of his vision with the text: "Roll and Shoot 30s", the numbers counting down to zero when he presumed the ability would be available again.

Mid-roll, he drew an arrow from his quiver and nocked it to the string. And the moment he came to his feet he drew and loosed the arrow at a tree 10 yards away that he'd selected as his target.

The arrow missed, surprising him; was that just his lack of skill, or did Roll and Shoot have a penalty to accuracy? Dare checked the ability's details and saw that it did, one that increased with distance.

It was obviously intended to be used defensively against enemies that were right on top of you. And he was just fine with that; he'd been getting sick of running around like a lunatic fumbling for space for another shot when the enemy only had one hit left to die.

Dare had two points for Level 5: he put one into Bows 2 as an obvious choice. For the second one he was considering Forestwalk, although he was leery about putting a point in something that was limited like that; there were a lot of other terrains besides forests.

Then he noticed that the bite to his bracers in his earlier fight, which still had his hit points at 99%, had unlocked Leather Armor 1, which increased the damage mitigation of leather armor by 5%. That would be more useful than Forestwalk, and he planned to craft a full set of leather armor soon. It was tempting to toss a point in that.

But ultimately, after some consideration he chose to put the last point into Improved Bow Making, which made it so every new bow he crafted would have a fairly decent increase in quality. It had just become available with his new level, along with plans to craft a Level 5 bow. And none too soon; his Level 1 bow's damage was becoming less and less impressive with every level, and he had a boar to kill.

He'd debated the ability since he assumed that at later levels, he'd buy bows from professional crafters that were much better than his basic bow. Which would make this a waste of a precious point.

On the other hand, he really, really needed a better bow right now, and he was going on the assumption that the creators of this world's system had provided some leeway where people could waste a few points here and there without completely trashing their optimal build.

Dare hoped.

In any case, he could always make basic bows to sell. The lack of bows in the village meant people might be willing to buy them, especially if they were the highest possible quality he could manage. And he'd get new plans to craft a bow every 5 levels, which meant he'd be able to make basic bows no matter how high he leveled.

Granted, it'd be impossible to sell basic bows at higher levels in places like Lone Ox, where nobody that he'd seen was above level 15.

At the very least, his ability to craft bows also let him repair them, including crafted ones he bought. Improved Bow Making affected bow repairs as well, making them as effective as any bowyer's, so it would never be completely useless even if he got to the point where he never made another bow.

Either way, the point was spent; Dare just hoped he didn't regret it in 50 levels.

Phoenix

Now that he *had* the ability, though, he was eager to make an improved Level 5 bow that would really help him kill the boar.

Unfortunately, the materials for the new bow included things he didn't have on him. Including a few things that dropped from monsters around this level. So he had a choice between crafting it today or going after the boar.

He sighed and got to work finding materials.

* * * * *

Dare had never been away from his campfire at night.

He managed to get the materials for his new bow right around sundown, and had to sprint to get back to his camp before full dark.

It was a reasonable precaution, since different animals came out at night and a lot of them could be pretty dangerous, and he assumed the same applied for monsters. That, plus the fact that he wouldn't be able to see and would have a harder time knowing if danger was coming and have more trouble fighting it off, had decided him.

At some point he probably *would* have to go out at night. But he preferred to know more, and be better prepared, before attempting it.

Besides, he had the materials he needed to craft his bow. And he wanted to get a good night's sleep so he could be up bright and early in the morning to kill the boar and finish the quest.

Thankfully he encountered no wandering monsters this time, and reached his camp while there was still a glow on the horizon. Although his bow ended up taking until almost midnight to create, so he didn't get the early night's sleep he was hoping for.

The bow itself was beautiful though, at least to his eyes. Longer, better carved, better polished, with a nicer grip and a more tightly bound and springy bowstring. It did more than double the damage of his previous bow, and its other stats were better too. Especially range.

Collisa

Better yet, the next morning when he crafted a dozen arrows to make sure he'd have enough for the boar fight, his Arrow Crafting skill ranked up and gave him Level 5 arrows. They didn't give him double the damage like the bow had, but it was a decent damage bump.

And a significant durability increase, probably because the better materials required included a harder type of wood and metal jags looted from monsters for the arrowheads. Which thankfully he had several of.

Given the pleasant surprises of his new level, it looked as if he'd need to keep Bow Crafting and Arrow Crafting up to his current level in the future so he'd be able to make upgrades as soon as they became available. At least until he could afford to buy better gear from crafters.

Either way, with this the boar fight would go from taking forever to taking an irritatingly long time. And that wasn't that bad.

Dare created the improved arrows, arranging them in his quiver so he'd use them first, then set out directly for the boar clearing. He reached it quickly, and after inspecting the boar again to solidify its information in his mind he began preparing.

He decided to perch between two branches in a tree for the fight; it was a great place to shoot a bow from safety at enemies who had no ranged attacks and no way to get up at him.

Which is why he was pretty sure it wouldn't work.

After all, if the people of this world could exploit such an obvious advantage to farm most of the types of monsters that spawned, they would. The world's system probably had some way to prevent it.

Maybe the monsters would knock him out of the trees, or knock *down* the trees, to get him on the ground. Or there were some games where if you attacked a mob from a place it couldn't reach, it basically became invulnerable until you moved to some place where it could attack you.

Maybe it was reckless to test what this world did about the potential exploit while fighting a boar that was twice as tough as any other monster of that level. But even if Dare did get knocked out of the tree, shooting from up there might give him some extra shots. And his Fleetfoot would help get him safely to the ground.

And if worst came to worst, he had his new Roll and Shoot ability to keep him away from the boar's tusks. Sure, the 30 second cooldown might make things a bit dicey if the boar was able to keep up with him, but he'd make it work.

Dare also planned to put down all of his spike traps.

At first he'd considered it broken that you could lay down as many traps as you wanted, which in most games wasn't allowed for balancing issues. But then he'd realized that if hunting a monster represented an investment of time, and creating traps represented an investment of time, then it all balanced out.

Of course the traps made hunting safer so you weren't as likely to die, but on the other hand they took a lot of time to make given the paltry damage they did.

If anything, he'd be better served using his time to farm gold so he could buy a better bow and arrows and do the damage that way.

At least his snares were actually doing something; he'd caught a rabbit and a rock chuck in them. Which were pretty humble finds considering he could go out and shoot a deer or pig or other large animal any time he wanted. But it was a start.

It would be nice to find a higher level Hunter if he could, though, to tell him if Create Traps was worth investing any more time into. Along with a slew of other questions.

Dare spread the traps in front of the tree he'd chosen, then climbed up to his perch and unslung his bow. His hand was steady as he pulled out one of his better arrows and nocked it, taking aim at the big animal across the clearing.

"Please don't let this kill me," he whispered. It was becoming a habit before every difficult fight. One that he should probably consider breaking before he joined up with other people, if he ever did.

He held his breath and loosed.

And missed by a few inches, his arrow thudding into the ground.

Dare bit back a curse, waiting to see if the boar would react. He'd missed first shots on a target before, and it was a tossup whether the enemy would notice and aggro him or ignore it completely. He wasn't sure whether there was a situational awareness roll or if it depended on how close the arrow was, or how much noise it made, or how close *he* was to his target, or what.

Thankfully, this time he got lucky; the boar glanced over at the arrow, then snorted and got back to rooting around the base of a tree.

Instead of grabbing one of his ready arrows, he drew one from a quiver in his backpack. Then he took aim again and hit the boar right in the side, in or near its vital organs.

The big animal squealed and charged the tree Dare was in, while he began plucking his ready arrows and loosing off more shots. He did it perfectly, no fumble or delays, but even so his target's health bar went down in what felt like tiny chunks.

The boar was still at around 60% when it hit the spike traps, which dropped it down to 40% in a matter of seconds. But it didn't so much as stumble from the damage as it continued forward and slammed into Dare's tree.

He cursed and hugged the trunk just in time to avoid being thrown to the ground as the branch beneath him shuddered violently. As soon as it settled he fumbled for another arrow to get a second shot off, but before he could the boar backed up a few feet and

Phoenix

slammed the trunk a second time, forcing him to get cozy with the tree trunk again.

The boar hit the tree again, then again, giving him no chance to get in a shot.

Okay, was this the mechanism the world's system used to prevent farming monsters from inaccessible locations? But at best it was a stalemate, not allowing him to act while the enemy was also locked in place.

And while he'd eventually have to eat or drink or sleep, the boar faced the same issues. Better yet, it drained its stamina every time it slammed the tree; would it eventually drop from exhaustion?

Another time tradeoff? You could hunt the monsters from the safety of some high place, but you'd waste so much time doing it that it wouldn't be worth the effort?

The boar slammed into the trunk below again, but this time there was a sharp *crack* and the entire tree lurched violently. Then, with a deep groan, the entire thing began to fall.

Or the world system gave you some time to change your mind about the exploit, then booted your ass to the ground either way. And probably with perches that couldn't be knocked over, like the top of a cliff or something, it would have other solutions to prevent exploits.

Dare just had time to leap to the branch of the next tree over, although he lost all his ready arrows. The boar snorted and circled the trunk, hitting more traps that dropped it down to 35%, and made a beeline for the trunk of the new tree.

Well, the experiment was over. Time to get serious.

He jumped towards the trunk of a tree deeper into the woods, landing with his feet against it and his arm swinging him around the trunk. He leapt again, hit the ground with barely a stumble, and nocked an arrow to the string as he turned.

Collisa

Just in time to loose an arrow at the boar as it hit the second tree.

It squealed in fury and tore after him, and he realized that its low, powerful body was custom built for maneuvering through forest underbrush.

Dare ducked around a tree as he fumbled for another arrow. The boar shot past him, confirming that it had quick acceleration but not quick deceleration or turning. That presented an opportunity.

Although not a great one. He didn't have time to shoot the boar as it recovered and closed on him again, but it bought him a little space. He repeated the maneuver a few more times, ducking around trees and using its weaknesses against it.

It took a while and some frantic scrambling, but finally he had enough breathing room to loose an arrow. Then he had to repeat the process and do it again.

It actually became a race, his stamina bar against the boar's health bar as it dropped with glacial slowness. Dare actually found himself getting worried as the minutes dragged on; he hadn't encountered this risk before.

What happened when his stamina ran out? Was his speed reduced to a crawl and he lost access to his abilities, or did he pass out? Was it possible he even dropped dead, like in some games?

Given the way he'd begun panting like a bellows, he assumed the stamina just marked his actual ability to keep going like this in a real world situation. Which meant he'd probably begin stumbling in exhaustion, then finally drop as his strength gave out.

Either way, he didn't want to find out. He needed to get even more creative with this fight.

Dare had an idea after he loosed an arrow and leapt aside, and the boar nearly slammed into a tree behind him. The next time he had time to shoot he positioned himself in front of a tree, and when he dodged the boar slammed into it.

Phoenix

He'd seen before that when the boar hit a tree it delayed it by half a second or so. That half second didn't seem like much, but in the frantic adrenaline of a fight like this they added up.

A half second represented a few less trees he had to scramble around to buy time. A few less seconds of running and dodging. A few less stamina points wasted when every one counted.

The boar's health dropped to 15%. Then 10. Then 5. And finally, finally, he loosed his last shot and the beast stumbled and collapsed with a final strangled grunt.

Dare stumbled over and stared down at the boar, chest heaving.

A Boaring Request his ass. That thing might've been a Level 5, but its power was more like a 7 or even 8. Then again, he supposed he was one to talk since his Fleetfoot gave him a huge edge over similar levels.

Not as fun to be on the receiving end of things, though.

He crouched to inspect the boar's tusks, which were definitely huge and had almost gored him to death several times. "That knife better be the best Level 5 knife in the world," he muttered as he got to work harvesting the tusks.

In spite of his complaints, though, he couldn't wait to get it. The first thing he was going to do was craft a new bow with it, then maybe farm a bunch of leather and get to work crafting a high quality cloak and full set of leather armor.

Including better shoes than the basic ones he'd started with, if the ones he could craft were nicer.

Dare also looted a large hide and a bunch of meat from the boar, including the portion that was used to make bacon.

He stuffed it all into his pack, overloading it, and then with a grunt set off straight for Lone Ox at the best run he could manage.

He wanted that knife as soon as possible. And hey, maybe

afterwards he'd celebrate by stopping by the tavern to see if they could make him a BLT.

Although about a mile from the village all thoughts of anything but lettuce were driven from his mind, when he heard plaintive cries coming from a clearing ahead. When he investigated he found an injured woman collapsed on the ground.

Not a human, though. Not with that impossibly pale skin and those long narrow ears rising from the top of her head.

Chapter Six
Helping Hand

It was a bunny girl. A real life, actual bunny girl.

Her skin was paler than even the palest redhead's, a tone no human could ever manage. Literally the color of cream. It meshed seamlessly with the long white hair that fell down to her waist, flowing free and looking as soft and shiny if it had just been thoroughly brushed. And the fine, velvety white fur on the long, slender ears that rose above her head in place of human ones, and the white cottontail perched adorably above her curvy ass.

Other than that she was completely hairless. Which Dare knew because the bunny girl happened to be completely nude, and breathtakingly gorgeous.

With her sprawled on the grass like that he couldn't see much, but he caught a glimpse of small pink nipples on her large breasts, the same shade as her full, luscious lips.

Her body, while he judged her small at about five feet in height, was nonetheless perfectly proportioned. As in, the sort of proportions you never saw in real life, only in idealized artwork.

The only exception to that, if it even was one, was that her legs were thicker and more muscular than he would've expected for a woman of her size and proportions. But then again, she *was* a bunny. And that thickness was appealing in its own way, exotic and inviting him to run his hands along the smooth pale skin, tracing the contours of her muscles.

Dare sternly shook himself. The issue of whether or not it was gentlemanly to be staring at a naked woman in the woods took a backseat to the fact that she was injured and needed his help; the poor girl was clutching at one leg, rocking back and forth in clear distress.

He would've rushed out to help her, but he was a bit hesitant because of her nudity, not sure how to treat it or what to do.

But then the bunny girl began to make whimpering noises, tears swimming in her large blue eyes, and occasionally swiping the back of her hand across her adorable button nose. She began calling out in barely above a whisper, a single word over and over, as if simultaneously pleading for help and afraid of drawing danger to her.

That was too much for Dare, and he cautiously stepped out into the clearing. "Hello!" he called gently. "Do you-"

The bunny girl squealed in fear and tried to leap to her feet and run away. She only made it a step before collapsing on her injured leg, sprawling to her hands and knees. That left him with a perfect view of her round, curvy ass, and between tense thighs quivering in fear an adorable little pussy with perfect pink inner labia, pouting open just enough to reveal a generous sized clit and the beginnings of a glistening pink hole.

In spite of himself he couldn't help but gape for a moment, practically salivating at what looked like the bunny girl presenting herself invitingly to him. Then he shook himself sternly and looked away, calling out again in a gentle voice. "Wait! I don't want to hurt you, I want to help."

The bunny girl either seemed to trust his tone, or she realized she couldn't escape and gave up. Either way she rolled to face him, pulling her knees up to her large breasts and hugging them tightly with her slender arms as she stared up at him with wide blue eyes.

Once again, that gave him a view of her pussy. The wetness he'd seen in her hole seemed to have spread to her creamy pale outer lips, making them glisten in a way that just begged for him to run his tongue along them.

Phoenix

Dare forcefully pushed aside those thoughts before his cock could become uncomfortably stiff in his pants, and focused on helping the bunny girl. He lowered his backpack to the ground and slowly approached, one hand held out reassuringly and murmuring soothingly the entire time.

The bunny girl quivered, looking torn between hope and fear, but remained almost frozen as if petrified as he carefully dropped to a crouch in front of her.

"It's your ankle, right?" he asked.

She stared at him in blank incomprehension; she didn't speak his tongue, which was small surprise given the . . . natural way she seemed to live out here. He held out a hand. "May I?"

Again, she didn't understand, but she didn't put up a fuss as he gently took her leg. Her skin was warm and impossibly soft beneath his fingers, and he had to resist the urge to slide his hands up her calf.

Then go even higher, up those muscular thighs, until he could run his fingers over that perfect little pussy.

Focus. He began gently probing her ankle. "Does this hurt?" he murmured.

He didn't see any signs of swelling or other obvious injury, but the bunny girl abruptly winced and cried out softly in pain as his fingers touched a certain spot. That, plus her inability to put weight on it, probably meant a break or at least a sprain.

Or so he thought . . . he wasn't a doctor, he'd just seen people do this in movies.

Still, a splint seemed like a good idea. He quickly found two straight sticks, and using a bit of hide for a wrap and strips of leather from his pouch got to work.

As he did he kept up a constant inane babble in a gentle tone to reassure the bunny girl. He only glanced up at her face once, and to his surprise saw her expression had changed from fear to bafflement. Although he almost thought he caught hints of disappointment on her milky white features.

Maybe even annoyance.

He was almost done with the splint when the bunny girl let her other leg drop to the side, as if shifting to a more comfortable position. That had the effect of making her small pussy lips pout open, giving him a clear view of her generous clit peeking out from beneath its hood, the tiny hole of her urethra, and the visibly wet walls of her sweet love tunnel beneath it. From this angle he could see almost straight into it, the smooth surfaces glistening pink and inviting.

Dare took a shuddering breath and tore his eyes away, again lifting them to the bunny girl's face; that seemed the safest place to look right now. "I'm almost done here, and then I can-"

He cut off, confused.

Her lovely, delicate features were twisted in clear annoyance as she glared at him. "You're really just going to help me, aren't you?" she said in perfect English. Or whatever the language of this world was.

He gaped at her in shock. All this time she could've talked to him? Why hadn't she? "Um . . ."

The bunny girl bounded easily up onto her one good leg, and with the balance and grace of a dancer reached down to rip off the splint he'd painstakingly applied. "Do you even have a cock, you pathetic joke?" she snapped, pouting sullenly. "You suck!"

Without another word she turned and stormed off into the forest.

As Dare was staring helplessly after her, wondering what the hell had just happened, he heard pealing laughter from behind him.

Phoenix

He whirled to see the farmwife he'd fucked, Ellui, standing at the edge of the clearing. In one hand she held a wide, empty basket, and it was clear she was out gathering.

He'd avoided the plump woman since their encounter, not wanting to tempt another compromising situation with a married woman. But now he walked over to her, shaking his head in bewilderment. "What was that?" he demanded.

"You really aren't from around here, are you?" Ellui chortled. "Gallantly coming to the aid of a cunid in the forest? If I didn't personally know better even *I'd* wonder if you had a cock."

Dare flushed, angry and embarrassed. "So why did she act like that? What's going on?"

She sobered, although her eyes still danced in amusement. "Cunids, although most call them bunny girls, are one of the most fecund races on Collisa. They breed like rabbits, in other words. And since they have a female to male ratio of like 7 to 1, the females are always out looking for males. Even males of other races . . . they're not picky. And considering bunny girls are adorable, obsessed with sex, and always horny, they usually don't have trouble finding one."

The farmwife abruptly scowled. "In fact, I'm sure Brennal's always hoping to run across one when he's out here." She jerked her head in the direction the bunny girl had disappeared. "Actually, I wouldn't be surprised if he's bred that little slut before."

Dare ignored that. "If she was trying to seduce me, I definitely would've been up for it."

Ellui's good humor returned in a flash, and she let out another peal of merry laughter. "Again, you really don't know cunid. Bunny girls don't seduce. They like to be chased and taken. Maybe because rabbits are prey animals and it gives them a thrill."

He frowned. "Taken as in?"

"As in they'll find passing travelers, then pretend to be caught or injured nearby in the hopes that the traveler will be overcome with desire and mount them in their helpless state."

Dare stared at her incredulously. "Bunny girls like to be-"

She laughed even harder. "Taken, like I said. They go wild at the feel of a powerful man pinning them down and giving them the forceful sex they want." She bit her lip coyly. "And I'll admit I enjoy that sort of thing myself sometimes, in controlled situations. Although cunids are a lot more daring in seeking it with strangers."

The farmwife gestured to where the pale bunny girl had disappeared. "So there's no need to look so shocked about bunny girl sexual preferences, or concerned for their welfare. While they may pretend to be helpless they're in complete control of the situation . . . if you know anything about how well they can run and jump, you should realize that if they really wanted to escape they easily could."

He thought about how effortlessly the pale little woman had hopped up onto one foot from the ground on a single muscular leg, and decided Ellui was probably right.

The farmwife gave a last chuckle as she shook her head. "Yeah, bunny girls are always up for it. They'll even let ugly, fat men chase them. Like Brennal, for example. Being chased, caught, and mounted is what turns cunids on. They'll even play with women, sometimes, if the woman's aggressive enough in dominating them. And since everyone knows what bunny girls want it's like a game we all agree to. Or maybe roleplay . . . people out in the wild see a cunid pretending to be stuck bent over in a bush, they know they're in for a good time."

She smirked. "Aside from you, that is. And given that everyone knows how bunny girls are, she probably thinks you found her ugly and didn't *want* to mount her, so you just pretended to be nice and help her instead."

"I definitely don't think she's ugly," Dare snapped. "She's probably the most gorgeous woman I've ever seen." He winced slightly in chagrin, glancing at the farmwife who he'd just so happened to have also bedded. "I, um, I mean . . ."

Ellui snorted. "You're an ass for saying it, but I've got eyes." She grimaced down at her plump body. "Only a fool woman tries to compete with a bunny girl for looks." She smirked at him again. "Not that you'll get a chance to compare us."

He was well aware, and cursed inwardly, staring in the direction the bunny girl had gone. He hadn't known he'd missed an opportunity; how many more opportunities might he miss because of his ignorance?

Oh well, maybe the opportunity would come again. If bunny girls really were that obsessed with sex and bred like rabbits then there were probably plenty of them around. Although he had reservations about chasing down and mounting a relative stranger . . . he'd probably have to at least talk to her first, make sure of what she wanted.

"Thanks for letting me know," he said heavily. "I guess better luck next time."

Ellui grinned and cupped a breast invitingly through her dress with her free hand. "Well, if you were really hoping for some fun, I'm here now . . ."

Dare scowled. "You know I'm not going to."

She sighed, although a smile still quirked her lips. "In that case, maybe you're more lucky *this time* than you think." She pointed behind him. "I think the bunny girl likes you."

He whirled to find the pale girl from before standing in the trees, just in view, looking at him with narrowed eyes.

Dare felt a surge of hope, cock twitching and starting to grow in his pants at the voluptuous curves on display; he could even see her little slit between her legs, slanted to one side due to her cocked hip and still glistening damply.

Collisa

Phoenix

"Or more likely she's desperate enough for a good lay to give you another chance," Ellui continued. "You *do* realize she's been listening to us this entire time, right?"

He hadn't. "What, um, do I do?" he whispered.

The farmwife smirked. "You think she can't hear you, with those ears of hers?" Laughing, she motioned to the cunid. "Now you chase her. Although considering how you just insulted and annoyed her, she's probably going to make you work for it this time."

Dare's cock twitched eagerly, although he found himself hesitating. "So I should go after her?"

The bunny girl threw up her hands in exasperation. "Okay you know what? I give up." She bounded forward with surprising speed, getting up in Dare's face with a finger in his nose. "It's obvious you're not going to make the roleplay feel genuine . . . you don't know my kind well enough, and you seem too kindhearted to really get into it even now that you know."

"I'm sorry," Dare said lamely. She was probably right; he wasn't sure he'd be comfortable chasing the bunny girl down and roughly dominating her the way she seemed to want.

The cunid smirked. "But you're probably the most perfect thing I've ever seen walking on two legs, and that's saying something since I have a mirror, so I want to play with you anyway. So if you need more to make you comfortable, I'll play along." She held out a pale, delicate hand. "Hi, I'm Clover."

He shook her hand formally, trying to act casual about this gorgeous naked woman standing very very close to him and obviously wanting the same thing he wanted. "Good to meet you, Clover. I'm Dare."

"Hi, Dare." The bunny girl grinned and eagerly rubbed her thighs together. "Okay, now that we're friends we can have sex, right? Humans are super slow about this sort of thing sometimes but I think that covers it."

Still watching off to one side, Ellui snickered.

Dare felt his face heating at her frankness. And more so at the unwelcome audience. "Right, um, right here?"

Clover shrugged. "Wherever." She brightened. "Or hey, how about let's play tag! That way I still get to be chased, and we can go somewhere else. We can even make it a challenge." She playfully bopped his nose. "You're it! Tag me before I get away and I'll try out making love with you the way humans like it, all gentle and romantic and stuff like we're life-mates."

"Actually, I sometimes enjoy getting pounded into the mattress like a nail under the hammer," Ellui said.

"Whatever." The bunny girl whirled, laughing lightly, and with a flick of her fluffy white cottontail bolted away. "Can't catch meeeeee!" she called at him as she disappeared into the woods.

Ellui belted out another laugh. "Better go, you idiot, before she leaves for real!"

Dare grinned and sprang after the pale girl, running awkwardly with his half chub until it thankfully receded. He bolted into the forest using every bit of his gifted speed, straining to go faster with every step.

Up ahead he saw the bunny girl loping through the trees, muscular legs carrying her with easy grace as she nimbly slipped around obstacles. He couldn't help but admire the way the contours of her ass shifted with every step, or the occasional glimpses of her generous breasts undulating.

Clover briefly glanced back, and her blue eyes widened with surprise when she saw how close he already was and how fast he was moving.

I'm better than most at tag, he thought with a wide smile, getting into the spirit of things.

His smugness vanished a moment later when the pale woman sprang effortlessly over an obstacle of knotted underbrush and fallen trees higher than her head, graceful as a leaping deer. From the angle of her jump he judged it would take her over fifteen feet forward, and she hadn't even seemed to be trying.

Dare cursed and bolted around the obstacle, only to skid to a halt in surprise when he realized the bunny girl had disappeared. He'd only been ten or so feet behind her and closing fast, but even though he could see for dozens of yards in all directions she was nowhere to be seen.

Was she that fast? Or had she gone to ground?

A flash of white caught his attention, and between two tree trunks up ahead he caught sight of a twitching cottontail, framed by wide hips and a voluptuous ass with just a hint of a delicate pink pussy between white thighs. Then she sprang away with a giggle, bolting through the trees.

Yep, it looked as if Clover was going to make him work for it.

Dare took up the chase again, straining for speed, and quickly realized that even though the bunny girl had gone to ground before, she really *was* that fast. Even moving as quickly as he could without poking out his own eye on a hanging branch, she effortlessly stayed ahead of him. And occasionally she'd surge forward in an impossible burst of speed, or leap impressive distances and heights as if she wasn't even trying. As if just to show off that she could.

But in spite of that she never seemed to get very far ahead of him.

In fact, as he started to flag, panting like a bellows, she slowed down a bit. Maybe realizing that if she kept this up, he wasn't going to have the energy to have sex after he caught her.

Dare groaned with relief at the reprieve, slowing down himself as he struggled to catch his breath. He was at least gratified to see that Clover's creamy skin was covered with a light sheen of perspiration, and her tantalizing breasts were heaving with her slightly labored breathing.

He closed again to within thirty feet, then twenty.

Only a minute or so later she burst out into a clearing, similar to the one he'd first found her in, covered with long, soft grass and wildflowers and with a stream flowing at one end of it.

Halfway across it the bunny girl stopped and turned to him with a giggle. "Okay, last chance to tag me!" she teased, bouncing eagerly from foot to foot.

Dare threw himself forward, channeling all the times he'd played tag, all his work on the track team in high school. Clover darted to one side, cleanly dodging him, and with a giggle forced him to chase her around the clearing.

Finally, though, she "stumbled", slowing down just enough for him to tap her lightly on the shoulder. At which point she gave a happy shout and flopped down to the ground. Dare couldn't help but notice that she conveniently landed right where the grass was thickest and softest, and his heart began hammering in his chest.

Looked like the game was over and she was ready to really play with him.

The bunny girl rolled over onto her tummy, coyly kicking her legs and making her cute ass jiggle. "I'm all yours, cutie. Hop on."

Nervous but eager, Dare gently climbed on top of her, straddling her thighs. He couldn't resist the urge to run his hands up and down her silky soft back, fingers gliding easily over warm skin slick with a sheen of sweat.

"Mmm," Clover sighed. "I like massages as much as the next bunny, but is that really where you want to be touching?" She playfully wiggled her hips. "Or where you think I want you to be

Phoenix

touching?"

He didn't need a second invitation, sliding his hands lower to caress the sides of her wide hips and thick thighs, then up to her plump ass. He was as hard as his pants allowed as he squeezed those perfect globes, luxuriating in the way his fingers pressed into her soft flesh.

She wiggled again. "Okay, enough foreplay. Whip your bad boy out and do whatever you want with it."

That was enough foreplay for her, huh? He supposed he couldn't really complain about her wanting to get straight to the point; he enjoyed taking the time to explore a woman's body and make her feel good, few opportunities as he'd had to do it in his previous life.

But right now he was almost desperate to bury his cock in Clover's tight little pussy.

Fumbling with the ties of his pants, he yanked his rigid cock free and shoved it between her tightly closed legs, starting out with thigh-fucking the gorgeous woman. His passage was eased by the surprising amount of her nectar coating her inner thighs, and even more so when his throbbing tip gathered more of her juices as it brushed past her silky soft petals.

Dare resisted the urge to just slam his length inside that delicious pussy, wanting to savor the experience, so he spent a while thrusting between her tightly pressed together thighs. Between her silky soft skin and the slickness of her juices, not to mention the feel of her plump ass beneath his hands, the sensation was almost as pleasurable as sex.

In fact, he'd rate it much better than fucking a slime girl. And he hadn't even felt her soft pink walls around his shaft yet.

Finally the temptation proved too great, and he pulled back and positioned himself at her glistening opening. "Ready?" he asked.

Clover's answering moan of pleasure made his cock twitch.

"Nature's bounty, yes. Shove it in me already, and don't treat me like glass."

Dare adjusted his position slightly atop the pale woman, then with one smooth motion pushed steadily inside her until he'd bottomed out at the end of her sweet tunnel. The sensation of tight warmth, combined with the squelch of her copious juices and the fact that her walls were already rippling in pleasure, tore a groan from his throat as well.

The bunny girl moaned again and bounced her hips upward impatiently, until he got the message and stopped just sitting there reveling in the pleasure of being inside her tight, warm tunnel.

He slowly withdrew, then pushed back inside her a bit faster and harder. Then again, speeding up a bit more. But on the third thrust, when he thought she'd be anticipating his actions, instead of speeding up gradually he abruptly thrust into her more powerfully.

The bunny girl squealed, silken walls clenching tight around him in surprise. "Goddess of Fertility, yes! Do that more!" She eagerly pushed herself back into him.

Dare grabbed her luscious hips and began thrusting into her fiercely, luxuriating in the feel of penetrating her tight warmth while she lay flat on her stomach beneath him. He'd never tried this position before in his old life, but the angle of his entry plus her legs pressed firmly together made her little pink pussy even tighter in an incredible combination.

It must've been doing something for Clover, too, because she writhed and bucked her hips more and more wildly by the second, giving out the most delicious moans every time he slammed into her. His cock was constantly squelching as her nectar flowed freely, splattering everywhere with every powerful thrust, and her heavenly walls began rippling faster and faster.

Then they clenched tight around him again, and the bunny girl gave another squeal as his cock was drenched in a fresh flood of her juices. "Goddess, that massive cock of yours was made to please bunny girls!" she moaned as she twitched beneath him.

Her sweet pussy's powerful contractions felt like she was trying to milk him, and with a groan Dare felt his self-control strain at the overwhelming sensation. "I'm going to come," he gasped.

He would've sworn his lover's orgasm got more intense just from those words, her walls clenching even tighter. "Oh Goddess yes!" she panted. "Paint my insides with your magnificent seed. Fill up my little bunny pussy!"

It took everything he had to hold back for a few more seconds in the face of that sort of sexy talk. "Is it safe?"

"What?" The bunny girl craned her neck to look at him, giggling as if he'd made a joke as she continued to tremble in a powerful climax. "Of course it's safe, silly!"

Right. She wouldn't be out trying to fuck random strangers if she hadn't taken precautions. Or more likely humans and bunny girls just couldn't have children, which is why they felt so free to tempt random travelers.

Dare pushed hard, bottoming out again and grinding the tip of his cock against Clover's core, and with a last ragged grunt of pleasure released powerfully inside her.

They both froze in position for what felt like forever in their shared climax. Then he slumped down on top of the beautiful woman, burying his face in her silky white hair.

He wasn't sure if it was the sheer pleasure of their coupling, or the fact that his unseen benefactor had given him a healthy libido, but as he pulled out of the bunny girl, releasing a flood of their combined juices, he realized that his erection wasn't going down.

He wasn't done yet.

Dare flipped the bunny girl onto her back, and in response to her look of slight disappointment that it was over he slapped her stomach with his massive cock, drawing her attention to its state. She looked down, her eyes widened, and with an excited grin she spread her legs almost wide enough to be doing the splits.

Her freshly fucked pussy gaped open obscenely, delicate lips flushed rosy, their combined juices flowing out and soaking the grass beneath her.

God, she was hot.

He caught Clover's slender wrists and pinned them over her head with one hand, making her back arch and her erect nipples jut out proudly on her luscious breasts. With the other hand he guided his cock to her glistening opening, teasing her clit with his sensitive tip in a way that made them both squirm and gasp with pleasure.

Then, grinning down at her beautiful face, he pushed inside in one swift thrust with such force that her body quivered all the way up to her long, soft white ears.

The curvy woman moaned again and bucked her hips wildly. "I'm so glad I c-came back," she panted.

"Let's see if we can make you even happier." Dare leaned down and kissed her parted lips, slipping his tongue into her soft mouth. He encountered large, blocky front teeth, like he'd expect to see in a rabbit, and teased his tongue over them before going in deeper to wrestle with her tongue.

Then he began moving inside her with slow, powerful thrusts, gradually speeding up but grinding into her hard every time he bottomed out.

The bunny girl moaned into his mouth and undulated her hips, making sure his invading cock found all her most sensitive places as he built up the pace. He felt her pussy clench around his girth and her juices flood around his cock as she climaxed, then less than a minute later felt it again.

Phoenix

It was hard to tell for sure but from the way her pussy rippled around his cock, milking it eagerly, and her small, perfectly proportioned body beneath him stiffened and quivered, he judged that she climaxed at least three more times.

He hadn't thought it could get any better after her last one, in which she clenched her quivering pussy down until it was so tight he could barely continue to thrust in spite of his best efforts. But then the bunny girl wailed in pure rapture, and the sensation of wetness between them became a drenching flood.

At first he thought Clover was climaxing again but the fluid was too thin, too watery, and had too much pressure to be even a powerful squirt. Within moments a familiar sharp tang reached his nostrils.

Dare pulled back enough to look at where his cock obscenely stretched her pink little pussy into a tight ring straining to accommodate his size. Sure enough, from just above their joining a thick stream of pale yellow fluid gushed out, soaking their crotches, thighs, and the ground beneath them. Not to mention his pants and part of his tunic.

The bunny girl, fully sunk into the depths of her pleasure, had lost control of her bladder.

Holy shit.

When he was in the mood he found girls peeing surprisingly sexy. Although in his old life he never would've dreamed of asking to be peed on, or for that matter to pee on a lover. But in this situation the sensations pierced right to the most primal part of him, overpowering his restraint.

Dare growled and gave Clover two final, savage thrusts, hard enough to push her almost a foot along the grass beneath them. Then he pushed as deep as he could go, tip scraping against the door to her womb, and with a cry of release began to empty his seed inside her.

Collisa

When the bunny girl felt him climaxing a second time, she slumped down into an almost languid pose, smiling in satisfaction, her long ears quivering with delight.

Dare rode his orgasm with clenched teeth, then finally gasped and collapsed on top of her, rolling to one side and gathering her into his arms to cuddle her.

Clover panted against him for almost a minute, licking at his sweaty shoulder and arm with a small, pink tongue as he ran his hands over her silky smooth, pale skin. He hadn't had a chance to really explore her body before, and now that things had settled down he took his time savoring her luscious curves.

But to his surprise and disappointment, after just another minute the bunny girl squirmed free of his embrace and rose to a crouch, then flew a good ten feet in a powerful hop that took her across the clearing.

She stood there staring back at him, one hand on a hip cocked to the side, his seed leaking out of her pink pussy joining her juices and urine on her glistening thighs. Then she grinned widely to reveal the large, blocky, perfectly white front teeth he'd felt with his tongue.

"Thanks, Dare, that was incredible," she told him. "Let's do it again sometime."

Without another word Clover turned and scampered away, not looking back. Dare's last view of her was of her cute little round ass disappearing into the trees, her fluffy white cottontail twitching cheerfully as if to reinforce her invitation to come play with her again.

Grinning like an idiot, Dare hauled himself to his feet and made his way over to the stream to wash up. If it had just been the bunny girl's sweet nectar moisturizing his cock, he might've been tempted to simply pull his pants up and go retrieve his pack so he could savor the sensation for a while.

But her cooling urine was starting to smell more pungent, and hot as it had been in the moment, and although he'd heard urine was sterile, he didn't exactly want to walk around drenched in it.

Especially not in a forest where monsters and dangerous predators could potentially be found; going about his day marked with the scent of a woman who shared characteristics with a prey animal seemed like a really stupid thing to do.

He stripped off his clothes and got them soaking, then crouched to splash water on his flushed face before he began cleaning himself off.

"Looks like you tagged her," a voice from behind said, making him jump.

Dare whirled to see Ellui grinning at him. "You followed me?" he demanded, resisting the urge to cover his exposed cock.

She smirked and held up her empty basket. "If it's a choice between grubbing about for mushrooms and greens or watching you take a bunny girl like a stud, it's not really much of a choice at all." She looked a bit disappointed. "Too bad I missed it."

The farmwife glanced down at his cock and her smile widened again. "Although I still get a bit of a show." She snickered. "Is that her piss all over you? You must've really given her a good time."

With an effort of will he ignored her leering and continued bathing, using the bit of soap he'd purchased in the village. "You know, if you spent half as much effort working on your relationship with your husband as you did chasing me, your marriage would probably be a lot happier."

She scowled. "Funny." She abruptly smiled again, a spiteful expression. "So are you one of those pleased at the thought you'll have a child running around out here, but won't have to do anything to help raise it?"

Dare froze, then whirled towards her. "What?"

Collisa

Ellui smirked. "You came inside the bunny girl, of course. In the heat of the moment everyone does. Not that most men need much encouragement to come inside, regardless of the consequences."

He stared at her in horror. "I asked her if it was safe and she laughed like it was a joke! I thought it was because humans and cunids couldn't produce offspring!"

She laughed at him. "Of course they can. Most humanoid races can breed together. What kind of idiot doesn't know that?" Her smile widened. "And you heard me say how fecund bunny girls are. Just a hint of cum anywhere near her pussy and she'll get pregnant for sure."

"Then why did she tell me it was safe?" Dare demanded, raking his fingers through his hair.

The farmwife sobered slightly and gave him a curious look. "Did she say she wouldn't get pregnant?"

He hesitated. "Well no. I said I was coming, she talked dirty about me doing it inside her, and I asked if it was safe. She laughed and said it was, then called me silly."

Ellui had started to laugh again as he spoke, and as he finished she fell to the ground and began rolling around in unrestrained mirth. "She probably didn't understand the question, and thought you meant the potential for danger from a wandering predator!" she gasped. "Bunny girls don't consider pregnancy a risk, they consider it a great success! They'll go out of their way to make it happen since they're always eager to have children. Usually just the precum will do it, so if you penetrate her or even touch her entrance with your cock at all, it's almost guaranteed you've knocked her up."

She gave him a mock sympathetic look through her chortles. "Unless she's already carrying some other horny local's child, which doesn't seem likely given how desperate she was for you to mount her, you'll be a father in five to ten months."

Phoenix

Dare glanced helplessly into the forest. "Should I go after her?" he asked uncertainly. "I mean, if she's carrying my child then it's my duty to take care of them." Honestly, while it would disrupt his plans for his life in this world, or at least significantly change them, the prospect of marrying the gorgeous bunny girl wasn't the most unappealing one he'd ever heard.

Ellui scoffed. "Such a noble sentiment, if you mean it. But you really don't know anything about bunny girls, do you? Remember how I said there's 7 females for every male? They don't really get the concept of marriage and certainly not monogamy, and are usually content to raise their children alone or as part of a warren with mostly other females and children."

That was a relief to hear, although he still felt guilty. "But will they be okay?"

She motioned derisively at the forest around them. "Did you see her teeth, by any chance? They're herbivore teeth. Grass eater teeth. Cunids have no problem surviving out in nature, and prefer to live a carefree, natural life. Usually close to humans or other intelligent races, who'll hunt the dangerous monsters and provide them with plentiful lovers."

Dare mulled that over. A more primal part of him was pleased at the thought that the pale woman was carrying his child. And imagining the voluptuous bunny girl round with his baby made his cock twitch appreciatively.

Still, he felt a bit guilty at the thought that he wouldn't be part of his child's life, and wouldn't be able to help out with it.

Then something Ellui had said snagged in his mind. "Wait, what do you mean five to ten months?"

The farmwife looked at him like he was a halfwit. "Five months, as in how long it would take for her to give birth to a cunid child. Obviously."

Collisa

Dare silently cursed his lack of knowledge of this world. "Could you explain it all for me? You know I didn't even know humans and other races could breed."

She shook her head. "My dear, sweet, ignorant trapper. You're lucky you're so cute and have such a big cock, or I might lose hope in you." She sighed. "Almost all humanoid races can breed together. To the point that females of smaller races, even much smaller ones, can accommodate far larger cocks to make it happen without any discomfort, just like she was a woman of that larger race. And childbirth for a smaller female having a larger race's offspring will be just as safe as for a female of that larger race. It's a ##### ########."

He blinked as her last words fuzzed, just out of comprehension. "A what?"

The farmwife looked at him impatiently. "A ##### ########. Part of the foundation of the world that defies rational explanation."

Was she trying to say something like world feature or game mechanic? Something everyone was probably at least in some way aware of, but that the system wouldn't allow to be openly acknowledged because it would break immersion?

"Anyway," she said, "with most of the races, mating results in an equal chance to have a child of either race. A few races can produce hybrids, for instance goblins that produce hobgoblins with humans, but races like that are rarer and cunids aren't one of them. Same with other beast folk."

Ooh, other beast folk. Did that mean there were catgirls and dog girls and fox girls and lizard girls and maybe dragon girls out there? Or even others?

Dare nodded thoughtfully at her explanation. "So Clover could either have a human or cunid child?"

Ellui shook her head again. "Bunny girls are one of the

exceptions. They'll usually have a cunid child, and probably a girl with the 7 to 1 female to male ratio. On the rare occasion they have a baby from the father's race, with whatever female to male ratio that race is known for, the warren works together to raise a child that has more challenging dietary needs. The child is welcomed into the warren, and only a few ever opt to leave and seek out their own race."

He couldn't blame them. Especially if the child was male; in the warren he'd never want for lovers offering wild sex, and they'd all live carefree and happy.

Hell, if Dare had the option he'd probably be happy to live among bunny girls too.

Then a thought struck him with sudden uneasiness. Babies weren't the only consequence of sex. "I hate to ask this, especially after the fact," he said slowly, "but do I have to worry about STDs?"

The farmwife stared at him blankly. "Estedees?" she repeated in bafflement.

"Sexually transmitted diseases," he clarified. "Diseases carried only through sex that usually affect the genitalia and are often incurable."

She shuddered. "Gods, what an awful thing. I've never heard of it before and wish I hadn't."

Dare perked up, feeling a surge of excitement. "So you've never heard of anyone getting a disease from having sex?"

Ellui looked bemused. "Not unless they fucked a monster that spreads a disease debuff or something," she said wryly. "Although no idea why anyone would ever do that."

That was great news. Especially since Dare had already fucked two women and a bunch of slimes without even considering the possibility; STDs didn't tend to come up in most fantasy games.

Collisa

One of those nasty real world things you wanted to escape when you played them.

Dare finished cleaning himself off, wrung out his soaked tunic and pulled it on, kicked into his shoes, and bundled the rest of his clothes under one arm. Then he started for the clearing where he'd left his pack. "Well, take care," he told Ellui as he passed her.

"Ah, don't be like that," she said, hurrying to fall into step beside him. "I'll keep you company, and you can tell me all the juicy details!" She nudged his arm teasingly. "Did you take her from behind? From the front? Did she squeal? Was her pussy tighter than mine?"

He grimaced. "I don't want to be rude, since you've been very helpful to me with information," he said as politely as he could. "But you're married and I fucked you without knowing that fact, which makes being around you right now really uncomfortable. So I'm going to leave now."

The farmwife laughed. "What, you're going to run away like a little boy?"

"If you say so." Dare sped up to his usual jog, which he doubted the plump woman could keep up with for more than a few minutes, if at all.

"What, you'll just leave me out here where there might be monsters or bandits, you son of a bitch?" she shouted.

Considering she'd already been out here, she must not think it was all that dangerous. Still, Dare slowed down enough to keep her just in view, in case she really did run into trouble.

He needed to wait for his clothes to dry a little before he went into the village anyway.

Chapter Seven
Healer

The trip to Lone Ox was awkward with the unpleasant woman following behind, always smirking when he glanced back at her. He retrieved his pack, walked on to the outskirts of Ellui's farm, and once there dressed in his wet clothes and continued on, giving the place a wide berth.

Nassor was out on his porch again when Dare reached his house. Although the older man immediately perked up when he saw the tusks poking out of Dare's pack. "So you got them, lad!" he called eagerly. He whistled in appreciation. "Good ones, too . . . I'm going to be able to carve some truly fine pieces with them."

Dare wasted no time handing over the tusks. Almost as soon as he did he heard a triumphant trumpet sound and the text "Quest completed. A Boaring Request. 500 experience earned" popped up.

Nice. That was way better experience than for the basic achievements he'd gotten so far. Although still not a huge amount compared to what he needed to reach Level 6.

The woodcarver handed him his knife, and Dare took a moment to admire it.

Utility Knife, Level 5, Journeyman quality. Six times the damage of his stone knives. Dramatically more durability. No quality penalty for skinning and crafting.

It was beautiful.

He pulled his main hand stone knife from the leather sheath he'd crafted for it and tossed it in his pack, replacing it with his Utility Knife. "Thanks," he said, offering his hand.

Collisa

"And thanks to you," Nassor said, admiring the tusks. Then he set them aside briskly. "Suppose you've got some more things to sell me?"

Dare did. He sold a bundle of Boarite tusks and a few other bits of monster loot. The Woodcarver seemed a lot more amenable to buying things now that he had his tusks; a reputation boost from the quest?

He even paid more.

"Take care, now," Nassor called as Dare walked off, their business completed. "You see any more boars like that one, think of me for the tusks. I can't give you another knife but I'll give you its value in silver."

Good to know.

Dare made his way to the tavern next, selling the boar meat and a few other pieces of monster loot. Then he asked the tavern keeper whether he had all the ingredients for a BLT on hand.

To his delight the man did, aside from mayonnaise unfortunately. Although he had butter, which was a decent substitute.

The man seemed fascinated watching Dare slice bread (with his new knife), then put the ingredients between the slices to make a sandwich. Apparently that sort of thing wasn't done in Lone Ox. Although after watching Dare's obvious enjoyment, it was likely the tavern keeper might copy his idea.

And he'd have plenty of bacon with the meat Dare sold him.

The final stop was the Mayor's, where Dare reported his progress on the bandit camp. Or lack thereof. The portly man was disappointed to hear Dare was going to have to gain more levels before he could even consider doing anything about the place, but he accepted it.

He also held to his agreement to buy all of Dare's trash monster

Phoenix

loot.

Dare headed back to his camp excited about his first quest completed, his new knife, and the superior items he'd be able to craft with it to replace his inferior gear. It would take some work, but it would be worth it in the long run.

He checked his snares, harvested a few small game and a lucky catch of a deer, cured the meat, hides, and sinew, and then called it a night and went to bed.

* * * * *

Dare gained 3 levels over the next ten days.

It was, understandably, taking longer with every level. Not quite double the time with each, but close.

First things first he'd made a better bow using his Utility Knife, as planned. It actually received quality bonuses twice, since he skinned the leather and chopped and carved the wood with it, which all received a bump in quality, and then used the knife to make the bow, again giving it a quality bump.

The upshot was that his new weapon had a modest bump to damage, which let him level up that much faster.

He moved camp to be closer to higher level monsters on the fifth day. For leveling he was doing most of the same things he had been: rotating between spawn points for sentry monsters, and locating another spawn point of slime girls so he could farm monsters coming to get off in them.

Luckily the transparent monster girls seemed to be fairly common. These ones were even Level 6, not that he had any plans to farm them. And green instead of blue, although thankfully still non-toxic. And they'd taken the form of a few other races and body types to enjoy with them.

Another efficiency bump occurred when he came to the

realization that hunting game took time away from hunting monsters, while his improved snares passively did the work for him while he could do other stuff. They might bring him game slower, at least until he made a bunch of them, but the value in time saved was by far worth the work.

So he made another concerted effort to make and set more snares.

The upside was he soon had plenty of meat and leather. He was able to make a full set of basic leather armor, and from it rank up the crafting ability enough to be able to make the Level 5 ones once he had enough leather and other materials. He also had plenty of trade goods for when he visited Lone Ox on the fifth day, soon after moving his camp.

He'd have to wait until Level 10 to be able to make a better bow, which seemed like a long ways away. He could only assume that bows he could buy from vendors and crafters filled the in between levels, and honestly with their qualities might've even made the basic bow inferior even at the level it could be made.

Although he was able to make a better knife at Level 8. It required rare gem drops from monsters or that could be found along the river, which would all be combined to make a sturdier blade than stone. Again, it made absolutely no sense but fit with a world designed around video game mechanics.

Unfortunately, that knife was barely better than his Utility Knife. So Dare ignored it and set his sights on Level 10.

That, or he'd wait to buy weapons in the village, or even in the town Nassor had mentioned nearby, now that he seemed to be farming more and better trade goods with his snares and monster hunting.

Speaking of which, it was the tenth day and he had enough trade goods he was actually needing to sort out which ones were least valuable and could be left behind. So it was time for another trip into the village.

That could wait until evening, though, when the villagers would be done with the day's work and more inclined to chat and trade. In the meantime, Dare wanted to do some scouting.

He'd seen a Level 11 bugbear visiting the new slime girls he'd found (which had prompted such a horrifying mental picture he wanted to bleach his brain, even though he hadn't actually seen anything). It was the highest level monster he'd seen, and would point him towards new spawn points to hunt once he gained a few more levels.

So he was going to go explore in the direction the bugbear had gone when it left the river, see what was out there. And if he saw any monsters close to his level he'd kill them while he was at it.

Dare actually found himself looking forward to exploring, even though it slowed down his leveling and he almost never discovered anything that would give him the paltry experience reward. It was just so enjoyable to explore this new world and see everything that was out there.

All the varied terrain even in what was largely a forest setting, the interesting landmarks he found like lakes and waterfalls and craggy hills. The varied monsters, some of which he'd never heard of in any game he'd ever played.

And of course the prospect of what might be over the horizon. The same thing that had him eagerly playing a game late into the night, ignoring hunger and thirst and anything else in his singleminded immersion.

Except this was a million times better.

Dare found the bugbear camp without too much trouble, the monsters inside ranging in level from 10 to 13. And they were monsters; bugbears were usually classified as a subset of hobgoblin in a lot of games, and were often intelligent (for a given value of intelligence) in them.

But on this world they were monsters, slightly different looking than most bugbear art from Earth and apparently with no relation to goblins. Similar to the Boarites.

Two levels higher was still more than he wanted to challenge most of the time, especially since the bugbears had a ranged attack called Throw Debris. Which he guessed meant they grabbed the nearest rock or handy heavy object and chucked it his way.

Dare moved on, finding more spawn points for some sort of venomous flying snake called a Slithin (Level 12-14), a squat, brutish animal called a Dolid Trouncer (Level 9-12) that resembled nothing he knew of from Earth.

He picked off a couple of the Level 9s and found that they were manageable, although their Quake ability had a surprising range and nearly threw him off his feet, as well as applying a debuff that slowed his movement and weapon attack speed.

Speaking of Boarites, he found another camp teeming with Level 15 to 19 ones, as well as a few much higher level leaders. Along with the higher levels, it was a more serious looking place that could've encompassed several of the previous Boarite camp he'd found, and had some odd totems and other decorations as well as a few large structures.

A Boarite city, if a crude one?

Dare marked it on his map with a wide circle for where the outer sentries and patrols roamed, then another circle even farther out for how close he was willing to get to the intimidating place; if he ever cleared it, he'd either have to be much higher level or part of a large raid group.

He backed away from the place and continued his exploration, swinging wide on his way back to his camp to check an area he hadn't searched yet.

Phoenix

Which was when he heard a frantic, distinctly feminine voice screaming deeper in the forest, causing him to twisted towards the sound in surprise and nearly drop his bow. There was pain as well as terror in that scream.

Along with words that, while in another language, clearly marked the person as intelligent.

Dare cursed and sprinted towards the obvious cries for help, ducking between trees and vaulting undergrowth with all the speed his reflexes could give him. Even so he nearly slammed his face on a few branches as he reached for an arrow and fit it to the bowstring.

Given his panic at the urgency of the situation and the fact that he was running at breakneck speeds, he should've fumbled and dropped the arrow. But his abilities must've come into play, because while inside he was freaking out his movements were calm and quick.

In a small clearing ahead he saw a large black cat, a jaguar or panther, holding a tiny green woman in its mouth by the shoulder and savagely worrying her. The woman was curled up on herself trying to prevent her neck from breaking, choked voice gurgling with fear and pain.

She'd gotten lucky that the cat was toying with her, but if Dare didn't act soon she'd be dead.

At the same time, it was dangerous to just run in. He'd never seen a panther in these woods before, so he quickly pulled up his Adventurer's Eye.

Then he cursed. "Panther, level 12. Animal. Attacks: Pounce, Bite, Claw, Pin, Savage."

Since it was 4 levels above him its threat color was Pink, but that was a bit deceptive since it was only one level away from being Red. Dare knew from careful study and painful experience that for enemies, every level above his own meant a significant jump in power.

It wasn't just the power that came with being that higher level, either. He'd also noticed that the few higher level enemies he'd faced gained a modifier for being higher level than him, so his attacks did less damage and their attacks on him did more.

And with every level that modifier grew.

It made sense in a way, to keep lower level adventurers from getting a decent level tank and then mobbing down much higher level Silver Sickle monsters in a horde. But it meant that whoever had created the system on this world very much didn't want adventurers fighting significantly higher level enemies.

More importantly right now, it meant that if Dare tried to help that tiny green-skinned woman, he was probably going to die. He very much doubted he had the gear a Level 8 should, so he was even weaker than his level suggested.

But he had to try. He doubted he'd be able to live with the guilt if he didn't.

He raised his bow and drew the fletchings back to his cheek, surprised to find his arms were still steady. Maybe he wouldn't have to fight the panther, he could just distract it and use Fleetfoot to lead it away so the green woman could escape. Then somehow find a way to shake the big cat and come back to help her.

It didn't seem likely, but it might be a better option than trying to fight it.

Please don't let this kill me, he thought in his usual mantra as he took aim and loosed.

His arrow buried in the panther's neck, and it flung its tiny victim away with a yowl of pain and whirled towards him. Dare already had another arrow nocked and was preparing to draw, but before he could the cat blurred towards him.

Phoenix

Pounce, he thought grimly, cursing his carelessness. Like other Charge abilities it would allow the enemy to more swiftly close the distance with a target. Only this ability let the big cat move *much* faster, almost like a teleport.

Even with Fleetfoot he barely had time to drop his bow and leap aside before the panther landed where he'd been. The predator seemed slightly surprised to find him not there, buying him a split second to act.

Considering his options, Dare drew his main hand Utility Knife and offhand stone knife and darted in. He couldn't run from the Pounce ability, and he no longer had his bow and wouldn't have time to shoot an arrow anyway. Which just left trying to stab a higher level panther to death with comparatively low damage weapons.

He was so fucked.

Dare dove into a roll past the cat as it whirled towards him, barely twisting aside from a flashing paw. He landed behind it and had just enough time to slash at the back of one of its legs before leaping backwards to escape another lighting quick swipe.

Without Fleetfoot he'd already be in trouble.

Text scrolled across the edge of his vision. "Melee ability unlocked: Hamstring." Which was all fine and dandy if he'd bothered to put any points into his melee attacks, but he'd focused mostly optimizing damage with his bow and beefing up his defensive abilities.

He might have to change that if enemies kept closing on him before he could get off more than a shot or two.

Dare leapt into the air, transferring his stone knife to grip in his teeth as he caught a branch and swung up onto it. The panther snarled and began swarming up the trunk of the tree as quick as a squirrel, but he had time to check it with his Eye.

Its health was still almost at full, but he noticed it had two status effects: Critical Bleed and Snare (25%). He also noticed that Pounce no longer showed up on its list of attacks.

Because it was on cooldown, or because taking out one of the panther's back legs disabled the ability?

Considering how the world's system responded to trying to exploit high places, Hamstring's snare effect probably only lasted for a short time. Still, it opened up a possibility and gave Dare an idea.

One that would cheese the fight to hell and back, but he was fighting for not just his life but the life of the wounded woman below.

The big cat reached the branch he was perched on and leapt for him, and Dare dropped down. But rather than falling to the ground below he once again caught the branch and swung up, just in time to slash at the hamstring on the panther's other rear leg with his Utility Knife, tearing a yowl of fury from the animal.

He was vaguely aware of gaining proficiency in Hamstring as he finally dropped to the ground below.

The panther dropped down a second later, limping heavily now with its speed reduced 50%. That allowed him to maneuver into position and dart in quick to hamstring one of the panther's front legs, then vault over the panther as it momentarily collapsed and go for its final leg.

The panther's status effect changed from Snared to Rooted, and the animal rolled awkwardly on the ground to face him, snarling, as he dove for his bow.

Dare came up with an arrow nocked, drew, and from practically point blank range shot it into the panther's neck. He kept unloading arrows into his target as quick as he could, stacking the Critical Bleed. The damage from the arrows was pitiful on a Level 12, but its health bar began ticking down slowly but surely from the Damage over Time effects.

Phoenix

The panther's first injured leg healed and it immediately began dragging itself towards Dare at 25% speed; he'd been right that a crippling injury in the real world would just be a minor inconvenience here.

He fired another arrow before jumping in to slash the leg again, reapplying the Root effect. Then he hung around and kept slashing at the big cat with both knives instead of going back to shooting his bow, waiting for the other legs to heal so he could Hamstring them again.

It went just fine with the other back leg, but Dare got punished when the first leg healed as his enemy immediately slashed at him with all its blinding speed.

He barely had time to start to leap back before claws raked across his ankle, tearing his pants and leaving lines of fire across his skin. No way to tell how bad the wound was, but he still had use of his leg, no bleed effect, and had only lost 4% of his hit points.

Dare growled and leapt in to Hamstring the front leg, then for good measure crippled the other one again as well before leaping backwards and switching to his bow, emptying his quiver into the panther's neck.

So far so good. The predator's hit points were down to around 50%, and he seemed to have a working strategy for taking it down. A dangerous one, as he'd just seen, but way better than trying to go head to head against it with his knives.

He was just starting to become optimistic when he saw that the back leg he'd first injured was already moving again.

Diminishing returns, a common mechanic for snare, root, and crowd control effects.

Damnit. That meant he'd only be able to keep the panther rooted in place for so long before it basically became immune to both Snare and Root from Hamstring.

Collisa

Dare checked the Critical Bleed, relieved to see that it, at least, didn't seem to be suffering from diminishing returns; all the stacks that should've been there were there, while the ones that had completed their duration had dropped off. He checked their damage per second, then the panther's remaining health, and did a few quick calculations.

Time to change strategies.

He began running away sideways, so he could continue drawing and loosing arrows at the panther while still managing a decent speed and being able to see where he was going. He soon got to the point that he couldn't accurately hit its neck and switched to its body, back to plinking away at the Pink's health.

The big cat's second leg healed and its pursuit speed increased. Then its third leg healed. And since Dare had crippled both front legs before backing off it should be healing soon too, which would unlock Pounce.

He turned and ran.

A glance back saved his life as he saw the panther blurring towards him again. He dove to one side, caught himself on a tree trunk, and leapt up to another branch. The predator could get up to him terrifyingly fast, but it bought him a bit more time than running and dodging on the ground, and he could see the animal coming easier since it had to either leap up to the branch or use a tree trunk.

He began hopping from branch to branch, all the while keeping an eye, or an Eye, on his enemy's hit points. He watched as they ticked down towards 0, the bleed rate slowing down as the DoTs gradually fell off.

Dare knew he'd put enough Critical Bleed stacks on to kill the panther and then some, but as its hit point loss slowed to a crawl below the 50 mark he began to fear that he'd miscalculated. And as it was he was barely staying ahead of the big cat; one mistake and he'd be toast.

Phoenix

Or if its Pounce cooldown finished.

Those final few ticks of the DoTs seemed to take forever, and he had to resist the temptation to try to find time to shoot a final arrow. Instead he kept running until he heard the panther give a final plaintive yowl behind him, and the crash as it fell off a branch and slammed into the ground below.

Dare sagged against a tree trunk, panting, as he checked with his Eye to confirm his enemy was dead. Its hit points showed 0, status (DEAD), and with a gasp of relief he turned and ran back towards the clearing where he'd left the injured woman.

He would've loved to see what sort of cool loot a Level 12 panther dropped, but he'd have to come back and hope the body was still there once he knew she'd be okay.

When Dare reached the clearing he saw that the green woman had dragged herself over to a tree to lean against it, breathing labored and eyes clouded with pain.

Now that he had a better look at the little creature he concluded she must be a goblin. She was tiny, probably no more than up to his belly button standing, a few inches shy of being 4 feet tall. That was what he'd expect for a goblin, but while most goblins in art were depicted as painfully scrawny and hideous, this woman was anything but.

For one thing, while it was obvious she was malnourished she had the sort of curvy body any college coed would envy. Proportionally perfect for her short height. Aside from her breasts, that is, which strained against the tattered cloth wrap covering them, large and firm and absolutely gorgeous.

She had jet black hair falling to her shoulders in a matted tangle, and her pale green skin made him think of the inside of an avocado. Also she had short pointy ears.

Actually, her face was pointy everything. A short, slender nose that ended in a surprisingly sharp tip, a pointed chin, and a slightly wide mouth that revealed sharklike teeth bared in pain or fear. Even her cheekbones were prominent to the point of having points of their own.

In fact, it seemed the only thing soft about her face were her huge, pale yellow eyes, wide and vulnerable and unexpectedly lovely as they stared at him.

Which wasn't to say that her sharp features were ugly, simply unfamiliar. Originally they'd been a bit strange, maybe, but the longer he looked the more he could see an exotic beauty there.

She was shivering, although probably not with cold on this sunny day, even though her only clothes were the cloth wrapped around her large breasts and a ragged loincloth. It was obvious that she was terrified and suffering, and his heart went out to her.

Dare only had a moment to take in her appearance, since his attention was quickly drawn to the deep, nasty scratches on her bare thigh and back. As well as an ugly wound on her shoulder from where the panther had held and savaged her.

They looked really bad. As in, potentially life-threatening bad. He quickly pulled up his Eye to inspect her.

"Goblin, adult female. Humanoid, intelligent. Class: Level 7 Healer. Attacks: Bite. Dagger (unleveled, unarmed)."

Her hit points were listed as at about 60%, steadily dropping as her wounds bled. Unlike with monsters and animals, it looked as if serious bleed effects for intelligent creatures didn't have a short duration; unless treated or you got lucky, you could bleed to death.

Just like back on Earth.

Dare looked around helplessly. He didn't have any medicine or potions, assuming those existed on this world, and he knew no healing spells. But he had to do *something*. At the very least he could wash the wounds with clean water from his water skin. And since

Phoenix

she lived in this world, maybe she'd have some idea of how to care for herself.

Didn't some primitive tribes from his world use mud or something like that? It seemed like a terrible idea that would just contaminate the wound; probably better to just tear strips off of leather from one of the pieces in his pack and bind the wounds.

He stepped forward, and the goblin's bared teeth became distinctly warning. She tried to scuttle away on her hands and feet, but whimpered in pain as her wounds dropped her back to the ground.

"Easy," he said gently, holding out a hand in what he hoped was a universal gesture. "I'm not going to hurt you. I want to help."

"Help?" the tiny woman said in a piping, timid voice, the word heavily accented. She relaxed slightly.

"That's right, help." He pulled out his water skin and offered it to her. "Here, water."

The goblin's sharp ears quivered. "Watuur."

Dare nodded, smiling. "Here." He poured some out onto his hand to show it was clean, then held it out to her.

She took it and briefly inspected it, then dropped it weakly and looked up at him, yellow eyes pleading. "Watuur." She made a feeble gesture that could've been a fish swimming.

"You need running water?" he asked. "A stream?"

"Watuur," the goblin said weakly, eyelids drooping.

"Let me take you to water." He stepped forward again, and to his relief this time she showed no reaction. He gently reached down. "I'm going to pick you up."

She didn't struggle as he carefully lifted her into his arms, mindful of her wounds. She was as light as he'd expected given her size, no burden at all to Dare's new body.

To his surprise her skin, covered in blood and filthy from being dragged across the ground by the black cat, was nevertheless smooth and as soft as he'd ever felt. It had a slightly oily feel, as if she'd just applied lotion, but it wasn't unpleasant.

It was only when he was holding her that he noticed her loincloth was damp, as were her legs, and the sharp scent of urine reached his nostrils; she must've soiled herself in her terror during the attack. Beneath the smell was another, musty and not quite pleasant, and he realized her loincloth and chest wrap were unwashed and filthy.

As was she, most likely. Still, she didn't smell as bad as he expected. In fact, as he draped her arm around his neck he caught a whiff of her armpit, hairless as if she either shaved or was naturally hairless there.

The scent was distinctly feminine, with a strong musk.

So this was a goblin. A real member of another race, in his arms. And dependent on him for help.

Dare quickly set aside his curiosity and offhand observations and rushed back through the trees to his campsite, the closest source of water he knew of, using every bit of speed he could muster with Fleetfoot and his Hunter abilities.

He carefully carried the tiny goblin over to the stream. Once there she motioned for him to set her down in the water. That seemed like a bad idea considering her open wounds, but when he hesitated she squirmed so hard he was afraid he'd drop her. He quickly stooped and gently set her so she was sitting in one of the shallower parts of the stream.

At that point he saw something amazing.

The tiny woman began to chant in a strange, chirping language that he assumed was Goblin. The water she sat in began to glow and flow around and over her, and then he watched in disbelief as the

Phoenix

ugly wounds on her thigh, back, and shoulder began to fade. Within a minute they were nothing more than thin white scars on her pale green skin.

She sighed in exhausted relief and slumped back into the water, listlessly splashing it over her skin to wash away the blood. The tiny woman looked too exhausted to do anything but lay there, but after a moment she glanced at Dare, then with an groan of weary reluctance sat up.

He smiled uncertainly and waved. "Hello." He pointed to himself. "Dare."

She stared at him blankly for a few moments until he repeated the gesture and his name, then she hesitantly pointed at her own chest. "Zuri," she said in her piping voice.

"Zuri." Dare smiled more warmly and motioned to the fire. "Are you hungry, Zuri?" He pantomimed putting food in his mouth. "Food?"

She nodded eagerly, so he stood and offered her his arms to carry her back to the fire if she was too weak to stand.

The tiny goblin held up her hands in a clear "wait" gesture, then got back to chanting in her language as the water around her started glowing again. But while before it had been a sort of whitish green, now it was a bluish purple. The goblin flopped around in the water, which confused him until he realized that she was trying to submerge every part of herself.

Then the glow faded. Panting wearily, Zuri pushed to her feet and hobbled over to the fire. Dare rushed to offer her a hand, which she stared at in confusion for a moment until he took her elbow and helped her over to sit on a log.

As she slumped there wearily he grabbed his bedroll and unrolled it by the fire, ushering for her to lay down and rest. She gratefully complied, and it was only when she sprawled atop it that

Collisa

he realized she was clean.

Not clean as in just rolled around in a stream, but clean as in as freshly washed and scrubbed as if she'd just had a long bath. Not only that, but her tattered loincloth and chest wrap were pure white. Still ratty and barely fit for use, but as clean as if professionally laundered.

So Zuri knew not only healing magic, but cleaning magic as well. Both very useful in everyday life, he had to say.

Dare looked thoughtfully at the tiny woman.

Goblins tended to be a wild card in games; in most fantasy worlds they were stupid, blindly aggressive, and usually classified as evil.

Of course Zuri didn't look evil. Actually, at the moment she looked scared, vulnerable, and surprisingly cute. And there was certainly no sign of blind aggression.

As for stupid . . . from what he'd seen she was just the opposite, able to understand what he was trying to tell her without a shared language, and express herself surprisingly well.

Which pointed to her being more like the goblins in games that classified them as just another humanoid race. One with its own customs and culture. Often those goblins were very intelligent and clever artisans, although reckless inventors that made dangerous devices that often got themselves or others killed accidentally.

Or intentionally, in war.

Either way, she needed help and Dare wanted to help her. He just wasn't sure how.

"How can I help you?" he asked. "Do you have a family you need to get back to? A tribe?" She stared at him blankly. "Goblins?"

Zuri nodded in comprehension. "Goblin," she said, pointing at herself.

Phoenix

He shook his head wryly. He was just glad the humans he'd met seemed to all speak a language he understood, or he'd be going through this with everyone. For months or even years probably.

He pointed at the forest around them. "Other goblins?" he repeated, then pointed at Zuri. "Your family? Friends? Tribe? Somewhere for you to go?"

She finally seemed to understand. "Zuri," she said, pointing at herself and nodding. Then she pointed out at the woods as well. "Goblin . . ." She shook her head.

So she was alone. "Then how did you get out here?" he mused, more to himself than the little goblin. He pointed in the direction of the village. "Lone Ox? Village?"

She looked at him blankly.

Dare sighed. Well, wherever she'd come from and whatever her situation, it was probably too late to help her get back to where she belonged tonight. Which meant he needed to worry about her immediate needs.

He tossed some steaks on the cooking rack and got them roasting, then began pulling the trade items he'd carefully gathered out of his pack. It would probably take most of the leather to outfit Zuri with the basic necessities, but that was fine; he could farm more in a few days.

The first thing he crafted for the tiny goblin was a tunic of the same design as his own. For her comfort and to see she was properly clothed in cool weather, of course, but he also had to admit that he was finding all her exposed skin unexpectedly distracting.

She was definitely a woman, and her curves were pleasant to look at. He did his best to be a gentleman and focus on her face, but he was only human.

Zuri watched him curiously as he worked, although her gaze kept darting to the cooking steaks, her yellow eyes longing as she licked her full lips with a pale pink tongue.

However, Dare had her full attention when he completed the tunic, tailored to her size thanks to game mechanics (although not a perfect fit due to quality), and held it out to her. "Here."

She was slow to take it and actually began trembling slightly. "Zuri?" she asked, pointing at herself and then the tunic.

"Zuri's tunic," he agreed, pressing it into her hands. "A gift."

The timid goblin smiled hesitantly, showing her sharp teeth, then quickly pulled it on over her head as if afraid he'd change his mind. She smoothed it until it hung right, then looked down at it admiringly with a more genuine smile.

Dare had to admit the tunic looked cute on her, although the leather still hugged her curves in a way he was going to have to do his best not to stare at.

Yellow eyes shining, she babbled a few words that he assumed were a thank you, then dropped to her hands and knees in front of him in some sort of submissive pose. Dare wasn't sure what that was about, but he shook his head and motioned for her to lay down and rest again until she finally complied.

Maybe the pose was a goblin thing.

Well, he'd find out sooner or later. Smiling at how happy the simple tunic had made her, he got to work on shoes, a goblin-sized tent, and a bedroll for her.

Zuri similarly went nuts over each as he presented them to her, seeming stunned and a bit dazed by the gifts. She also assumed that same odd pose after every gift.

Dare managed to finish all her new items just before the meat finished cooking, and while she was still admiring her new gear he got out the crude plate he'd carved from a large piece of bark and loaded it with a steak and a few foraged mushrooms and greens. He placed one of his stone knives next to the steak, laid the fork he'd carved on the other side, then held it across the fire to Zuri. "Here."

She stared at it in blank incomprehension, as if she couldn't believe he was giving her all that food. She looked up timidly, as if to confirm he'd made a mistake, and he smiled reassuringly and set the plate on her lap.

"Here, eat," he said, pantomiming cutting the steak and using the fork to lift it to his mouth.

The tiny goblin hesitantly complied, staring at him with huge eyes as she eagerly devoured the food; she was obviously starving.

It felt nice to see her enjoy the food, and Dare couldn't help but smile as he snagged another steak off the rack with his Utility Knife and used it as a skewer as he gnawed off a bite.

He realized Zuri was staring at him, her eyes darting down to the plate and fork he'd given her then back to him, expression baffled. "I only had the ones I use," he explained sheepishly. "And you're a guest." He motioned to the food again. "Go ahead, eat."

She got back to eating, although she kept staring at him thoughtfully.

A somewhat uncomfortable silence settled as they ate. "I wish we could communicate," he finally said regretfully. "I bet there's so much about this world and about your people that you could tell me." He gave her a rueful smile. "Besides, it's a bit awkward not being able to talk."

Zuri looked at him blankly for most of that, but brightened at the end. "Talk," she agreed. She hesitated timidly, looking as if she was almost shaking with nervousness, then abruptly blurted, "Dare save Zuri, help Zuri, food Zuri." She motioned to the tunic and other things he'd made her, although she couldn't seem to think of a way to describe him giving them to her. "Help Zuri," she finally said again.

Then her yellow eyes looked into his, shyly but with solemn

sincerity, and she tapped a fist against her generous chest. "Save, help, food. Talk Zuri lots."

Dare smiled back at her. In spite of the awkward caveman speak he had a good idea of what she was saying. And honestly, that fact that she only knew a few words but could find a way to express herself that eloquently suggested the tiny goblin was smarter than her primitive garb had suggested.

"I'm just glad you're all right," he said. She stared at him blankly, and he bit back a sigh and reached to the spit to pull off another cut of meat, offering it to her. "Here, you still hungry?"

She looked at the food with obvious longing but didn't take it, expression timid. So he took her plate and set the steaming meat on it, then firmly pressed it into her hands. "Go ahead, there's plenty and it looks as if you haven't had a good meal in days."

Zuri nodded and tapped her chest again, which he assumed was a sign for gratitude, then eagerly tore into the steak with her sharp teeth.

After she finished eating the tiny woman settled down on his bedroll, and soon after fell asleep. Dare didn't have the heart to wake her to move her into her own bedroll in her set up tent, so he wrapped the fur blankets around her.

After he was sure she was comfortable he climbed into his tent, using the small bedroll as a pillow with his leather cloak wrapped around him.

He'd slept worse when he'd first arrived.

Not that he was quick to fall asleep. He wasn't sure what to do about Zuri, and spent a while fretting about it.

If he'd understood her correctly there were no other goblins around. No tribe for her to get back to. And she hadn't seemed in any hurry to get anywhere. But that might've just been due to exhaustion.

Phoenix

He'd try again tomorrow, see if she showed any urgency to get back to wherever she'd come from. Or if not, try to communicate with her that he could take her where she wanted to go.

Although the nagging thought chased his tired mind that if the tiny goblin had been out in the middle of nowhere all alone, dressed in rags and completely defenseless, it was possible she had nowhere to go.

What would he do then?

Dare wanted to help her, but he wanted to level and farm gold and materials and eventually become a powerful and successful hero on this world. She might be able to group with him and they could level together, since he'd seen her healing ability and knew she could be useful. But it would mean he was basically taking responsibility for her, or at least to be her companion for who knew how long.

And he had no idea what Zuri wanted or was capable of.

In the end he decided all his internal debate was pointless. He'd been planning to go into Lone Ox anyway to trade, so he might as well take her there and see if anyone knew what to do. Or better yet, find someone who spoke Goblin and ask her directly.

Yeah, that was the next step.

Dare gave the sleeping goblin by the fire one last look over his shoulder to make sure she was still doing okay. He couldn't see anything but an unmoving bundle under the blankets and assumed she was still asleep, hopefully comfortable and resting well.

Yawning, he rolled over, pulled his cloak tighter around him, and drifted off to sleep.

Chapter Eight
Companion

Dare woke up the next morning to find that Zuri was already awake.

He wasn't sure how long she'd been up for, but she was outside his tent on her hands and knees, waiting patiently. He just hoped she'd only taken that position after she heard him stirring, and hadn't been there long. Especially since a light drizzle was coming down.

Although judging by her soaked hair, the damp patches on her tunic, and the water beaded on the leather, she probably had. Also she was trembling as she stared at the ground, as if afraid that his kindness yesterday had been a fluke.

Dare sighed. "Got to be honest," he said lightly as he ducked out of his tent, "even if it's a cultural thing, not a fan of you bowing like that. Especially if you're miserable out in the rain." She stared at him blankly and he offered her a gentle smile. "How about breakfast?" he asked, pointing at the burned out campfire. "Food?" he pantomimed eating.

The timid goblin looked up, expression turning hopeful. "Food?" she agreed. She tapped her chest with her fist.

Shaking his head, he led the way to the fire.

It had rained several times now, although usually at night. When it rained during the day he usually either just did his best to ignore it, since his leather gear was decently waterproof, or he found a tree or ducked into his tent to wait it out.

Since Zuri was waiting for breakfast that wasn't an option, and he wanted to get a quick start to Lone Ox anyway. So he hastily rigged up a hide cover over the fire, then got some meat roasting

Phoenix

over it and retreated to lean against the trunk of a large overhanging tree as he waited for it to cook.

The goblin followed him, settling down beside him, and he motioned towards Lone Ox. "After we eat I was thinking we'd go to the nearby village, Lone Ox. We can see if anyone knows you or has talked to anyone looking for you, or if nothing else if anyone there speaks Goblin."

"Goblin," Zuri agreed, probably because it was the only word of what he'd said she understood.

"Talk Goblin," Dare corrected, pointing at the village. "Find where Zuri came from and what you want to do."

Her brow furrowed. "Zuri talk Goblin," she said, then pointed at him. "Dare talk Haraldaran." She shook her head and tapped her generous chest. "Zuri talk Haraldaran . . ." She shook her head vigorously.

Well, that wasn't exactly a revelation. He'd have to do his best to try to teach her at least the basic words so they could communicate while they were together. He gave an exaggerated nod and pointed at his nodding head. "Yes," he said. He shook his head just as dramatically. "No."

He pointed at himself. "Dare yes talk Haraldaran." He pointed at her. "Zuri no talk Haraldaran. Dare no talk Goblin, Zuri yes talk Goblin."

She nodded in understanding. "Yes," she said, and tapped her chest with her fist.

Dare smiled at her and settled back comfortably against the tree trunk. Then he grabbed a rock and drew his Utility Knife, activating the ability to sharpen it.

He did it until his knife's sharpness was classified as "razor", which it would quickly dull from with use until it was sharp, then after far more use drop down to dull. That quick dropoff from razor to sharp, combined with the fact that it only added a slight bonus to damage, didn't make it worth the effort in fights.

But he wasn't sharpening it for a fight.

He dug through a leather pouch he'd made and pulled out a shiny bit of metal he was using for a mirror, as well as the bit of soap he'd bought in Lone Ox. Then he drew his Utility Knife and, after lathering his several days' worth of stubble, began carefully shaving.

Zuri watched curiously as he scraped away every bit of facial hair, checking his face in his crude mirror until he was satisfied. Then he reached back with effort to grab a hunk of his hair, which had grown annoyingly long in the last few weeks, and began hacking it off.

At that point the goblin caught his wrist, looking alarmed. "Zuri help," she said, pointing at herself.

Dare grinned. "A Healer and a barber, Zuri?" He handed her the knife. "I doubt you can do any worse than I would. Thanks." He tapped his fist to his chest.

Zuri brightened in realization. "Thanks!" she repeated, tapping her own fist to her chest. "Zuri thanks Dare!"

"You're welcome." He patted her head, then sat straight and let her get to work.

Her hands moved confidently, and she *seemed* to be doing a neat, uniform job. When she finished a few minutes later he checked in his mirror, satisfied at what looked like a good cut considering it was done with a knife.

"Okay, looking good for our trip to town," he said brightly. He tapped his fist to his chest again, and the timid goblin beamed with pride.

They had breakfast, Zuri again digging in eagerly and packing away more than he thought her little body could hold. "You storing

Phoenix

it all in your chest?" Dare joked as he watched her go, feeling safe since she didn't understand him.

She paused. "Chest?" she repeated.

He felt his cheeks heat. "Never mind." He left her to finish her meal and began gathering trade goods.

Soon after that they were on their way, Dare loaded down with a heavy back and several bundles and Zuri carrying her own full pack, although with a much lighter load.

When she'd realized he was going to be carrying a burden she'd timidly but firmly managed to convey, with gestures and repeating the word "help" over and over, that she wanted him to make her a little hide pack so she could carry some of it.

He could appreciate that she wanted to do her fair share, so he complied. Her contribution was modest, but he respected her for it.

It felt strange to be moving at almost a snail's pace with a companion, when he'd usually be jogging or even running through these woods at 10 miles an hour or better. Especially since while Zuri's legs were proportionally long and elegantly slender, they were also half the length of his. She had to walk along briskly to keep up with Dare's slowest walking speed, with Fleetfoot just widening the gap between their normal walking paces.

Although to the tiny goblin's credit she made it to Lone Ox without needing to stop for rest, even with her burden, and when Ellui's farm came into view her breathing was barely labored.

The farmwife was out in one of her fields as they passed, hard at work with a hoe. Although the moment she spotted them she dropped the tool and headed for her fence.

"We meet again," she called. She glanced at Zuri and smirked. "What's with the goblin? Slimes and the random bunny girls not enough to satisfy your cock, so you got yourself a pleasure slave?" Her slightly mocking smile widened. "You made a good choice . . .

goblins are almost as fertile as cunids, so they're just about as horny, too. She should be able to keep up with you just fine."

Dare didn't hear anything after "slave".

Son of a bitch, slaves existed on this world? He supposed he should've expected it, since his unseen benefactor had warned him Collisa could be a brutal place. And most fantasy worlds took place in a medieval setting, where slavery was still common.

Besides, in spite of the best efforts of countries that knew better, slavery still existed on *his* world. The vile practice was an evil as old as time.

That didn't mean he was pleased to hear it. "She's not my slave," he said firmly. He did his best not to glower. "I don't believe in slavery."

The farmwife looked at him in bafflement. "Like, that it doesn't exist?" She laughed. "Because it definitely does."

Dare glanced helplessly down at Zuri, her big yellow eyes looking staring back up at him making his heart break. "I mean I don't approve of the practice and I don't want any slaves." He stopped short of adding that he thought it should be abolished; he doubted he was going to convince her, and she'd probably tell him to get off her property.

Ellui stared at him as if he was an alien. Which, he supposed, he technically was. "If she's not a slave then what is she?" she asked, pointing at Zuri.

That was a good question. "I don't know. I saved her from a panther in the woods. Now I'm trying to find her family or tribe or whatever."

"There aren't any goblin tribes in this region," the farmwife said with a frown. "They mostly infest the mountains to the north or west, or the jungles far to the south where they breed like flies. Aside from the occasional marauding band most goblins in Haraldar are slaves."

Phoenix

She motioned at Zuri. "Your goblin's most likely either a runaway or a survivor from some band of travelers. Either way, you should probably find out before you're accused of theft."

Dare moved protectively in front of the little goblin. He wasn't about to turn her over to some master for a miserable life of drudgery or worse. But Ellui was right that he should probably find out what Zuri's situation was so he knew what he was dealing with.

"Where can I find out?" he asked.

"The Mayor, of course," the farmwife said. "He gets regular reports from Driftwain a day's travel to the north. Things like bounties and wanted criminals, notices about escaped slaves, announcements for raiding parties to hunt dangerous monsters, and stuff like that."

"So I guess you haven't heard anything about a missing goblin?" Dare asked, just to be sure.

She laughed again. "You think anyone around here can afford a slave?" Her lip curled as she stared at Zuri, who was peeking around Dare's leg. "Not even a pukeskin . . . they might be common and cheap enough that nobles and wealthy merchants toss them aside like garbage on a whim, but we're all living hand to mouth here."

He flushed. "What did you just call her?" he asked quietly.

The farmwife just laughed harder. "What, insulted on her behalf? You'll hear her called worse. And end up beaten half to death in a ditch if you try to defend a gobbo's honor."

Dare shook his head, giving up. "I could call you worse too, but I'm polite enough not to." He motioned to Zuri and started past the farm towards the track leading into the village.

"Wow, I keep on forgetting what a smug, superior bastard you are!" she yelled at his back. "When you finally give in and come back for another taste of me I'm going to have to hate fuck you."

Collisa

He ignored her and sped up, Zuri seeming happy to keep up to get away from the unpleasant woman. Once Ellui finally stopped shouting the tiny goblin looked up at him and babbled something.

"You said it," Dare said, patting her head.

They got odd looks as they made their way through the village, along with a few hostile ones. Dare assumed that even if goblin slaves were common, the villagers probably didn't see many.

When Dare knocked on Durrand's door, there was no response for almost a minute. Then the Mayor pulled the door open dressed in a sleeping robe and night cap, yawning into his fist. "This better be good."

Dare felt a moment of chagrin; it was midmorning, and he'd assumed everyone would be awake. Good thing he'd been traveling slowly with Zuri or the man would be even more pissed off.

"I'm sorry, Mayor," he said. "I didn't realize you'd still be in bed."

Durrand glowered. "Well I'm up now. What's this about?"

Dare motioned at Zuri. "This is Zuri. I saved her from a panther in the forest, and now I'm trying to figure out if there are people who are missing her."

"An escaped slave, huh?" the Mayor mused, looking the goblin over. "I imagine someone's missing her. She's good breeding stock so she'd be valuable . . . for a goblin."

"We don't know she's a slave," Dare said, not pleased about the reminder of one of the ugliest sides of slavery. Or the insult to Zuri's race.

Durrand stared at him with a look of bafflement Dare was becoming familiar with. "What else would she be? There's no wild goblins in this area."

Again, Dare wasn't overjoyed at that term. "She could have been freed. Or part of a caravan that was attacked and her master died. Or-"

The portly man held up his hands to stave him off. "Okay, okay, lad. Finders keepers, especially if she was about to be ripped apart by an animal. If nobody's missing her then you're free to claim her as your own."

"I don't-" Dare started to say, then gave up. If he was free to claim her then he was free to free her as well.

"Come on," Durrand grumbled, opening the door wider for them. He led them over to the same sitting area near his office space in one corner, where he ushered Dare to the same seat as before. Dare motioned Zuri towards the other seat, but Durrand quickly interrupted him, aghast.

"Let the goblin sit on my wife's good furniture?" he demanded. "Are you insane?" Zuri whimpered at his tone and huddled against Dare's leg; he could feel her trembling.

The Mayor saw her reaction, along with Dare's disapproving scowl, and sighed. "She doesn't look filthy, at least," he grudgingly allowed. "I suppose she can sit on the carpet. And goblin or not, I should be a good host." He raised his voice. "Maritha! Tea for three!"

Dare didn't like that compromise, treating Zuri like a stray dog even though she was probably the cleanest person there thanks to her spell. But he needed the man's help and couldn't afford to antagonize him.

So he nodded at her silent request to sit on the carpet, and she settled down.

Durrand began rifling through a stack of papers on a side table: most had large block letters with crude drawings in the center and looked like notices, complete with reward offers. An uncomfortable silence settled as he searched the stack, and Dare filled it by teaching

Collisa

Zuri more words in Haraldaran, ignoring the Mayor's occasional looks of disgust.

A few minutes later a plump older woman wearing a robe over a nightgown hurried in with a tea service, bustling around pouring them tea as she filled the air with warm chatter meant to put guests at ease. She didn't seem to care for Dare particularly, and only grudgingly gave Zuri a cup of tea, sternly admonishing the tiny goblin not to spill on her carpet.

But she showed at least the veneer of politeness, which was something.

Finally Durrand stepped away from the stack, shaking his head. "Nothing with any goblins of her description." He reached into a box and pulled out a finely cut piece of rose quartz hanging from a thin steel chain, slipping it over his neck. He turned to Zuri. "Who's your master?"

"She doesn't speak-" Dare started to say, but Zuri was already chattering back at the Mayor in her high, chirping language.

Interesting. Was the quartz some sort of translation artifact?

"I see." Durrand turned to Dare. "She says her master abandoned her in the wilds because she was no longer useful to him."

Dare looked at the tiny goblin. So she had been a slave, but had essentially been freed, if in a really cruel way. That was good, right?

"It might even be true," the Mayor continued. "Goblins have such low value that unless her owner was poor, he probably won't raise a fuss about her." He waved at the stack. "I'll keep an eye out for the next few weeks, but otherwise it looks as if you've got yourself a new slave."

Dare frowned. "I don't want a slave."

Maritha looked up from the tea service. "Are you selling her? I've just been pestering Durrand to start saving up for a-"

Phoenix

"I don't want to sell her either," he said, doing his best not to snap. "If she's mine I intend to free her."

They both gaped at him. "Free her?" the Mayor's wife said as if he'd suggested bringing pigs to a cocktail party. "Why in the world would you do such a thing?"

"Even if you're one of those fools who thinks non-humans should be allowed to operate in Heraldar same as humans," Durrand argued, "you do realize the moment you set her free someone else would just snap a collar on her, and probably send her straight to the breeding pens or an arena as a runaway. And if she tries to go it alone in the wilds she'll end up in a monster's belly like she already almost did."

Zuri, who of course had understood everything the man said, cried out and scurried over to Dare, spilling her tea as she went. She threw her arms around his legs and began babbling at him, face frantic and big yellow eyes full of terror.

"Hey, hey, it's okay," he told her gently as he patted her back. He lifted his head and glared at the Mayor. "You didn't have to scare her like that."

Whatever the man might feel about goblins, he still looked a bit guilty. "I forgot I was still wearing this," he mumbled, fingering the rose quartz hanging around his neck.

"Well what's she saying?"

Durrand shook his head grimly. "She's begging you to keep her as a slave. Saying she's always been a good and obedient worker and that it wasn't her fault her master abandoned her."

Zuri was still babbling frantically and Dare turned his attention back to her. "It's okay," he told her. "Dare help Zuri." That seemed to calm her a bit, although tears still streamed down her cheeks.

He looked up at the portly man. "Tell her that of course she can stay with me. I would never just abandon her like that. But she'll stay as my free and equal companion . . . she gets to choose what she wants to do, and I won't try to make her do anything. And if she ever wants to leave she can."

"Equal with a goblin?" Maritha exclaimed. "Of all the foolishness!" She snatched up the tea set and strode out of the room, bristling with affront.

"You aren't by chance touched in the head, are you lad?" Durrand asked. Dare just glared at him until he sighed and turned to Zuri, repeating the words.

The tiny goblin calmed down as she listened, although she also stared at Dare in bafflement. "Your guess is as good as mine how much of that she understood," the Mayor said when he was done. He grimaced at the mess Zuri had made with her spilled tea and sighed, reaching for a cloth to begin cleaning it up. "Mari's gonna kill me."

"Sorry about that," Dare said, gently extricating himself from Zuri and moving to help.

The Mayor waved him away. "If there's nothing else I won't keep you," he said with forced politeness. "Got lots of things to do today."

Dare hesitated. "There is one thing . . . could I ask about your necklace?"

"What, the translation stone?" Durrand said, fingering the large quartz. "Handy thing. It's enchanted to allow me to be understood by people speaking most of the common languages on Shalin, and to understand them as well. Better yet, you get a dozen people wearing these speaking different languages in a room and everyone hears everyone else in the whichever one they know best."

He chuckled. "Although it can get overloaded if too many people are speaking at once, leading to some hilarious garbling and translation errors."

Dare stared. He'd assumed the stone just allowed the Mayor to speak Goblin, but that was infinitely better. So good, in fact, that

Phoenix

getting one for himself should be a priority. "That's quite the valuable enchantment."

Durrand looked startled. "I suppose it is, now that you mention it. Not that I have much use for the thing here." He chuckled. "Benefit of living in a quiet place in the middle of nowhere."

"Was it expensive?"

"This?" The Mayor fingered the translation stone again. "Not too bad. Twenty silver, although I haggled this one down to fourteen."

Dare could afford that. And while there were other things he needed more, if he was going to be stuck with Zuri then it was essential.

He immediately felt guilty when he thought that; it wasn't fair to consider it that way. Especially since the poor goblin was in an even worse situation. And he couldn't begrudge her desire to stay if he was willing to help her, especially if the alternatives were being taken as a slave again by someone, or going back out into the wilds and potentially getting eaten by a panther.

Besides, even if they couldn't talk right now Dare found himself enjoying her company. He hadn't realized how lonely he'd been, even with his regular trips to the village.

And he *was* willing to help her. He just needed to find a way to do it where she had a chance for the life she wanted, and he was able to accomplish his goals on Collisa.

"Can I buy one around here?" Dare asked.

"What, in Lone Ox?" Durrand laughed easily. "Like I said, not much call for them here. And even the more prosperous villagers don't have twenty silver to drop on something that's not going to be useful for them."

He scratched his chin. "You may be able to find some in Driftwain, but I wouldn't hold my breath. Since these things have such a specific use anyone who needs one usually already has it, and isn't willing to sell. Especially since the only person in the region who can make them, an Enchanter a week's travel away in Kov, is willing to deliver them via courier for a nominal fee."

Dare perked up. "What if I wanted to order one? How long would it take to reach me?"

The Mayor chuckled. "Well the order would have to make its way to Kov through merchants or travelers passing along messages. Then the Enchanter would put you in his client queue, and then the courier needs to deliver it." He touched the quartz. "Mine took a couple months . . . your best bet is probably to head to Kov and order in person if you're in a hurry."

Damn. Dare probably wouldn't even be in this area in a few months at the rate he was leveling. He sighed. "I suppose I'll be passing through there at some point, or visiting some other place with an Enchanter who can do it." He paused, eyeing Durrand's necklace. "Unless . . ."

The portly man laughed. "Sorry. I may not need it often, but when I do need it I can't afford to not have it." He mock glared. "Besides, you've already got something of mine that you've yet to earn."

The map for his remaining quest. Right.

Dare nodded sheepishly. "I'm leveling up as fast as I can, and looking into getting a group together to take the bandits out. I've already scouted the camp and learned a bit, although I've needed to be careful."

The Mayor perked up. "Show me what you've found," he said, moving to his own map of the area. "You can consider the information rent on my map."

Fair enough. Dare ushered Zuri up onto the chair he'd vacated, defying Durrand to protest again, and moved over to join him,

Phoenix

quickly describing what he'd found and his thoughts on the bandits.

Durrand wasted no time politely inviting them to leave once he had the information, although Dare insisted on him keeping to his word about buying monster loot. It was selling for more now that he was Level 8, giving him almost 5 silver with the trash loot alone.

Then he left the Mayor to his morning routine and toured all the people willing to buy from him, selling what he could. Zuri stayed quiet by his side the whole time, curiously looking around and watching him haggle.

While the villagers stared at her (or glared in some cases), nobody made a fuss about her being there.

"Don't mind their glares," Dare told her when one big man's particularly fierce scowl made her duck around to his other side and clutch his leg fearfully. He patted her head, smiling. "I think you look cute . . . anyone who's rude to you is probably a jerk anyway."

The timid goblin gave him a tentative smile, although she kept holding his leg as he tried to continue down the street. He offered her his hand instead, and for most of the rest of the time in the village she held it.

Occasionally her small, soft hand with its lotion-like slickness would squeeze his in sudden fear when she met eyes with a glaring villager, but for the most part the contact with him seemed to calm her down.

Soon enough Dare's business was done. He bought a few simple items like a pot, a pan, a pottery jug, and more soap, as well as a ribbon for Zuri that was the same bright yellow color as her eyes, so she could tie up her long inky-black hair in a ponytail or whatever other style she wanted.

The goblin seemed to love the simple gift, treating it with far more reverence than it deserved. She even tried to get on her hands and knees again in gratitude.

"No," Dare said gently, pulling her up before she could. He hadn't thought to ask Durrand about it, but he was almost certain that was a slave position. Or if not that, at least a subservient one. "You never need to do that again."

"Zuri no?" she asked timidly.

"No." He gently lifted her pointed chin, then raised his own and assumed what he hoped was a proud and independent pose. "You're free now, Zuri. Free." He pointed at himself. "Just like me. Free. No kneeling."

She looked at him blankly. "Zuri no?" she clarified as she made as if to kneel once more.

He nodded. "Zuri stand tall," he said, lifting her chin again.

The woman who'd sold him the ribbon was staring at them in a mixture of bafflement and disgust. "Is this some kind of mummer's show?" she asked.

Dare ignored the villager and offered his new companion his hand, leading her back towards the forest. "Come on, back to hunting and adventuring, if that's what you want to do." Zuri stared at him blankly and he smiled and pointed straight up to indicate midday. "We can get back to our camp by noon and have lunch. Food?"

"Food!" she agreed happily.

He couldn't help but grin at her enthusiasm. For so much of the time she seemed so nervous and timid, as if waiting for the other shoe to drop in a world where they fell like rain. But he caught glimpses, more and more as time went on and he slowly earned her trust, where he could see the bright and sparkling person she could've been if the world had been a kinder place to her.

And still could be, he hoped, if she was free to pursue it.

"Hey," Dare said as they reached the edge of the village. "Want to see something cool?" She just stared at him curiously, and he grinned and pulled out a silver coin. "Watch." He casually flipped it into the air, making no move to catch it as it fell towards the ground.

Then it disappeared.

His new companion shouted in surprise and began looking around on the ground for it, and he couldn't help but chuckle. "Zuri," he said. She looked up, and with a grin he reached behind her short pointy ear and pulled out the coin, showing it to her.

She stared at it in a combination of wariness and awe and babbled something in her language.

Dare chuckled. "It's something from my world called a magic trick. Except I guess in this world it would just be a trick, or sleight of hand, since there's no magic involved." He twirled his hand and made the coin disappear, and Zuri shouted again and grabbed his hand, searching it closely.

Did he spoil the trick, or keep having fun? With a laugh he pointed his arm downwards and flicked it, and the silver coin dropped from his sleeve to fall towards the ground.

Then disappeared again; nah, no spoiling tricks here.

Zuri babbled some more in disbelief and pointed at his bow, as if to point out that he was a Hunter and couldn't do this. Dare chuckled again and made the coin appear one last time, then very slowly and obviously put it in his pouch.

She looked almost disappointed when she realized the show was over, although happy enough to take his hand again when he offered it. As they continued down the street she kept shooting curious, hopeful glances at his pouch, as if expecting silver coins to start appearing and vanishing around them again at any second.

To be honest Dare had only been a mediocre magician in his own world. At best. It had been a hobby he'd been just good enough at to amaze kids and people who weren't really paying attention. One he practiced every now and then while he was bored watching TV or waiting for something.

Although it turned out that when the hand was quicker than the eye, having 34% increased speed made magic ludicrously easy. He might even be a solid prestidigitarian in this world, assuming there weren't abilities that might see right through him.

Maybe literally.

Still, it had been nice to make Zuri smile, see the wonder in her big eyes and the excitement on her sharp features; he'd have to brush off his old skills and see what else he could do. Maybe some of the tricks he'd struggled with before.

Dare looked down at his new companion, walking along contentedly with her hand in his. He wasn't sure what she wanted, and wouldn't be until he could get to Kov and get a translation stone. But she'd made it pretty clear she wanted to stay with him, so he'd just need to adjust to how his life had unexpectedly changed.

Looked as if he wasn't solo leveling anymore.

Chapter Nine
Unpowered Leveling

After a lunch of mushrooms and greens fried in his new skillet with some of the choicest bits of meat from a boar Dare had hunted a couple days ago, it was time to get down to business.

He wanted to level. And since Zuri was close to his level and a Healer maybe she could level with him. The first member of his party?

She might've even done some leveling herself at some point in the past, since she was slightly higher level than the people in Lone Ox who hadn't gotten levels from anything but organically gaining experience from living their lives. Like Ellui.

And it was best to ask her now, so he could see whether she was going to accompany him in hunting monsters or, he supposed, hang around camp while he was gone.

Dare gathered his weapons and traps and checked his armor. "Do you want to go hunt monsters?" he asked Zuri has he slung his mostly empty pack on his shoulders. She stared at him blankly. "Level up?" he tried.

Still nothing. He sighed and tried making the triumphant army noise that sounded when you leveled up.

To his relief comprehension dawned, and she babbled a reply in Goblin. "I'll take that as a yes," he said. He went into the command screen and found the party invite command he'd noticed in his earlier explorations, inviting Zuri to his party.

To his bafflement, the timid goblin's pale green skin went darker green in a blush and she almost immediately turned down the invitation.

Collisa

Dare stared at her. "Kill monsters?" he asked again. "Level up?" He drew an arrow and shot it at a nearby tree, then took a stone knife and gently pressed it into her hand, closing her fingers around it. He led her to the tree and had her stab it.

"Hunt monsters?" he repeated again. "Level up?" He made the level up noise.

She nodded, and he smiled in relief and tried inviting her to his party again.

Again she immediately turned him down, looking embarrassed and nervous. As if afraid he'd be angry with her.

Dare sighed and gave up; being grouped would be nice, but she knew this world better than he did and must've had some good reason for refusing the invite. "Hunt monsters," he said again, retrieving his arrow and motioning for her to follow as he started off into the woods.

Zuri followed without hesitation, walking close at his side as they went in search of enemies to level up on.

* * * * *

As it turned out, a Hunter and a Healer made a terrible two person party.

If Dare had been a melee class, especially a sturdy tank class, then being healed as he went toe to toe with an enemy would've allowed him and his healer to level more swiftly and efficiently. But he was a ranged damage dealer, who needed the enemy to stay far away and not interrupt his attempts to shoot it.

If he was getting hurt it meant he didn't have time to use his bow.

Combined with the fact that if Zuri had any offensive spells or abilities besides biting with her sharp teeth, she hadn't shown them yet, it meant that she was basically reduced to stabbing enemies with the knife he crafted for her. And while she could gain more proficiency in daggers same as any ability, she didn't get any extra class bonuses to her fighting stats or any special abilities in daggers.

He assumed that if this world was like some games then her weapon was supposed to be a stat stick, empowering her with enchantments and passive stats. And also the last desperate defense for a caster class, or maybe a way to strike a killing blow on a mostly dead enemy without wasting more mana.

But either way, it meant that Zuri basically couldn't do much but sit there as Dare hunted.

The other huge headache was experience distribution.

The simple solution was to be in the same party. He didn't know how the party system worked on this world, or how the experience would be divided in it, but if it was like most party systems in games the experience would be evenly divided, with maybe some weighting for level difference.

Unfortunately, Zuri kept refusing his party invites.

It completely baffled him. Especially since every time he invited her she stared at him in bafflement. Like he'd grown a second head.

He couldn't understand her reasoning, and since he couldn't talk to her he had no way of finding out for the moment. But it was what it was, which left the only other option available to them: solo leveling and sharing experience on monster kills.

Dare wasn't even sure it was possible since in some games it wasn't, and only one person got the experience no matter how many people attacked the enemy. Usually the person who hit it first. In those games, having more people attack a monster just incurred an experience penalty for the single person getting experience, because they weren't doing 100% of the damage.

It was a measure to prevent power-leveling by high level players in a way that would break the game. Same as the way that partying up with a higher level would usually mean the lower level didn't get experience, because it was all weighted towards the higher level player.

Anyway, Dare had to do some experimenting to figure out how experience distribution worked on this world. Which turned out to be a surprisingly aggravating process since he only knew how much experience *he* was gaining, so he had to design experiments to see how much he gained in different scenarios, assuming the same applied to Zuri.

The process was made even more aggravating because he had to get her cooperation for his experiments, which meant he needed to find a way to tell her what he needed her to do. It led to a lot of baffled looks, and a few close calls even though he'd chosen the weakest Level 1 monsters he could find for his experiments.

Basically, for his experiments he first killed the monster to see how much experience it gave. Then he had Zuri stab the next one once, making sure she took off some hit points. Then he killed it and checked his experience.

Sure enough, it was lower than what he'd gotten on his own. Which he hoped meant Zuri had also gotten a little experience.

Next he stabbed a monster once, using the same knife and hoping he did at least somewhere near the same damage. Although he knew his basic and combat stats would both make his damage much higher. Then he did his best to distract and grapple the monster while Zuri laboriously stabbed the thing to death.

Which took forever; he was having both of them use his Utility Knife, but even so she just couldn't do much melee damage given her class.

Luckily, this was just for the experiment. Hopefully the actual leveling process would go more smoothly.

With the second monster that Zuri did most of the work killing, he found that he only got a sliver of experience. Which he hoped

Phoenix

meant she got the lion's share. He then repeated the experiment but this time had Zuri get the single *last* hit, since sometimes that gave more experience. And then he had Zuri solo a monster and got the last hit himself.

As he'd hoped, the last hit got a small bump in experience. Although it was still not great.

He tried first and last hit both, and the experience gains were slightly bigger. Although that might've just been from doing two hits instead of one. Then he had them both try to do about 50% of the damage, and found the experience to be a roughly even split.

Dare hoped, since he didn't know what Zuri was getting. If she was even getting anything at all.

He tried asking her, and after a frustrating few minutes of her staring at him blankly finally thought to try to copy the noise made when leveling up. Then he pointed at the dead monster, made the noise, and pointed to her.

Understanding dawned, and she nodded hesitantly; she was getting experience.

Unfortunately, the most efficient way to level would be for her to get the last hit on enemies while he did the rest of the damage. It would be a slow, inefficient pain in the ass, but any other option would be even slower and more irritating.

And he had to level Zuri.

Not just because he hoped to someday have a better party composition where her skills would be invaluable, but because he was leveling himself. He wanted his new companion to stay with him, and given how she determinedly stayed by his side he hoped she felt the same.

But if he leveled too high above her, and had to go into areas with higher level monsters, then if Zuri was a lower level she'd aggro the monsters at twice the distance and get herself killed.

Collisa

He flat out wasn't about to let that happen.

Zuri at least seemed to realize he was trying to help her level. She even did her part, and when he had a monster well occupied or if he managed to cripple it in some way, she'd dart in and try to do more damage with his Utility Knife. Which he'd given her so she'd have every advantage possible.

At one point, after several hours of leveling, the timid goblin growled in frustration and made the level up noise. Surprised, Dare checked her with his Eye only to see that she was still Level 7. Then he realized she was pantomiming casting a spell, after which she stabbed her knife into the monster they'd just killed.

She had to repeat the sequence of gestures once, and then he thought he understood. "The next time you level up, you'll put a point into an offensive spell?" he asked. He pantomimed casting himself, then pointed at the monster and said, "Zap!"

Zuri nodded and grinned. "Zap!" she agreed, seeming to like the word. He supposed it was an onomatopoeia, which helped make comprehension easier.

He couldn't wait for that boost to her damage, because right now they were going *slow*. He was getting experience at half the speed he'd managed on his own, which would've been fine if Zuri was also getting that much experience. But she wasn't; she was getting much much less.

Over the next week Dare gained a level and a half in the time it took his companion to level once. But as soon as she did, she selected an ability that to his Eye showed as an attack called "Mana Thorn".

The next monster they fought Zuri began pelting with the spell, which didn't do much damage but was definitely way better than the dagger. Especially since she could stay a safe distance away.

To his amusement, every time she cast it she shouted, "Zap!"

Phoenix

As soon as the monster was dead he swept her up in his arms and hugged her, unable to keep from laughing. "You are just too cute," he said to her baffled expression, kissing her pointy cheek.

Her expression remained confused, although after a moment she smiled hesitantly and hugged him back with surprising fierceness, large breasts pressed to his chest. "Dare abur Zuri?" she asked almost shyly, lovely skin going a slightly darker green in a blush.

Dare had no idea what that meant; she hadn't said it before that he could recall.

He chuckled and set her down. "Okay, this changes everything. Now we can both level up at much closer to the speed I was leveling on my own." It would still be slower, but compared to their previous glacial pace it was a massive improvement.

Zuri stared at him, expression clearly disappointed. "Dare no abur Zuri?"

"Sorry," he told her. "I wish we could understand each other, and I know I should be trying harder to learn your language. But right next to a bunch of Boarites isn't the place to play pantomime . . . you can ask me back in camp."

She brightened; at this point she recognized most words he used frequently, and camp certainly counted. "Dare abur Zuri camp?"

"Yes, you can tell me all about Dare abur Zuri back in camp." He patted her head and pointed to a sentry in the distance. "Let's keep going."

Grinning, Zuri ran over and began pelting the monster with her Mana Thorn while Dare hurried to keep up. Unfortunately, when he used his Eye on his companion after they killed the Boarite he saw something that put a damper on his good mood.

Mana was something he hadn't thought much about, since as a Hunter he didn't use it. He hoped eventually he'd unlock some universal abilities that did, just so he could use his own mana pool, but for now it just at there.

In fact, he hadn't really even paid attention to his mana pool, except to note that it grew slightly with every level.

But now that Zuri was in his party and using offensive spells on every enemy, he quickly realized that her mana pool wasn't limitless. In fact, he discovered that she took 14 or 15 Mana Thorns to completely kill a monster of her same level, and that she could only cast about 90 or so total before draining her mana pool. Or in other words kill six or at most seven even level monsters.

He supposed that was understandable; healer classes shouldn't be good damage dealers.

With them both sharing damage that was a bit better, and he also discovered that if she got more than 30% of the damage her experience gain jumped up to 40% of the total. Which was such an obvious sweet spot that he began having her try to do that much damage from then on.

With his Eye he was able to determine exactly how much Mana Thorn cost. He also saw that her mana slowly returned over time, so that she got back enough to cast the spell again about every half hour. He also saw that when she slept her mana pool fully charged.

Which, as it turned out when he experimented with it a bit, meant that if he had her sleep for four hours her mana pool would fill up, and then if they emptied it hunting monsters and she slept again for another four hours, it would fill up again. Four hours seemed to be the minimum sleep required to fill up your mana pool, but it still meant that by disrupting their sleep schedule they could double their efficiency.

Zuri seemed surly at first about being woken up, but once she realized what he was doing she became excited at the discovery.

All those tricks and tactics combined allowed Dare to do what he loved best in games: min/max. In this case, by optimizing an efficient leveling system for them.

Unfortunately, even his best efforts meant that Zuri still couldn't go a full day hunting with him. He had her switch up to using the knife on crippled enemies, and also to finish off seriously wounded or almost dead enemies, so she could do damage without using precious mana.

It helped a lot, but even so by the end of the day the timid goblin was reduced to using the knife entirely, while occasionally she'd be able to shout "Zap!" and fire off a spell.

The good news was, since she was lower level the 40% experience she got meant she still leveled faster than him, since her levels required less experience. That would change once she caught up to his level, when he'd slowly outpace her again. But at least she'd always be able to stay at worst a level behind him.

More importantly, she'd be close enough level to his that she'd continue getting experience.

Dare completely forgot about her earlier innocuous question while he was hugging her, and Zuri didn't bring it up again at camp that night. Aside from maybe looking at him very expectantly, which he completely failed to notice at the time.

In retrospect if he'd known what she'd been saying he probably would've paid a lot more attention to her.

A day and a half later, he reached Level 10.

The level up notification was quickly followed by a list of everything he'd gotten for the level, including the bonus ability points he'd been anticipating.

Then he saw "Class ability unlocked. Rapid Shot: Arrows can be loosed at melee range while ability is active. Hold up to four arrows in bow hand to increase their draw and loose speed by 25%-"

Dare put a point into the ability without even finishing reading the text.

Finally! After dodging around enemies like a moron because he couldn't use his bow while they were trying to rip him apart, he finally had something that would help. Combined with Roll and Shoot, he'd be able to do enough damage at melee range to finish off the tougher even level mobs, as well as a lot of the ones that were a level higher. Not to mention it was a clear damage boost.

"Yes!" he shouted, pumping his fist. With a laugh he activated the ability, noting its one minute cooldown.

In that strange way of abilities, almost of its own accord his hand dipped into his quiver and slipped four arrows into the hand holding his bow, almost faster than the eye could see. Then he was able to fit those arrows to the string and draw at a blurring speed, sending all four into the trunk of a nearby tree in about the time it would take to shoot two from his quiver.

Best yet, the ability remained active for 15 seconds, so he'd have more time to shoot enemies at melee range even after he'd shot the four arrows.

This was *huge*!

Zuri clapped her hands and shouted as she watched him use his ability. She might not know the specifics of it, but his obvious delight wasn't lost on her.

And her adorable toothy grin wasn't lost on him. With a laugh Dare once again dropped his bow and swept his tiny companion up in his arms, this time kissing the top of her head. "We should spend some time picking quality foraging ingredients and selecting our highest quality meats and have a feast tonight," he told her.

The little goblin didn't answer, just hugged him back tightly with her face pressed to his shoulder. And when he tried to set her down she just held on even tighter.

The celebratory embrace started to turn awkward. Zuri might be on the tiny side of petite but she was very much a woman, and Dare became more aware of her large perky breasts pressed against his chest by the moment. Her slender but curvy little body was starting to feel better and better in his arms, and he felt himself subconsciously stroking up and down her back.

When he realized what he was doing he felt his cheeks heat and again tried to put her down, relieved when she finally let go. At which point he saw that her skin was darker green in her own blush.

He hastily cleared his throat. "At Level 10 you'll probably get an awesome ability too," he told her. "I can't wait to see it."

She enthusiastically made the level up noise and beamed at him, delicately sharp features adorable; he couldn't believe he'd ever thought they were off-putting.

Also, Dare couldn't help but notice that she was gaining more weight and muscle definition after over a week of getting plenty to eat. Where she'd been almost painfully skinny before now she was slender, her womanly curves more pronounced.

All in all Zuri seemed healthy and happy. Which he was pleased to see, glad that his companion was doing so well.

And she got another chance to eat even better that night, as Dare spent an hour preparing a feast just like he'd promised. Which considering the ability system, as it applied to cooking, was the equivalent of spending all day in the kitchen at home.

He'd recently found some super high quality mushrooms, the first food he'd found so far that gave a status buff when eaten. Which of course he'd tested with his Forage tree's Test Edibles ability, which he'd now improved to the point that he didn't even have to wait to see if something was safe.

Using the mushrooms for dinner was a waste, since the buff would wear off before morning without them getting any use out of it, but he didn't care. This was a celebration and they deserved the treat.

For the appetizer there was salad, although unfortunately with no dressing. It was accompanied by a thick juice, or more accurately pulp maybe, made from berries that he'd carefully squashed in the pottery jug.

For the main course he fried up mushrooms, boar and venison chunks, and a couple types of chopped tubers that very vaguely resembled turnips and carrots, along with herb greens for flavor. He even learned a new recipe with his cooking ability from it.

For dessert, he'd purchased a few pieces of hard candy back at the village when Zuri wasn't paying attention, as a surprise to give her later. He gave her one now, enjoying her delighted reaction, and showed her how to suck on it to make it last instead of immediately chewing it up.

It was a good evening. Probably the best he'd had on Collisa so far. Food and good companionship; sure, he would've liked some beer or a few shots to make the celebration a real party, and he wouldn't have said no to a warm body next to him when he went to bed, but it was still great.

Although he ended up getting one of those things after all.

Zuri matched his cheerful mood with surprising exuberance, and after filling their bellies with all the delicious food they began trying to find ways to entertain each other and make each other laugh without communicating.

Which worked surprisingly well.

His goblin companion was so adorable that every face she made, even the fiercest, just made him want to hug her. He tried his own silly faces, and was gratified when she rolled around on the ground, high pitched voice filling the clearing with peals of carefree laughter.

It was wonderful to hear.

Phoenix

After the laughter died down Zuri motioned eagerly to Dare's coin pouch, and getting the hint he spent a half hour or so showing her magic tricks. He even showed her how to do one or two herself, to her delight.

She was surprisingly dextrous and learned quickly, confirming his opinion of her intelligence. Although while she was clearly excited to learn and delighted when she got it right, she seemed slightly disappointed that there was no actual magic involved.

His companion didn't seem to want the celebration to end, but finally Dare had to give in to his exhaustion. He motioned to his tent and pantomimed sleeping, standing firm against her obvious disappointment as he headed to bed.

Zuri made for her tent too, which she'd taken to setting up right beside his. But to his surprise she only ducked inside long enough to pick up her bedroll, carrying it purposefully towards his tent.

"Umm," he said uncertainly.

She looked at him pleadingly with those big yellow eyes as she pointed back at her tent. Then she shivered as if cold, and hung her head as if sad.

Was she saying she was lonely in her tent? He supposed he couldn't blame her, since he understood the feeling all too well.

Maybe it was a bad idea to let her sleep in his tent, especially considering his growing attraction for her, but he couldn't refuse that pleading face.

Besides, he was no saint. Hadn't he specifically told his unseen benefactor he wanted to sleep with as many women as he could? Or at least hinted at it. Or maybe she'd told him to do that . . . it had been long enough since his conversation with her in that unnerving gray void that he was starting to forget.

But none of that was the point. He was happy fucking slime girls and bunny girls for enjoyable casual sex, but Zuri was his friend. A companion he'd fought beside for over a week, building a bond of trust and camaraderie until he'd gladly put his life in her small hands. Someone he'd spent contented evenings beside the campfire with, just enjoying each other's company even if they couldn't really communicate.

Someone he'd found himself starting to deeply care about even though they'd only known each other for a short time. If he planned to take the next step with her he wanted it to mean something, for her sake as much as his.

Or maybe he was just falling back on the same uncertainties that had torpedoed his relationships on Earth.

So he took the coward's path. "Want to cuddle?" he asked, pointing at his tent. He then carefully made sure she was snugly tucked into her blankets on one side of the small space before climbing into his own bed.

Although after a few long seconds of awkward silence she silently scooted over to press against his side, and he couldn't resist the temptation to wrap an arm around her and pull her close to him over his covers.

"Good night, Zuri," he whispered.

He could see her disappointment that this all that was going to happen, but she still made a contented noise as she pressed her face to his blanket-covered shoulder.

"Zuri mizzen egoka abur Dare," she murmured tenderly, nuzzling his shoulder through the cloth. Then she closed her eyes and drifted off to sleep.

Content in the peaceful feeling of holding the beautiful goblin woman in his arms, Dare soon joined her.

Chapter Ten
Abur

Dare had finally found a slime he hated.

Specifically, it was a Level 12 Vampire Slime. It didn't even pretend to take a pleasing form, oozing furiously after him as a giant blob. And rather than being transparent it was the hideous red of dried blood. As if there was a barely scabbed wound over its entire surface that seeped a viscous, blood-like slime that stretched out towards him in writhing pseudopods.

But what probably made it the most awful was that its attacks were almost the exact same as a slime girl's: Envelope, Stimulate, and Devour Gore, with only the last one being different. Except in this case he guessed that after being enveloped by the Vampire Slime, it would get his blood pumping wildly in agony and terror, then likely begin to drain him from every surface of his skin until he was shriveled up like a raisin.

It had another ability the slime girls didn't have, though: Split. Which Dare assumed meant that when it had consumed enough blood it would split into two of itself and go searching for more victims.

The oozing creature was surprisingly fast, too. Dare had decided to risk fighting the higher level enemy because its existence was a disgrace to the peaceful and helpful slime girls, only to realize that with its combination of sliding and rolling it could move faster than some lower level creatures using Charge.

So after he figured that out when he shot the thing, he was reduced to playing the part of tank and running around while Zuri nuked it from a distance. Even worse, the arrow he'd shot and his dagger attacks both did minimal damage to the monster.

Collisa

He'd even whipped out Rapid Shot at one point when he'd managed a bit of breathing room, only to watch them sink into the foul slime without much more effect than a few trickles of blood from the monster and a few percentage points of health lost.

Dare and Zuri did have a few things going for them, though. The first was that the slime seemed drawn to the nearest enemy, so he had no problem kiting the hideous thing around so Zuri could do damage without issues.

The second was that when he said she was nuking the monster, he meant it literally.

The thing had to be vulnerable to Nature damage, the type Zuri's spells fell into, because while Dare's attacks seemed to do half their usual damage, hers did well over double. With every "Zap!" she shouted the Vampire Slime's health chunked down a healthy amount, and at this rate it would be over soon.

Sooner than he thought, it turned out.

When the monster was at 10% health it abruptly stopped chasing him and began to convulse and quiver with an alarming gurgling sound. Dare watched the bulges within its scab-like exterior churn and roil with increasing speed, and felt a sudden sense of foreboding.

"Look out!" he shouted, crossing the clearing with all his speed and throwing himself protectively over Zuri as she stood staring in shock.

A moment later the Vampire Slime exploded, coating every surface of the clearing and surrounding trees, including Dare, with a splash of putrid, viscous gore that reeked like meat left to rot for days in a swamp.

Was this its last ability, Split? A final "fuck you" to whatever killed it?

He didn't see any status effects on himself or Zuri, and the vile substance didn't seem caustic. It was just gross to the point he

Phoenix

wanted to empty his guts.

"Gah," he growled as he pushed to his feet and helped Zuri to hers. "I fucking hate that thing so much."

Thankfully his companion had been spared the worst of the Split, with only a few splashes of gory slime on her tunic and skin. She began gingerly picking her way across the fouled ground to escape the mess.

Dare followed, swiping the blood off his reinforced leather coat. "I need to wash up right now, or I'm going to puke." They reached blessedly clean ground, and he glanced in the direction of the nearby river, barely visible through the trees, then at Zuri. "Could you stay here for a second? I'll be right back."

She just stared at him, of course, so he gestured for her to stay put and headed for the river.

As he went he peeled off his armor, coat, tunic, and pants, pinning them under a rock in the water to soak before dunking in himself. He could see crimson streaks drifting away downstream as the filth covering him and his gear washed off, and floated facedown for a moment enjoying the sensation of cool, clean water over his skin.

Then he felt the water begin to warm up and swirl around him and his dirty clothes, and saw the bloodstains begin to fade.

Gasping, he surfaced and turned to see Zuri standing on the bank, casting her cleaning spell. Of course; in the heat of the moment while all covered in bloody slime he'd forgotten his companion had the spell.

His cheeks began to flush in embarrassment, and the flush deepened when he realized she was staring at his manhood with huge eyes.

Dare hastily covered himself; it took two hands. "I thought I told you to stay back while I bathed," he said, trying to sound stern but coming off as more sheepish.

Zuri didn't seem to hear him; her creamy avocado skin began to flush a darker green, her pupils slightly dilated as she ran her eyes over his body, and she began very gently biting her lip with her pointy teeth, thighs rubbing together slowly. One hand started to move between her legs, then abruptly stopped.

Dare felt his blush deepen; he couldn't deny his growing attraction for his beautiful companion, nor was he blind to the fact that at the moment she was practically eye fucking him.

She was obviously horny, and he had to admit that he was more than a little horny himself. He hadn't visited the slime girls or gone out looking for bunny girls since finding Zuri; partly because he was reluctant to just ditch her so he could go get his dick wet, and partly because she was just as reluctant to be away from him and her watching him fuck would be beyond uncomfortable.

Ten days now, and he had a far more healthy libido on this world than he had on Earth; the sight of Zuri openly struggling not to jill off while staring at him was making his cock stir.

His companion finally seemed to snap out of it, flushing an even deeper green color in embarrassment, and she hastily motioned to him, saying a word in Goblin in a questioning tone.

"Clean?" he guessed, picking up his clothes and covering himself with them.

"Clean?" she repeated back at him; of course she had no idea if that was right. But she waved at her tunic, which had a few splashes of blood even though she'd been farther back, then at the river. "Clean," she repeated.

He nodded. "Yeah, I think we got the right word."

She nodded absently, the way she sometimes did when she couldn't understand a word he said but wanted to show she was listening. Then, to his consternation, she kicked off her shoes and began pulling her tunic over her head as she stepped into the water.

Dare stared for a moment longer than he should've, as the long sexy legs he remembered from before giving her the tunic came into view. Then he hastily fled the water.

"I'll, um, leave you to it!" he called over his shoulder as he headed for the safety of the trees.

"Dare!" Zuri called after him impatiently.

He stopped but stayed with his back to her. "What?"

Her voice became even more insistent. "Dare!"

Dare reluctantly turned, then his clothes slipped from limp fingers as he stared in shock and amazement, even though he should've expected it.

Zuri stood in ankle deep water, tunic discarded beside her. She'd also unwrapped the cloth covering her large breasts and let it fall at her feet, and now stood naked aside from her loincloth.

Her pale green skin looked soft and inviting, the small body he remembered from the first day now far more curvy and, without a doubt, sexy.

Dare swallowed, then dropped his eyes to her breasts.

They were beautiful perky globes, with small dark green nipples that were quickly stiffening in the chill of the water and the breeze blowing across them. And arousal, maybe. He was almost entranced staring at their perfection, pleasantly aware of his cock stiffening to attention to point straight at her.

Zuri, her eyes once again going huge at its sheer size, gave a pleased smile and stepped out of the water. She started towards him with a swaying walk, sexy hips drawing his gaze with every graceful movement and large boobs shifting hypnotically.

"Zuri," he said in a strangled voice, cock visibly twitching.

Collisa

Phoenix

"Shh," she said sternly, yellow eyes fixed on his huge manhood. "Dare abur Zuri."

Oh. Ohhhhh. He remembered her saying that before but having no idea what it meant. And now he thought he had a pretty good idea.

He closed his eyes with a quiet moan when his tiny companion, not seeming so timid at the moment, reached out and took him in her small hands, skin impossibly soft and gliding smoothly over his shaft thanks to its lotion-like slickness.

There was a benefit to having sex with a goblin who was barely taller than his waist; she could stand up straight as she delicately ran her tongue over his tip while continuing to jack him off.

"God, you're beautiful," he said as he stared down at her yellow eyes looking up at him with gentle adoration as she bathed his already clean cock, coating it with warm saliva.

She smiled at him eagerly as her tiny hands jacked him off more quickly with a surprisingly firm grip. "Dare abur Zuri?"

"Fuck yes," he moaned, resting his hand on her head and luxuriating in the silky soft feel of her jet black hair.

The tiny goblin wrapped her arms around his legs and with some effort took his massive girth into her mouth.

At first Dare was a bit nervous about that, thinking of her shark-like teeth. But ten days of putting his life in her hands had earned her a show of trust. And also the feel of her lips making a tight ring as she pushed onto the head of his cock was incredible.

Thankfully, in spite of his trepidations all he felt when he slid into her mouth was a wet tongue, then soon afterwards the sensation of the head of his cock pressing against the back of her throat.

Then, making him gasp with shock and pleasure, the indescribable feeling as, with a grunt of determination, Zuri pushed her lips farther and farther down his shaft as she forced it down her tiny throat, until finally her pointy little nose was pressed into his pubic hair.

Holy shit . . . Dare didn't think even a human woman with a lot of experience could so casually deep throat his monster.

His tiny lover gagged, the muscles of her tight esophagus rippling down his shaft in a way that made him grunt with pleasure in spite of her discomfort. He could see his enormous size as a bulge all the way down her slender throat, below the base to where he had to be close to the entrance to her stomach.

It seemed anatomically impossible, or at least unbelievably uncomfortable. But when he considerately tried to pull back her little arms wrapped around his legs held on stubbornly.

Maybe it made sense after all. At first he'd assumed Zuri was barely chewing her food because she was ravenously hungry. But thinking about it more, with a predator's sharp teeth she'd be more adapted to swallowing her food in big chunks, or even whole.

She was certainly swallowing his massive cock whole.

Dare settled back to enjoy the sensation as his tiny lover, breathing frantically through her nose, began sliding her throat up and down his shaft, constantly swallowing down her gags in a way that made it feel like the tight space was milking him. Now that he was letting her have her way she let go of his legs and lovingly ran her hands over his thighs and up to his ass, rubbing and squeezing his solid muscles with a grunt of obvious admiration.

The sight of his massive tip visibly moving up and down her slender throat as she bobbed on his shaft was so overwhelmingly erotic that he was sure he'd spurt then and there, and had to force himself to think of other things.

Then Zuri started humming in enjoyment, the vibrations rippling all along his length, and the battle was lost.

Phoenix

Dare groaned and grabbed the back of her head, holding her as she continued to smoothly glide up and down on his shaft with her impossibly tight esophagus milking him eagerly.

He only lasted a few more seconds under that pleasurable assault, especially after ten days of abstinence, before with a last gasp of pleasure he held her head still. His cock began jerking wildly as he emptied himself down her throat, and when his tiny lover felt it she made delighted sounds around swallowing and gagging as she took it all in.

Afterwards she beamed up at him, gasping for breath, face the deep green of an avocado skin and huge yellow eyes glistening with tears. She looked so proud of herself that he couldn't help but lift her into a hug.

"That was incredible," he murmured, pressing his lips to hers. They were smooth and soft, with a slightly sweet taste.

Zuri didn't kiss him back, and when he opened his eyes she seemed confused; did goblins not kiss?

Well, if not they probably did the thing he'd been wanting to do ever since she pulled the wrapping off her gorgeous chest. Dare smiled at her, then lifted her a bit higher so he could bury his face between her large firm breasts, luxuriating in their silky feel.

She moaned in delight and wrapped her arms around his head, pulling him harder against her.

"God you're sexy," he said, moving to suck a nipple, which quickly grew to the size of a pencil eraser in his mouth.

Her skin tasted sweeter than he expected from sweat, with a slight but heady musk, and her hard nipple was delightfully rubbery as he pushed it around with his tongue before giving it a good firm suck.

His tiny lover quivered and moaned, hips undulating to rub her loincloth-clad crotch against his chest. Dare could smell her arousal, which filled his nose with a musky but surprisingly heady scent. It smelled so good he found himself longing to taste it, and after the incredible blowjob Zuri had just given him he wanted to return the favor.

He was just about to lower her to the ground and tear away her loincloth, eager to get his first glimpse of her tiny pussy, when he heard a viscous, bubbling sound behind them. He whirled with Zuri to see another Vampire Slime oozing their way through the trees, ruining the moment.

He really hated those things.

Zuri squirmed out of his arms and they hastily grabbed their clothes and ran, dressing when they'd escaped the presence of the monster. At that point a slightly awkward silence settled as they looked at each other, not sure exactly how to address the sudden change to their relationship.

Then his tiny lover offered him her hand and made the leveling up noise. "Hunt?" she asked.

Dare grinned; he'd found that as soon as she learned his method for optimizing experience gain and leveling up, she was just as businesslike about leveling up as he was. "Hunt monsters," he agreed.

However their relationship had changed, they could explore it when they got back to the safety of camp. He could admit he was looking forward to it.

* * * * *

Although they might've put the plug on getting too frisky out in the dangerous wilds, Dare noticed that he and Zuri were both far more affectionate with each other and more comfortable with intimacy.

She would often run over and throw her arms around him, and when possible would hold his hand and walk with her little body pressed contentedly against his leg. She'd also nuzzle his hand or his thigh, making happy noises.

For his part Dare couldn't resist the temptation to pick her up and hug her, even if there was nothing in particular to celebrate. He'd sometimes carry her around when they were moving from place to place, just to enjoy the sensation of holding her in his arms. He even tried kissing her a few more times, and while she still seemed confused by it, she didn't object.

And when it came time to head back to camp, he finally tried something he'd been wanting to do since he traveled to the village with the little goblin that first morning.

They were both well aware that Zuri couldn't move as fast as him. Dare had been content to move as fast as she was able, and when they traveled to and from camp, or from one monster spawn point to another, she would run at a fast pace with surprising endurance to keep up.

But he still mourned the opportunity loss of those extra minutes adding up here and there.

He'd respected her dignity, and her personal space, too much to suggest carrying her while he ran before now. But if he could convince her to try it then they might have as much as an hour a day of extra time to level.

It didn't take much to convince her.

Dare started off holding her in his arms as he took off at his usual trot. Which was enough to make Zuri squeal in delight and turn her face to the mild wind of their passage. She patted his shoulder and said something in Goblin, and he tried going faster, which made her even more excited.

Just for the fun of it, he tried going all out across a large clearing, blowing past 25 miles per hour.

Instead of shouting in amazement at the speed Zuri went quiet, expression awed as she squinted her eyes against the strong wind blowing in her face. "Sebur itig megatik!" she whispered, hand on his shoulder stroking gently.

He slowed down to a walk and grinned at her. "You like that?" He moved his arm as if he was still running. "Zoom!"

"Zoom!" she shouted, pointing insistently ahead in a gesture to for him to keep going.

Laughing, Dare kissed her again and affectionately rubbed her lower back. "You are absolutely adorable."

Back in camp they immediately headed over to the pool they'd made a few days ago by damming it in a good spot, dipping into the water while Zuri began chanting.

In spite of the filthy and bedraggled condition he'd first found the tiny goblin in, it turned out she was very clean and neat when she didn't have more important things to worry about like not starving to death or being eaten by a monster. And so, although they did their best to save her mana for Mana Thorn so she could level up, his new lover still insisted on using her cleaning spell every evening when they got back from camp.

Dare agreed fully; hygiene was important, even if this world seemed to be kinder about illness and infections than Earth. And honestly it just felt nice to be clean when he fell asleep.

After his "bath" Dare got to work cooking another good meal. Speaking of quality of life improvements, he'd eaten way better since Zuri joined him, motivated to make better food than the simple steaks and uncooked greens and mushrooms he'd mostly subsisted on before.

He enjoyed eating well as much as the next person, of course, but with his focus on leveling up and increasing his proficiency in abilities he hadn't bothered with even a lot of simple comforts, let alone luxuries.

Phoenix

Now, though, he was finding new recipes and improving his cooking skill with every meal, and Zuri seemed to appreciate the effort.

So much so, in fact, that while they waited for the food to cook she climbed contentedly into his lap and began kissing his chest through his coat and tunic. Or maybe she'd just wanted to do that anyway.

Much as Dare enjoyed it, after a few minutes of cuddling he reluctantly set her down. "I have some work to do," he told her. "And I think you're going to like it."

He'd been trying for a while to figure out how to craft a collapsible camp chair out of wood, leather, and cloth scraps looted from monsters. He hadn't managed to make one that would hold his weight, but he thought it would be much easier to make one for Zuri.

She watched curiously as he took the materials for the larger chair and cut them down to fit her size. Then she frowned and motioned to his busy hands. "Dare no, um . . ." she trailed off, brow furrowed adorably.

Then she brightened and pointed at the fire, mimicking the clacking rocks together gesture of the ability used to make it.

Dare nodded in realization. "Not using a crafting ability," he agreed. "No, this is something I thought of myself, based on something from my home."

His tiny lover watched with interest as he kept working. Then she said something in Goblin and pointed to the sky, moving her arm as if tracking the sun moving. Again, he thought he knew what she was saying. "Yeah, it takes a lot longer than using an ability. Welcome to the real world."

That seemed like a dickish thing to say considering this world was as real as his own, and he hastily added, "Or my world at least. Where everything is a huge pain in the ass, and your efforts usually fail until you spend a stupid amount of time getting it right. At which point it probably wasn't worth the effort in the first place. In a lot of ways this world is ridiculously easy in comparison."

Again he felt like a dick, looking at a woman who'd been been starving and half naked in the forest when he found her, being eaten by a panther. "I mean . . ." He shook his head. "This world is dangerous and can be cruel, like my unseen benefactor told me when I first came here, but some things are definitely a lot easier."

His tiny lover just stared at him blankly, then pointed at his hands to remind him he'd stopped working. He chuckled and got back to it.

By the time the food finished cooking he had a good first attempt on her chair, and backed away to present it to his tiny lover.

She circled his creation, looking at it in fascination, and he showed her how to collapse it into four fur and leather-wrapped sticks that could easily be carried in a pack, then open it up again into a chair with a comfortable fur seat. She seemed to get a kick out of it, and delayed actually using the chair to open it up and close it a few times.

But finally she climbed in, and Dare quietly braced himself for the entire thing to collapse like it had with him.

But although it creaked a bit it held firm, and she beamed at him in delight as she rested her hands on the padded armrests and leaned her head against the leather back. She murmured something in Goblin, then curled up in a surprisingly tight ball on the seat and made a contented cooing sound.

At which point he had a pleasant surprise as text appeared on the edge of his vision. "Congratulations! New crafting pattern created: Collapsible Chair for small humanoid races and children. 100 experience awarded."

Had Dare's invention just been put into the world's system? He supposed it made sense, because people were going to be coming up with innovations every day. Unless the world's creators wanted the crafting system to quickly become obsolete, it would need a way to integrate those innovations.

And the integration was so precise that it acknowledged that his design wouldn't work for larger and heavier people.

To his amusement, after just a short while enjoying the chair Zuri left her gift behind and climbed back into his lap. "Thanks," she said, tapping her chest with her fist. "Zuri thanks lots." She hesitantly leaned up and kissed him, the first time she'd initiated it.

His tiny lover was awkward and clumsy and slightly off-center on his mouth, but he still enjoyed it just for what it meant.

His inner timer, nothing tangible but just a sense he'd developed in this world for when things were done, especially with cooking, turned his attention to the fire. With a sigh he reluctantly pulled away from Zuri's warm embrace, motioning. "Food's done."

She was happy to climb back into her chair as he handed her a plate loaded with steaming meat and vegetables. He leaned back on the log with his own plate, and aside from the occasional sounds of enjoyment they were mostly quiet as they dug in.

As Dare ate he couldn't help but sneak glances at his tiny lover. After dinner would come bedtime, and after today's events he was both eager and nervous at the prospect that tonight when they shared the tent, they might be doing more than sleeping.

Zuri caught him looking and smiled back shyly, yellow eyes glowing warmly in the firelight. Then she put aside her empty plate and patted her belly with a sigh of contentment, before hooking one leg up over one of the chair's armrests and settling back with a happy smile. Then, giving him a sidelong look and biting her lip, she shifted an bit and lifted her leg even higher over the armrest.

Dare still had a few bites left of his own food, but as he was

Collisa

lifting his fork to his mouth he glanced over at his goblin lover and nearly dropped it in surprise.

With her legs spread like that he could see beneath her tunic, and she wasn't wearing her loincloth.

The gentleman in him wanted to look away, but the stronger (and more lecherous) part of him desperately wanted to see what she looked like down there.

Besides, her underwear didn't just fall off by accident, and he doubted she'd spread her legs like that to give him a full view on accident, either.

Confirming his suspicions, Zuri boldly met his eyes and with a small pleased smile very deliberately pulled up her tunic, giving him a better look. At that his lecherous side won the day, and he dropped his eyes.

The sight took his breath away, because it might've been the most perfect little pussy he'd ever seen.

Her delicate petals glistened with her nectar, opening like a flower to reveal the beginnings of a soft pink tunnel flowing with her arousal. Above it her tiny pearl stood out proudly from its hood, practically throbbing with her excitement as if begging him to play with it.

Dare stared, feeling his cock stirring until it was rock hard in his pants. Especially when, still biting her lip, his little goblin lover stood, slowly and deliberately, and stared at him with smoldering eyes as she began to lift the hem of her tunic.

He watched eagerly as she slowly revealed her long (proportionally), sexy legs, her glistening pink slit, her curvy hips and small, firm ass that was just begging him to grab and squeeze it. Then her almost ridiculously narrow waste, soft flat tummy with an adorable little belly button, and finally her round and perky breasts, no sign of her cloth chest wrap to be seen, with the dark green nipples already standing out proudly.

Dare noticed her avocado skin slowly flushing a darker green as she bared herself to him, her juices slowly dripping down her thighs. As she lifted the tunic over her head her chest heaved with her excitement.

Zuri tossed the garment away and stepped past him with a sexy swaying walk, teasingly trailing her fingers across the back of his hand as she went. He turned to watch, still gaping like an idiot, as she made her way to his tent.

She didn't need to do more than duck slightly to enter it, but she went down onto her hands and knees anyway. She even lifted her small ass slightly to make sure he had a good view of her glistening little pussy as she started to crawl inside.

Then she paused and looked over her shoulder, staring at him expectantly. "Dare abur Zuri?" she said, her piping voice throaty.

That was his cue. Dare swallowed and started for the tent, heart pounding in excitement. And, if he was being honest, nervousness.

He wasn't a virgin, of course, hadn't been even on Earth. And since coming to Collisa he'd certainly had his share of new sexual experiences.

But fucking mindless slimes in the form of women that were basically life-sized sex toys, or bunny girls just looking for a quickie, was a far different thing from his first time with a woman he genuinely cared about.

He could admit he was worried he'd screw it up.

But he wanted to hold his little lover. Wanted to touch her, and be touched by her, and share the wonder of exploring each other's bodies and sharing everything.

So he stripped off his clothes and ducked into the tent.

As he awkwardly crawled in to lie down beside Zuri she slid

under his arm, cuddling against his chest with her head buried in his neck. One slender leg slipped up over his.

In that position her small pussy was pressed against his thigh, and she made a soft whimpering noise and rubbed against him, the already plentiful nectar of her arousal coating his skin and dripping down onto the blankets. The interior of the tent quickly grew heavy with her musk, sweet and heady.

Dare was as hard as he could ever remember being, cock throbbing with need as her soft leg pressed against it.

His self control was strained to its breaking point as Zuri's small hands began roaming across his chest. The way she'd wiggled under his arm had left his hand brushing against her lower back, the skin softer than anything he'd ever felt with that lotion-like slickness.

Dare closed his eyes, enjoyed the tiny woman humping his leg, and with a hungry groan moved his hand to cup her ass.

It was small but firm, one cheek fitting easily in his palm. He rubbed it, savoring the silky smoothness and slightly oily, slippery feel. Zuri whimpered again and doubled her efforts grinding against his thigh.

He bent over, lifting the little goblin's chin, and pressed his lips to hers. She kissed him back eagerly but awkwardly, as if she still wasn't quite sure what she was doing.

Dare started to slip his tongue between her lips, and felt a bit of amusement when she jumped in surprise. Her wide eyes found his, a silent question, and he nodded reassuringly as he invaded her mouth with his tongue.

He trailed it over her sharp teeth, careful with the tips, then moved past them and found her small soft tongue, pushing against it teasingly. Instead of pushing back her tongue writhed as if trying to escape, moving to one side then the other as he chased her.

Zuri finally pulled away with a gasp, looking confused, and

fumbled to take his cock in her hands.

Considering his size, he felt even more huge as her tiny fingers closed around him. Her slightly oily skin made them glide up and down his shaft like silk, and he groaned again and thrust his hips into her pleasurable touch.

His tiny lover let out a whimper that went straight to the primal part of his brain, then she shoved him onto his back with surprising strength and climbed on top of him, so slight he barely felt her weight.

Dare felt warm wetness drip down onto his cock, making him shiver as she positioned herself above him. She rubbed her sex up and down his shaft, the plump lips parting around it, and it was all he could do not to erupt.

He closed his eyes, focused on ice cold showers and football plays and the hideous Vampire Slame he'd fought earlier, and clenched his fists at his sides to resist the urge to reach up and smother her plump breasts in his hands.

If he did, if he did anything at all but lie there, he was sure he'd lose control and shoot off like a rocket.

Zuri moved more urgently, bouncing up and down so the tip of his cock mashed against her clit. Her breathing was ragged, coming out in a desperate whine, and she finally gave a high-pitched cry of release, a sound that transcended language or culture barriers. She clamped her thighs against his hips with desperate strength and his cock was drenched in her warm nectar as she climaxed, dripping down his thighs to puddle on the leather blanket beneath him.

Finally she collapsed forward onto his chest, trembling and whimpering as she gave in to her pleasure.

Dare wrapped his arms around her tiny body, hugging her close as she came down from her orgasm. He felt her lips brushing over his collarbone, then the warm wetness of her tongue as she traced

Collisa

down his chest to his nipples, swirling around them.

He grunted and pushed his hips up, sliding his cock against the sopping lips of her tiny pussy.

That seemed to be all the signal Zuri needed. She positioned himself over his cock again, but this time moved his tip to her entrance and, panting with excitement, eagerly pushed down.

He was almost shocked when he slid inside with ease, while she moaned in ecstasy and jabbered something in Goblin.

It didn't seem possible that his massive cock could fit inside her tiny pussy, especially not without some work getting her used to it. But then he remembered what Ellui had told him about the world system making it so the women of smaller races were able to accommodate the cocks of larger races without discomfort.

Thank the deities of Collisa for that.

Incredibly, though, while Zuri was able to fuck him as if she was a normal sized human woman, sliding up and down on his massive shaft with whimpery little gasps, her tiny pussy still felt like he thought it should for its size without the difficulty or discomfort.

And it was so crushingly tight it was like a vise, pleasurable to the point of pain.

Even more than that, he could see the bulge of his huge cock moving up and down her flat tummy as he bottomed out inside her with half his length still outside. It was the most erotic thing he'd ever seen, and between that and her impossibly tight, slick walls he wasn't sure he'd be able to hold out long.

His goblin lover seemed to feel the same, because she only managed half a dozen humping motions before collapsing on him with a squeal of pure joy, her vise-like pussy clamping down even harder as she milked his shaft in her powerful orgasm.

That was enough for Dare as he felt his balls boiling. "I'm about to come," he warned Zuri, trying to lift her off him.

She shook her head and held on with surprising strength. "Dare abur Zuri," she said stubbornly.

He grit his teeth and struggled to hold back. "You might get pregnant," he argued, trying to pull his hips back and lifting her harder. "Baby? Child?"

His tiny lover held on with a fierce grip, staring at him firmly. "Dare abur Zuri!" He wouldn't have expected this kind of stubbornness from the timid goblin, but unless he wanted to hurt her trying to pull out, it looked as if he was stuck.

As for giving him permission to come inside her . . . if anything she was demanding it.

Actually, now that he thought about it he might already be too late; hadn't Ellui said that goblins were almost as fertile as cunids? And she'd also said that if he so much as touched a bunny girl's pussy with his cock he'd pretty much definitely knocked her up.

Zuri might've gotten pregnant as soon as she started rubbing against his tip and got his precum all over her little pussy.

"Goddamnit," Dare groaned. Hopefully the farmwife had been lying or he'd get lucky, but it looked as if either way he was going to have to deal with the consequences. And honestly, part of him was excited to fill up that crushingly tight little pussy with his seed.

With a resigned but eager grunt he heaved his hips upward, which served no purpose other than to lift Zuri's small ass higher into the air, and erupted inside her.

She cried out in pleasure as she felt the powerful jets spray her walls, arms and legs hugging him tight. Dare wrapped her in his arms and held her with equal fervor, grunting as his balls strained to push his seed into the tiny opening his cock was trapped inside.

In spite of that his orgasm lasted twice as long as any he could remember, and he was certain he fully emptied his balls into the little goblin. She continued to hold him, trembling with pleasure, and he leaned down and kissed her jet black hair, working his lips down to a small pointy ear and nibbling on the tip.

They lay like that for a few minutes. Dare's cock, still trapped in Zuri's sweet vise, took what felt like forever to shrink, and he wasn't sure whether to be relieved or disappointed when it finally slipped out of her with a soft *plop*, drenching his crotch in their combined juices.

The soft sounds of deep breathing confirmed his tiny lover was already asleep on his chest, which he had to admit was a bit disappointing; her arousal hung heavy in the tent, less sweet than a woman's, more tangy and with a slight musk.

But it must've been absolutely loaded with pheromones, because it made his head spin more the longer breathed it in, encouraging an extra rigidity to his member even after just coming. It practically made him salivate, craving the overpowering scent almost like wine, and he couldn't wait for the chance to dive between her sexy little thighs to taste her to his heart's content. And see her quivering in a climax he gave her.

He'd definitely have to do it tomorrow.

Kissing the top of her head again, Dare pulled his blanket up over them both and allowed himself to drift off as well, loving this new world he'd been given a second chance at life on and the beautiful goblin woman he'd found here.

Phoenix

Chapter Eleven
Gone

A bit after dawn Dare was awakened by Zuri wiggling out of his embrace.

"Hey come back," he protested, blindly reaching for her with his eyes still screwed shut. "I wanted to snuggle a bit." Sleeping with her warm, lotion-slick little body pressed against his, arms wrapped around each other and her head on his shoulder, had been blissful.

She ignored him, tugging on his foot and then on the blanket beneath him. "Clean," she said firmly.

Right, they had made a bit of a mess last night. With a sigh he allowed himself to be dragged out of bed and helped her haul his bedroll to the pool, where Zuri cast her cleaning spell on everything.

As he was about to take his bedroll out to dry, however, his new lover caught him and pulled him back. Guiding him over to a grassy area on the bank, she pushed him onto his back and straddled his hips.

Then she began urgently grinding her delicate petals against his quickly stiffening cock; apparently at least part of her motivation for cleaning them had been so they'd have more fun getting frisky again.

"Dare abur Zuri?" she asked in a playful voice, yellow eyes sparkling.

He paused suddenly, remembering last night's concerns. "Zuri, are you okay with getting pregnant?" At her confused look he patted her belly, then pantomimed it growing, then finally cradling a baby in his arms. "Baby?"

Realization dawned in her gorgeous eyes, and she gave him a

reassuring smile and pointed at herself. "Zuri."

Um, what? Dare stared at her blankly, and she pantomimed casting a spell and patted her tummy. "Zuri," she said again. "Kizzag mig meshald."

"Yes . . ." he said slowly. "You're a Healer, so of course you'll be able to take good care of a baby if it gets hurt or sick."

Zuri seemed to realize he hadn't understood, because she shook her head. "Zuri kizzag mig meshald!" She began casting a spell, hands over her lower stomach, and he watched as a green glow spread from them to her skin there.

Dare stared as realization dawned, hardly daring to believe. "Is that a spell that prevents pregnancy?" he asked. He made the cradling gesture again. "No baby?"

"No baybee," she agreed.

"Oh thank the gods," he said, hugging his tiny lover tight.

He felt like a weight had been lifted off his chest. Much as he cared about Zuri, and although he thought he could see himself having children with her at some point, he wasn't ready to settle down just yet. He still wanted to level up, get strong, and become someone important on this world. Thrive in it the way he had in the games he played.

And even if it made him an asshole, he could admit he still held out the dream of fucking women of every race on this world. He wasn't a saint.

Assuming Zuri was on board with it, of course.

His goblin lover hugged him back, looking pleased about making him happy. Then she hesitated, expression almost shy, and began sweeping her arm across the path of the sun as if to indicate passing days. "Baybee yes Dare?" she said, making more rotations of the sun and several level up noises.

Phoenix

Dare laughed and kissed Zuri firmly. "Some day, yes, I'd like that. But for now we don't even have a house, or money to buy what we need to make sure the child has a good life and every opportunity."

She stared at him blankly, and he patted her stomach gently. "No baby, not yet. Dare talk Zuri, Zuri talk Dare. Then baby when . . ." He made several of his own level up noises.

Zuri nodded, seeming satisfied at that. "Dare abur Zuri?" she said, beginning to grind her soft little pussy against him again.

Dare grinned. He would've been up for it anyway, as he'd proven last night, but now that he knew they were being responsible he was even more excited about it.

He rolled them over with a delighted giggle from his goblin lover, and began kissing and caressing her as he positioned himself between her glistening petals to push inside.

* * * * *

Dare heard "Dare abur Zuri" a lot over the next five days.

It didn't take a genius to figure out what the words meant. Especially since the statement was usually immediately followed by wild sex with his tiny goblin lover.

He supposed that Ellui *had* said that goblins were as horny as bunny girls. And Zuri was certainly eager to go several times a day, in a way not even the honeymoon period of their relationship could account for.

So much, in fact, that sometimes he'd turn away from taking a leak against a tree and she'd immediately jump on his dick before he could put it away. Taking him down her throat and expertly working him until he came like a firehouse while she eagerly swallowed it all.

Then she'd tuck him into his pants and do up his ties, and happily continue on with whatever she'd been doing.

Collisa

She became more and more passionate in their lovemaking as well, although her pussy continued to remain crushingly tight. It didn't take long before she was bouncing up and down on him with delighted sounds, or urging him to pound into her.

Dare had discovered something else in that time, too; he could keep up with his insatiable goblin lover. Maybe she was just that good at getting him hard, but he suspected this body his unseen benefactor had given him had incredible stamina along with all its other amazing traits.

He could come again and again and never feel like he was pushing his limits. In fact, a lot of the time he made love he could even fuck right *through* the refractory period after coming, allowing him to go for over a half hour sometimes without stopping even though he came once or twice during it.

And it was a good thing he could, because Zuri's vise-like pussy and mind-blowing deep throating always had him spurting within minutes in spite of his best efforts to hold out.

One thing their shared intimacy didn't seem to change, however, was his goblin lover's obstinate stance about grouping up.

The day after they made love for the first time, as they were preparing to set out to hunt monsters, Dare tried to invite Zuri to his party again. He was baffled when she again turned him down. Although this time she held her arms up until he crouched, then threw them around his neck and looked into his eyes, speaking solemnly in Goblin.

Her expression and tone were loving, and he was sure she had a great explanation for him if only he could understand her. "Well, I suppose I'll figure out what's going on with you and joining my party when we finally get our translation stones," he said, leaning in to kiss her.

Only a few hours later the long anticipated event finally happened, and Zuri turned Level 10. Dare had hoped that it would jump her up in power the same way it had for him, and give her a useful new ability.

But even in his wildest dreams he couldn't have expected what she got.

With the next monster they hunted, a large snake, his tiny lover darted in and cut the reptile with her Utility Knife. Then she backed away to a safe distance, took some blood from the blade, and crouched to mix it with dirt from the ground, water from her flask, and one of her own strands of long black hair. Then she began molding it into a figure while chanting in Goblin.

A few seconds later, holding a recreation of the monster they fought, she bent it into a loop while her chanting became harsher and more commanding.

At which point the snake spasmed and gained a debuff. "Nature's Curse: Reduces movement speed by 25%, 5% chance each second to apply a paralysis effect for 3 seconds. Gain active ability with one time use during duration of Nature's Curse called 'Voodoo Spite: stun the enemy for 2 seconds'."

It had no time limit, suggesting it would be active as long as Zuri held the spell. Even better, Nature's Curse didn't take her full attention; she was also able to cast Mana Thorns as she kept the debuff up, damaging the monster down.

Dare stared in amazement as he worked to keep the snake occupied and damage it down alongside his lover.

Forget what he'd thought at first about Healer and Hunter being one of the worst class pairings . . . Zuri's class was awesome and so was she!

It got even better, because apparently her voodoo-like magic had two different abilities she could use. On the next snake she did the same thing, only instead of the support spell, this time she applied a damage over time effect called "Nature's Rebuke".

Collisa

That one, unfortunately, required her full focus to maintain. And it didn't do as much damage as if she was spamming her Mana Thorn spell. But it cost a quarter of the mana and, if Dare slowed down his own damage and kited the enemy for a while, would do the required 30% of the damage faster than her combination of Zaps and stabs.

And especially faster than when she was out of mana and was reduced to only the knife.

Dare couldn't help but regret that he hadn't selected Healer himself; Nature's Rebuke might be of only limited value for a Healer who wasn't grouped with someone who could keep a monster occupied, but with his speed he could've just zoomed in, cast it on several enemies at a time, then run circles around them until they died.

Of course, he could do the same thing with his arrows. Still, with Zuri's incredibly versatile, powerful new spell they were able to level far faster and more efficiently. So much so that four days later they both reached Level 12 within hours of each other.

At that point Dare decided it was time to move on.

Technically they could keep pushing out farther and farther from Lone Ox, finding higher and higher level enemies to farm. But Dare didn't like that for multiple reasons.

First, this was a dangerous world. Along with monsters there were marauding tribes of other intelligent races, bandits and other criminals, vicious animals who would've been hunted and chased away from settlements, and probably natural hazards as well.

None of the villagers knew much about what was beyond five or so miles from them, aside from what could be seen on Dare's map of basic topography. In the face of that ignorance he wanted to err on the side of caution and avoid blundering into anything.

Better to stick to places other people had explored recently so he knew exactly what he was dealing with.

Phoenix

For another thing, the farther he got from a settlement, even a small place like Lone Ox, the farther he'd have to lug his trade goods. That, or hoard it all and find a way to cart it en masse. He also wouldn't be able to buy gear and necessities to help them level and make their lives more comfortable.

But ultimately, the main deciding factor was that he wanted to head to Driftwain, then if necessary Kov, to get a translation stone for Zuri. He'd saved up more than enough by this point, assuming his next load of trade goods sold well, as well as enough to buy amenities like food and lodging if necessary.

So the next morning he got to work packing up. Not just the trade goods but the tents and bedrolls and Zuri's collapsible chair and the cooking rack and plates and utensils and everything else.

Zuri watched him, brow furrowed. "Lone Ox?" she asked, pointing in vaguely the right direction.

"To start with," he said, patting her head. "Then Driftwain." He drew a picture of a necklace with a large stone in the dirt, then pointed at it. "Translation stones. Like Durrand had. For you." She stared at him blankly. "So Dare can talk Zuri, and Zuri can talk Dare."

Realization dawned, and her face lit up as she pointed at the stone. "Zuri talk Dare?"

He grinned. "Yes."

She shouted happily and leapt up as high as she could, wrapping her arms around him. He laughed and caught her, pulling her up the rest of the way into his arms. "I want to talk to you so I can tell you how much I love you," he told her, stroking her silky black hair. "And I'm sure we've both got so many other things to talk about after weeks together."

With all their gear they both ended up loaded down like pack mules and plodding along at a snail's pace. At least as far as Dare was concerned, after spending the last several days running around at his preferred speed with Zuri riding on his back or held in his arms. But at least it would get better when they sold all their trade goods and extraneous camping gear, ie Zuri's tent and bedroll.

She didn't really need them anymore.

Because of the difficulty of the hike Dare decided to stick close to the river for as long as they could, so at least they could drink up and refill their water bottles in the heat of the day. It also tended to have fewer monsters along it, which seemed counterintuitive but he wasn't complaining.

The route also happened to take them right past the green slime spawn point, where Dare couldn't help but pause.

Slimes were usually common in games, and no doubt he'd find more on his travels. But there was no guarantee they'd be slime girls. So he looked at the beautiful transparent monster girls oozing along the riverbank, thinking back fondly on the good times they'd had.

He'd only meant to say a brief, silent goodbye before moving on, but when he turned back to Zuri he saw her smiling at him knowingly. "Dare abur slime?" she asked.

Dare felt himself blushing, but nodded. "If Zuri say yes?" He loved Zuri, but there were a lot of different types of women on this world he wanted to fuck.

Best to see now if she had a problem with that.

But his tiny lover just laughed. "Dare abur slime, yes," she said, shrugging out of her pack, then tugging on his as if to tell him to do the same.

She helped him undress, smirking at his already hard cock, then took his hand and pulled him towards a slime that had taken the form of a bunny girl. The transparent green monster dropped down on her hands and knees as they approached, teasingly presenting her ass.

Phoenix

"Does this mean you don't mind me fucking cunids, either?" he joked.

She gave him a blank look and pointed at the slime. "Dare abur cunid slime?"

Well, he'd ask her again when they could actually communicate. In the meantime he wasted no time stepping up to that tempting transparent green ass.

He hurried, both because they had a long way to go and because he was aware of Zuri standing over by their packs waiting. She didn't seem to mind him going to town on a slime girl's ass, and in fact was unashamedly rubbing herself beneath her tunic as she watched.

That turned him on more than he expected, and with a groan he emptied himself in the slime bunny girl faster than he'd meant to.

The monster didn't seem to mind the quick snack, contentedly moving to cover him and clean away his sweat before oozing off in search of another horny meal. He returned to Zuri and pulled his clothes back on, then shrugged into his pack and helped her into hers.

"Sorry for the delay," he said.

She grinned at him. "Dare abur, Zuri rest." Then she grimaced as the weight of her pack settled on her small shoulders.

Well, they'd be in Lone Ox soon.

An hour and a half or so later, they came in view of Ellui's farmhouse. Dare supposed he shouldn't have been surprised to find her working out in the fields as usual, and considered going around to stay out of her view.

But his pack was getting heavy and he wanted to get to the village already. Besides, poisonous as the woman could be she'd been helpful too, and he supposed it was only polite to give her a proper goodbye.

Collisa

Unsurprisingly, the farmwife immediately came over when she spotted them passing by her fence. "Unusually big load," she called. Her sun-blistered lips pulled upward in a smirk. "Of course, I could've said that the first time we met."

Dare rolled his eyes. "It should be since I brought everything with me."

Ellui nodded thoughtfully. "So you're leaving, huh? Not surprised, I guess . . . adventurers always wander to find stronger and stronger monsters. And trappers and hunters wander more than anyone." She gave him a speculative look and twitched her skirts up slightly to show him her pale plump legs. "Last chance to have me before you go."

Zuri gave him a confused look. "Dare abur human galeka?" she asked, pointing.

The farmwife gave the little goblin an ugly look. "What did the pukeskin just say about me?"

He lost his patience with the toxic woman. "Probably something much kinder than you said to her. Which is to be expected."

Her scowl deepened. "What's that supposed to mean?"

"Exactly what it sounds like. Zuri's a good person and she deserves better than your spite. Which is why I'm not going to miss you."

Ellui glared at him. "Get the fuck off my land. You and your goblin sex toy. I never want to see either of you again." She stooped to pick up a rock, waving it threateningly.

Dare moved protectively in front of Zuri in case she threw it, and set a quick pace down the road in the direction of the village.

"Gods curse you, you smelly, ragged tramp!" the farmwife shouted after him. "What makes you think you're so great anyway? Who cares if you have impossible good looks and the body of a god and a giant cock, you're still trash! That's why you fuck trash like goblins!"

"Don't listen to her," he told Zuri.

The timid goblin looked at him uncertainly. "Human galeka zaburazed?"

"Very zaburazed," he said with a laugh, hoping he wasn't saying something stupid.

She smiled tentatively and slipped her hand into his.

The village was more tense than Dare expected, women standing in doorways and leaning out of windows to talk to each other, children huddled by their sides. And rather than going about their chores, the men were all gathered at the big table on the tavern's patio, hunched over mugs of ale in spite of the early hour and talking grimly.

Whatever the excitement was, it probably wouldn't have much to do with him and Zuri. And he wanted to sell his and Zuri's loot and be gone as quickly as possible, so he could hopefully carry her and run the distance to Driftwain before nightfall.

It was a day's walk for most people anyway, so even with a late start it should be easy.

As they passed the table Dare nodded politely to the men seated around it, most of whom either nodded back or ignored him. But to his dismay, just as they came abreast of the final seat the big fellow perched on it rose ponderously and moved to block Dare's path. He had thick arms, big fists, and a pronounced beer belly, and Dare's heart sank as he recognized the man he'd seen visiting the slime girls.

Ellui's husband, Brennal.

"What're you doing parading your pukeskin sex slave around our streets?" the big man said belligerently. "Lone Ox is a decent town."

Dare glanced at Zuri, who was cowering behind his leg. The clothes he'd crafted her were as decent as any woman's in the village, and she'd simply been walking quietly at his side, bothering no one.

He was furious on her behalf, and would've liked nothing more than to pound the big farmer into the ground. He wouldn't hesitate to defend Zuri with his life if it came to it, but his parents had taught him that you didn't answer words, no matter how vile, with fists, except in very clear cases of imminent physical danger.

It usually just made the situation worse.

Just in case Brennal had any ideas of starting trouble, though, he quickly used his Eye on the man: Level 14 Tiller, by far the highest level in the village. Which might've been explained by the farmer's Brawler subclass; Dare hadn't realized people with non-combat classes could have a combat subclass.

But he supposed it made sense, since as a combat class he'd been given a Leatherworking subclass. Although with a penalty to quality and probably other things as well. That was probably the case for a combat subclass as well, although it would still be a good alternative for people who didn't want to spend their life adventuring but still wanted to be able to defend themselves.

The man's hit points were fairly impressive, and his attacks included a decent arsenal of punches, tackles, and grapples. Even so, Dare wasn't worried about him.

"You have the wrong idea," he said as calmly as he was able. "Zuri isn't my slave, she's free. And she's my friend." He wasn't about to talk about his love life with this lout.

Even so, his declaration drew a chorus of harsh guffaws from men around the table, as well as from a few villagers who were emerging from their houses to watch the confrontation. It briefly relieved whatever tension had the town in its grip.

Brennal laughed loudest of all. "A goblin friend? What, you play

Phoenix

cards with the pukeskin? Tell it all your hopes and dreams? Punt it around like an inflated pig's bladder when you're bored?"

"Don't listen to him, Zuri," Dare told his trembling lover, patting her shoulder. He turned back to Brennal. "We have some business in the village, then we'll be gone. You probably won't see us again."

The farmer's face turned ugly. "The pukeskin doesn't go a step farther. Send it outside and fetch it when you're done."

His parents may have taught him not to answer words with fists, but they'd sure as hell also taught him not to back down, either. Especially when it came to defending his loved ones. "No," Dare said evenly.

Brennal slowly cracked his knuckles. "I don't think you're listening to me, adventurer. The only good use for a gobbo is seeing how far you can punt it." He drew back his leg and started to drive his big boot towards the tiny woman's face. "Like th-"

Dare kicked out with impossible speed, knocking the farmer's foot aside before it could hit Zuri. Brennal stumbled, and without giving the man time to recover Dare stepped in close and began raining punches on his face.

He was already fast thanks to his body's heightened traits and Fleetfoot, but he added to it by using chain punches; his fists were an almost impossible to see blur as he struck over twenty times in the space of a second.

Brennal stumbled back a step with a strangled grunt and Dare stepped in to keep up the attack, punishing the shocked Brawler's face until the man finally fell flat on his ass.

It all happened in a manner of moments, so to an observer it would've looked as if Brennal went from trying to kick Zuri to rolling on the ground, cursing as blood streamed from his broken nose and split lips and bruises formed on his cheeks and around his already swelling eyes.

Collisa

Which was why for a moment everyone could only stare in shock at the man 2 levels below the farmer, who had just cleaned his clock faster than they could even see.

Dare looked around at the gathering crowd, labored breathing more from anger than fatigue from the brief fight. "Lone Ox has been good to me, and I'm grateful to you," he called. He hardened his voice. "But anyone who tries to harm my friend will end up on the ground, and lucky they're not six feet under it. Am I clear?"

Some people, especially Brennal's friends around the table, quickly looked away. But most just stared silently.

Dare gently guided a trembling Zuri past the prostrate farmer, keeping her on his other side just in case. "Now, we're going to complete our business in Lone Ox, then be on our way," he continued in the same loud voice as the onlookers muttered to each other. "Anyone have a problem with that?"

The crowd abruptly quieted, and Dare followed their turning heads to see Durrand storming down the street towards him, expression furious. "Adventurer!" he shouted.

Dare quickly raised his hands. "He started it."

The Mayor glanced at Brennal and snorted derisively, although that didn't lessen his fury in the slightest. "You think I care if that lout finally picked a fight he couldn't win? This is about the bandits."

Dare nodded apologetically. "I know I've been taking my time-"

"Fuck that!" the portly man shouted. "You need to kill them now! Last night they raided a farm and murdered everyone there, aside from the farmer's daughter and a fieldhand's young wife, who they took back to their camp." His expression twisted, looking almost sick. "I don't suppose I need to tell you why."

Shit. Dare had actually put the bandits out of his mind, not wanting to take the risk even if he was now higher level. But it looked as if his procrastination had led to the suffering and death of innocent people.

He couldn't take too much responsibility for that, since he'd only told Durrand he'd fight the bandits if he could, and it looked as if the Mayor and villagers hadn't taken any steps to protect the village themselves.

But now that he knew the bandits had hostages, and were likely hurting them, he couldn't just ignore the girls' plight.

"Of course I want to help them, but me and Zuri can't take the camp by ourselves if they're all gathered up," he said. "We need more people."

"I'll go," Brennal said, wiping his bloody nose on his sleeve as he finally stood.

Dare stared at the Brawler in shock. "You'll help me after I just got done beating your ass?"

The man glared murder at him. "Fuck you and your pukeskin whore. Harand was a friend of mine, same with most of the others working his land, and Telliny and Yena are sweet girls. I'll do it for them."

Dare stared thoughtfully at the Brawler, then turned to Zuri and pointed at the man. "Could you please heal him?"

She stared at him blankly, either not understanding or surprised by the request.

"Let me," Durrand said, motioning to the translation stone around his neck. He quickly explained the situation to Zuri, who looked a bit frightened as she hesitantly took out her water skin, dumped it over Brennal's face, then cast her healing spell on him.

"She's scared to go up against a dozen humans, even if they're lower level," the Mayor explained. "And she's not wrong . . . this won't be like fighting monsters or animals in the wilds."

Yes, which was why Dare had been taking his time finishing up the quest; he didn't want to get swarmed by intelligent enemies. And he hadn't wanted them to know he was hunting them until he was ready to attack, which was why he'd given their camp a wide berth after first scouting it.

Dare looked around at the crowd, picking out a Level 8 and a Level 9. "Either of you want to help?" Both shook their heads fearfully.

Brennal chuckled dourly. "Looks like it's the two of us then."

"Guess so." Dare turned to the Mayor. "Can you tell Zuri I'd like her to stay in the village, and take care of her while I'm gone?"

Durrand had only repeated half of that when Zuri yelled "No!" and grabbed Dare's leg. She babbled desperately at the Mayor, who stared at Dare's face the entire time with a neutral expression.

"She might be scared, but she'll go with you." the portly man said, shaking his head. "That's one loyal goblin you've got there."

Dare nodded reluctantly; he would've preferred she stay safe here, but he had to admit he needed her help. And he could think of a plan that would hopefully keep her out of danger.

Brennal strode over to the tavern's patio and retrieved an ugly cudgel that was leaning against the railing. "All right, let's go," he growled, slapping the weapon into his palm.

* * * * *

Dare took out one bandit on patrol and one sentry as they snuck up on the camp, a Level 8 and a Level 6 respectively. The one on patrol had some sort of Stealth ability that applied to vision but not sound, which allowed them to find and kill him before he could raise a warning.

The sentry was actually asleep, the careless idiot. He was dead before he woke as they all struck at once.

Then they were at the camp, the dozen-ish bandits whittled down

Phoenix

by two.

Dare made them hang back and hide while he climbed a tree and tried to get a good view of the camp without being spotted. They were all gathered around a tent, drinking and laughing.

As Dare watched a man emerged from the tent tying the laces on his pants. Another man eagerly ducked past him through the entry flaps, and a short while later Dare heard the soul-wrenching sound of a woman's broken scream, quickly cut off.

Fuck.

His instinct was to rush in and start killing to try to save the poor girl before she could suffer any more at the hands of these monsters. And from the looks of it Brennal, fist clenched murderously around his cudgel, was about to do just that.

Dare dropped down to the ground and caught the man's arm. "We can't save her by committing suicide," he whispered. "They're all paying attention to the tent and drinking heavily . . . if we sneak up we can kill several before they even know we're here, then finish off the rest."

"I'll tell you what, adventurer," the farmer growled, straining against Dare's grip as another scream pierced through the trees, a different woman's voice. "I'll march over there *quietly*, but as soon as I reach that camp I'm going to start smashing in heads."

Dare grit his teeth; the man's refusal to work with him might get them all killed, and at best would just make the battle more difficult. "Fine. Try to hold off at least two minutes."

Without waiting for a response he picked Zuri up and began dodging through the woods, keeping underbrush and trees between him and the camp. He did his best to avoid making noise, aided by his Hunter abilities. But honestly with the frequent haunting screams and the harsh guffaws of the bandits, he probably could've been snapping sticks with every step and not drawn attention.

He finally reached a spot where they'd be approaching the bandits from behind as they faced the tent, and there was a clear shot to the camp of almost twenty yards for his arrows. Dare took up position there and motioned for Zuri to stand beside him.

"Dare shoot starting from the left," he whispered, motioning to the leftmost bandits and shaking his bow. "Zuri "Zap!" starting from the right." He gestured to the rightmost enemies.

"Zap," she agreed, face pale but determined.

Dare sighted in on his first target, nocked an arrow and drew the fletchings to his cheek, and . . .

Brennal chose that moment to rush into the camp, roaring to alert the bandits to his approach of course, and slammed the nearest ruffian with his cudgel.

Motherf-

Dare loosed his arrow, transfixing his target as the bandits all scrambled to react to the Brawler's attack. Then he activated Rapid Shot and brought four arrows to the hand holding his bow, swiftly loosing them at every target of opportunity he had a clear shot at.

Which was made a bit more difficult with Brennal running around like an idiot as if deliberately trying to foul his shots.

He saw a dark green bolt shoot towards the camp as Zuri joined in, casting Mana Thorn at bandits as quickly as she could. Her sharp features were set in fierce determination.

The Brawler stumbled back, beset by four bandits at once, although none were higher than Level 8. They were still managing to chunk away his health as one slashed at him with a short sword and the others jabbed at him with spears.

Just as the farmer was starting to regain his footing, the flaps to the tent burst open and a brawny man wearing only undershorts stormed out, bearing a wicked-looking black greatsword.

Phoenix

The bandit leader had leveled up to 11 at some point since Dare last saw him. Beyond that his size and physique must've given him good stats, because he was more powerful than he should've been for his level. His attacks included Charge, Maim, Overpower, and Fury.

Dare saw the man and immediately focused on him, loosing an arrow at his chest.

The shaft hit the bandit leader in the thigh, but the man barely reacted to it, his Fury ability making him go nuts as he made a beeline for Brennal.

The farmer, for his part, took one look at the bandit leader and fled, although it was futile since the man's Charge quickly closed the distance.

Dare hit the huge bandit with an arrow to the leg, applying a small Snare effect, while one of Zuri's Zaps hit him in the chest, slicing deep across the flesh of one bulging pectoral. The bandit leader took one more step and slashed at Brennal's back.

The Brawler used some sort of evasion ability and spun away from the attack, barely avoiding the razor-sharp tip. Then he darted in and slammed his cudgel into the big man's gut, doubling the bandit over in spite of his solid abs.

The bandit released his wildly swinging sword with one hand and backhanded Brennal across the face, sending him flying backwards a few feet, momentarily stunned. Dare's next arrow buried in the leader's upper chest, a Critical hit, and Zuri's next Mana Thorn hit the man in the side of the head, shaving a wide strip of his hair off and leaving a deep wound in his scalp that bled profusely.

The huge boss ignored the attacks and raised his sword over the Brawler. As if that wasn't bad enough, Dare noticed the other bandits were ignoring that fight and rushing through the trees to either side of the open space to get to him and Zuri.

Damnit. Brennal had made his bed jumping right into the

hornet's nest like that. "Zuri, in the trees!" he shouted, pointing with an arrow before nocking it and shooting at the closest bandit.

His improved reflexes gave him just enough time to twist aside as a bandit in the woods to the other side of the open space hurled a throwing axe at his head. Or maybe it was just a hatchet. Either way the haft slammed into his temple, dazing him, and he fumbled and dropped his next arrow.

Zuri pelted the bandit who'd thrown the axe with a Zap, making the man stumble clutching an eviscerated belly. Then she turned and bolted as three more of the ragged men came within ten feet of them, closing the distance fast.

Good girl; she knew from long experience hunting with Dare that he could handle himself, and she should prioritize her safety.

Dare had time to loose one last arrow, hitting the nearest bandit in the head, then used Roll and Shoot to hit another in the side. As soon as he loosed the arrow he dropped his bow and drew his stone knives as the last man, twirling a spear in an aggressive attack pattern, lunged at him.

The Level 7 might as well have been moving in slow motion as Dare sidestepped the blow and dropped low, slashing both blades across the man's belly. One snapped halfway through the slash, but the other cleanly sliced through the bandit's thick shirt and deep into his flesh, hitting vitals.

Dare spun away before his enemy could counterattack, if he even could with that wound, and went after the bandit he'd hit in the side, who was soldiering through the pain to come after him with a dagger in one hand and a short sword in the other.

It turned out that dual wielding might've been a bit advanced for the man, since he couldn't handle either weapon properly while trying to use them both. Dare kicked aside the sword and ducked beneath a clumsy swing of the dagger, getting behind his assailant and using Hamstring on both his legs.

Phoenix

Humans and other intelligent creatures didn't recover from crippling wounds the way monsters did; with a nasty arrow wound in his side and both legs useless, he was effectively dead.

That just left the spearman. Who was on his knees, face ashen as he held his ruined midsection. "I surrender," he groaned through gritted teeth. "Healer, please."

Dare wiped his knife on the man's shirt as he walked past to retrieve his bow. "I'll check on you after I save the women you were raping. Although your fate's ultimately in the hands of the villagers, so even if you survive I don't like your chances."

A roar from the camp drew his eyes, and he watched the bandit leader swing his greatsword at a prone target with a powerful downward slash. Brennal cried out, and the sword rose bloody.

With another roar, the big ruffian whirled away from the farmer and locked furious eyes with Dare.

Shit.

Dare raised his bow and loosed an arrow that hit the bandit leader in the eye: Critical hit, the man's health chunked down to 40% and he got a perception and defense debuff. Although what should've been a fatal or at least incapacitating injury barely gave the bandit pause under the effects of Fury.

From off to one side, deep in the trees, a dark green bolt emerged to slam into the big thug's crotch, which also barely seemed to faze him even though he started bleeding heavily from his groin.

With a snarl the bandit broke into an out and out sprint towards Dare, sword raised overhead. He was coming fast, and still had enough health to close the distance before dying.

Dare's Rapid Shot cooldown ended, and he activated it and buried the four arrows in the bandit leader's torso. That was about all the time he had before the big man reached him, sword whistling.

Collisa

He started to activate Roll and Shoot to one side, but on some instinct rolled backwards the full distance instead. A good thing, because the bandit leader's overhead slash became an entirely different move, slashing low to the ground in a circle right where Dare would've been.

Maim?

Dare came up with an arrow nocked thanks to the ability and drew and loosed, burying the shaft in the bandit's gut. Then he turned and fled.

His Eye confirmed that his enemy had no DoTs on him, just a slew of debuffs that his Fury ability was mitigating in exchange for reduced defense. He still had about 10% health left, and given his dangerous skill with that massive sword of his Dare wasn't going anywhere near him to try to slash him with his stone knives.

The bandit leader snarled and swung, his greatsword somehow managing to close the distance between them like magic; either Dare had misjudged how far behind him the man was, the bandit had put on a burst of speed, or the sword's blade was just that long.

He desperately dodged, then tripped on a root and stumbled. His enemy roared in triumph and brought his weapon around for another swing.

One Dare wouldn't be able to dodge in time as he struggled to keep his balance.

In an even more desperate move he went limp and dropped to the ground, the blade hissing as it cut the air just above his head. But now he was out of moves; he couldn't roll away from a sweeping attack from that long blade, and this bandit was no fool; he'd take advantage of an enemy's weakness.

Dare lifted his bow and knife and braced himself to try to stop the coming attack, knowing it was as useless as trying to stop an avalanche.

Phoenix

Then the bandit leader abruptly jerked and spasmed with a cry of pain, going stiff as a board and dropping hard to the ground beside Dare.

The paralysis proc from Zuri's Nature's Curse ability; she must've managed to get her hands on some of the man's blood.

Never one to ignore an opportunity, Dare immediately rolled to slash at the back of the bandit leader's nearest leg. His stone knife broke halfway through the attack, doing slight damage but not applying Hamstring's Snare effect, and Dare cursed.

He didn't have time to grab his other knife from his pouch, so he did a kip-up (a move he could never get close to doing on Earth but was able to manage easily here), coming to his feet smoothly and shooting the bandit leader in the back from point blank range as the big man lay prone.

Then the 3 second timer on the paralysis ran down.

The bandit leader roared and rushed to his feet, throwing a surprisingly fast punch his way. Just before the blow connected Dare used Roll and Shoot to go straight backwards, shooting another arrow at the big man as he came up. Then he turned and ran again.

The bandit leader didn't have a hope of catching him now that he was slowed by 25% and infrequently getting paralyzed. And all the while Zuri was pelting him with her Mana Thorns.

When the paralysis effect triggered again Dare was ready to spin and shoot, then paused when he saw that the brute was down to a sliver of health.

So he lowered his bow and let his goblin lover take the last hit and the experience bonus; she'd more than earned it.

A final Mana Thorn sliced in, right across the bandit leader's throat in a Critical Hit, and with a shudder the big man escaped the paralysis effect just in time to go limp in death.

Collisa

Chapter Twelve
Hero's Reward

Dare breathed a huge sigh of relief when Zuri scuttled out of the trees to join him, rushing to meet her and dropping to his knees to wrap her in his arms. "Are you okay?" he asked, checking her over.

"Zuri okay," she replied, similarly searching for wounds. "Dare okay?"

He rested a hand on her silky hair. "I'm fine thanks to you," he told her. "You saved my ass."

"Ass?" She looked at him in concern and began running her hands over his rump, in a way that he thought was out of place hanky panky until he realized she was checking him for injuries. "Dare ass hurt?"

Dare laughed sheepishly; right, he'd used that word a few times during lovemaking, so she knew it. "Not hurt. It's an expression." He motioned for the camp. "Brennal's hurt though."

"Brennal, yes," she said, starting for where they'd last seen the man at a run. Dare kept up with her, looking around warily in case more bandits had been out in the trees as patrols or sentries.

If so they must've run away, because he didn't see any enemies as they reached the large clearing the camp was situated in.

Brennal was sprawled on the ground a stone's throw from the big tent the captured women were in, blood sheeting across his chest. Dare and Zuri hurried over to the farmer, although considering the ugly wound he feared the worst.

But just before they reached Brennal the man unexpectedly sucked in a ragged breath and his eyes flew open.

Phoenix

"Still alive?" Dare asked, crouching beside the man.

"Fuck you," the Brawler growled. He started to sit up, then grit his teeth around a cry of pain and fell back, panting. "Healer," he said through gritted teeth.

"You mean the woman you tried to kick in the head because it's fun to punt goblins?" Dare asked savagely. But he was already motioning for Zuri to help the man.

She grabbed his and Brennal's waterskins and dumped them out on the man's chest, then began chanting as the water swirled around the wounds. It took a long time, longer than he'd ever seen for the healing spell, and he watched her mana swiftly drain as she healed the serious wound.

Finally, though, the farmer was left with just a long, jagged scar across his chest and abdomen. He had a weakness debuff from blood loss and the severity of the wound, which even after healing would take days to recover from, but other than that he was much improved.

Brennal dragged himself to his feet, then swayed and grabbed his head as if dizzy. "Thanks for leaving me to singlehandedly face that big bastard while you stood around holding your dick," he growled balefully while glaring at Dare through his fingers.

Dare snorted. "I fought two bandits hand to hand because I let them get close while trying to focus on their leader to help you. If you didn't want to face the entire camp alone, maybe you shouldn't have *run into the middle of it yelling to let them know you were coming.*"

The farmer flushed. "Fuck you," he said again, turning to scowl at the scene of carnage around them. "So, you get them all?"

Dare did his best not to look too closely at the bodies around them; he thought he'd be desensitized to this sort of thing after watching violent shows since he was a kid, but in real life it was far more horrifying. Especially since now that the fight was over he had to face the knowledge that he'd killed real people.

Scum who murdered and raped innocent villagers, but still people. And most likely it wasn't going to be the last time he'd be forced to this recourse.

This had been justified, and had saved two young women from unspeakable abuse, slavery, and possibly death. But the bloody scene among the tents would still haunt his nightmares.

He kept his focus on Brennal to avoid seeing more than he had to. "Unless there were any patrols or people who ran, I think so. But I'm keeping an eye out just in case." He glanced over to where he'd been forced to fight hand to hand. "Oh, and two seriously wounded who are out of the fight and surrendered."

The Brawler looked at him incredulously. "So?"

"So I'm not in the habit of killing injured, defenseless people after the fight is over. I'm a Hunter, not an executioner."

Brennal snorted contemptuously. "Bandits are kill on sight in Haraldar. Nobody would fault you for it . . . in fact, they'd give you a reward."

Dare didn't back down. "The bandits are dealt with. I'll leave it to the people of Lone Ox to decide what to do with those two."

"Fine, then on behalf of the village . . ." the big man leaned down and hauled up the bandit leader's wicked black greatsword, dragging the tip on the ground behind him as he strode towards the injured men.

Dare didn't stop him; the man's points were valid, and even if Dare himself didn't want to kill those men, he wouldn't go out of his way for bandit scum whose deaths the kingdom had authorized.

Besides, Brennal might've been focused on his butchery, but there was a more important consideration.

Phoenix

"Come on," Dare told Zuri, starting for the big tent at the center of the camp. Inside he could hear moaning and quiet sobs, and his stomach churned at the vile acts people were capable of.

His unseen benefactor had warned him that this world could be brutal. Although honestly this horror happened on Earth as well. An evil as old as time.

In the distance he heard a bandit's scream suddenly cut short, and barely flinched at it.

"Telliny, Yena?" he called gently. Inside the tent the women went abruptly quiet. "I'm Dare, a Hunter who lives nearby. I'm here with Brennal. We've killed the bandits and you're safe now. When you're ready we'll lead you back to the village."

A pained voice answered. "Thank the gods. Can you, um, help us? Those monsters kept us bound while they-" she cut off with a broken sound.

Dare turned to Zuri, wanting to preserve the dignity of the poor girls. "Could you . . ." he motioned to the tent. "Help humans?"

She nodded her understanding. "Zuri help." She motioned to the nearby stream. "Dare watuur."

Right, the poor women would need healing. Dare hurried to gather two buckets from beside the fire and went to fill them.

When he got back Brennal was at the tent entrance, speaking to his friends inside through the cloth. Dare wouldn't have thought the big Brawler could sound so gentle, but the man surprised him.

"I have water, Zuri," he called.

The little goblin quickly ducked out to laboriously haul in one bucket, then the other. The tent began to glow a whitish green as she healed them, and then she raised her voice so he could hear her. "Zuri help humans."

"Telliny, Yena, you feel up to the hike back to the village?"

Collisa

Brennal called.

In answer the flap opened and the two women emerged, Zuri trailing them. One looked to be in her late teens, around Dare's age, the other a few years older. They wore torn clothing with soiled blankets wrapped around their shoulders, and while they showed no visible injury they walked with hunched shoulders and hesitant steps.

A sign that healing the outward injuries could do nothing for the mental and emotional trauma they'd suffered.

At the sight of their empty, hollow expressions and haunted eyes, Dare felt a new surge of fury at lawless thugs who would do this to innocent people.

If bandits were all like this then kill on sight was what they deserved.

Brennal stayed near the two women, lending his support and clear show of protection without coming too close and triggering his traumatized friends. Zuri walked behind them murmuring supportively. That left Dare to lead the way.

Although they hadn't gone far before the younger girl broke away to make for the stream running beside the camp. "Just a second," she mumbled, face lowered in shame. "I can't . . . I need to wash . . ."

The other woman shuddered and nodded, hurrying to join her. The two splashed into the water side by side, turning away as they struggled to wash away the physical evidence and doubtless also the memory of the horrors they'd suffered.

Dare turned away as well to give them privacy and knelt beside Zuri. "Zuri," he said solemnly, motioning to the two women. "Cast clean spell, and no baby spell?"

Beside him Brennal, who had also turned away, sucked in a furious breath at the thought of his friends having to carry children from the abuse they'd endured. "Yes, please Zuri," he said quietly.

Phoenix

"After all they've suffered, they shouldn't have to suffer that as well."

Dare was pleasantly surprised hear the man call Zuri by name, with no show of contempt; amazing how some shared experiences caused people to set aside petty prejudices.

Zuri nodded solemnly. "Clean humans. No baybee humans." She started for the stream, already casting.

As she worked Brennal led the way over to stand behind a tent, giving the women some privacy. They waited there in tense silence for a few minutes until the women rejoined them, the younger one holding Zuri's hand as they walked.

Brennal once again accompanied his friends protectively, while Dare led the way. It was a long, somber walk to the village, with frequent stops for rest and water for the exhausted women.

When the first houses came into view the older of the two women broke into sobs and bolted for one, calling out her parents' names. Several people swarmed out the front door to surround her, hugging her close and crying in relief at her safe return and grief for her husband and the others who'd died at the farm.

The younger girl, who seemed to have no family of her own left, hesitantly followed and was pulled into the hugging, crying group.

Word spread quickly through the village, and as the two women were ushered into the house to rest and recover a quiet but exuberant celebration broke out. Casks were broached at the tavern, mugs passed around, and people cheered the defeat of the bandits and the return of their people.

Brennal was the hero of the hour, strutting around with a grin as his friends and neighbors cheered him. Ellui wasted no time latching on to his fame, showing no sign of her contempt for her husband as she clung to his side and soaked in the adulation.

Dare was also showered with hugs, backslaps, and handshakes

from grateful villagers. He also found himself the center of attention for most of the village's young, single women. And even some that weren't so young or single.

More than a few found opportunities to surreptitiously whisper invitations in his ear, the more coy ones asking him on a private walk to get some air, while the aggressive ones simply offered him their beds if he wanted to "rest" and maybe have some fun.

He was certainly interested in the offers from some of the prettier girls, although he politely turned them all down; he wasn't sure how he'd explain to Zuri that he was ditching her to go get laid, and he highly doubted any of these girls would want his goblin lover to tag along.

And if they weren't willing to accept Zuri he wasn't really interested anyway.

Not to mention Dare still needed to get her a translation stone and have a talk to her about a whole slew of things, one of which was whether her encouragement for him to screw a slime girl extended to all women.

He should probably find out if she'd be on board with him pursuing his dreams of being with as many women of every race as he could.

Speaking of his lover and the celebration, even Zuri received smiles, praise, and occasional head pats from the happy villagers. A few younger girls even made the goblin a string of flowers to tie into her long inky black hair, helping her braid them in.

Zuri looked as if she didn't know whether to be pleased by the jubilant crowd or nervous at the press of bodies, all much taller than her aside from the children. She stayed close by Dare's side the entire time.

He could admit himself that after so long basically alone in the woods, then his time with Zuri, the crowds were a bit much for him

Phoenix

too. Luckily they were eventually pulled away to take care of the business with the bandit camp.

Mayor Durrand was called on to adjudicate the splitting of the loot and his own offered quest reward, and the portly man, Brennal, several of the farmer's friends, and Dare and Zuri all headed out to the camp to scour it for everything of value.

Although given the dangerous nature of the wilds, they simply packed up pretty much the entire camp and carted it back to the street in front of the Mayor's house, where they got to work assessing it and negotiating who got what.

The rules of loot sharing were very clear that possession was 10/10s of the law. Ie, anything stolen by monsters or bandits, pirates, and other condemned criminals was fair game for any adventurer who killed them. Even if the previous owner was still alive and could make a claim, they were SOL; the kingdom apparently prioritized stopping the criminal over reimbursing the victim.

In spite of that rule, Dare and Brennal both agreed that anything taken from the farm should be returned to Telliny and Yena.

As for the rest, the surly Brawler unsurprisingly insisted on half. Which was ludicrous since he'd basically just run in and got his ass kicked, killing one or at most two of the bandits and maybe distracting the bandit leader for a couple minutes.

But the rules were very clear, and on top of that the villagers were on Brennal's side. The best Dare was able to negotiate was that by those same rules, since he'd declared Zuri free and she had contributed to the fight, she was entitled to her share.

That didn't go over well with any of the villagers. Ellui, who'd showed up for the negotiations after avoiding Dare during the celebration, accused him of trying to cheat her family.

Dare was adamant, however, even going so far as to point out that he and Zuri had killed almost all the bandits as well as the bandit leader. And finally Mayor Durrand decided in their favor, albeit grudgingly. He split the 14 silver, 50 copper of the quest reward three ways, handing out 4 silver and 83 copper to Dare and Brennal, and 4 silver 82 copper to Zuri. All the while staring at Dare as if silently challenging him to protest.

Dare saw no reason to do so over 1 copper. Especially since he had the map as part of his reward as well. Which, unsurprisingly, Brennal and Ellui were sour about. But since the deal for the map had been agreed on beforehand they couldn't manage to wrangle any extra coin out of it.

"As per the rules, this 4 silver and 82 copper goes to the goblin Zuri," the Mayor said, smirking at Dare as if expecting him to try to take it for himself. For her part Zuri's eyes got huge as the portly man began dumping copper into her upraised hands, causing many to spill to the ground, then carefully placed 4 silver atop the pile.

Zuri knew what Durrand was saying thanks to the translation necklace, but even so she tried to give the money to Dare. "No, it's yours," he told her firmly. "Put it in your pouch, and spend it on whatever you like." He motioned to the Mayor to translate.

She looked at him as if he was insane, shifting nervously as if afraid of a trick. Then she reluctantly stuffed the coins into the belt pouch he'd crafted for her.

As for the bandit camp's loot, including all the tents and equipment and weapons, it was estimated at 53 silver. They again split it three ways, this time with Dare and Zuri getting 17 silver, 66 copper and Brennal getting 17 silver, 67 copper.

If the goblin had been confused and dismayed about getting around 5 silver, she practically soiled herself at getting almost 18. She was much more insistent about trying to give it to Dare, and when he finally convinced her to put the money in her pouch she took it off her belt and pushed it at him, jabbering firmly.

"She says she wants you to hold it for safekeeping," Durrand said. "And that if you decide to keep it for yourself, she won't mind."

"Tell her I definitely will return it to her when she wants it, but I'll keep it for safekeeping." Dare took the pouch and tied it on under his tunic, alongside his own; with his speed he'd probably be able to stop pickpockets, but no sense tempting them.

That concluded the business with the bandits, and Dare got a "Quest Complete. Bandit Brutality: Slay the bandits operating east of Lone Ox. 1000 experience earned" text notification on the edge of his vision.

Ellui and Brennal seemed eager to head back to the party, and once they had their coin the farmwife started tugging at her husband's arm in the direction of the tavern.

Ignoring her, the big Brawler paused to offer Dare his hand. "You're an asshole, Hunter," he growled. "But many of the men I'm proud to call friend are."

Dare wasn't inclined to forgive the man after he'd tried to kick Zuri, but better to leave on friendly terms than as enemies. So he nodded politely and returned the handshake.

The farmer grunted, then grudgingly turned to Zuri. "Got to say you're okay, for a gobbo. What you did for those girls was kind, so thank you for that." He shifted uncomfortably and looked around, then lowered his voice. "And, um, I'm sorry about this morning."

That was . . . unexpectedly civil. Maybe there was some small hope for the man yet.

The little goblin just stared at Brennal blankly, half hiding behind Dare. "Brennal thanks Zuri?" she asked him. He nodded, and she smiled shyly at the Brawler. "Zuri yes help."

Dare grimaced. He really needed to teach her "you're welcome", along with a ton of other words and phrases. He kind of sucked as a language tutor. But in his defense he'd sort of been slacking off, hoping a translation stone would solve the problem for him.

Collisa

Which was just lazy and not very smart if he was being honest.

Meanwhile Zuri always listened to him intently, ears practically quivering as she struggled to figure out words and learn so she could speak to him. And in return he just found ways to more creatively express himself with grunts and gestures, instead of putting that same energy into useful work at long term communication.

"Well, looks like the message got through to her," Brennal said. "Farewell wherever you two go, and good hunting." He nodded at them with a hint of respect and finally gave in to the insistent tugging of his glaring wife, heading back to the party.

Durrand was kind enough to stick around so Dare could finish selling basically everything he didn't strictly need, to lighten his pack for traveling. The man's gratitude for dealing with the bandit camp meant he was unexpectedly generous with his offers, too, netting Dare another 14 silver and change.

Dare kept the money for anything he'd made through trapping, skinning, and crafting, as was fair. But he gave Zuri her share of the coin for the monster loot, as well as all the coin for the sale of her tent and sleeping pad, since they belonged to her.

"Some reason you're selling the goblin's camping gear?" Durrand asked with forced casualness.

Dare felt his face flush. "None I'd like to say."

The Mayor grimaced in distaste as if coming to his own, likely accurate, conclusion, but dropped the matter and began counting out coins.

Dare split his and Zuri's shares, then showed her coins to her as he put them in her pouch. "These are also yours for your half of the monster loot and for selling your bedroll and tent," he told her, Durrand translating.

It seemed she'd given up trying to refuse the money, because she just nodded as he put the coins away.

Phoenix

The Mayor glanced longingly at the party still going strong at the tavern. "Will you stay for the celebration, Hunter?" He paused, then added reluctantly. "You and your sla-companion are welcome to sleep in my guest room tonight."

It was tempting to relax and enjoy the exultant atmosphere. Dare looked down at Zuri. "What do you think? Stay, eat good food and drink some mugs of ale, and sleep in a bed? Or start on our way to Driftwain and hunt monsters as we go, camp out again tonight."

Durrand translated, and both of them blinked in surprise when Zuri immediately replied, "Hunt, camp."

Dare shrugged. "Got to admit, I hate taking breaks from leveling myself." He offered his hand to the Mayor. "Thank you for everything, Mayor Durrand. I can't say if I'll make it back to Lone Ox, but I'll always remember it fondly as a welcoming place."

The portly man firmly returned his handshake. "No, Master Dare, thank *you*. You've done great good for our village, and we won't forget it. Should you return you'll always be welcome."

"Cool." Dare crouched and held out his arms to Zuri. "Zoom?"

"Zoom!" she replied, grinning eagerly as she hugged him around the neck and wrapped her legs around his waist.

He straightened, gave a final nod to the Mayor, then trotted down the street in the opposite direction he'd come from. He'd never left the village in this direction before, and was amused to get an exploration achievement only a short ways past the houses, earning his paltry 25 experience.

The forest soon gave way to hilly plains, with patches of woods scattered across the terrain, and Dare grinned at the change of scenery, hugging Zuri tighter as he sped up to a faster run, causing his little lover to squeal in delight.

They were going to a new place, with the prospect of new sights and new enemies to fight. New people to meet and new quests to complete.

And their first stop would be the first town he'd seen on Collisa, with a decent amount of coin in their pockets. With any luck they'd find a translation stone there and soon he'd be able to talk to his lover.

Dare laughed freely, not trying to quiet his voice, as he pelted down the road towards Driftwain. "Ready for the start of a new adventure, Zuri?" he asked, hugging her closer.

"Zoom!" Zuri replied, laughing too.

"Zoom!" he shouted back, speeding up to his fastest sprint for a while as they left the village of Lone Ox behind them.

Chapter Thirteen
Driftwain

Early the next morning they packed up camp immediately after a quick breakfast, then Dare picked Zuri up and started jogging towards Driftwain at a pace he could maintain all day.

They'd eventually had to put the hunting on hold, since the farther down the road they went the stronger the monsters became, up to Level 18 before he gave in and decided to set up camp.

Thankfully the spawn points were all far from the road and their monsters not likely to aggro, but it was clear trying to find enemies to hunt in this area would be a waste of time. He only hoped that as they got closer to the town the monsters' levels would drop again.

Although even if they did he wouldn't hunt them right away; it was time to quit dicking around and get to Driftwain.

The only exception to the high level monsters were along the infrequent smaller roads, which he guessed led off to villages like Lone Ox. Some of the villages must've been close enough to the Driftwain road that the lower level monster spawn points around them reached it, because along some of those roads he could see familiar weak monsters in the distance.

The villages were a bit tempting. They probably all had their own quests, which he could knock out quickly and reap the generous XP and rewards. And he could get more variety by wandering around to all the spawn points around them that were his level, seeing what sort of monsters they had.

On the other hand, every village he went to was one more possibility that people would be jerks to Zuri. Which they could handle if necessary, fingers crossed, but he still ran on past those roads.

His priority remained to get a translation stone for his lover. To the point that he had to keep slowing down because he found himself running faster, eager to get to Driftwain as soon as possible. Which would ultimately slow down their progress with necessary rests.

It was a good day to put some miles behind them. The sky was clear, sun shining bright. The packed dirt road was reasonably well maintained, letting him go at a constant pace. The scenery around them was beautiful, giving him constant new things to look at.

And as he'd hoped, the monsters capped at Level 20 and then began to gradually drop back down as the hours passed and they got closer to town.

According to the villagers of Lone Ox it was a day's travel, but at the speed Dare was traveling they'd reach it in closer to five hours, after the distance they'd traveled yesterday.

In fact, as the monster levels dropped to 13-15 he wondered if he should change his mind and suggest they do some hunting after all. They had plenty of time before nightfall, and many of the monsters were ones he'd never seen before.

Then he looked at Zuri, who was holding him contentedly with her face buried in his neck, and his determination to go straight for the translation stone if it was there to be found was renewed.

In fact, he thought he could go a bit faster without running out of energy before reaching the city, so he picked up the pace.

About five minutes later someone entered Dare's perception circle, approaching from a grove of trees to the right of the road. Which seriously alarmed him.

The alert system for his Adventurer's Eye only triggered for monsters, dangerous animals, or other similarly hostile enemies. And since it hadn't picked up this presence at double the distance like it otherwise would've, and gave no warning, that meant this had to be a human or other intelligent creature.

Unfortunately, what the Eye designated as "hostile" wasn't for emotion or intent; for the intelligent races, the designation seemed to be based on a reputation system with the kingdom, region, or local area. Which was why bandits showed as hostile because of their crimes.

It was the greatest weakness in the Eye, the fact that it wouldn't warn him if he was in danger from a thinking being that meant him harm. Such as now.

A man appeared through the trees, dressed in fine black leather armor adorned with multiple pockets, belts, and pouches for items and reagents. He held a wickedly sharp side sword in one hand and a long dagger in the other, and moved lightly and silently as he swiftly approached the road.

Dare's Eye identified him as "Human, adult male. Class: Duelist Level 26." There were a dozen nasty sounding attacks the man could use, including Backstab and Maim.

In other words, if it came to a fight they were screwed.

Zuri whimpered and held Dare tighter, shaking like a leaf; if he hadn't been there he had a feeling she would've already bolted.

"I hate to say it, but your money or your life," the man said as he stepped out onto the road in front of them.

Dare swallowed, wondering if he could talk his way out of this. "If you're conflicted about this-" he began in as friendly a tone as he could.

The Duelist looked surprised. "Conflicted?" He laughed. "Oh, because I said "I hate to say it"? I'm just getting sick of that salutation . . . I really need to think up a better one that's just as short and to the point."

The man flicked his sword impatiently. "Anyway, let's have your

Collisa

coin and anything else of value you might have. Including the knife and the slave."

Well, that settled things. Dare had no chance of beating someone 14 levels higher than him, but he'd die before letting the man take Zuri.

"I kind of need my things," he said. "And Zuri is my friend, not my slave." As if to shield her protectively, he held her tightly.

Zuri was still trembling like a leaf, eyes huge with fear. But she seemed to realize what he planned, because she shifted slightly and held him tighter with her arms and legs, head tucked into his neck, prepared for him to go maximum speed.

The Duelist laughed loudly. "You have a goblin friend," he said. "I don't know if that's hilarious or sad."

Dare shrugged. "Even so, I won't let you take her."

The tall, lean man shook his head wryly. "You've got balls, friend. Some would slit your throat just for mouthing off to them. But you honestly don't think you have a choice here, do you?"

Dare shook his head. "It does kind of look like I either give you what you want, or die."

"Good, then shut up and-"

"But like I said," Dare interrupted, shrugging to make sure his pack was seated firmly on his shoulders, "You can't have Zuri, and you're slow as balls."

Without waiting for a response he turned and bolted back the way he'd come, using every ounce of speed and reflexes Fleetfoot gave him.

Over the wind of his speed, he heard the Duelist curse behind him and the thud of footfalls as the man took up the chase. The would-be highwayman was burdened only by his light armor and weapons, had long legs, and had selected a class based on speed. He was no slouch in a footrace.

Meanwhile Dare, who was the same height and also a class based on speed, was loaded down by a heavy pack and Zuri. Who in spite of her best efforts bounced around a bit at the speed he was going, slightly throwing off his balance.

Even so, he easily widened the gap between them and the mugger. He had to keep his eyes on his feet to avoid tripping or losing his balance with the weight he carried, but with every glance back he saw the Duelist falling farther and farther behind.

The man interrupted his stream of curses to shout after them. "How the hell? Hunters don't unlock a movement speed ability until Level 30!"

Dare hadn't known that, although now that he did he was looking forward to when he'd be able to go even faster. But he didn't waste breath replying as he reduced his speed slightly, to a pace he could keep up for the few remaining hours to Driftwain.

Where hopefully the mugger wouldn't follow.

Although at the moment they were headed back towards Lone Ox, taking them farther from safety unless he wanted to go all the way back to the village. Which wouldn't be any sort of sanctuary because this Duelist could slaughter the entire village, or at least send everyone running, without breaking a sweat.

Shit. Dare was going to need to leave the road and find a way to circle back north as soon as possible. Probably ducking around much higher level monster spawn points and avoiding roaming monsters and bandits and who knew what else.

At least once they got around the Duelist they could return to the road and follow it. Assuming there weren't any other highwaymen lying in wait.

Godsdamn bandits; he'd have to inform the guards about the Duelist when they reached the town.

Collisa

Although for all he knew the man was shedding the cloak of bandit whenever he reached a settlement or city, robbing people along the roads and maybe killing them to eliminate witnesses, then sleeping easy every night in taverns and traveling through towns and cities with no guard so much as giving him a second look.

Hell, the Duelist may even be doing quests, hunting dangerous invading monsters, and securing a reputation as a hero. All while preying on innocents wherever he traveled.

How dangerous was a Level 26 overall? How hard was it to reach that level? And once you got powerful enough, did you just get to wander around doing whatever you wanted and nobody had the power to stop you?

Criminals on Earth didn't exactly have the option to level up until they could slaughter an entire squad of guards and walk away unscathed. That had to make crime, interpersonal dynamics, and all sorts of other things more complicated on Collisa.

Like, for instance, did high levels grant immediate prestige, or at least fear?

"Doing okay, Zuri?" he asked, stroking her hair.

"Zuri okay," she said, although she still trembled slightly. "Human no help."

Dare chuckled. "No, he was definitely not helpful." He kissed her head. "I'm going to leave the road and try to circle around him. Pay close attention for monsters."

She just looked at him blankly until he veered away onto the hilly plain at a right angle, at which point she clutched him tighter and buried her face in his neck.

Over the last month and a half or so since coming to this world, Dare had carefully observed the monster spawn points he encountered. At this point he could almost see the probability line around each spawn point, beyond which monsters wouldn't spawn and couldn't cross aside from the rare roamer.

So he was able to weave through the spawn points and stay far away from any monsters that might aggro. Better yet, if the Duelist wanted to chase them along anything close to a straight line he'd have to go right through the spawn points himself. A bit of extra protection courtesy of the world's system.

Which was a relief right up to the point when Dare glanced back and saw his pursuer running right across a probability line, then straight through the center of a spawn point without the slightest hesitation.

The monsters, a weird insect-lizard hybrid with vicious teeth and wicked claws on its six legs, mostly ignored the sprinting Duelist. Aside from the cluster near the center that began chasing him in a group of four, with the man not even showing the slightest concern.

Right, their pursuer was 9 levels higher than those monsters. He could probably fight that group all at once and survive.

"Fuck," Dare muttered, speeding up to his fastest sprint again.

"Abur," Zuri agreed, watching the Duelist and his train of monsters cut their lead by a few dozen yards.

In retrospect, it wasn't as close as Dare worried. Sure, he basically had to turn two right angles, going in a big curve around their pursuer. Which meant the man should've been able to catch up to him. Especially considering the need for Dare to weave between spawn points.

But in spite of his reckless chase and best efforts, the Duelist never got closer than ten yards. Dare repositioned Zuri so she could look over his shoulder and shout a warning if the man tried to throw a weapon, just in case, but otherwise he began to calm down as he passed the closest point of pursuit and began gaining ground on the mugger again.

"I think we're good," he told his lover. "Back to the road."

Collisa

From behind came a furious, defeated shout, and Dare glanced back to find that the Duelist had given up his and turned back to engage the monsters chasing him, dancing around to keep from being surrounded as he cut them down.

Looked like he'd given up the chase.

Dare breathed a sigh of relief and slowed to a trot, making his way back to the road and continuing along it. Although even though he'd relaxed a bit, he noticed Zuri continued to keep a wary eye on the Level 26 until they were out of sight of him.

Thankfully, after that close call there were no more incidents the rest of the way to Driftwain.

They began to encounter travelers the closer they got to the town, mostly farmers pulling carts or driving oxen-pulled wagons full of produce, or craftsmen bearing packs or carts full of trade goods. Dare was cautious around all of them, in case some were bandits in disguise, although he was reassured that none showed a level higher than 10.

Unless there was an ability to change what level you were shown as, they were probably good.

The travelers all seemed more than a little surprised to see him running past at what for them would be a sprint, with a pack on his back and a goblin in his arms. And even more surprised when he left them in the dust without collapsing in exhaustion.

Dare called out warnings to all of them about the Duelist, hoping he wasn't leading the bandit right to innocent people. Then again, they were getting close enough to Driftwain now that these people should hopefully okay.

Especially once he reached the guards and warned them of the Duelist's activities on the road.

He and Zuri both breathed a sigh of relief when the walls of the town came into view. He'd been warned it was small, and he wasn't disappointed; it had fifty homes and buildings at most, maybe a few hundred people total not counting travelers and merchants.

There was a small line of people lined up at the gate waiting to be passed through, with two guards inspecting goods and apparently issuing some sort of entry tax. Dare was surprised to see that they were only Level 20; that seemed awfully low for even a small town like this, especially since he'd just run into a Level 26.

Of course, he was only Level 12 so what did he know?

He bypassed the line and headed straight to the armed and armored man and woman at the gate to give his warning, only to be stopped by a sharp glare from the woman. "Back of the line!" she barked.

"I need to warn you about-" Dare started.

"*Back of the line!*"

He gave up and took his place; it was a short line anyway, and if someone happened to get robbed in the couple minutes he had to wait, that would be on this guard's head.

After squabbling briefly about fees for trade goods with a farmer she seemed to know, the guard finally waved the last person in front of Dare through and motioned him forward.

He set Zuri down and stepped up to her. "I need-"

"State all trade goods," she interrupted in a bored tone. "And there's a traveling tax for slaves, based on estimated value. Goblins usually get taxed at 1 to 2 silver." She looked Zuri over with faint distaste. "She's a fertile breeder, attractive by the standards of her kind. 2 silver."

"Zuri's not a slave," Dare protested.

The other guard, leaning casually against the gate flipping and catching a knife to amuse himself, snorted at that. "As if we haven't heard that from half the rascals that pass through this gate hoping to avoid a tax."

The woman ignored her partner. "If that's true, you need to have an official document from a region or kingdom capitol to that effect. Do you?"

Dare shook his head and reluctantly reached into the coin purse on his belt, in which he only kept a few silver to make him seem poorer and discourage thieves, and fished out two. "I need to warn-"

"State all trade goods," the woman said doggedly, snatching the coins from him. She marked something on a ledger, then put the coins through the slot in the lid of a sturdy chest chained to the wall just inside the gate. Same as the other taxes she'd collected.

"I only have my camping gear, weapons, and armor," Dare said, giving up. "I might sell some of it if I can find better."

"Personal sales or sales under ten silver do not apply," the guard said. She smirked at his gear. "You're more than fine." She took another look at his face, opened her mouth with a slight smile as if to add something, then quickly looked away, cheeks turning pink.

"Can I give my warning now?" Dare asked. He wasn't interrupted again so he hurriedly continued. "About two hours-" He cut off, remembering his speed and endurance, and did some quick math. "That is, six hours out from town I was attacked by a Level 26 Duelist trying to rob me."

"Was it two or six, lad?" the other guard snapped.

"I travel fast . . . I was estimating time at a walk."

The woman ignored the exchange, spitting off to one side in disgust. "Duelist. Just a prettied up Rogue, you ask me. It's usually picked by nobles wanting to beat on commoners in a duel with rules that favor their class, or lowlifes who want to prey on others but also want to be able to stand against enemies in a head to head fight. Like highwaymen."

Phoenix

Her eyes narrowed as she looked Dare up and down. "But how do you know that's what he was? He wouldn't be stupid enough to tell you."

Shit. His mind raced for the best response. "He kind of was," he answered as confidently as he could. "I recognized his choice of sword and dagger as one that Duelists favor and guessed that's what he was. And since he was 14 levels above me he wasn't afraid to admit it."

He didn't actually know if Duelists favored that weapon combination, but if the guardswoman called him out on it he could always say it was different where he was from. Or better yet, play the ignorant yokel act.

After all, she seemed happy to cast him in that role.

But the woman just grimaced and shook her head. "Thank you for the alert, citizen. We'll pass it along and make sure this menace is dealt with. We can't have scum going after innocents on the road, disrupting travel and trade."

Dare glanced at the woman's stats again with his Eye. "Just out of curiosity, how do you usually deal with a higher level enemy?"

The guard leaning against the open gate straightened with a scowl. "You hear that, Tandri? Bumpkin wants to be clever about insulting our level."

The woman, Tandri apparently, nodded with a scowl of her own. "You're lucky the Commander just gave us a talking to about cracking skulls."

Zuri hid behind Dare at the guards' tones, and he quickly raised his hands. "I didn't mean to insult you," he said. "Like your friend said, I'm from a small village and don't know much about the world." The bluff woman's expression didn't change, and he tried the same smile that had seemed to work so well on the women of Lone Ox. "I'd be grateful for any help you're willing to give me."

Collisa

Tandri spat off to the side again. "We're here to keep the peace and stamp out crime, so in training they level us up just enough to do the job in order to save on expenses."

"Like with everything else," her friend grumbled. "Cutting corners on lodging, food, ale rations, what have you."

She ignored him and kept going. "You may have noticed, most people don't bother leveling up very high. We can solve pretty much any problem we run into in town." She waved vaguely over his shoulder. "As for more dangerous threats, we keep a small group of retired adventurers on retainer to deal with them."

"For ten times our pay," the guardsman said. "And most of the time they're not needed so they just sit around drinking, gambling, and womanizing." He shook his head and leaned back against the wall. "Lucky bastards."

Tandri shot her partner a disgusted look, then turned back to Dare. "Be on your way, citizen. And don't cause trouble or you'll see that even Level 20s can dish out a beating."

Of course they could, especially to someone his level. "Thank you," he said, inclining his head. Still carrying Zuri, he quickly ducked through the gate into the town.

Ten feet in he realized he hadn't asked about translation stones and bit back a curse. Oh well, he shouldn't have trouble finding them by asking around among the vendors.

Compared to cities on Earth, Driftwain was cramped, filthy, poorly planned and built, and utterly lacking in amenities. But even though it was roughly ten times larger than Lone Ox it was surprisingly similar to the village, aside from being more crowded and smelling much worse.

And having a market district in the center of the town, although a small one.

The houses were mostly thatched, with stone walls changing to wooden walls halfway up. He wasn't sure of the purpose of that construction, but he thought he'd seen it before. The larger buildings were mostly brick with slate roofs, and looked much neater and in better repair.

Dare didn't see any sign of beggars or obvious unsavory sorts as he made his way towards the market, and the people he passed all seemed clean and relatively prosperous. If for the most part humbly dressed in rustic garb, with the worn features of those who'd spent their lives doing hard labor to survive. A few were dressed in finer clothes, and one or two wore suits and fancy dresses.

He noticed most of the women shooting him second or even third looks, and a few offered him cheerful greetings or even approached to talk to him. The good looks his unseen benefactor had given him seemed to be working in his favor, and he wondered if he might be able to pick up a beauty to spend the night with.

An unmarried one, this time.

Of course, he'd have to explain it to Zuri and see if she minded. His unseen benefactor had told him harems were common here and most women were cool with it, and his tiny lover had practically pushed him towards that slime girl before they left Lone Ox.

Of course, getting off with a slime girl and a one night stand with some random woman who probably wouldn't be pleased to have Zuri tagging along were two different things.

Well, he'd play it by ear. And if he was able to find a translation stone and finally communicate with Zuri he'd probably spend the whole night talking to her, making it a moot point.

The market seemed to be mostly filled with farmers, so of course the majority of the wares were produce and livestock. Dare's heart sank at first when he saw that, at least until he made his way to the other side of the square and saw a decent-sized section for adventurers, with merchants eager to purchase monster loot and sell gear, reagents, and other useful and necessary items.

Collisa

Dare immediately made a beeline for a blades merchant, which boasted a surprising variety of bladed weapons with quality ranging from Trash to Journeyman.

The quality tier list was available in the command screens and went, from worst to best: Trash, Poor, Decent, Good, Journeyman, Exceptional, Master, and Fabled. There was a significant bump in stats for each tier, along with a bump in difficulty to craft or rarity to find from drops.

Apparently everything Exceptional and above could even have item bonuses, which could do things like buff the wielder or have added effects. They were different from enchantments, which could be placed on anything, and generally weren't as powerful. Just little stat perks and the occasional passive or active ability for the better ones.

None of these weapons had item bonuses, though.

After perusing the prices Dare purchased three Decent quality Level 12 knives. It took some fierce haggling to get the price down to something he was comfortable with, ensuring that he'd still be able to purchase at least a Decent bow and some arrows. Although he had to toss in his remaining stone knives for free and his Utility Knife for 1 silver to seal the deal.

But ultimately he came away with a weapon that would help Zuri level, and two for himself that would let him survive and prevail a bit better when enemies came into melee range.

Satisfied, he started for the bowyer. Only to have his tiny lover tug on his hand to stop him.

He looked down at her in confusion as she led him to a secluded space, then reached a small hand under his tunic. At first he thought she was getting frisky in an inappropriate location, but then he realized she was going for her coin pouch.

She dug in it and produced the money needed to pay for her

Phoenix

knife, then two more silver, he presumed for her tax to get into the city. She held the money out to him with the sort of flat adamant look that suggested she'd stand there all day if he didn't take it.

Dare didn't even hesitate to take the coins and put them in his pouch; he was happy to buy her gifts, but an important part of freedom was independence, and an important part of that was earning your own money and paying for your own things.

She was already doing the former, and he could see what a big milestone it was for her to be able to do the latter.

Taking her hand, he once again headed for the bowyer.

It had some good specimens, Good or Journeyman quality, but expensive, and some monster loot ones ranging from Trash to Decent. Most were in the 5-15 level range, with nothing crafted higher than that. The types available were short bow, hunting bow, long bow, recurve bow, and light and heavy crossbow.

Dare was interested to learn a bit more about the types of bow. The ones he could craft were hunting bows, unsurprisingly, somewhere between a short bow and a long bow in size and draw weight, with decent range and damage. They could pierce the hide of most game animals but weren't ideally suited for armored enemies or those with damage reduction abilities, and wasn't affected by Stealth.

Short bows were fast and had a short range and light draw weight, but their damage was proportionally worse than the others. They had a bonus to Stealth damage and the fewest penalties to detection when carried by a Stealthed person.

Long bows were the slowest and had the heaviest draw weight, but the highest range and proportionally the most damage. However, they got large penalties to Stealth detection and couldn't be used from horseback.

Recurve bows looked best across the board, with good speed and draw weight, good range and damage, small penalties to Stealth detection, and most of all extra damage when used from horseback. The biggest drawback, unless you were going for one of the specific benefits of a different bow, was that they were prohibitively expensive due to the extreme difficulty in crafting, with a bigger time investment and more materials.

Dare didn't have much interest in crossbows, but he noted that the light ones had moderate range and damage, the heavy ones had excellent range and damage, even compared to a longbow, and they got fewer damage reduction penalties against armored enemies. They also had the best accuracy of any of the ranged weapons, and gaining proficiency in their ability apparently went very quickly, so they were easy to learn.

The drawbacks were that they were slow as balls to reload and fire, had extreme Stealth penalties, and had a racial bonus for dwarves. Which wasn't really a drawback, just a kick in the nuts for other races.

Dare was debating between a Good quality longbow for a decent price, but it was Level 11 and he'd quickly outgrow it, or a Decent quality Level 14 recurve bow that was going to break the bank. He wasn't sure he wanted to invest that much on a weapon when he was going to level quickly and make it obsolete within a weeks.

But they were the best options.

He was pondering the choice when his eyes snagged on a dusty short bow in the corner. The details for it showed surprising stats, and he pointed. "Can I take a look at that?"

The vendor grimaced as he retrieved the weapon. "Ah, the albatross." He brushed it off with a cloth and proffered it.

Dare inspected it closely. It was Level 20, Exceptional quality and had amazingly good stats compared to other ranged weapons offered in that level range. Even damage, considering a short bow's usual weakness in that area.

Phoenix

Best of all, it had item bonuses: +5 agility, and an extra 10% shadow damage while Stealthed. The Stealth one wouldn't be much use, but the agility was nice.

In fact, Dare couldn't see any drawback aside from that its durability was in the red, which not only severely reduced its stats but also increased its chances to break on use to almost certain.

Still, items could be repaired, and this would be an extremely valuable weapon if it was. Dare frowned; was there something he wasn't seeing? "Why an albatross?"

The man grimaced. "No one in Driftwain has a crafting level high enough to repair it, and without that it's basically trash. Nobody wants to buy it for use, and it's too much bother to go looking for a crafter, which would probably mean traveling all the way to Kov, just to repair it for resale."

Interesting. Dare's bow crafting ability let him repair bows, and as far as he could see there were no penalties to it. One of the benefits of choosing a hybrid ranged/survival class.

Which meant he could buy this thing cheap, use it himself until he out-leveled it, then sell it at a profit. Zero downside.

"It might be useful in the future," he mused, setting the weapon down. "How much for your albatross?"

The vendor snorted. "Fifty silver."

Ouch. So that was the price jump for even a nearly broken Level 20 Exceptional quality short bow that the vendor was eager to unload. Of course, he had to keep haggling in mind; the first ask was always high.

"That seems . . . excessively high," he said carefully.

"For an Exceptional quality Level 20 weapon?" the burly vendor said incredulously. "It's a steal!"

"From what you've told me, someone stealing it is probably the only way it stops collecting dust in your stall," Dare countered wryly. "I could go 20."

"Then you can go." The man pulled the bow back to his side of the table. "I'll eventually get to Kov, or a higher level crafter will come by and I can hire their services. And there's no cost to sit on it until then."

The man didn't seem particularly desperate to sell, and Dare backpedaled a bit. "There must be a reasonable price somewhere in between we can both agree on."

"I offered you a reasonable price." The burly man glowered at him suspiciously. "You seriously want a bow 8 levels higher than you just to use in the future? *You'll* be sitting on it for years before you reach 20."

More like months, at most. Weeks, more likely, with proper gear for himself and Zuri. "Dress for the job you want," Dare replied glibly.

"What the hell's that supposed to mean?" The vendor glanced down at his clothes, as if he thought he was being insulted.

"It means take action now to reach the future you desire." Dare tapped the table in front of the short bow. "I'll eventually be able to use this, and it'll help me a lot when I can. I'm willing to make that investment."

The vendor sighed. "35 silver," he said grudgingly. "But only because I have a soft spot for adventurers and like your ambition." He glowered. "And 35 is as low as I go."

Dare frowned. He didn't have anything near that. It would break the bank even if he borrowed from Zuri, which he didn't want to do.

On the other hand, he and Zuri could stay here and farm money until he could afford it, and get some levels in the process. That would get him closer to being able to use the weapon anyway.

Phoenix

"I'll take the Level 11 bow," he said, decided. It was still a huge upgrade over his current weapon, and would help them in the moment. "How much you going to fleece me if I use it for a week or so, then bring it back repaired to top durability and sell it back."

The vendor looked miffed at his phrasing. "Top durability means newly made," he growled. "Even with ideal repairs the overall durability goes down each time. Nothing lasts forever."

"But you'd buy it back for a fair price?"

"All my prices are fair, but bear in mind I have to make a living." The burly man retrieved the weapon. "I never buy for as high as I sell."

Fair enough. He could consider it like renting.

Dare managed to haggle the price on the longbow down to 7 silver, 35 copper. In spite of the fierce haggling the vendor seemed satisfied when they shook hands, and Dare was excited to get back out and try his new weapons after they finished their business here.

While he was at the bowyer's he also bought thirty arrows. It turned out that the basic ones he could craft did shit damage compared to the ones on offer; which told him he either needed to start putting ability points in crafting to make better items, at least arrows if not bows and leather armor.

That would cost a lot of points, though, which seemed like a waste when he could buy the items, even if they came at a steep cost.

Still, knowing how bad his crafted arrows were gave him the sinking feeling that he should probably check a leather armor vendor, too, and see just how bad the armor he'd crafted for himself was.

Sure enough, a quick perusal confirmed his fears that the stuff he could craft without investing any ability points was all complete shit. Even the cheapest leather armor of his level, the Trash and Poor quality stuff, was vastly superior to what he was wearing.

He left the stall behind without making a purchase, since at the moment he was going with the play style of putting points in defensive abilities and relying on his speed; if he wasn't getting hit he didn't need to worry about armor.

That would change when he could afford things, and he was high enough level and his leveling had slowed enough that buying a set of gear could last him for months instead of weeks or even days.

He and Zuri visited a clothing vendor next. Not just because he wanted to see if they could find anything to help her, but because if he was shitting on his crafted gear, might as well see if the *clothes* he made were somehow inferior too.

As it turned out yes, yes they were.

Mostly the quality difference was in things like appearance, softness, durability, and other normal consideration for clothes. But some of the highest quality shoes also offered small travel perks, like a small decrease in stamina usage while moving over long distances, less chance to alert nearby enemies with noise, and even a 1% bump to movement speed.

Dare resolved to buy the best pair of shoes he could afford as soon as he had more money. The effects might've seemed small for the price, but he knew from experience that all the small advantages in games added up to make a difference.

Of course he'd need to buy the best weapons and armor before he could worry about nice shoes: the stat gains on those would be much more significant. He should also look into enchanting his weapons and armor, and whether crafters could improve them in any other ways.

But that was a consideration for the future, when wouldn't be replacing his carefully optimized gear every month. At the moment he'd be content to do what he could.

The cloth armor the vendor had on offer had no bonuses, so it wouldn't really help Zuri, whose play style also revolved around not getting hit. Although Dare, with a bit of embarrassment, did ask about undergarments for her, wanting to replace the literal rags she wore under his crafted clothes.

Zuri didn't seem embarrassed when the vendor brought out a few bras and panties and surreptitiously displayed them for her perusal. She selected the cheapest ones, which were plain, undyed, coarsely woven, and baggy.

Before the vendor could begin haggling on them Dare picked out a cuter pink set with lacy frills, made of much softer and more comfortable fabric. "These ones," he said, ignoring his tiny lover's protests in Goblin.

The vendor's lip curled. "Dressing up your pukeskin pleasure slave?"

Dare flushed, more in anger than embarrassment. "Take a silver off the final price for insulting my friend."

The man folded his arms. "I don't think I will."

Fine. "Come on Zuri, we'll find you something better than this trash somewhere else." He took her hand and walked off.

Zuri was quiet as they walked, looking a bit bothered. Not so much disappointed as . . . he wasn't sure. But to his relief after they'd gone a bit farther she brightened and rushed over to a different stall, showing him a bolt of plain but soft cloth.

She pointed at it, then pantomimed cutting and sewing. "Zuri make," she said. She blushed slightly and pointed at his crotch. "Make Dare, yes."

Dare blinked. He hadn't realized she had any crafting abilities. Then again, a lot of people picked Tailoring as a subclass, especially those too poor to clothe themselves any other way; apparently Tailoring let you make crude outfits out of leaves and grass if there was nothing better on offer, and every possible material up from that.

He hadn't considered underwear for himself as well, but he couldn't deny that it would be nice. Actually more than nice; chafing against even soft fur or leather while running 25 miles an hour was no joke.

And just as if not even more importantly, it would be nice to have proper socks.

He picked out the cloth and some sewing supplies, and with a bit of haggling got a decent price for it all. Then, pleased, he patted Zuri on the shoulder. "One last stop," he said. "Translation stones. Talk stones."

She brightened eagerly. "Zuri talk Dare?"

"Soon, hopefully." Taking his tiny lover's hand, he set off to see if anyone in Driftwain was selling the more niche item.

Phoenix

Chapter Fourteen
Catching Up

It took almost two hours of looking around, talking to people and pursuing possible leads all over town, before Dare was pointed to a merchant in the market square who dealt in sundry goods.

Frustratingly, he'd walked past the man's small table under a simple awning several times in his search, and nobody had pointed to him as a possibility.

Especially since the moment Dare asked about a translation stone, the man brightened eagerly and rummaged through a box of cheap-looking brass and tin jewelry, finally digging out a steel chain just like the one Durrand had worn, with a similar sized piece of plain quartz mounted on it.

Except this stone had a hideous crack lined with darker stone running almost all the way through it, nearly splitting it in two.

"Amazing things, translation stones," the vendor said, twirling the flawed gem. "You know the Enchanter has to get the knowledge about languages from somewhere? Most Enchanters who make translation stones spend their entire lives learning other languages and dialects and perfecting their skills with them. The best ones even get a whole team of linguists together and pool all that knowledge into every stone. They use precious gems like diamonds for their hardness and durability so their stones last practically forever, and charge large amounts of gold for every one."

He flicked the large quartz. "Our man up in Kov is no slouch, but of course he's not at that level. Which is why his stones are relatively cheap."

That was really interesting to hear. And made Dare decide he had zero interest in ever becoming an Enchanter, or at least one who made translation stones; he'd already confirmed he sucked at learning other languages.

"Speaking of cheap," he said casually. "That's got to be the ugliest piece of quartz I've ever seen." He honestly didn't care, and doubted Zuri would either. But haggling was all about driving down the price.

The vendor grimaced but didn't dispute the claim. "I know, that's why its last owner sold it once she'd got the one she custom ordered." He twirled the stone on its steel chain. "Still, people who've got shit to do aren't going to be buying one of these for its looks. And you look like a man who's got shit to do. You want the only functioning translation stone available for sale in Driftwain, you can have it for twenty silver."

"Ten," Dare immediately countered.

The man behind the stall flushed irritably. "If you weren't so obviously ignorant of these stones I'd tell you to get lost just for insulting me with that offer."

"The Mayor of Lone Ox said he got his for fourteen silver," Dare argued. "And his didn't look like a rock he'd just pulled out of his shoe."

"Good for the worthy Mayor," the vendor said sarcastically. "*This* one cost me money to purchase, and I need to make a living. Also supply and demand says I can pick my price. Twenty."

"From what I've heard, people who actually want one of these order it custom. Even the woman you bought it from. I bet that thing's been sitting on your table for months if not longer, gathering dust." Dare didn't improve his initial offer; he had the feeling the man was just as eager to sell the enchanted item as he was to buy it.

The vendor ground his teeth. "Eighteen, if you're going to be a dick about it."

Phoenix

"You always insult your customers for asking a reasonable price for inferior goods?" Dare asked. "I might go up to eleven, just in the spirit of being reasonable."

The man slammed his hand on the table, making Zuri jump and press herself nervously against Dare's leg. "You yourself said your friend bought his for fourteen!"

"Are you dropping your offer to fourteen?" Dare asked, quickly jumping on it.

"Hell n-" the man started to snap, them grimaced. "Fourteen," he agreed grudgingly.

Wow, the man really was eager to sell. "Twelve," Dare said.

"You-" The vendor took a deep breath. "I was reasonable with fourteen. Buy it for that or look elsewhere."

"Take a good long look at the stone," Dare said. "Think about how long it's been sitting on your table, making your other wares look like trash. I'll give you thirteen, it's up to you whether you want to tell me to get lost."

The man behind the table glared for almost fifteen seconds in silence, breathing through his nose. Then his shoulders slumped and he sighed. "Thirteen silver. But only because this thing is so damn ugly." He held out one hand with the necklace, and the other in a silent request for payment.

Dare hesitated. "You mind if I see if it works first? No offense to you, but it's an easy test and I want to be sure."

The man looked even more irritated, but it was a reasonable request so he grudgingly agreed. Although he watched like a hawk as Dare looped the necklace's chain twice so it wouldn't hang down to Zuri's belly button.

It was obvious the vendor expected him to try to run off with his wares, and he'd need to call the guards.

Collisa

Dare ignored the glares as he slowly, almost tentatively, crouched and placed the necklace around her neck. He could admit he was feeling a lot of nervous anticipation for this moment.

He wanted to talk to Zuri so much, but he was also a bit worried about how their relationship could change when they could actually speak to each other. Would a friendship and growing love that had been forged through their experiences thrive, or worst case even survive, when they were actually able to get a better idea of who their lover was and what they really thought about things?

He trusted it would, but there was still that bit of nervousness. And from the way his gentle lover trembled as he settled the stone against her chest, yellow eyes wide and eager smile almost a grimace, he thought she felt the same.

Dare gently put his hands on her shoulders. "Can you understand me, Zuri?" he murmured.

Her entire face lit up with joy, and with a happy cry she threw her arms around his neck. "Yes! Thank the ancestors, primal spirits, and Nature itself, yes!" She nuzzled his neck, laughing. "I was so sick of grunting and pointing like an orc raised by wolves."

He could feel her tears on his skin as she continued in a thick voice. "And I've wanted to really talk to you for so long . . . there's so much I've wanted to tell you. So many questions. So much I've been feeling for you, my mate."

"I've felt the same." Dare was vaguely aware of the vendor glaring at them in disgust, and he absently counted out thirteen silver with his fingers and tossed them onto the table full of wares as he stroked Zuri's back.

The vendor wasn't the only one looking, unfortunately; others in the market were beginning to stop to stare, and even pointing and making disparaging comments.

Zuri became aware of the attention, and it hurt Dare to see the way she hunched her shoulders, looking nervous as she pulled away. "This isn't the best place for this, is it?" she asked quietly, tugging on his hand and leading him towards a secluded park surrounded by buildings they'd passed earlier. "I don't want to get you in trouble for showing affection to a lowly goblin."

"Hey, none of that," he said firmly. "You're amazing, and I'd get into any trouble I had to for your sake."

She smiled timidly at that, but shook her head. "Still, we should continue this in private." Her cheeks flushed a darker green. "Besides, we have a lot to say to one another that I don't want a bunch of strange humans lurking around listening in on."

Dare stared at his tiny lover in amazement as they entered the park and stepped over to where passersby wouldn't see them.

Now that the excitement of discovering the stone worked was over, it was a bit of a shock to hear her using full sentences. Speaking so comfortably and naturally after all this time listening to her struggle to string words together to be understood. He knew she was very smart, but even so hearing her speak normally threw him for a loop.

And it wasn't only that, because she wasn't just speaking normally. He wasn't sure if it was a feature of the translation stones, or Zuri's actual skill at language, but she sounded . . . educated. Refined even.

"Were you a scholar before I met you?" he asked as he settled on the grass and pulled her into his lap.

His lover flushed even darker green. "In a way. My mother was a high priestess, and trained me to take her place one day. Or at least serve under her as an acolyte. And I did my best to read books when I was allowed to."

"You can read?" Dare asked, surprised; literacy was usually very rare in medieval and fantasy settings.

Collisa

It was her turn to be surprised. "Of course I can. Everyone can . . . how else would we use the ##### ######? In fact, the ############ ###### has a reading tutorial to make sure everyone has the chance to learn." She shook her head in bafflement. "That was a very odd question, my mate."

He shook his head as well, although in amazement. When put like that of course it made sense. "I just thought the information system's voice told you everything you needed to know if you couldn't read."

Zuri gave him the blank look he was very familiar with; apparently even now that they could communicate, confusion was possible. "What voice?"

That was . . . quite the revelation. Was the voice his unseen benefactor after all? Had she been there this entire time, talking to him while pretending to be the world system?

That was definitely something Dare would have to think through when he had time.

"Never mind," he said, kissing her forehead. "I'm guessing you read in Goblin?"

"That's right," his tiny lover replied. She smiled eagerly as she fingered her new translation stone. "Although this works for writing as well. So with it I can read and write all the languages the Enchanter put into it."

Wow, that made the item even more amazing, and even more of a steal at thirteen silver. Also even more of a priority to buy one for himself when he could.

Although Zuri was turning out to be even more amazing than he'd realized as well, and his opinion of her had already been high. The only way she'd know that about the translation stones was if she'd tried it before; Dare found himself again wondering, as he had so many times while trying to speak to his lover, about her past.

Phoenix

"Well it's an honor to meet an educated daughter of a high priestess," he said, bowing.

Zuri flushed, but not with embarrassment. "Don't tease me," she said quietly.

Dare looked at her in surprise. "Why would you think I'm teasing you, Zuri?"

"It took a long time to accept you letting me have my share of the money we earned hunting monsters, and you treating me as an honored mate and showering me with kindness and gifts. It still sometimes feels like you're teasing me or baiting me into a trap, even though I know you're sincere." She crossed her arms firmly. "But I won't have you bowing to me. It's too much . . . even if you don't mean it that way I can't help but feel like you're mocking me."

He hugged her closer, stroking her back. "I would never hurt you or try to make you feel bad," he said gently. "I want you to be happy."

His lover's big yellow eyes softened. "I am," she said. "As happy as I've ever been. You've been good and kind in a way I've learned not to hope for." She laughed softly. "You even pick stupid fights when people insult me."

She hesitated, some of her timidity returning. "Although I kind of wish you wouldn't . . . words can't hurt me like a lash or switch would, and I don't want you to get hurt trying to defend me from them." Her green skin flushed darker, and she added bashfully. "Although it makes me feel happy that you think I'm worthy of it."

Dare briefly pressed his lips to hers. "I'm so glad you're finally able to tell me these things, Zuri."

Instead of smiling she trembled slightly. "Actually," she whispered, blushing a deeper green, "speaking of telling you things, my name isn't Zuri."

He stared at her. "But when I told you my name, you said that was yours."

She shook her head and smiled wryly. "For goblins, it's customary for adventurers in the wild to introduce themselves by their class. I thought that's what you were doing, so I told you my class in turn." She shyly met his eyes. "My name is actually Ge'welu."

Dare chuckled ruefully. "So it was all a misunderstanding?"

"I guess so," his goblin lover said, smiling uncertainly.

"And I've been calling you Healer?" he asked, giving her an affectionate squeeze.

"That's right," Zuri, or Ge'welu he supposed, said.

"Well all right then, Ge'welu." The name felt unfamiliar on his lips, and to hide his awkwardness Dare rested his cheek on her soft black hair. "I'm glad I finally know your name. It's a pretty one."

To his surprise the timid goblin shook her head firmly. "Thank you, but I want you to keep calling me Zuri."

He tried not to frown. "But it's not your name. It's easy to switch to using your real name, and I don't want you to feel like you have to use another name just because it's what I know you by."

The tiny woman looked at him fiercely. "I want you to call me that *because* it's what you know me by." She pressed her face into his chest. "Ge'welu is the name I had in my old life. It was given to me by my parents, and so I treasure it, but at the same time it's the name I've heard from the lips of some very cruel people. Memories I'd like to forget."

She pulled back enough to smile up at him. "Zuri is the name you know me by. That's what makes me so happy to use it."

"But I don't know if I'd feel right just calling you "Healer," he protested. "You're a person, you're my beloved mate, and I care about you."

Phoenix

Her huge yellow eyes looked up at him, full of adoration. "Your name is a human word for courage, isn't it?"

Dare blinked. He didn't often think of the meaning of his name, especially since it was a nickname. "Something like that."

Zuri nodded in satisfaction. "You're proud to be called Courage. And I'm proud to be called Healer. Especially if I can heal you."

He rubbed her back, pulling her tiny body closer. "You really want me to call you Zuri?"

She mock scowled at him. "I won't answer to Ge'welu," she said as she cuddled against him contentedly.

"If you insist," he kissed her forehead. "But I still think it's a cute name."

His little lover smiled and pressed her lips to his, then giggled. "That's still such a strange thing to do," she said.

"Goblins don't kiss?" he teased, running a thumb over her soft lips.

She shook her head. "Mouths are for food." She hesitated, blushing. "Aside from when we offer it to our mate as a hole for his pleasure."

Dare laughed. "Which you do better than anyone I've ever met." He paused, then continued playfully. "Although I can show you a way my mouth can be used to pleasure you, too."

He'd been holding off on going down on Zuri because for one thing, she was usually so quick to either jump on his cock or take him in her mouth that he hadn't had the chance, and for another she'd been so nonplussed by kissing that he wasn't sure how she'd respond to burying his head between her legs.

And he meant holding off; after almost a week of smelling her heady arousal, so dizzyingly full of pheromones, the need to finally taste her was driving him to distraction.

Zuri blushed deeper and grinned. "Want to do it now?"

Dare wryly looked around the small park, with the path to the street in full view. "Maybe if we can find someplace more private." He grinned. "What do you think? I'd be happy to buy a room in an inn and treat you to a proper meal, then we can play on a proper bed. Or we could head out into the wilds and set up camp, play a bit before going back to hunting-"

"The wilds!" she practically shouted, grabbing his hand and tugging eagerly. "We've finished our business here, right?"

"Unless there was anything else you wanted."

She patted her dagger and the bolt of cloth sticking up from his pack. Then she gave him another loving look. "I have everything I want," she said shyly.

On impulse Dare kissed her, then pulled her close. She was just unbelievably cute. "I love you, Zuri."

Zuri stiffened as if she'd been struck by lightning. "Like lifelong mate feelings?" she whispered, trembling.

He hesitated; this seemed very important to her, and he wasn't about to treat talk of lifetime commitments casually. "I'm getting there," he said, leaning down to kiss her neck.

"Oh." She pressed her cheek to his. "I . . . I feel the same way. I would be very happy to be your mate for life, and give you many children."

"Once we're more situated with a house and the gold to see to their future, I'd like that too," he said. He gently picked her up, motioning. "So, ready to go?"

His tiny lover beamed. "Ready!" She pointed at the street leading to the gate. "To adventure and hunting monsters. Zoom!"

Dare couldn't help but laugh as he broke into a trot. "Zoom!" he agreed.

Phoenix

She gave him a curious look as they made their way towards the gate. "What does that mean, anyway? The translation stone doesn't give me anything."

"It means zoom." He smiled at her confusion. "It's an onomatopoeia for a sound the carts from my home make as they quickly pass by you."

"Ah, that fits." Zuri buried her face in his neck. "I've been wanting to say this to you for a long time, but now's a good time."

"That you love me?" Dare teased.

She laughed a bit shyly. "That too. But what I've wanted to say is that I think you're a very smart man, a genius even, given how you figured out a way for me to level with you and so many other things. But at the same time some of the things you say and do are very strange. I'm completely baffled by them."

"Probably because I come from another place," he said. "I hope you can live with my strangeness, because now that we can communicate you'll probably be noticing a lot more of it."

Zuri snickered. "Now that you can actually explain it all, I think that'll be fun. But when you were just grunting and gesturing and having me try strange things like sleeping four hours at a time for no apparent reason, I thought you were insane."

Dare joined her laughter and gave her a loving squeeze. "I suppose now's a good time to say that I've thought you were very smart from the first, too. I think that's why we were able to communicate so well without spending days or weeks teaching each other our languages."

She blushed in pleasure at the compliment. "Maybe," she said. She grimaced and fingered her necklace. "But I never want to have to talk to each other like that again. It's a huge pain in the ass."

"Seriously." He nodded at the guards as he and his lover left Driftwain behind, and they nodded back curtly as he started down the road headed north.

To new places they hadn't explored, and new adventures.

* * * * *

It took a half hour or so of running along the road to find monster spawns points around their level.

Dare found a good spot by a stream to set up camp, and was all ready make good on his promise to pleasure Zuri right then and there. But she insisted that they stick to leveling while there was daylight and save the fun for dark.

"Glad you're here to keep me on task," he joked, ruffling her hair.

She looked a bit miffed as she worked to straighten it. "You're obviously determined to level quickly, and honestly you're leveling faster than I thought was even possible. Especially while making sure I keep pace with you."

Dare chuckled and hefted his bow. "Well it's about to get even better." He hesitated. "Especially if you'll finally tell me why the hell you haven't been accepting my party invites so we can evenly share experience."

Zuri looked away, equal parts embarrassed and ashamed. "I know. Once I figured out what you were doing with experience, I realized that I was slowing you down by making you wait for me to do a third of the damage to every monster."

"Is there something I don't know about the party system?" he asked.

She was quiet for what felt like a long time. "It's just that the party leader has access to a lot of information about party members. And party members get some information about the leader and other party members as well. It's a tremendous display of trust."

Dare chuckled and lifted her into his arms, kissing her fondly

Phoenix

while playfully rubbing her small ass. "We're mates. I'd say that's a pretty serious display of trust too." She didn't smile back, and he sobered. "Zuri, I trust you completely. With my life . . . I have many times while we've been together. And I hope you know that you can trust me too. I love you."

His tiny lover buried her face in his shoulder and began to sob. "It's just when you told Durrand that I was free, I thought it was because you didn't understand the truth. I still don't know that, actually."

"Wait, what?" he asked incredulously. "Of course you're free. I've considered you my free and equal companion from the first."

"And I appreciate it, but am I really free?" She looked up and briefly met his gaze, big yellow eyes shining with tears. "When I join your party, you'll see that my official status in Haraldar is "Slave." She buried her face in his chest again. "I'm a slave, Dare. You might've thought that just because my master discarded me, that means I'm free. But I'm not. I can't be free unless the paperwork is done in a region or kingdom capitol. At best I'm your slave now, thanks to adventurer loot rules and possession is 10/10s of the law. Although you might have to contest your claim on me if my master ever tried to get me back."

Zuri paused with a hiccup, then continued in a tiny voice. "Now that you know that, is everything going to change between us? Will you stop being so nice to me and start treating me like a slave?"

Dare's heart broke for his lover. Was that something she'd feared all this time? "Zuri," he said gently, "as far as I'm concerned, you could never be a slave because slavery is wrong and nobody should have to live like that. I don't give a damn what some status text says."

She looked up slowly, big eyes hopeful. "Really?"

"On my life, Zuri," he said solemnly. "I'd do everything I could to make you happy no matter what your status was or circumstances are. I love you. And as soon as I can figure out how, I'll get you those papers from a capitol. Because you don't deserve to live in fear like this. You deserve everything good in the world, and I want to give it to you."

He gently stroked her hair. "Do you honestly think, after all the time we've spent together, that I'd suddenly turn on a dime and start treating you so horribly?"

"No," she said quickly, tone sincere. "But I was still afraid. This world is cruel and has no mercy, and I've spent my life learning to take no risks and trust nothing." She looked up at him, tears streaming down her cheeks. "Please don't be mad at me."

Dare kissed her soft hair, then her forehead, then lifted her chin and pressed his lips softly to hers; they trembled against his. "I'm not. I understand why you did what you did. But I promise that I'll never betray your trust, and I'll do everything I can to protect you from the cruelty of the world."

Zuri stared at him for a very long time, searching his eyes. Then she sucked in a sharp breath. "All right. Invite me."

He grinned as a thought struck him. "I've got a better idea. You invite me."

He couldn't believe he hadn't thought of that before, although he supposed there was no reason he would've. But if she was having trust problems, and justifiably given her past, then this was a good solution.

The timid goblin's eyes widened in shock. "You'd trust me with that?"

"I trust you with my life, Zuri." Dare kissed her again. "I trust you with my heart. I trust you with everything."

Her eyes filled with new tears, and she kissed him tenderly. "I don't deserve you," she murmured. "I keep on thinking one day you're going to see how worthless I really am and what a mistake you made being so kind to a lowly goblin."

He gently but firmly cupped her cheek with his free hand. "Zuri, I want you to listen to me very carefully." He waited until she nodded. "I don't care what anyone else says about you or other goblins. I don't care what they think. I've lived with you, I've loved you, and I see exactly how much worth you have."

Zuri sucked in a sharp breath as he gently dried her tears with his thumb. "You're beautiful, you're kind, and you're loving. And I'm honored that you think I'm worthy to be your mate and have your love. And when we have children, whether they're goblin, hobgoblin, or human, I'll love them equally and be filled with joy to be their father."

She hiccuped a shy little laugh. "I told you that you think and say such strange things sometimes. Things that just aren't thought or done here in Heraldar." She kissed his hand, then leaned in and kissed his lips again. "But wonderful things."

Dare smiled. "Invite me, Zuri. We've got better gear, we've got monsters in front of us. Let's be a party and really start leveling."

The timid goblin looked at him thoughtfully. "No." At his look of surprised disappointment she grinned impishly, showing more of the bold lover he'd given his heart to. "You need to know how the party mechanics work, and being the leader is the best way. That way you can put that genius to work figuring out the best way to use it, too."

She wiggled out of his arms and lay down on the grass, spreading her legs suggestively and holding out her arms in teasing invitation. "Invite me."

Dare smiled broadly as he stared up her tunic, admiring her long, slender legs. "After," he said with a grin. "There's something I want to do first."

"Oh?" She hiked up the hem and wiggled her hips teasingly.

Collisa

"Dare mate Zuri?"

He felt his cock lurch at the invitation, translated even though none had been needed, and dropped down between her legs. "Soon," he murmured with a grin. "After I taste you."

Grinning at her confused stare, he gently picked up her tiny, slender foot, pulled off her shoe, and began kissing his way up it, enjoying the silky feel of her soft, lotion-slick skin.

Zuri shivered at his ministrations. "Dare?" she asked, a bit breathlessly.

He paused and grinned up at her. "Want me to stop?"

"You're so strange sometimes, but spirits, no." With a shy giggle she ran her fingers through his hair, then pushed his head back down to her ankle.

Dare continued to kiss his way upwards, at the same time sliding his hands up her sexy little legs, pushing her tunic up around her waist and untying her loincloth to spread out beneath her small, round ass. Then he began running his hands up and down over the soft, lotion-slick skin of her calves and thighs as he continued to shower her with loving kisses, up to her knee now.

A few times Zuri tried to catch one of his hands and guide it between her legs, but he always pulled it away with a teasing smile and kept his slow but steady progress.

In spite of her eagerness for him to hurry, his efforts were definitely doing something for her; she was panting softly, legs trembling and pushing against his hands and lips. And while he kept his focus on his work, he wasn't blind to the fact that her delicate petals were flowing with her nectar, running down to dampen the cloth beneath her.

Like always, the scent of her sex tantalized him. Even in open air with a slight breeze, he couldn't help but breathe deeper to savor it. He kissed his way up past her knees and began alternating between

Phoenix

her inner thighs, moving quicker now in his eagerness to reach the source of that heady fragrance.

Even so, he took his time kissing around her tiny pink pussy, to either side of her lips and across her soft hairless mound. Zuri moaned and whimpered with need, shifting her hips this way and that, and her delicate folds brushed his cheek, coating it with her juices.

Dare broke away and smiled up at her. "You want me to get on with it?"

She stared down at him across her body, eyes slightly glassy. "You're going to kiss my pussy the way you kiss my lips, right?" she panted.

"I am." He grinned wider. "Unless you think it's too strange."

"No!" she squealed, lifting her hips towards his face. "I don't care if it's strange, please, please do!"

Grinning impishly, he winked at her and lowered his head to kiss her full on her nether lips, tasting her. Then he gave her a long, slow lick from bottom to top, finally pressing his tongue hard against the little pearl peeking out from beneath its hood.

Zuri went nuts, grabbing his head and shoving him harder against her as her hips bucked wildly. Her ecstatic whimpering sounds spurred him on in his efforts.

Dare began to lick her eagerly, filling his mouth with her sweet nectar and savoring it before swallowing; if the smell was enough to turn his head the taste was like fireworks going off in it, her tantalizing feminine musk stirring something primal in him.

It had a sour taste almost like lemons, slightly pungent, and made his heart pound and breath come in panting gasps as his cock throbbed against his pants, as hard as he'd ever felt it.

"God you taste incredible," he mumbled. The tiny goblin

moaned and looked down at him, sharp features enraptured.

Probing her soft pink folds with his lips and tongue reinforced just how small her pussy was, and how much it had to stretch to accommodate him. But in spite of its size it flowed a constant stream of her arousal, so he didn't so much lap at her labia as seal his lips to them and drink.

Time and again Dare filled his mouth with his tiny lover's heavenly juices, savoring the taste before finally swallowing so he could get more. His head was in a fog, and his cock throbbed against the ground beneath him, aching for action. If he'd so much as shifted position he had a feeling he would've erupted.

As for Zuri, she seemed to be engulfed in pure pleasure.

Obviously she'd never been eaten out before, and she spent the entire time thrashing and bucking against him, tiny hands clenching clumps of his hair, making constant gasping, squeaking noises.

He wasn't sure how many times she climaxed. He knew every time it happened from the way her widespread legs clamped shut around his ears, and her honeyed walls rippled and clenched around his invading tongue. A fresh surge of her love juices flowed every time he sent her over the edge, and he redoubled his efforts to get more.

Finally Zuri squealed and shoved his head away, although the effect was more shoving her tiny body away from him. Then, yellow eyes gleaming gold in the sunlight, she spread her legs wide and opened her arms in clear invitation. Her drenched pussy gaped open in an invitation of its own.

"I need you in me," she moaned, somewhere between a plea and a command.

Dare wasted no time climbing on top of her, eager to stretch her out some more. But to his chagrin, he was so aroused from the smell and taste of her nectar that the moment his throbbing member

Phoenix

touched her lower lips, parting them in a tender kiss, he groaned and began to shoot into the entrance to her pussy.

Zuri made a displeased sound and tried to push herself onto his erupting cock, but got the angle wrong. Instead her efforts combined with the slippery juices drenching her made his rod spring free, spraying across the tunic covering her flat stomach and large breasts with powerful jets of come that seemed to go on forever.

After his orgasm finally stopped Dare properly positioned himself and and pushed inside his tiny lover. This was only his second time today so he should easily be able to fuck through his refractory period. Especially considering his excitement in this situation; once again he silently praised the gift from his unseen benefactor that his body had so much stamina.

His massive cock slowly but surely parted her glistening folds, which formed a crushingly tight ring that stretched and strained around his girth, slipping over his tip and closing around his head with the gentle pressure of a velvet lined vise.

Dare grit his teeth around an almost overpowering surge of sensation, struggling not to cry out as the pleasure spiked until it approached torment. Zuri's almost painfully tight pussy was intense enough as it was, and with his tip super sensitive he almost couldn't bear it.

Especially as her vise-like walls clamped down with an intense surge of pleasure as she again climaxed, flooding their joined crotches with her heady ambrosia.

"Harder!" she moaned through gritted teeth, entire body trembling. "I'm not made of glass . . . I'm made to be bred. Breed me."

"Oh gods, your sex talk is even sexier when I can understand you," Dare panted. He began thrusting into her eagerly, ignoring his own discomfort as he let himself be more forceful in his tiny lover.

Collisa

He couldn't get more than halfway inside her before bottoming out with a jolt of sensation along his super sensitive tip, but that half was still a lot of pleasurable length. Especially when Zuri reached down and began frantically jerking off his remaining length with both hands in frantic desperation, her already slick skin constantly being lubricated by the arousal flowing freely from her depths.

"Harder!" she squealed. "Rip me in two with that monster of yours!"

Dare groaned and bottomed out inside her again as his balls boiled. He may have just come, but he couldn't hold back with her talking like that; he'd known his lover was a little sexpot, but she was at a whole new level now that he could understand her.

"I'm coming," he gasped.

"Yes!" Zuri moaned, collapsing in her most powerful orgasm yet, limp as a rag as his cock stretched her little pussy obscenely around her squirting juices. "God yes, fill me up."

He did, his entire body tensing in jolts of pleasure like electric shocks as he released one powerful spurt after another. So much, in fact, that he was certain he felt the volume steadily pushing his cock out of her tiny pink tunnel.

Finally he collapsed beside her, rolling them around until she was on top, still impaled on his shaft. They lay panting like that for what felt like a detached, blissful eternity.

Then Zuri giggled and wiggled her hips. "Dare," she cooed.

"Mmm?" he panted.

"You're not going soft." She giggled and began undulating her hips, moving him around inside her in a way that made pleasure ripple down his cock and through his abdomen. "You must've really enjoyed it to still be iron hard after painting my little womb twice." She tenderly kissed his chest. "Then again, you go can longer and harder than any man I've ever met."

Phoenix

Dare bit back a tired moan, flexing his exhausted muscles as he prepared to flip her back over and go again. "You want me to-"

"No!" His tiny lover put a small hand on his chest to forestall him, reaching down with her other to begin rubbing her button as she began gliding up and down his shaft.

He slumped back to the ground again, enjoying the tight, slick sensation. "I love you," he breathed.

Zuri paused her efforts, staring at him for a few seconds with her large yellow eyes. "And I love you," she said, the first time she'd said the words.

Then she got back to riding his cock, moaning in pleasure.

Collisa

Chapter Fifteen
The Rhythm of Things

"I've been wondering, Dare," Zuri murmured.

She was panting against his chest, bare skin to bare skin, after finally coaxing a third orgasm out of him after almost ten minutes. His limp cock was still trapped in her tiny pussy, the juices of their lovemaking slowly seeping out to soak his crotch.

"Mmm?" he said, half dozing in post-orgasmic bliss.

"How are you so fast?"

Dare opened his eyes, grinning. "What? I know I have a hard time holding back from coming like a geyser in your incredibly tight pussy, but that last time I thought I lasted a good while before shooting."

She giggled. "I mean how you can move so fast. You moved with impossible speed when I first saw you as a Level 8, faster than you should, and you move faster than you should as a Level 12. I think that at any level you move faster than you should."

That was surprisingly observant of her. Although he supposed she'd had plenty of chances to watch him in action. "To be honest, I've been this fast for as long as I've been on Collisa."

"Ah, so you were born with it," Zuri said in satisfaction. "Everyone's born with different traits, some stronger than others. But it's very rare to be born with such a powerful one." She nuzzled his chest again and made a contented noise. "My mate is very special."

Dare felt his face heat at the praise. With a groan he gently lifted his little lover off him and sat up. "Speaking of levels, you feeling up to getting back to it?"

Phoenix

"Don't try to change the subject," Zuri said, climbing into his lap and staring up at him intently. "I've never seen a trait give more than a perk of a few percentage points. I can't know your exact details, but for you to move as quickly as I've seen when you're really going all out, the trait's percentage has to be at least in the double digits, and probably even over 20%. I didn't know that was possible."

"34%, actually," he said. No sense being coy with his observant lover, even if he had wanted to keep things from her. "To everything affected by speed. Including reflexes."

"Thirty-" She sucked in a sharp breath, eyes huge. "That's . . . impossible. Have you found some source of great power, or been blessed by a powerful spirit or elemental?" She shook her head. "*Are you a spirit, maybe of wind or fire, manifested in flesh??*"

"Of course not," Dare said with a wry laugh. "I'm not sure exactly sure who or what is responsible for my gift." That was true enough, since he didn't know who his unseen benefactor was or what process she had used. "I just know that I've had it for as long as I've been alive on this world."

"Well it explains how you're able to fight monsters so easily. Or how you could beat that panther that nearly killed me." Zuri gave him a thoughtful look, then climbed off him. "You're a mystery, mate. I'm looking forward to learning all there is to know about you."

"And I'll happily tell you everything I can." He wasn't sure if his benefactor would want him blabbing about coming from another world, where he'd died and then was given an awesome new body. "Anyway, ready to go?"

"Just about. Let me cast Prevent Conception."

Ah, so that was the "no baby" spell. Dare watched as she pressed her glowing hands to her belly. "Have I told you how incredibly useful your spells are?" he asked. "As far as I'm concerned, Clean and Prevent Conception would be worth picking the class for all on their own."

Zuri blushed darker green. "I'm glad I can help so much." She reached for her tunic. "Also the clean spell is Cleanse Target, castable on any valid target."

"Thanks, nice to get the proper terms." He reached for his own clothes.

Once they were dressed and geared up, ready to go out hunting, Zuri turned to him with a deep breath. "All right, invite me."

Dare found the familiar party invite command, and couldn't help but smile as he saw her accept, and a whole new command screen for party information appeared. Then he whistled as he saw some of that information.

His lover hadn't been wrong about the information party leaders were privy to. It looked as if it was basically anything that could remotely impact the survival of the party, including physical stats, health, etc.

A lot of it was incredibly invasive. Which maybe was reasonable since the leader needed to be able to trust his people when it was a matter of life and death, and joining a party was voluntary. But even so . . .

Some of it was stuff Dare could already find with his Eye, like a person's class, hit points, stamina points, mana points and abilities. But there were also things like statistics for performance and behavior in previous parties, criminal reputation for various factions in the kingdom and region, public achievements, and more.

For instance that Zuri was 20 years old, in excellent physical condition, and perfectly healthy. It also showed injuries or other things that had affected her body in her past that might affect her performance in the party.

Included in that list was something that immediately caught his attention: she'd given birth once before.

Phoenix

That was something he'd like to know more about, but at the same time it was her secret to tell. And she'd already extended what he now knew was a great amount of trust in him. Besides, they'd only been able to talk for a few hours, so she hadn't really had time to delve into serious, intimate topics like that.

He'd let her tell him when she was ready, if she ever was.

Feeling suddenly ashamed of his intrusion, even if his lover had tacitly give him permission, he stopped looking at her information. "Thank you for this show of trust," he said, cupping her cheek. "I'll let you invite me at some point so you can see my information as well."

Although come to think about it, with these sorts of specific details how was his history going to look? Like it hadn't even begun until several weeks ago?

He jumped in shock when text scrolled across the center of his vision, with the soothing female voice reading it. "A generic history has been populated for you. Nothing to make you stand out, but overall very positive."

"You can read my mind and just pop in and talk to me?" Dare asked the system incredulously. Then the obvious answer hit him: his unseen benefactor. "Is that you?"

There was no response.

Zuri was looking at him like he was crazy. "What are you doing?"

He felt himself flush. Right, he'd just stared off into nowhere and shouted at the sky. "Talking to the command screens for information."

She narrowed her eyes. "That's not a thing." Her eyes widened. "Were you talking to your patron spirit or god?"

"I honestly have no idea." Dare motioned to the nearest spawn point, which was full of rotting corpses aimlessly shambling around like undead should and ranged from Level 9 to 10. Their appearance was horrific in realistic detail, and Dare hoped they didn't smell as bad as they looked. "Ready to get started?"

"Sure." His tiny lover fell into step beside him. "You saw that being in a party gives all members an equal percentage of the experience they'd receive for killing that monster solo, according to their level?"

"I saw." Dare grinned at her. "I'm going to machine gun down these things as fast as I can."

Her brow furrowed. "Machine gun? That didn't get translated."

"Kill them quickly," he clarified. "You just focus on doing whatever damage you can and providing support with Nature's Curse."

Zuri jumped. "How do you know the name of my ability?" she said in amazement. "I couldn't have told you before now because it would've been the Goblin term."

He hesitated. "It's an ability I have."

"What ability?" She pointed at the monsters just ahead. "For that matter, how can you just walk up to every monster we find out here and know instantly whether it's safe to fight them or we should walk away? Did you memorize a complete monster compendium, and one for classes too?"

Dare gave her a sheepish look. "Well first off, what do you see when you look at that thing?" he asked, pointing to the nearest undead.

His goblin lover gave him the blank look he was so familiar with from before they could communicate; guess he could still earn it from her sometimes. "I see a walking corpse."

"Well yeah, but what information?"

Phoenix

Her brow furrowed. "None. Its ##### is blank."

Wow, nothing? Not even a health bar with a percentage meter so they could see how close their enemy was to death? That was super rough . . . no matter most people were afraid to go out and hunt monsters.

Zuri kept going. "So how do you do it? Everyone knows you can't just go out and hunt monsters. Even if you had one of the best compendiums and carefully researched what regions monsters usually spawn in, there are new monsters constantly appearing that the compendiums haven't recorded, and some elite monsters can be as much as 10 levels higher than their counterparts. You'd probably end up being killed by a Silver Sickle within the first few weeks."

"Then how do adventurers level up?" Dare asked.

"Very carefully. They prepare for years and only visit exhaustively explored and cultivated zones around villages and towns, where the monster levels are predictable. Usually with a hired guide to show them to each new spawn point for their level and babysit them in case they run into trouble. And at higher levels they get an ability that gives them a sense for the strength of monsters relative to their own, so they can venture out farther. Although even then they often run into a bad end because of the ability's vagueness and that it's limited to your perception circle."

Wow. So his unseen benefactor hadn't been joking about how valuable a gift Adventurer's Eye was. Apparently it was helping him even more than he'd realized, if others trying to level were so crippled by not knowing the strength of enemies.

"What if I knew exactly what level an enemy was, and what attacks it had?" he asked quietly. "Then I could hunt monsters confident I wasn't getting into a suicidal fight."

Zuri smirked at him. "What, you're going to tell me now that you have the spirit-cursed Adventurer's Eye? At Level 12 or even earlier? The legendary rare ability that no adventurer has ever gotten sooner than level 50?"

Interesting. So it looked as if the level cap went past 50, which was a level adventurers could and had attained before. And if his benefactor had told him that it would take centuries of constant effort to reach the cap, how much higher would it be? 100? 150?

Dare set aside that thought for now and looked at Zuri thoughtfully. It looked like she was getting overwhelmed by all the mysteries and impossibilities about him as they started to add up, and he didn't want to push her credulity too far.

So instead of answering he changed the subject. "What ability do people have to begin with? They must have some means of sensing danger, or everyone would've been killed by monsters long ago, and traveling would be impossible."

The goblin stared at him blankly. "You really know nothing about the world, do you?" she mused. "You're just nothing but confusions and oddities."

"Will you tell me about the ability?" he asked, reaching forward to rub the top of her head.

She puffed out her cheeks irritably, but he noticed she also leaned into his hand. "Fine, I'll act as if you're a small child." She stared off into the distance. "First, Silver Sickles radiate an aura of terror. You can feel them approaching and the direction they're coming from, and the higher level they are the more powerful the aura. Which gives you some idea of the danger."

Dare had never felt anything like that, although admittedly he didn't think he'd encountered a Silver Sickle yet. He had to wonder, though, if his Adventurer's Eye's warning system about approaching enemies was a replacement for sensing the fear aura.

"That seems pretty useful," he said.

Zuri snorted bitterly. "Sure, it just means you get ripped apart by an enemy 10 levels above you, instead of 11." She shook her head

Phoenix

and continued. "As for people being killed and travelers facing danger, roads and settlements seem to have some characteristic that keeps most enemies away from them. There are monster hordes and random attacks from roamers, of course . . . no place is truly safe. But you can usually trust that a road or village will be safer than the wilds. Also a campfire, but you seem to already know that."

Dare had sort of figured all that from his observations and conversations with people. It made sense, when he'd noticed that the monsters he'd encountered had all occupied their own spawn points, and had seemed to stick to set patrol routes and behaviors.

As if his lover knew what he was thinking, she continued. "Also, as a general rule lower level enemies will be found near villages, and the farther you go from where people gather the higher level enemies you'll encounter. With the exception of monster hordes and things of that sort, that is."

That was also consistent with what he'd seen, and also fit with most games he'd played. Although he wondered how it was implemented in a real world like this without marring the realism.

He opened his mouth to ask a question, but Zuri firmly held up a hand. "Please, can we go back to talking about you claiming you know monster levels without the help of a compendium?"

Dare sighed, giving up. "Okay, you're right. I was given two gifts by . . . someone or something. They never revealed themselves to me, just spoke to me with the same generic voice as the command screens use."

Zuri again stared at him. "The information systems don't have a voice."

Right, she'd told him that before. He still wasn't sure whether that meant his benefactor was basically communicating with him every time he used the screens, or if she'd just put her voice in the system to make them more friendly for him.

He glossed past it for now. "Anyway, she gave me an ability called Fleetfoot that increases my speed by 34%, as well as the Adventurer's Eye."

"So you *do* have the Adventurer's Eye!" Zuri shouted, expression full of wonder. "A very great spirit or god must have blessed you so, to prepare you for a great purpose."

Dare shifted uncomfortably. "Not that I know of. She said she just wants to observe me for her entertainment. Watch me level up and see my love life and such."

His lover was silent for a very long, very uncomfortable time. "I'm . . . going to assume she just wishes to be inscrutable in her purposes," she finally said carefully.

I hope not. She promised me she just wants me to live my life how I want so she can see what I do . . . didn't she?

Dare cleared his throat and pointed at the undead. "Well, daylight's wasting. Want to see how much faster we can go with a good bow and proper shared experience?"

Zuri looked as if she wanted to delve deeper into all the things he'd told her, but she also seemed relieved for the chance to let it settle and process it. So with a tentative smile she reached up and slapped his butt. "Let loose, my mate."

Grinning, he raised his bow and fitted one of his new purchased arrows to the string.

* * * * *

Dare quickly discovered two things that were awesome. Or three, although two were related.

First off, with his new bow and arrows he *shredded* enemies. He wasn't sure if he was supposed to be able to kill these monsters that fast, or if Fleetfoot plus a good rotation was working to his benefit. All he knew was that he hadn't had such an easy time killing an even

Phoenix

level enemy since Level 1, with the specifically weak starting monsters.

The other thing was that the undead seemed tailor made to be picked off one after another.

For one thing, they didn't pull adds. Not even when they were right next to each other, which he'd tested since they were so easy anyway. For another, they had no Charge or speed boost ability, which made them ideal targets for a speedy ranged damage dealer.

In fact, many of them had a movement speed debuff called "Shamble", which slowed them by 10%. It only affected the undead with broken or missing legs, unsurprisingly, and basically made that enemy a target dummy. Not that the normal speed ones were much harder.

Most of the zombies had weapons, which gave them a significant damage buff, but that was only a problem if they could reach him, which they couldn't. Even better, they had a small percentage chance to drop those weapons.

Which might've explained why the merchant in Driftwain had so many monster loot Trash and Poor quality weapons. The weapons had a "rusty" debuff and were in red durability, but no doubt with proper repairs they'd be serviceable.

Best of all, though, the undead dropped money.

Not much, somewhere between 1 and 8 copper. But considering the spawn point had around 30 of them, and they could clear it every 12 hours when respawns happened at 6 in the morning and 6 in the afternoon, as best he could tell without a clock, it meant they could make a tidy income from farming them. On top of the other loot and experience.

If Dare and Zuri hunted almost nonstop among these spawn points, and even higher level ones since he thought he could take them now with his bow, and if he also set his snares and hunted game, skinning and curing leather and meat, then he'd be able to make bank.

He could buy that Level 20 Exceptional short bow in no time.

Of course, right now he was looking at prices for basic low level items. No doubt at higher levels there'd be the highest quality gear and enchantments, magical items like dimensional bags to store loot, and other stuff that would cost huge amounts of gold.

Not to mention a house. And maybe a horse.

For that matter, at higher levels the monsters might become proportionally more powerful to make up for the access to superior gear. Or there'd be more monsters that required a party or even a raid to beat.

Dare actually kind of looked forward to that prospect; outside of his few romantic memories, participating in or even leading raids through some of the most difficult dungeons in a game were some of his favorite times of his old life. Sad as that might seem to others.

One step at a time on this world, though.

Another benefit of the undead was that they took increased damage from nature spells. No doubt holy spells would be even more effective, but even so Zuri was able to do a good amount of damage.

Since her most efficient spell was her Nature's Rebuke, and he killed things so quickly, the best way for them to hunt was actually to have her pick her own targets, always the slowest ones, and kite them around until they were dead. Dare kept killing his own undead as she went, and if needed buried an arrow in her target to finish it off and give her some breathing room.

That wouldn't work so well on faster enemies, where it would probably be better for her to use Mana Thorn on his targets. But for these they could both essentially solo level together. And their experience gains were insane; far better than even when he was

Phoenix

soloing at his best.

Although a good part of that was due to his bow.

It was almost a disappointment when they finished clearing the undead spawn point. Dare couldn't wait until they respawned, but until then he moved on to a spawn of Level 10-11 creatures that looked like weasels the size of large dogs and moved quickly. They also brought adds if they were too close together, which many were.

Even so, Dare confidently began pulling enemies, trusting he could bring them down fast enough. And if not, he'd get a chance to use his new knives.

He got that chance a few times, and even took a few nasty bites and scratches keeping them off Zuri. But she was always ready to heal him if needed, and while it took longer to clear the spawn point than it had for the zombies, they still gradually worked their way through it.

The giant weasels had a chance to drop high quality fur, super thin and soft, that Dare immediately resolved to turn into new clothes for Zuri. She seemed content with her tunic in the summer heat, but he wanted to make her a dress, leggings, and shoes.

So he asked if he could keep all the furs, giving her playful smiles when she poked into what he wanted them for.

The weasels mostly dropped trash loot aside from that, claws and teeth and stringy meat. Also, for some odd reason, lumps of shiny tin that looked like crushed cups and plates the monsters had scavenged. Probably a crafting material.

Looking at the sun, Dare judged they had time to go after one more spawn point, a sort of nightmare bull that had mangy skin, terrifying teeth, and long wickedly spiked horns. They ranged from Level 11 to 13, didn't draw adds, and had a Bull Rush ability that let it increase its speed per second while charging in a line, as well as increased damage on impact with its target the faster it was moving.

Collisa

It also had extra hit points and damage.

What it didn't have, unfortunately for it, was good deceleration or turn speed. Even though it could reach Dare before he could kill it, he literally just had to sidestep at the last second, then keep loosing arrows as it shot past and struggled to wheel back around at him. Kind of like a matador with a bow.

Without Fleetfoot he might've been in a lot more trouble, and he was very careful to make sure Zuri stood safely off to the side, and watched in case any of the nightmare bulls happened to rush her. None did, but if it had he would've swept her to safety.

The bulls dropped about what he'd expect; high quality steaks, thick hides, and hooves (which he assumed crafters could use to make glue). All fairly rare to make up for their value. Although their rarest drop were their huge horns, which no doubt were extremely valuable considering only one pair dropped.

Even if killing the bulls was relatively safe and easy, because of their increased health killing them took time. Less time than moving to another spawn point, but he and his goblin lover still only cleared about a third of the monsters before he decided it was time to head back to camp.

Dare and Zuri had been talking nonstop as they leveled, learning more about each other and, on his part, about the world. She was happy to tell him whatever he wanted about her personality and desires, her experiences leveling, and things like that.

But she was reluctant to talk about her past, especially her recent past. He got the sense she'd grown up in a village, probably with other goblins, but whenever he asked any questions about her life she'd grow quiet until he changed the subject, or change the subject herself.

It was obvious she had pain she didn't want to dwell on, or share with him just yet, so whenever she fell into that uncomfortable silence he'd pat her comfortingly and change the subject.

Phoenix

Back at camp Dare checked his snares and got to work curing hides and meat and cooking up some of the best bull steaks for dinner. Along with some new forage items he'd found on the plains, including potatoes.

Meanwhile Zuri got out the bolt of cloth and, with the mechanical competency of abilities, began crafting clothing. "You wanted my underwear to be sexy, right?" she said casually as she snipped the cloth into patterns.

He felt his face flush. "If you'll be comfortable in them."

"I will." She gave him an impish grin. "Turn around."

Dare obliged, using the opportunity to take the weasel leather and fur he'd just finished curing and secretly make her a dress, leggings, and shoes.

When he turned back around a while later, whatever his tiny lover had been crafting was nowhere to be seen, and she looked up at him innocently as she cut more cloth into patterns. "What?" she teased.

"Going to make me wait to see it?" he asked, peeking around her back.

"Maybe." She laughed. "I'm going to make your underwear sturdy and comfortable . . . you run around too much and too fast to get fancy."

"Sounds good." Dare looked at the bolt, which still had some left. "Can you make socks?" At her blank look he said. "Stockings, but only going up to the ankle or mid calf, depending on fashion and preference."

Zuri looked dubious. "I have the pattern, but aren't they a luxury item?"

He laughed. "With how much running around we do, more like a necessity. They'll help prevent blisters, rashes, callouses, and infections. And they'll also help our shoes stay good for longer and keep our feet from stinking."

She shrugged. "Okay. I'll take your word for it since half the time goblins don't wear shoes anyway."

Dare grimaced at the idea; their feet must be rock hard. "They keep the skin soft and smooth too," he teased. "More enjoyable to kiss."

His goblin lover blushed darker green, remembering what he'd done earlier. "I guess that does sound nice. I'll try to alter the pattern to make us some."

"Good." Dare pulled his hands from behind his back, revealing the ermine clothes he'd made. "Also, I made these for you."

Her eyes lit up as she eagerly accepted the items, running her fingers wonderingly over the soft fur and leather. "They're like a high priestess's finery, or the formal dress of a chieftain's concubine!" She flushed again. "Although I suppose that's right, since I'm the concubine of a great man."

He blinked. "You think I'm a great man?"

Zuri laughed. "How could I not?" She stood and pulled off her tunic, letting him feast his eyes on her large breasts, flat tummy, and long legs. At least until she began pulling on her new clothes.

Which, as it turned out, also hugged her curves and looked elegant on her lush body.

Dare grinned admiringly. "Crafting clothes is so simple and the materials are so easy to get, I'm going to have to make you lots of pretty things to wear."

She gave him a stern look. "Our packs only have so much room." But she spent a long time staring down at her clothes, running her hand over the soft leather and even softer fur, before finally settling down on his lap. Yellow eyes shining, she gently pulled his face

Phoenix

down to kiss him.

"Thank you, my mate," she whispered.

"Your smile is all the thanks I need." Dare wrapped his arms around her and slipped a hand under her tunic, rubbing her soft tummy. Then, grinning impishly, he slid his hand under the waistband of her leggings and trailed it down her soft mound towards her-

"Ho, the camp!"

Collisa

Chapter Sixteen
Visitor

Zuri leapt off Dare's lap with speed born of terror and ingrained survival reflexes. Although he was even faster, moving as soon as she was clear.

To an observer, or whoever was out there, it probably would've looked like they went from cuddling contentedly to Dare on his feet, three arrows clutched in the hand holding his bow with an arrow nocked to the string ready to draw, in the blink of an eye.

He had to use Rapid Shot, but in the face of a possible attack now was the time.

"Easy, friends!" the voice called. It was male, deep and calm and oddly reassuring. "I merely wished to share your fire for a time and talk about an opportunity."

Dare dropped into a crouch, bow still ready. "Get ready to jump on my back and hang on if I tell you," he murmured to Zuri. She nodded grimly, moving around behind him, as he raised his voice to the intruder. "You'll pardon my caution. I believe in guest rights and the sanctity of travelers sharing a campfire, but we've had run-ins with bandits before."

"Understood. But I assure you I'm unarmed and mean you no harm." The man sounded a bit amused, as if he'd made a joke. Although a friendly one.

Dare lowered his bow slightly. "Then approach slowly."

"As you wish." The voice slowly came closer, and Dare felt the man enter his perception circle. "A man who holds to noble traditions is one I can trust, and I'm willing to take steps to earn yours."

Phoenix

Collisa

He came into view and Dare looked him over: a short man in his late 20s, lean but muscled and with a sense of power like a coiled spring. Or maybe an undetonated nuke.

His head and face were shaved smooth, an odd tattoo of some mystic pattern inked along one cheek and stretching up across his forehead before disappearing over the crown of his head. He wore form-fitting tan and brown clothes, everything tied with cloth strips for ease of movement and silent passage.

As promised, he had no visible weapons. Which led Dare to conclude, based on the other clues, that the man was a Monk or some other type of combat-oriented Cleric.

Of course Dare didn't need to guess; he activated his Eye and saw "Human, adult male. Class: Monk Level 14". His attacks were all unarmed and included what sounded like abilities that channeled the power of the body into focused techniques.

That would explain the man's joke about being unarmed.

"I'm Ilin," the bald man said, stopping just within the circle of firelight. "A traveler from distant lands, seeking to explore the world while improving myself in body, mind, and soul."

Yeah, he even talked like a Monk.

People were people, of course, but generally members of a group that tended to be ascetics and sought balance and peace could usually be trusted. Dare lowered his bow. "Well met, Ilin. I'm Dare, and this is my companion Zuri."

Ilin bowed respectfully to him and, surprisingly, to Zuri as well. Which immediately made Dare more kindly disposed toward him. "Well met, friends." He motioned. "Might I join you?"

"Please." Dare motioned to a spot across the fire. "Come have a seat. We've got food cooking which you're welcome to share."

"That's very kind of you." The Monk approached and squatted

Phoenix

down across from them, looking comfortable and well balanced in that position. Like he could stay like that all night.

"So, what brings you to our fire?" Dare asked, turning the meat on the rack and stirring the potatoes frying on the griddle, which had been positioned to catch the fat dripping from the steaks.

"Aside from the joy of meeting new people and learning new things?" Ilin smiled slightly. "There is a monster camp a bit farther north. Kobolds . . . nasty creatures, sneak thieves and murderers of the weak and helpless who'll leave their spawn point if left for too long. But they also tunnel, and I've heard they have a chance to drop ores of precious metal, gold and silver, as well as uncut gems and semiprecious stones."

"A Mon-" Dare cut off, realizing the man hadn't revealed his class. "A monetary goal for one seeking enlightenment?" he said instead, tone light.

The man chuckled. "Even the enlightened must eat, if we would not be beggars or spend our lives in toil rather than exploration and service to others." He motioned idly. "And any wealth I do not have need of, I donate to orphanages and the like in cities I pass."

Reasonable enough. But Dare still didn't think it was that straightforward. "Generous of you to share this information with us."

Ilin scratched at his jaw. "Not just generosity, I'll admit." He leaned forward. "I can handle one or two enemies my level, and according to what I've heard these are within my range, 12 to 15. But the times I tried to draw one, no matter how isolated, three would accompany it."

Ah. "Not exactly a spawn point for solo levelers."

"No indeed." The Monk rubbed his jaw ruefully. "You may be a bit low for them, but your gear seems decent enough. In a group I think we could handle four of the fiends." He nodded at Zuri. "Especially if your companion is a healing class, as I suspect."

"I think we could," Dare agreed, leaning close to the fire to begin portioning out the food. "Want to check it out tomorrow?"

Ilin took a small camping kit with bowls and utensils from his pack, accepting his portion with a murmur of thanks, and dug in with gusto. "Aye." He paused, giving them a curious look. "Just a heads up, it's a large spawn because the kobolds are guarding the entrance to their mine . . . a dungeon that randomly spawns at that point and is currently active."

Dare perked up. He'd assumed, or at least hoped, that dungeons would exist in this world. But this was the first he'd heard of them. "I think I've encountered a large spawn before," he said, thinking of the huge Boarite city he'd avoided. Although he hoped the kobold one wasn't nearly as large or intimidating or even the three of them wouldn't stand a chance. "Never seen a dungeon before."

The bald man nodded, pausing from taking a bite to respond. "The lowest ones I've heard of are Level 21, which I assume this one is considering the location and level of the entry guards. Most require a party of at least six of the same level, maybe four or five if they're well geared, have good class synergy, and work well together. At higher levels fewer could probably manage it, with care."

Dare scratched his jaw as he mulled that over. So the entry guards were lower level than the dungeon; that wasn't too out of the ordinary. "Guess we'll be steering well clear of it, then," he said with a wry smile.

Zuri nodded emphatically. "From what I've heard, dungeons eat more adventurers than party rated or even raid rated monsters." She shivered. "They go in and never come out."

"I've heard the same," Ilin agreed soberly, tearing into another steak. "Although the loot is good."

"So it may take longer than usual to clear out the spawn point?" Dare guessed.

Phoenix

"A great opportunity for loot and experience, as long as we're careful." The Monk looked between them. "Speaking of which, we should probably agree on some things." He smiled wryly. "I doubt you'd be willing to join my party."

Definitely not. "We're already in a party," he said carefully.

"Ah." Ilin nodded. "I have similar reservations about joining your party. Party leaders generally need to either find a group of close friends or develop a very solid reputation for integrity to have any success finding members." He gave them a respectful nod. "Always heartwarming to see such trust between companions."

"Thank you," Dare said, returning the nod. "I have a system for optimizing experience between people outside a party. It won't require much extra effort, and it'll be better for you . . . with how the party experience sharing works you'll end up getting 40% of each monster's experience, while me and Zuri each get 30%."

The bald man shifted uncomfortably, chewing and swallowing before answering. "I wouldn't want to take so much more than you."

"Actually, with how experience sharing works outside of parties, if we tried to distribute it evenly we'd just get a bit more while you got a lot less. This is fine."

"Dare figured that out with just a few experiments," Zuri said proudly. "I bet most people don't even consider trying to figure out how experience sharing works, outside major adventurer's guilds and adventurer factions who try to optimize everything."

For a moment Dare wondered why everyone didn't immediately do such simple tests. Then he remembered that they couldn't see health bars; without that they'd have to basically guess based on the damage of their items and abilities, and how many hits it took to kill a monster.

Still, while it would be more difficult it wasn't impossible. Which would explain why the factions did it to give their people an advantage.

Or maybe those guilds included a high level person who had access to Adventurer's Eye, and helped them. Or they'd obtained the information from some person in history who had the Eye.

Ilin was eyeing him thoughtfully. "A sharp young man," he said. "And more knowledgable than you seem."

Had he noticed Dare's slip earlier where he'd almost identified his class? "I'll keep track of how much damage you do to each monster to ensure we all get our share of experience," Dare said. "And we'll split the loot three ways. Fair?" He held out his hand to shake.

The Monk hesitated. "I hate to be churlish after your generous offer with the experience. As well as your even more valuable information on how you manage to split it so evenly, which will aid me tremendously in the future."

"But?" Dare asked.

"But I'm two levels higher, better geared, and I was also the one who gave you the information about the kobolds." Ilin offered his own hand. "Let's stick to the theme and say 40, 30, 30?"

Dare immediately shook his head. "We would've probably found the kobold camp eventually, since we're headed north in the direction of Kov leveling as we go. As for you being higher level and better geared . . ."

He grinned wolfishly. "Let's make a bet. You and me will single out two equal level kobolds and each have a race to see who kills theirs first. You win, we'll split it your way. I win, even split."

Their prospective companion frowned. "As a rule, members of my order frown on gambling."

Dare waved that away. "A challenge, then. To the victor go the spoils."

Ilin perked up a bit at that, then his expression soured. "There's also the fact that you're ranged. I have no doubts I could best you in a fair fight, or in your little race if we could both begin damaging our targets at the same time. But as it is you'd kill it before I could even do damage. Also there's no way to make sure they're the same level, and on top of that they come in groups of four . . . your "challenge" would never be feasible."

That was a good point. Dare was confident he could think of a way to arrange it so they could both began damaging their enemy at the same time, but it wouldn't do much good if Ilin didn't believe the monsters were the same level. And he wasn't about to tell a complete stranger about his Adventurer's Eye, even if he thought the man would believe him.

"Okay then," he said with a grin. "How about a footrace?"

Zuri looked startled for a moment, then giggled knowingly.

Ilin also looked startled, then roared laughter. "You want to race me?"

"I do."

The man kept chortling. "I don't believe in tricks or deceit, so I should warn you my class is Monk. We hone our bodies through a lifetime of intense training and meditation to push ourselves not to the limits of what we're physically capable of, but beyond."

He looked Dare over. "You're tall, and your body looks like it was sculpted by a god to be the perfect athlete, but you have no idea the kind of speed and power I'm able to call upon."

The Monk obviously expected Dare to be surprised or impressed by that revelation, maybe even intimidated. But he just nodded blandly. "Okay."

"Okay?" Ilin repeated in disbelief. He glanced at Zuri, but she also had an impressive poker face. "You don't have any speed increase abilities at your level. No archer class does, and from your camp and clothes I'd say you're a Hunter, which I'm confident doesn't."

"Nope," Dare agreed. "Aside from a small bump in the woods, but we're on the plains."

"And you don't have high quality boots with a speed bonus," the man pressed.

"Not that it would be significant, but no."

The Monk stroked his jaw thoughtfully. "All right, I'm intrigued. If for no other reason than to see what kind of secret you're hiding that makes you so confident." He offered his hand. "Deal. If you win, an even share. And if I win, 40, 30, 30 in my favor."

Dare returned the handshake firmly and found Ilin's grip to be crushing. And the man was clearly holding back; that didn't do much for Dare's confidence. "How does five miles sound?" he asked; anything that pushed the body beyond its limits wouldn't be sustainable for long.

Ilin chuckled knowingly. "A hundred yards sounds better."

Dare was confident he'd be just fine at that distance too, but no sense making it too easy for the Monk. "One mile?" he compromised.

The man nodded and glanced at the fading light. "How does bright and early in the morning sound? We'll use the road."

"Next morning, then," Dare agreed.

The Monk finished his last few bites of food, then stood and bowed politely. "Thank you for your hospitality. I'll camp closer to the road. You can find me by taking a straight line back there."

With that he was gone in the night, stride brisk.

"You have a mischievous side, my mate," Zuri said, grinning.

Dare chuckled. "If you've got it, use it."

Phoenix

"Mmm." She smirked as she looked pointedly at his crotch. "Speaking of which, I still haven't shown you my new underwear." She motioned to their tent. "Ready to turn in?"

He eagerly wolfed down his last few bites. "Yup."

His tiny lover slipped past him on her way to their bed, and he hurried to join her.

Her new bra and panties turned out to be *very* sexy. Although they didn't stay on for long.

* * * * *

Bright and early the next morning Dare and Zuri packed up camp and headed for the road.

True to Ilin's words, the man had a camp set up. Or more accurately, a fire; the man had simply set his pack aside, and by all appearances had then settled on the grass in the lotus position to meditate. He'd probably been like that all night.

Dare couldn't imagine doing that himself, but then again he wasn't a trained Monk who'd spent a lifetime honing his self-discipline.

Ilin opened his eyes as they approached, but didn't otherwise stir. "Sorry to interrupt your meditation," Dare called.

The man again looked surprised at his knowledge before smiling ruefully. "We meditate when we may, so we can act when we must." He came lightly to his feet in an explosive motion. "Now then, I believe you've presented me a challenge?"

Dare nodded. "Mind if we leave our things here during this race?"

"By all means."

They laid their packs by the Monk's, then Dare moved to the road and began stretching. Ilin watched with quiet amusement, standing in an at ease position that seemed completely relaxed but also ready to explode into action in an instant.

"Not going to stretch?" Dare asked the man.

"No need to limber your muscles when you never allow them to stiffen."

Wow, this guy was actually pretty hardcore. Assuming he wasn't just talking big.

Dare finished his stretches and looked along the road. "I'll run out and put a marker down for the finish line."

"No need." Ilin motioned to a nearby pair of rocks on either side of the road, a thin white line drawn between them. "I've put chalk lines there at the start, as well as at the quarter, half, three-quarters, and the finish." He smiled. "Anything else you need to get ready?"

"Nah, I'm good." Dare positioned himself at the white line, trying to copy the position he remembered from his days in track a decade in the past.

When, ironically, he'd been about this age.

"Runner's starting pose," the Monk said, nodding in approval as he moved to stand beside him at the line. There the man stood at ease, taking no position himself.

Well, if the guy didn't want to optimize his race that was on him. "Want to do the honors?" Dare asked Zuri. At her uncertain look he smiled. "Just count down from five."

"Okay." She looked nervously between them and then down the road. "Um, do your best! Five, four, three, two, one."

Dare shot forward, accelerating to a sprint and then pushing faster and faster. He'd never tested how quickly he could go from standing to max speed, but it turned out the answer was-

Ilin was ahead of him.

Phoenix

The man must've pushed off with unbelievable power, at a sprint in an eyeblink while Dare was still speeding up. He was already running at 25 miles an hour or better.

Dare grit his teeth and pushed to go faster, closing the gap until he was running side by side with the shorter man.

Ilin looked over, and if Dare had been surprised at the Monk's speed, the other man looked absolutely shocked at his. "An elite athlete," he said, smiling widely. He didn't seem to be struggling. "I believe we're approaching the fastest speed a normal human has ever run."

With a friendly wave, the Monk sped up. "And . . . now I'm past it. Which means that even though you put up an impossible fight, this about the point when you start to fall be-"

He cut off as Dare once again caught up to him. Although Dare was starting to get worried; he was barely managing to keep this pace. If he went full out, pushed himself harder than he ever had, he could go a bit faster, maybe get close to 30 miles an hour.

But not for long.

Ilin looked over and his smiles were gone. As was his wasting breath talking. His face assumed a look of extreme concentration, and after a few seconds a violent shiver swept his entire body.

He must've unlocked some sort of gate or barrier within himself, because with a roar of effort he began to pull ahead again.

Dare watched him increase the gap in disbelief; holy shit, Monks really had access to these sorts of short term bursts? How did that square with balancing between classes?

He looked ahead, after a few seconds spotting the finish line his competitor had set. It was approaching faster than he'd like; at these speeds they could go a mile in a bit over two minutes.

But he still had a bit of breathing room to try to keep this pace until they got closer, then push himself to the limit for a final burst.

They crossed the halfway mark, and Ilin's movements started to become the slightest bit jerky, as if he was finally struggling. Dare couldn't feel much smugness about that because he was panting as hard as he could and still straining to get enough air, and his legs burned so badly he was afraid they'd cramp.

The three quarter mark. Dare let out his own cry of effort and pushed to go faster than he ever had before, the ground blurring beneath him. At this speed the wind stung his eyes to the point he couldn't see much more than a blurry outline of the road through his tears, and the slightest unevenness in the dirt beneath his feet made him feel like he was going to crash and burn.

He closed the gap with Ilin, who didn't take the risk of looking back, all his energy and focus on the blurry white line ahead. The man's lead shrank to fifteen feet, then ten, then five, and the line flashed past.

Dare was dimly aware of the Monk tucking into a series of rolls that somehow bled off all his insane momentum, but he was past before he could see the man stop. He was struggling to slow down himself without leaving a twenty foot skid mark made of his skin down the road, and was well past the line before he finally reached a speed where it was safe to veer off the road and collapse into a tumbling roll on the grass.

He lay there desperately sucking in air, every muscle in his body on fire and his lungs burning, and for thirty or so seconds the pain was almost unbearable.

The soft pad of footfalls on dirt distantly reached him through the noise of his own panting and throbbing heartbeat, and he opened his eyes to see Ilin standing over him.

The man was breathing hard, but that was it; he could've just paused a relaxed jog to chat with a neighbor.

Phoenix

"Guess . . . you . . . win," Dare gasped out, looking up at the blue sky overhead.

Ilin was slow to answer. "Every day of my life from when I was a very young boy," he said in a neutral tone, "I've pushed my body to its limit. I've honed it to the closest peak of perfection I thought physically possible. Then I meditated for countless hours to balance my lines and open the Locks within myself."

He reached down to give Dare a hand up, speaking in that same tone. "I opened the Third Lock during the race to reach that speed. At my current level of mastery over self I would've risked serious, perhaps even permanent, injury to open the Fourth, or to maintain that speed for very much longer. And even then, I heard you only steps behind me as I crossed the finish line."

Dare took a few more panting breaths, then accepted the help up to his feet; the man lifted him as if he weighed nothing. "A good race," he told the Monk. "I didn't expect it to be that close."

Ilin threw back his head and laughed, no anger or bitterness apparent. "Very much the same, my friend." He clapped him hard on the back. "I think we both surprised each other back there."

"To be honest, I surprised myself too . . . I don't think I've ever run that fast. I probably couldn't have without you up ahead pushing me to do it." Dare clapped him on the back in turn. "It's worth losing that extra share of the loot to see someone who's gone so far above the pinnacle of human ability in action."

"Ah, right." the bald man turned him, starting them back down the road to where they'd left Zuri. "I'm happy to take your extra share, to the victor goes the spoils, but I have a lot more respect for you and your goblin friend after this. It's only fair that she, at least, get an even third."

Dare didn't want to do the math for that more complex loot distribution with his brain fried from the race. But he was more pleased about the man giving Zuri her fair share than would account for the extra . . . 3.33%, right, that she'd be getting.

"Thank you," he told the man quietly.

Ilin chuckled and looped an arm around his shoulders, tapping Dare's chest with his knuckles. "It's only a small amount in the end."

Dare shook his head. "I meant for treating her with kindness and respect. I've yet to see that from others."

"Ah." The Monk's smile faded to soberness. "Our order believes that if you can see a person's level, see that they're a thinking being, their soul is precious. Anyone capable of intelligent thought is a miracle from the gods, deserving of kindness and friendship."

"I'm glad I'm not the only person in the world who thinks that way," Dare said, smiling back.

"Yes, it's always a pleasant surprise to meet someone who can see other races as equals." Ilin paused, looking at Dare closely. "You should consider joining my order. It's composed of more than simply Monks, and a man with an open mind and a kind soul is always welcome."

Dare chuckled. "I would be honored, but I don't think I'd be good at denying self as an ascetic. I intend to sleep with as many women of as many races as I can in my life. An entire harem of beautiful wives, as I can support them. And I want to enjoy the finer things in life with them."

The Monk joined his laughter. "Ah, a generous and kindhearted hedonist. A joy to meet, but yes, sadly probably not a good fit for my order."

Dare glanced ahead. "Besides, I could never abandon Zuri." He sheepishly rubbed the back of his head. "Actually, I still need to run the entire harem thing by her."

Ilin shook his head, smiling slightly. "You care deeply for Zuri. You see her value when others see only a lowly goblin."

Phoenix

Dare nodded fiercely. "I'm blessed to have her in my life."

"As you've unquestionably been a blessing in hers." Ilin chuckled and clapped his back. "Don't be too worried about broaching the subject of sleeping around with Zuri. Most goblin women prefer to join the harem of a wealthy and powerful male, and tend to get along well with everyone."

His grin widened. "Honestly, most women of most races are happy with the arrangement. In a world full of uncertainty and danger, having a high level man who can protect and provide for you and your children is bound to draw plenty of interest among the fairer sex."

"So I've heard," Dare said, thinking about the words of his unseen benefactor. He'd still have to ask Zuri when it came up, but it was a relief to know she'd probably be on board. Hell, from how much she'd seemed to enjoy watching him with the slime girl, she'd probably be happy to join in.

He glanced at Ilin with a rueful smile. "I guess as a Monk you'd know all about this subject?"

His new companion laughed outright. "There's a reason vows of celibacy are so popular with the leaders of my homeland. More women for them."

Up ahead Dare spotted Zuri coming down the road to meet them and waved. She waved back eagerly and broke into a run. "You're smiling!" she called. "I knew you'd win."

He chuckled. "Actually Ilin kicked my ass." He motioned to the grinning Monk. "He's agreed to let you have your fair share of the loot, though."

Her eyes got huge. "He *beat* you?" she said incredulously. "How?"

"I'm more interested in how he came so close to beating me." Ilin clapped his hands briskly. "But now that we've had our fun, the day

Collisa

is wasting and kobolds need killing . . . shall we gather our gear and be off?"

Chapter Seventeen
Dungeon Mouth

To Dare's relief, the "large spawn" of the kobold camp wasn't nearly as huge as the Boarite city he'd seen near Lone Ox.

In fact, that place might've been some sort of dungeon in its own right. He asked Ilin but the man couldn't be sure if it was a mega spawn, a dungeon, some sort of faction capitol for the monster type, or something entirely different.

"I'd have to see it to be sure," he said. "Although if they're that numerous and high level, it probably needs either an extremely high level adventurer or a raid in that level range to clear them out."

That was a concern for another time, if Dare planned to address it at all that was.

In the meantime, the kobold camp basically had two sections. The first was an outpost a bit farther out on the plains, with a dozen distinct groupings of four kobolds patrolling or sitting outside crude dugouts or what could generously be called tents.

The second, larger section abutted a tall hill with a very visible entrance leading underground. It had maybe a hundred kobolds, all in groups of four, and most of them were doing tasks around the mine entrance or patrolling.

There was also a regular stream of weaker Level 8-10 kobold laborers pushing carts full of dirt and rocks out of the entrance. They'd dump the carts in haphazard piles all around the camp, then scurry back into the mine while the bored higher level guards jeered and occasionally pelted them with dirt clods or debris from the mine.

The scene could've been taken right out of any number of RPGs Dare had played, which either spoke to their realism or this world's similarity to those games. But when it came right down to it, it meant there were a good 37 groups of 4, or 148 total, that they could hunt.

Ilin was right, that was a good opportunity. Especially if they dropped good loot. And they could take out the laborers too for good measure.

Assuming that didn't aggro whatever was in the dungeon; with instanced dungeons that wouldn't happen, but Dare hadn't encountered any sort of boundaries in this world. Aside from the soft boundaries keeping monsters away from campfires, roads, and settlements, as well as in their spawn points, that is.

Although if you aggroed something, he knew from experience it would basically follow you anywhere you went. At least until you'd gotten far enough away to be out of its sight for several minutes, or you got more than a couple miles from its spawn point and were outside of its perception circle.

Which meant that if some jerk did it right, it was highly possible for them to pull high level monsters to cities and leave them to wreak havoc. Which might even happen for all Dare knew.

They started at the smaller outpost camp, with him planting a few traps around Zuri, just in case. Then he waited for nods of readiness from his companions and pulled the nearest group.

The four came charging out, and he and Zuri got to work downing his first target while Ilin prepared to intercept any survivors.

Because they were higher level it took a bit longer to down the monsters. Although not too much longer; with Dare being able to obliterate even level enemies these weren't that much worse, especially with Zuri's help. And the kobolds weren't exactly a threat, since their only movement buff was a slight increase to speed when they were enraged below 50% health.

Phoenix

He and his lover killed the first kobold and had almost finished off the second by the time the kobold group reached their new companion. Dare used Rapid Shot to finish off their second target, then with his remaining arrows got started on a third with Zuri.

Meanwhile Ilin expertly took down the fourth, all the time keeping it between him and the third one as he kited both to keep them away from his teammates.

True to form, the Monk attacked his enemies with a flurry of punches and kicks that hit with surprising force, while at the same time using his hands and knees to slap aside the clumsy attacks from the kobolds, who were mostly armed with pickaxes or shovels.

He also employed acrobatics, leaps to land his kicks and rolls to maneuver, along with surprising twists and dips of his upper body to dodge attacks, all the while keeping his legs rooted solidly as tree trunks.

Even beyond that, the bald ascetic seemed to have a mastery of anatomy that let his blows land solidly on vulnerable spots, scoring what looked like frequent critical hits. And a mastery of physics, or at least redirecting force, that let him use the momentum and strength of his enemies against them.

Ilin took down the fourth kobold while Dare was still working on the third, and smoothly switched to that one while not getting in Dare's line of sight. Together they finished off the last enemy in seconds, then took a moment to assess the fight.

"Glad I didn't accept your wager," Ilin said with a grin. "Even with the Healer's help, you basically took down three to my one."

"I bet you could've gone faster if you'd exerted yourself," Dare said. There'd been no sign the man had opened an inner Lock for the fight, or used any advanced techniques.

Their new teammate shrugged. "There is the issue of experience . . ."

"Right." Dare settled on his haunches, scraping in the dirt. "Now that we've assessed the enemy by fighting a group, here's what we do." He quickly detailed how he and Zuri would damage each kobold down to 30%, leaving Ilin to finish the enemies off as they came close to him. As for any that Ilin fought solo, if possible he'd try to do that 30% and then run or fight defensively until Dare and Zuri could finish it.

"Interesting," Ilin mused. "I didn't realize you could get that much extra experience for doing 30% of a shared kill." He rubbed his jaw. "Alternatively, though, you realize that with that last fight we got close to getting the same split of experience?"

Surprised, Dare paused as he thought it through.

The man was right. By killing two for Ilin's one, and then doing 70% of the last one while Ilin did the rest, they *had* pretty much split the experience. And even more evenly than it would be otherwise, since the split was uneven on only one enemy instead of all four.

And it was way less of a hassle than trying to balance damage on every mob.

"You're right," Dare said, grinning. "Guess my experience sharing technique isn't so great after all."

"Plenty valuable in its own right." The Monk clapped him on the shoulder. "We'll still stick to your way for individual monsters, if we run into a higher level officer or roamer or whatever."

It turned out the kobolds, like the undead, dropped a small amount of copper coins. Although to their disappointment none dropped the hoped for ore or uncut gems. It was probably rare to make up for its value.

Over the next few hours they settled into a routine, getting the work of killing the groups of four kobolds down to a science. There were rarely any injuries, with Ilin taking the brunt of them, but Zuri quickly healed him and they continued.

Phoenix

They managed to clear the outpost and about half the main camp before lunch time. The experience had been great, bumping Dare and his lover that much closer to 13, and they had a couple handfuls of silver ore, a few chunks of gold ore, and one rock that might've contained a geode or deposit of semiprecious stone inside. They'd also got a few rusty picks and shovels that could be sold.

Dare suggested they pause for lunch and began handing out dried meat and mushrooms. Then they all settled on the grass outside the aggro range of the remaining monsters to rest and eat.

"Does the camp respawn every 12 hours, like other spawn points?" he asked.

Ilin shrugged. "The person who told me about it didn't say, one way or another. I guess we assume so until see proof otherwise."

The man took a few more bites, then paused and gave Dare and Zuri a long look. "You know, my friends, it seems we're all traveling north to Kov," he said casually. "You two do remarkably well together." He chuckled ruefully. "Probably even well enough to take the kobolds without my help, with a bit of preparation and some extra effort."

"You want to travel together?" Dare asked.

"Why not?" the Monk said with a broad smile. "I get to sit back and enjoy ranged teammates doing most of the work for me, while you get the reassurance that if any enemies do reach us, you won't have to worry about running around like idiots trying to cast spells or shoot arrows."

There was something to that. Their leveling always slowed to a crawl when an enemy reached them, with Dare usually having to kite the monster while Zuri finished it off, with help from his cooldowns if they were available.

And there was always the chance of aggroing more adds than they could handle; having another teammate would make things safer.

"I don't suppose you'd reconsider joining our party?" he asked without much hope.

Ilin laughed. "Not just yet. We're doing well with the arrangement like it is, are we not?" He leaned forward eagerly. "But I'd like to stay around this camp for a while so we can farm it every respawn, at least until we level enough that it's no longer worth the effort. And any other good monster spawns nearby during the rest of the time, assuming we can test them to be sure they're not too high level or dangerous for their level."

Dare glanced at Zuri, who nodded. "I'd be fine with that," he agreed. "We want to focus on leveling more than traveling or exploring, and anyway I don't want to get too far from Driftwain until I can afford a Level 20 bow that was on sale there. And maybe a Level 14 bow in the interim to help us get to that level faster."

"Then it's settled." The Monk leaned forward, offering his hand to each of them in turn. "Here's to friendship, safety in numbers, leveling like madmen, and making a fortune."

"In the grand tradition of your esteemed order," Dare said wryly as he accepted the handshake.

Their new companion laughed. "I'm young and low level, yet. My teachers may have instilled the proper values in me from childhood, but I won't have to worry about perfecting Stoicism to get to the next stage of my abilities until I'm much higher level."

"Speaking of lack of stoicism . . ." Dare glanced at his lover. "We'd welcome you into our camp, but privacy would be nice and you probably wouldn't want to hear what we get up to anyway."

Ilin laughed even harder. "Don't worry. I meditate when I'm not doing anything else, including all night. And in that state my subconscious mind is open to the world around me but pays attention to none of it . . . in meditation I only register threats or cues that it's time to come back to awareness." He grinned at them. "You could literally be rutting on top of me, and unless one of you tried to bite me or kick me I wouldn't notice."

Dare shifted awkwardly. "We'll still try to keep it quiet, assuming you want to camp with us."

"If you'll have me I'd be honored. And of course I'll respect your privacy, and do my share of tasks around camp and all the rest." The Monk dusted a few crumbs off his clothes and sprang to his feet, motioning to the camp. "Ready to finish this place off and go find something else to hunt?"

Zuri swallowed the last bite of her jerky whole and joined Ilin, and Dare tucked the rest of his food away and stood as well. They made their way to the next group of four kobolds, ready to resume the hunting.

He'd considered a lot of events to be the start of his adventure. And maybe that's because there were many starts. Or that he was having such a good time on this new world that everything felt new and exciting, a constant adventure.

Either way, he was ready to start the next phase of his adventure with Zuri at his side. And more lovers to come in the future, he was sure.

Collisa

Epilogue
A Gift

This wasn't a dream.

Sure, Dare remembered falling asleep, and he was aware that dreamers usually didn't realize they were in one. But he knew.

He was in a room with pure white walls, floor, and ceiling, perhaps ten feet by ten feet. There was no door, and the substance of the room's surfaces was hard to determine but was flat and smooth like alabaster.

The space was completely empty aside from the bed he was currently lying flat on his back on, a futon on the floor in the center of the space. Just a normal black futon, almost uncomfortably firm, especially resting on a stone floor, complete with rumpled sheets as if he'd been tossing and turning in his sleep.

He was completely naked, although the air didn't feel cold on his bare skin. Or warm, for that matter.

Dare had been momentarily frozen in place, disoriented and confused as he looked around and tried to figure out what the hell was going on. He was starting to get his bearings now, but as he made to sit up he froze again.

A shadow was growing on the wall, like a distant person backlit by a bright light slowly approaching. It had a woman's shape, a *naked* woman's shape, curvy and voluptuous and tantalizing in the fact that he couldn't see more than vague details.

The silhouette reached human size, giving the impressing it was just on the other side of the wall. He should've been terrified by what was happening, like some sort of horror movie, but instead he felt a sense of peace and comfort.

Phoenix

Still, it was a fucking shadow person on the wall, while he was trapped in a bizarre completely white room with no doors or windows that he didn't remember entering.

Dare tried to look at the shadow with his Adventurer's Eye ability, but it didn't register as anything. Which seemed impossible; every living thing he'd encountered so far had at least been recognized by the Eye, even if many of them just showed up as "critter, normal stats".

Was the shadow woman alive? Was this some sort of hallucination? Maybe a magical attack? Was it actually a dream, even if his mind adamantly insisted it wasn't?

So far the shadow wasn't doing anything. But even as he thought that, as if waiting for a cue, it began moving gracefully in a very erotic dance. Or she did, because she was very obviously trying to entice him.

As she dipped, swayed, and twirled, movements designed to exaggerate the hypnotic motions of her breasts, hips, and ass, he glimpsed perky nipples stiffened from either cold or arousal. As well as the occasional glimpse of plump, pouty lips between her legs when the angle was right.

In profile her face was elfin and delicate, a small nose and full lips just begging to be kissed. Her hair fell loose halfway down her back, flowing with her graceful movements and occasionally fanning out behind her as she twirled.

In spite of Dare's disorientation and the oddness of the situation, he felt his cock stir as he watched the sensual display. Soon it was standing tall and proud, obscuring his view of the shadow woman's dance.

At which point the shadow flowed off the wall and onto the floor, the woman moving as if crawling towards him, except in two dimensions.

Collisa

Phoenix

In spite of the feeling of calm and warmth, and the fact that he was rock hard, he couldn't help but scream at that.

But it turned out that he hadn't just been frozen by confusion; it felt like some sort of sleep paralysis, with only his head able to move. And his cock, he supposed, although that was completely involuntary.

Almost as if chagrined, the shadow paused. Then it moved to stretch out beside him on the bed and just lay there quietly, as if trying to reassure him.

Dare abruptly realized that the shadowy woman was shivering slightly. Was she nervous, excited? Somehow that simple gesture made her seem more human, or more whatever she was, and he started to calm down.

Especially since she was just laying there next to him, facing him head-on so he couldn't see any of her features in profile. Which was actually a bit unnerving, reminding him a bit of the motionless faces of the slime girls.

He quickly tore his eyes away and inspected the rest of her, and in spite of himself couldn't help but find the sight even more appealing up close.

What he could see of the shadow woman's curves from this angle were lush and alluring. In fact, he'd almost go so far as to say she had the exact body shape he most liked. His cock, which had wilted slightly, rose to full rigidity again and began to throb.

The shadow tentatively stretched out a hand, as if offering it to him, slim and elegant on the futon between them. Dare knew he was probably being stupid, but maybe he was just a sucker for a face lost in shadow and a pretty body. And it wasn't like he hadn't taken reckless risks before in order to get his dick wet, like with the slime girls.

Either way, he slowly extended his own hand until his fingers touched the shadow woman's.

They were slightly cool and had an odd texture. Not so much smooth but as if there was a complete absence of friction. However, even though he couldn't see anything but flat surfaces and profiles from the shadow, he could feel the shape of her slender fingers beneath his.

Or at least, the odd sensation of frictionless resistance.

To his surprise the shadow hand rose off the futon, lifting his with it. It became three-dimensional as it did, and the cool, frictionless fingers closed around his delicately, maybe even tentatively. It was a weird sensation, pressure but no friction, but not an unpleasant one.

"What are you?" he whispered gently.

As if in answer, the shadow slipped towards him. She raised slightly off the futon, hip, shoulder, and side briefly becoming three-dimensional and showing the sort of curvy shape that would make any man's mouth water.

Then Dare bit back a scream as she flowed smoothly on top of him.

The sensation was odd, like being covered by a cool, heavy blanket. He hesitantly ran his hand across the top of the shadow lying across his chest, and was baffled by the same cool, smooth sensation he was feeling from below.

Did the shadow woman only have shape when she raised herself off the ground?

His confusion and questions faded as the shadow atop him . . . *undulated* was the only way he could describe it. The sensation across his gooseflesh-covered skin was like he was being massaged along every contact point.

It was oddly soothing and pleasant, and in spite of the

Phoenix

bizarreness of the situation and his fear that this entity might be some sort of threat, he felt himself relaxing.

The shadow head had been across his upper chest, but now it lifted to hover over him. He still couldn't see any features since she was facing him head on, but as the head lowered towards him he felt the cool, frictionless sensation of her lips pressing against his.

The rest of the shadow continued to undulate, massaging him and lulling him into a relaxed state. The smooth sensation of the shadow moving across his bare skin was pleasant, and in a strange way arousing as well.

Probably because he knew the sensations he felt were of a naked woman, albeit a shadowy one, basically doing a full body grind against him.

Through it all the shadowy lips continued to brush his. To his shock he felt a hint of wetness as they parted, then a cool, wet tongue teasing against his lips with that same frictionless feel.

He kept his mouth shut; he had no idea what that wet substance was, especially not produced from a disembodied *shadow*, but he sure as fuck wasn't letting it in his mouth. The shadow didn't seem disappointed by that, although the cool lips moved away from his mouth and began running along his chin and neck, then across his collar. From above he could see the hint of long hair falling this way and that as the shadowy head moved.

As this was going on the undulating shadow below his waist finally went for the kill.

He felt his massive erection smothered by the cool smoothness. The rippling sensation engulfed him and massaged his length in the same way it was doing every other part of his skin the shadow touched, and Dare groaned.

The sensation was unlike anything he'd ever experienced before, but he couldn't deny it was pleasurable.

Collisa

He lasted longer than he could ever remember under the gentle ministrations of the shadow. A languid, even peaceful process that washed over him like waves on the beach, lulling him into an odd mixture of drowsy and tense with arousal.

Perhaps he drifted, but his eyes immediately snapped open when he felt cool wetness flow over his crotch. He immediately looked down, but the shadowy head was still nibbling at his collarbone.

What? But that would mean . . .

Dare lifted himself onto his elbows and looked down, amazed but not surprised to see that the shadow over his crotch had lifted, forming into the silhouette of a perfectly rounded ass rising slowly up and down as the sensation engulfing his cock continued its gently rippling massage.

The shadow was fucking him.

He tentatively reached down, gathering up some of the cool liquid on his thigh. It had warmed slightly with the heat of his arousal, and between his fingers felt just like he'd expect from the nectar from Zuri or any of his other lovers.

He raised it to his face for a better look, seeing a glistening wetness coating his skin. It had no smell he could discern, and he certainly wasn't about to taste it, but for all that it certainly *felt* like juices from a woman's arousal.

And yet even as he watched the glistening area shrank, then faded away as if it had an incredibly low evaporation point. Dare looked back down at the gorgeous shadowy rump rising and falling over his cock with increasing speed.

Was his mysterious lover a ghost or something?

He started with surprise when the peaceful, almost soothing sensation milking his cock became a series of tightening ripples. The shadowy head sliding over his chest abruptly jerked up into three-dimensional perspective as the woman's back arched, and for a brief

Phoenix

moment he caught the right angle to see his shadow lover's mouth open in rapture.

Well, good to know he could make odd ghost/shadow women climax too.

As she came down from her peak Dare decided to try something. He wrapped an arm around the shadow blanketing his chest and rolled over, hoping to take her with him. To his pleasant surprise the shadow, like a real woman, followed his movements, creating a faintly defined pool of darkness beneath him as he positioned himself above her.

He could still feel the cool, frictionless inside of the shadow woman's drenched pussy around his cock, and looked down to see shadow legs spread wide to either side, as if she was doing the splits. A peek underneath his raised hips showed the junction between her thighs still there in stark relief, glistening with ethereal arousal.

Dare grunted, pleased, and then began to thrust into his lover.

The shadow flowed beneath him, but the soothing undulations were nowhere to be seen. Instead it flowed and pressed desperately against his skin as he pounded the upraised shadow pussy with increasing vigor. He felt coolness slip around his sides and to his back, her arms clutching him and holding him close.

Then he gasped in surprise and involuntarily jerked his hips in an extra hard thrust as he felt cool lines of fire draw across his lower back.

Was she . . . clawing his skin in pleasure?

Dare looked down again, and as if the woman had intended it her head was turned to one side, showing her face in profile. Her delicate features were scrunched in passion, mouth open in panting gasps, and the once-soothing grip of her delicate walls tightened to a rippling vise as she once again climaxed around his cock.

He grunted, struggling to distract himself with any thoughts other than the sheer pleasure and eroticism of this bizarre experience. But it was a losing battle, and before long he gave a cry of release and thrust into her one last time, letting his blazing hot seed spray her cool insides.

She quivered beneath him like she was convulsing, icy lines of fire raked his back a final time, and then with abrupt suddenness the shadow vanished.

Dare nearly fell flat on his face even though he'd been supporting himself solidly, shocked at unexpectedly finding himself alone again. His last couple spurts sprayed the futon, and he could already feel the cool wetness of his disappeared lover's arousal beginning to evaporate off him.

He collapsed onto his side, sucking in huge breaths.

"What the fuck?" he asked once a bit of his composure had returned. "What the absolute fuck?"

The empty white chamber answered his question with silence. Then it slowly faded away, taking him with it.

* * * * *

Dare woke up slowly and languidly, feeling oddly refreshed and satisfied.

Zuri was curled up against his side, small hands wrapped lovingly around his limp, sensitive cock. From her position and the dampness on his stomach he assumed she'd discovered him hard in his sleep and had stroked him to another climax. Which would explain his dream.

Except it hadn't been a dream, he was sure of it. And he had a sneaking suspicion it was related to the curiously helpful system commands that spoke to him in the same voice as his unseen benefactor.

He didn't think it was a coincidence.

Phoenix

Gently disentangling himself from his sleeping goblin lover, he pulled on his pants and slipped out of the tent. The night air was pleasant this time of year, fresh with the smell of grass and a cooling breeze blowing in from the west to dry his sweat-slick skin.

Dare glanced over at Ilin, who was seated facing the fire, motionless as he meditated. Then he turned and strode into the night, out to the edge of the protection the campfire offered and hopefully out of earshot of his companions.

Once there he looked up at the sky, brilliant with stars as well as numerous phenomena that not only seemed scientifically impossible, but also statistically improbable they would all be visible from the surface of this world. Like a binary system where the larger star was eating the smaller in a brilliant display, or a black hole and its accretion disk, or a nebula glowing a soft but brilliant blue. Or several spiral arms of a galaxy clawing across the dark sky like fingers.

Was this world even in the same universe as Earth?

Dare pushed that thought aside for the moment; he had other questions he wanted answered right now. "I want to know about magic resistances," he said firmly.

It wasn't exactly a trick question. But he'd already discovered in previous searches that there was no information on magic resistances available. Presumably because they were abilities he hadn't unlocked because he'd never been the target of a spell.

He half thought the disembodied voice, or world system overseer, or whatever he'd been interacting with would either tell him no information was available or just ignore him.

Which was why he was shocked when he received a full screen of information on magic resistances. Including his current resistances for his level, how gear mitigated magic damage, and how increasing his proficiency in different magic resistance abilities would reduce damage received from those schools of magic.

Collisa

The immediate conclusion to this was that he should start having Zuri pelt him with Mana Thorns a few times a day to build up his Nature resistance. And if any of Ilin's abilities used magic, he could maybe get a few whacks from the Monk too.

But more importantly, this wealth of information seemed like pretty clear proof that whatever talked to him through the command screens wasn't just an automated system.

Dare looked at the lines of text hovering in front of him. "You talk to me more than to others of this world, don't you?" he asked. "In fact, I don't think you talk to them at all. Certainly not aloud."

There was no response, but he continued stubbornly. "I doubt you're this helpful to everyone. Especially since some of what you've told me seems like stuff you wouldn't tell the average denizen of Collisa. And you'd never give them information they haven't unlocked just because they asked."

After a long pause, new lines of text quivered in the air in front of him, and the soothing female voice replied in amusement. It was the first time she'd shown emotion since he'd come to Collisa. "Well, I've already given you so many other little edges over the others of this world."

"And big edges," he said, thinking of Fleetfoot and Adventurer's Eye. Or his nearly perfect body, for that matter.

"Very big," she teased, giggling in an almost naughty way before continuing in a sober voice. "You're lacking in decades of knowledge you would've gained organically by living here. It's only fair I help you out when you really need it."

"That makes sense," Dare admitted. "Thank you. I don't even know who you are, but I owe you so much. Everything, really, since you gave me a second life and brought me here."

"You're welcome," the voice said, sounding amused. "I'm going to transfer you over to the default system now, unless you have something else you need to say."

"Just thank you again."

She replied with a peal of lighthearted laughter. "And thank *you* for taking good care of me tonight. It was a pleasant new experience."

Then she was gone.

Dare looked up at the sky, smirking. As he'd suspected, the shadowy woman who'd seduced him in his dream had been his benefactor.

On the one hand, he was reassured knowing it was her. That it hadn't been a dream eater or nightmare demon or some other monster that attacked you in your sleep, and she hadn't meant him any harm.

On the other hand, it raised an entire slew of new questions and worries.

Like, what if she came to him again? Given her powers she was probably some sort of god of this world; now that he knew who she was, how was he supposed to just bend her over and give it to her like any other woman?

What if she didn't enjoy it the second time around? Would she smite him on the spot?

Dare wasn't sure whether to be excited or nervous at the prospect of another visit from the shadowy woman. And it again raised the question of whether she had some secret purpose for him that she wasn't admitting to.

He wasn't about to believe he was such a good lay that she'd saved him from death and brought him here and made him an entirely new body, just to get a good fucking.

Sighing, he headed back toward the tent. He doubted he'd be getting more answers from his benefactor tonight. He'd just have to

Collisa

wait and see, and enjoy the adventure as he went.

Slipping through the entry flaps, he crawled up beside Zuri and pulled the blankets back over him, pulling his little lover tight.

Tomorrow was a new day.

End of Collisa.
The adventures of Dare and Zuri continue
in Kovana, second book of the Outsider series.

Phoenix

Thank you for reading Collisa!

I hope you enjoyed reading it as much as I enjoyed writing it. If you feel the book is worthy of support, I'd greatly appreciate it if you'd rate it, or better yet review it, on Amazon, as well as recommend it to anyone you think would also enjoy it.

As a self-published author I flourish with the help of readers who review and recommend my work. Your support helps me continue doing what I love and bringing you more books to enjoy.

Collisa

About the Author

Aiden Phoenix became an established author
writing stories about the end of the world.
Then Collisa called, a new and exciting world to explore,
and like the characters in his series he was reborn anew there.

Printed in Great Britain
by Amazon